FAERIE

FAERIE

DELLE JACOBS

Montlake
Romance

Published by Montlake Romance
P.O. Box 400818
Las Vegas, NV 89140

ISBN-13: 9781612185934
ISBN-10: 1612185932

The best revenge might be happiness, but the greatest happiness comes from the love and support others give. And for that, my thoughts always come back to my children, Andy, Lori, and Jeannie. With that kind of happiness, who needs revenge?

PROLOGUE

"THAT ONE," SAID THE CRONE. ONE LONG, BONY FINGER emerged from her dark green sleeve to point into the courtyard beyond the shadowed arcade. Tall, gaunt, old, and ashen-faced, she was everything Rufus was not.

He frowned, but quickly hid it. No one told him what to decide. He, William II, son of the Great Conqueror, was King of England.

It was an odd demand she made. Of all the king's knights, only Philippe le Peregrine wanted no fief, no wife, no family, only to roam at the king's will, to fight and make peace at the king's command. In return, Rufus had given the Peregrine his word to honor the knight's wish, and Rufus made it a point of honor to keep promises to his knights.

Still, as he studied his favorite knight from the obscuring shadows of the colonnade, he began to see the possibilities. Aye, it just might do. In fact, he could not have dreamed up a better opportunity himself.

Again he frowned, this time purposely, as if she had angered him. But his mind was spinning with thoughts on how he could use her demand. "He will not do it," he replied.

"Oh, he will, Red King," the crone said, her gravelly voice crackling. "He is bound to you, just as you are bound to me by your father's oath. You know what will happen if you do not keep it."

He rubbed the crisp curls of his red beard. Aye, he knew, and he needed her. She knew he would comply. He honored his father above all men, and that first Norman King of England had trusted this strange old woman implicitly, enough to give her free rein in the promise she exacted.

So, then: His own promise betrayed to honor a prior one of his father's making. It would not be the first time a king had not kept his word. "So it shall be," he replied at last. "But how to do it? It will not be easy."

The crone laughed, but she did not smile. "You will know," she said, and again the rough chuckle shook the bag of bones that was her body. She focused her gleaming green eyes on him, and Rufus tried to look away, only to be caught in their compelling intensity. A chill rippled down his spine. She did not possess the Evil Eye, nor was she a witch—he had met his share of evil beings and had a sense for them. But in some indefinable way, she was magical. For what she knew, Rufus would pay her price, any price, just as his father had done.

With a jerking gait that made him think of walking sticks, she passed through the pale arcs of sunlight and shadows of the colonnade to the stone wall between Rufus's private courtyard and the palace bailey. She glanced back, then pulled the hood of her moss-colored cloak over her straw-like hair. Her cloak blended with the shadows, then faded into the morning mist.

The mist thinned and vanished. The crone was gone. Rufus tilted his head and squinted. Nothing was left. Only the wall.

For a moment he wished for her strange powers. Imagine a king who could walk through stone. Imagine a king standing in a room when no one knew he was there.

CHAPTER ONE

THE FOREST HAD ALWAYS BEEN LIKE A FRIEND TO HER. NOT
that Leonie minded the hot sun in the meadow, and the bright,
hot weather was a boon that would bring plenty to sustain the
castle and village through the coming winter. But the forest was
her place, as if she had been born with an affinity for its cool
shade and deep green, quiet majesty.

In fact, like all of the Faeriekind, she had a kinship to the forest, but that was the secret she dared not share with any human.
Only old Ealga knew. And the old woman who had been hand-
maid to Leonie of Bosewood since the girl's birth lived in constant fear that Leonie's carelessness would someday betray her.

In the meadow that lay between the woods and Castle Brodin,
the sun bore down in blistering brightness on the burned necks
of the villeins harvesting the grain. But beneath the canopy of
leaves, the air stirred into a cooling breeze. Leonie let her veil fall
to her shoulders to cool her scalp, for no one was in the forest
except her and her favorite little boy, Sigge, the curious dreamer
who always wanted to know everything and do everything.

Other times of year, Leonie and her little friend might roam about the forest for other reasons. But now was the time to harvest the club moss she used to make green dye for the prized Castle Brodin wool. And it was Leonie who made the perfect green dye. But the secrets of other colors—the perfect scarlet, the brightest yellow, or a blue as bright and clear as the summer sky—eluded her.

Leonie grinned as she spotted a clump of club moss, growing like a tiny fir tree beneath the first of the year's fallen leaves. "Sigge, come here," she called, focusing her gaze on the clump as she knelt.

"In a minute," the boy responded.

She frowned. The child was uncharacteristically quiet. "No, come, Sigge. You need to see what it looks like and how it hides beneath the leaves if you are going to help me."

"Coming."

She smirked in silence at the rustle of noise. That was more like him. She swept back the leaves, unable to contain her own exuberance any longer. "This is just right, Sigge," she said, gently fingering the succulent branches of the moss. Her fingers worked into the dark, cool, loose soil beneath the plant, carefully dividing it so that she would leave some of the plant to regrow. Already she was imagining the rich green dye simmering in the pots over the castle hearths.

The calm air shattered with the child's scream. "Leonie! Help! Help me!"

Terror sliced straight to her heart. She jumped to her feet and turned to see the little boy hopping on one foot, blood pouring from the other one into a spreading blotch in the dirt. His face was already paling.

She leaped up and ran. "Sit down, Sigge! I'm coming!"

"It hurts, Leonie!" The child sank to his knees just as she reached him. She plopped down, scooped him into her arms, and turned the sole of his foot upward. Bile rose in her throat at the bright red blood gushing out.

"Aye, Sigge, I know," she said and glanced around her. She could stop it. Just touch and let the healing flow through her hands. She knew never to do it. But.

Frowning, she pulled off her veil and dabbed at the wound. She couldn't wipe fast enough. Her stomach sickened at the thought of her favorite little boy bleeding to death.

She fought her fears to find a calmly pleasant tone for her voice, as if nothing were seriously wrong. "What happened, Sigge?"

"A piece of metal. Ow!"

"Metal? In the forest?" Strange. Nobody discarded valuable metal. "Someone must have lost it."

"I saw it and I thought I could dig it up. But I didn't see the other part."

Sigge gasped hard, and tears flowed down his cheeks. For all her calm appearance, Leonie's heart was pounding rapidly. From her infancy she'd been taught never to show her strange skill, lest she be thought a witch. The old Celtic part of her knew what she had to do. But her Norman half screamed at the danger. Normans did not understand such Celtic things.

No one else was in the woods outside Castle Brodin. She could close the wound and no one else could. There was no choice, and she knew it.

"Leonie!" Leonie jerked her head toward the meadow beyond the wood and the sound of her cousin Claire's voice. "Leonie, where are you? You must come now!"

Leonie gritted her teeth. Why now? Claire would be within the wood in no time. Close as they were, Claire was only an ordinary human and knew nothing of Leonie's secret. She had to move fast, now. Just enough to stop the blood. A swift swipe of her thumb. Tricky, but if she did it right, not even Sigge would suspect.

Sucking in a breath, she swept her thumb over the wound and the light-headed, foggy feeling filled her head as if part of her life abandoned her. But it was nothing like the near faint that had overcome her as a small child when old Ealga had first discovered Leonie's hidden talent. Ealga would turn white from fear when she learned she had once again been disobeyed.

"Oh, look, Sigge!" Leonie smiled as sweetly as if she were pointing to a fawn bounding across the meadow. "It's stopping already. I told you it would be all right." But before he could really see, she wrapped her veil tightly around the child's foot. "Now, hold your thumb against the cut while I get my basket."

He shook his head, and his voice trembled. "I can't. It hurts."

"I know. Imagine yourself a brave knight. You've always wanted to be a knight, haven't you? Well, now you must act like one. We'll keep the bandage on tight, and you mustn't walk on it, and by tomorrow, you will be much better." For the rest of this day, she must mask her worry. Pretend it only looked like a lot of blood. Pretend there was nothing to fear. But that was not new to her.

Leaving the boy where he sat and grimaced, she hurried back to the beeches and snatched up the basket she had spilled. She rushed back to the boy. Already he looked better.

"Up, now," she said, and lifted him to her hip. With his arms wrapped around her neck, they started out of the woods just as Claire came running up the path.

"Leonie, where have you been? I've been calling for you." Then Claire stopped and gasped, her pretty blue eyes round like plates.

Leonie looked at her blood-soaked kirtle and grimaced. "He's cut his foot," she said. "It bled a lot at first. He will be all right now if he doesn't walk on it."

"But your clothes! What will Mama say? Papa has visitors. The king's knights!"

"I'll hurry up and change, then."

"But your veil!"

"I'll wash it myself." That was not what Claire was thinking, Leonie knew, but it would deflect her for now. Claire was like her mother sometimes.

With long strides, Leonie bounded over the meadow toward the castle, knowing Claire's short legs would have to work hard to keep up. "What do you suppose is so important that the king sends his knights?"

"Maybe he's chosen a husband for you. 'Tis about time."

Leonie shook her head and snickered, once again playing the carefree maiden. "He wouldn't send knights to tell us that. More like, he has his mind on war. Again."

Claire giggled. "Or trouble in Normandy. Again. And the king seeks a new levy to pay for it."

Leonie smirked. "Uncle Geoffrey will not be pleased."

"Mama will be angry with me, Leonie," Sigge said, tightening his hold around Leonie's neck.

"Your mama loves you, child," Claire said, patting the boy's shoulder. "She worries when you sneak off to the wood."

"I was only helping Leonie. And looking for mushrooms."

Leonie shuddered. "And don't you do that again. You don't know a good mushroom from a bad one. It's not the time of year for the good ones. A bad one could kill you."

She strode past grazing sheep toward the castle, Claire panting behind her. Pausing at the edge of the village, Leonie spotted the brightly garmented knights approaching, with the king's flamboyant pennon of gold and crimson signaling their status. Helms, swords, and shields flashed bright stars of sunlight. Apprehension tickled in her chest. This was no ordinary visit. Everyone would be expected to be in attendance of the guests. She must not embarrass her uncle with her disheveled appearance.

"I'll go through the postern gate and up the back way to the solar," she said to Claire. "You go around to the barbican."

Claire gasped for breath and nodded, probably grateful for the easier route. Claire was not the sort to tromp about in the wood like her cousin, nor run up the steep hill, but Leonie could walk even faster if she didn't have to worry about Claire. With Sigge's legs locked about her waist, Leonie climbed the steep steps on the castle's north side to the postern gate.

She emerged into the lower bailey, but too late, for she could already be seen by the knights who had passed through the barbican and now dismounted in the bare ground. Sigge's father, the black-smith, broke away from the gathering crowd to run to his child.

"He is not hurt badly," she said as Harald took the child from her arms. "He has a kinship to metals, I think. His foot must have found the only piece of discarded metal in the entire forest. Do not unbind his foot for a day, and do not let him walk on it, and he will be fine."

"My thanks, lady."

If Harald followed her directions, he would never know how bad it had been. If he ignored them...

Well, she had done what she had to do.

Leonie turned to sneak past the upper bailey gate, intent on the outer steps of the hall that led to the solar. But Uncle Geoffrey caught her eye and motioned to her to join the crowd. She sighed. She was not fond of looking foolish. As it was she was different enough, with her long, thin legs and arms, funny pointed ears, and wild hair that looked like curly straw.

With her eyes downcast in a vain attempt to look maidenly, she sidled toward the back of the crowd, hoping to be unseen. An interesting feat since she stood head and shoulders above every woman and most of the men.

"Mother in Heaven, girl! What has happened to you?"

Aunt Beatrice. Leonie's face heated, knowing the rumpled, blood-streaked, dirt-smudged state of her kirtle. Sigge was not the cleanest child who inhabited the castle.

"She had to rescue Sigge, Mother," said Claire, still gasping deeply as she hurried up. "Again."

"Again? What will that child do next? Where is your veil, Leonie? Your hair is a shambles!"

"Wrapped around Sigge's foot," she mumbled, her face growing even hotter, remembering how she had left off the veil for most of the hot afternoon to let the occasional sultry breeze toss her long curls. Even after entering the cool shade of the forest, she had left it draping over her shoulder.

Aunt Beatrice flung the back of her hand to her forehead, and although she was not one to faint, Leonie feared this time she might. "You'll be the death of me, child. Of all the times, Leonie, why now? It is the king's Peregrine himself who has ridden all the way from Gloucester to sup with us."

Oh no. The hot flush fled Leonie's cheeks as fast as it had come on her. Philippe le Peregrine. It wasn't bad enough already. Did it have to be him?

Aye, there he was, standing beside his great brindled grey warhorse, the knight of her dreams and her nightmares, his huge, brawny body dwarfing his companions.

He lifted off his helm and handed it to his squire, then shook out his tousled golden hair—Viking hair, more golden than the sun. But he had Frankish eyes, warm and mellow brown like meadow honey, and they made her feel as if her bones were melting.

She'd been but thirteen years old, barely budding into adulthood, when she had so thoroughly humiliated herself over him that she had hoped never to see his face again. Now, here she was, with her disheveled kirtle and hair tossed like a tumbled haystack, once again about to make a fool of herself.

If only she were a true Faerie, not merely a secret halfling! For then—so Ealga had told her—Leonie would have been born knowing how to fade into the stones at her back and be safely unseen and forgotten. But she didn't know. All she could do was stand there, tangling her slender fingers together like spun wool attacked by a kitten.

The Peregrine scanned the castle folk surrounding him. Leonie hunched down. But her height, her great bane, betrayed her once again. In the entire courtyard, no man save the Peregrine towered over her.

She cast down her gaze again, forcing herself to focus on her unsteady hands, but her eyes rebelled. Again and again, they shot back up and sought out the knight.

The compelling brown eyes landed their gaze on her, questioning, assessing, perhaps laughing at her once more.

Why? Couldn't he just forget he'd ever met her? She was nothing to him. She knew the stories told about him, the knight who wandered, by his own desire having no fief. Monkish in his ways, vowing never to let a kiss pass his lips, but explaining nothing. People said he remained faithful to his murdered wife. He would never love another, they said.

Leonie certainly believed it, and was certain that love would never be hers. When last he had been here, she had foolishly challenged him and beaten him at targets. All the castle had known what the Peregrine had not, that she was the best archer for miles around. It was bad enough that she had so easily beaten him, but then, even more foolishly, she had demanded a kiss as forfeit.

"*Take my bow, my arrows, my quiver. Take the ring from my finger as your prize. But I have no kisses to give to guileful maids.*" Then he had turned and stalked away.

That was how she had learned. Up to that moment, what fun it had been to play the silly trick on him! But from then on, her cheeks would turn red with shame at the mere thought of him.

Five years had gone by since then, and even now, the sight of him brought fire to her face.

Philippe le Peregrine advanced on his quarry. She squirmed.

He sauntered easily, not like his namesake hunter that could dive from the sky faster than a horse could run, but with the grace of a cat, his square, masculine hips lightly swaggering. Hoping at least to hide her stained kirtle, Leonie slipped behind Ealga, who was as short as Leonie was tall. But Ealga knew her place. No servant would stand where a knight wished to go. With a meek bow, the elderly maid stepped aside.

A deceptive softness warmed the Peregrine's honey-brown eyes as a smile curled on his lips. It made her want to trust him. To please him, to melt. It was said he could talk the birds out of the sky, and she believed it, but when forced to fight was as fierce as his namesake falcon. The men of this keep trusted him as completely as did the king. Everyone did.

She did not. She had seen how he could turn.

"Ah, Leonie," he said. The smile broadened, as if he had come to a friend. "The little lioness of Castle Brodin."

She licked her suddenly parched lips. "None other calls me little, sir knight, though surely your great height excuses you."

The brown eyes widened and lost some of their softness. "Ah. Have you claws now, little lioness? But you have grown. Even taller." He ran his gaze over her.

She was no stranger to the assessing eyes of men, as if they wondered whether such a long-legged woman might be fair enough in bed. She swallowed. Her great height, with her ugly, gangly legs. Folk rarely mentioned it, but she knew they all measured her difference by it.

"Do you still play at targets, little lioness?"

"Aye." She gulped and hung her head. Did he have to bring that up? "It's but a game, sir knight." She need not mention she practiced every day.

"Is it? And can you still best a man?"

Leonie licked her dry lips again, but her mouth was equally dry. Did he challenge her or insult her? "If the man has neglected his practice, haps. Though not many a knight trifles with a bow, I'm told."

"I do."

Uncle Geoffrey stepped up, chuckling, and took the knight by his arm. "You ought not try her again, Philippe," he said. "Would that I had a hundred archers who could shoot as straight. My men best her only in their strength. Come now, let us be off to the hall, where it is cool. This heat is fine enough for harvest, but not so fine after a long ride."

Philippe's dark eyes sparked with the boldness only a great knight would have. "Later, then, little lioness, but I cannot let my honor go unchallenged."

"Better to let it go unchallenged than to face defeat at a woman's hands, no?" A smile skimmed over Uncle Geoffrey's face as he again tugged at the knight's arm.

"Not I," Philippe replied, but he returned Uncle Geoffrey's smile. "I confess, I would rather be bested by a woman than let my chance for redemption pass me by."

The king's knights were eager for the ale and cool air beneath the high roof of the hall, and they clapped Philippe on the shoulder and begged him to hurry. He turned away from Leonie, suddenly immersed again in the knightly camaraderie. The attention she had not wanted now felt cruelly absent. Her throat tightened and ached.

When the Peregrine disappeared through the high, rounded doors into the hall, Leonie whirled around and sprinted toward the chapel and up the outer stairs along its wall to the solar, taking them two at a time. She dashed through the solar to the ladies' chamber she shared with Claire.

Ealga had reached the chamber before her. Leonie turned her eyes away. Nothing could be hidden from the elderly Scot servant who had been with her all her life, and with her mother before, but that didn't mean Leonie had to brandish her humiliation.

Ealga squinted suspiciously at her. "'Tis a good thing ye dinna have the gaze."

Use the gaze on Philippe le Peregrine? "I—I would not, Ealga. Even if I had it."

Ealga wiped her brow. The old woman always worried too much. But Leonie had few of the Faerie talents. She had the Faerie sight that lit the dimmest night like the light of the full moon, and that ability that so vexed the Peregrine, to shoot better than any man. The closing of wounds—well, they didn't know where that had come from. Ealga said Herzeloyde had had no such talent to pass to her daughter.

"And not him, anyway," Leonie added. "I do not want him. I do not like him."

Ealga harrumphed. "Ye're too careless with your ways, lassie. Someday ye'll be finding yourself roasting on a fire like a suckling pig."

Aye, she knew. The gaze was the power, Ealga said, that had bound her father to her mother, but it had brought only tragedy and hatred in the end.

She wondered, had her mother left for fear of burning as a witch? Had her father accused Herzeloyde? She would never know. They were both gone, and Ealga knew too little, or would not tell.

"Ye'll be wanting your green kirtle," said the old Scotswoman, nodding toward the high bed where she had laid out the garment.

The kirtle was Leonie's favorite, dyed from the forest's club mosses. Beside it lay a pale green veil that could all but conceal her face when they supped with the castle's guests, if she adjusted it just right. Tonight she would be more than glad for it.

"'Tis a brutal hot day, though," Ealga continued. "Ye'll be wanting to wash up first, and then I'll comb out your curls. Comb 'em about me fingers, round and round, make 'em the most glorious mass of curls a man has e'er seen. Ye'll do your uncle proud."

Leonie sighed and submitted to Ealga's gentle help. Soon enough, she must return to her uncle's hall to sup and tend his guests. Somehow she must manage to appear properly demure, almost an impossibility for her. For though she was only half Faerie, sometimes it seemed she was not human at all.

Philippe le Peregrine paused at the door to Geoffrey's hall, catching a glimpse of the girl racing toward the chapel in an unseemly fashion. He shook his head, trying to remember when he had ever met one so unmaidenly. No other maid shot a bow so well. None drew one, for that matter. Even riding up the winding track to the castle, he had recognized her from a distance as she strode across the meadow in long, manlike steps, carrying a child in her arms, unseemly though it was for an heiress so wealthy. Any other maid would have sought a servant to carry the child.

Everything about her was unseemly.

"A beauty, is she not?"

He frowned as he looked at the girl's uncle. Not a beauty, yet she caught and held his attention like no woman had in many a year. Too thin, too tall, yet with breasts too full and ripe, in ways they had not been when they had first met. Too much hair, enough for three maids, with its long and wildly tangled ringlets that reminded him of golden wheat spread willy-nilly on the threshing floor. Huge eyes, far too green, like the very depths of the forest. Everything about her beckoned, but was not beautiful. Nose, ears, eyes, everything. She was too—everything.

"Nay," he replied. "I cannot deny there is something about her, but I do not find her beautiful." And he became as hard as granite immediately, imagining those long legs wrapped around him.

"I would not have guessed." The lyrical tone of Geoffrey's voice spoke of amusement.

Philippe's face instantly reddened. He was behaving like a moonstruck youth, and he should have known the older man would notice.

"Still, men cannot keep from gaping after her."

Philippe shook his head, knowing he had been gaping too, with heart speeding and entire body tensing. He ordered his mind to squelch the lurid thoughts. That was the way of men, but he had forsworn such things. He would have no love, ever again. And it was not wise for a man sworn to be celibate to have such thoughts. "But she is an heiress," he said, "not a common woman. A knight would wish a more modest wife."

Geoffrey sighed. "I know the world is changing, my friend. But this is still the North. Here a lady does not merely sit with her embroidery. I am not ashamed of either of my girls, who will know how to do much more than manage a household when they marry."

"Make her cover her hair. It's too intriguing. And she should be more demure. I saw her walking with a child, striding like a man. The boy must have bled on her clothing."

"Aye. Sigge, the blacksmith's boy. The lad has a way of finding trouble and seems it's always Leonie who rescues him."

Philippe shook his head. "In all my travels, I've never seen a woman like her."

"She has her mother's look, although Herzeloyde's hair was paler. She was Saxon, you know. Many here in the North still admire those Saxon women who were not afraid to fight alongside their men. It is from her mother that she has the archer's skills. She has none of her father in her, and though he was my brother, I happily say I am glad for it."

Geoffrey led him deep into the cool hall, which sent a sweet chill over Philippe's sweat-drenched scalp.

Philippe stopped as his squire came up, and he stood still while the boy helped him out of his hauberk. The weight of the mail garment removed from his shoulders was as refreshing as the coolness.

"What happened to her mother?" he asked as he and Geoffrey resumed their journey the length of the hall.

"She walked into the wood one day and disappeared. The baby girl was sent to us, and her father never saw her again."

"Many men have no interest in daughters."

"Aye, more's the pity."

"You don't agree, then?"

"Did I agree, I would not have taken her in. She has become as dear to me as my own daughter. I pity the man who cannot love his kin. His life is an empty shell."

Philippe had to smile at Geoffrey's revelations. Powerful baron though he was, Geoffrey of Brodin was not as wealthy as most, for he was too good-hearted. He trusted too much and gave away too much.

"And what of you, my friend?" asked the baron. "Do you still choose a solitary life?"

"Aye," he said quietly.

"It has been a long time."

Philippe frowned in his silence. Six years. And like yesterday. Not a night passed that he did not relive in his dreams the horror of his wife's flaming body falling from the double-arched window. Not a night passed that he did not hear her screams.

"Do you not long for family of your own?"

Nor did a day pass that his heart did not ache so deeply, he thought it would rend itself from his chest. Nor one that he did not dream of revenge and ridding the world of the sorcerer Clodomir's evil. Someday he would find Clodomir and make him feel pain never before felt by any man. But in six years he had found no sign or clue of the man.

"Nay," Philippe replied, making his voice bland, and he smiled lightly. "I am doomed to wander."

Philippe detected sadness in Geoffrey's smile. But he could not know; he thought his own path was the one every man should walk.

"Ah," replied the baron with a hand to Philippe's shoulder. "Well, haps you would like to go refresh yourself before the evening meal. You have been riding long on a very hot day."

Philippe nodded. "We are all too drenched with sweat to make good dinner companions. I saw a place in the beck where it forms a pool, just beyond the rapids. A likely spot for us to bathe, sheltered so as not to offend the womenfolk of the castle."

"If you chase away the laundresses. Remind your men I want no spare babes to support next spring."

Philippe raised a brow. "You would not turn them out?"

"I take care of my own."

"An unscrupulous man might take advantage of your generosity, knowing his bastards would be cared for."

"Unscrupulous men, I kill."

"But not the king's knights."

"Over them, I would treat with the king. He gives me justice."

Ah, and that was why he liked Geoffrey of Brodin so much. A man of wisdom and quiet courage. "You need not worry, my friend. My knights are under my control. They do not raid like Danes, nor even carouse like Normans."

Leonie stepped out the solar door and glanced in all directions at the castle folk, who were all too busy providing for the king's knights and supper. And the knights had left the castle to bathe in the river. She could surely get to the forest and back and find that stray scrap of metal that had cut Sigge's foot. She knew the boy too well. If she didn't find it first, his curiosity would compel him to look for it, and she had no doubt he would manage to cut something else.

Ealga would have a fit, after all her hard work getting the tangles out of her curls. Leonie promised herself she would just be careful. She slipped down the stairs and crossed the courtyard to the postern gate and the steep steps down to the harvested fields and the meadow. Already the cows were turning back to the village for their milking. She would have to hurry.

As soon as she stepped into the woods, the breeze turned cool, a welcome change from the stifling air in the solar. She hurried down the path to the huge old beech where Sigge had cradled his bleeding foot.

His blood still stained the ground. Frowning, she followed the drops of blood. A rusty scrap of metal could be hard to spot amid the dry leaves that littered the forest floor. Carefully, she pushed the leaves about with a stick. She saw nothing.

A sharp breeze tossed the branches of the old beech and something metallic flashed. Not rusty at all, but bright, shiny, as if it had been dropped only yesterday. The glint vanished as the sun shifted behind a cloud. She knelt and began sweeping the leaves with her hands, cautiously, lest she also cut herself.

There it was. The point of a knife, protruding from the earth. It was honed so sharp she was surprised Sigge had not cut his foot off.

But it couldn't be. Anything buried here would have been here a long time, perhaps from the Danish invaders so long ago. It would have to be rusted, wouldn't it?

With her stick, Leonie scraped away the leaves and dirt along the sides of the blade. The sharp edge, showing more and more as she dug, slanted into the soft soil, a longer and longer blade. A sword, one with an old, plain look to it, not like the decorated ones knights carried today, yet it was as shiny as if it were new.

Puzzled, she kept on digging, and as the dry soil crumbled back into the channel she had dug, she widened her hole, scooping the dirt aside. She found a bigger stick and dug the hole deeper.

She hit a rock. Using the big stick like a spade, she carved out the soil from around the edges of the rock, slowly exposing its rounded white surface.

White? It was not the color of any rock she had seen. She frowned and renewed her efforts, instead concentrating on the lower end of the sword, for it was nearly free of the soil now.

Bone! The bones of a hand, wrapped about the hilt of the sword!

Her heart pounded as she returned to the rock near the sword's point, scraping and digging rapidly, and scooping away the dirt. Who was this who had been buried so shallowly? Recently? Very old? The stick gouged around the outer edges, and the outline of a skull became visible. She dug around a jawbone. With her hand, she smoothed away the soil from the face, revealing nose bones, teeth, eye sockets.

Two bloody eyeballs stared from their sockets at her.

She shrieked, sat back, scrambled to her feet. It could not be! But it was! A skull, its jawbone gaping, but with eyes that followed her!

Leonie dropped everything and ran, the pace of terror pounding her heart.

To the beck! She'd be safe there. She could circle around back to the castle, away from that corpse thing. Dodging low branches along the narrow trail, she fled through the forest toward the increasing sound of raucous male laughter, toward the slowly brightening light and the sandy banks of the beck.

She stopped cold.

No, wait, she couldn't go there. The knights were bathing. She could hear them.

She leaned against a skinny young oak, forcing herself to take several deep, slow breaths.

How silly she was! She was a mature woman of eighteen winters, yet she still imagined things like a hare-witted maiden. It was all wrong. There couldn't have been a shiny-bright sword buried in the soil, even less a skeleton! Everyone knew one did not bury bodies at the foot of a tree. The roots would get in the way. It was nigh impossible. People were always buried in the churchyard, anyway.

Unless someone died and the tree grew up over him.

Her heart started to pound wildly again.

Nay, it was still nonsense. The sword would be rusty. She'd better get control over herself, now. She inhaled deeply and laughed at herself.

The eyes.

Rocks that looked like eyes. Had to be.

But she shuddered. And now she had a worse problem. How was she going to get back to the castle without the knights thinking she was spying on them? Oh, she would die of embarrassment if the Peregrine saw her!

She relaxed, bit by bit, telling herself it was all nonsense. Once she calmed, she'd go the long way around to the castle.

The knights splashed about in the sparkling water, some swimming, some wading waist-deep, and others standing near the shallow water or on shore. Clothing littered the banks of the beck and draped over branches of bushes by the forest's edge. Their flesh was not the pale white of hers beneath her kirtle, but the golden hue of skin that had seen many hours in the sun. She suspected they made a habit of bathing in streams on hot summer days.

Near the bend in the beck, Philippe le Peregrine emerged from the water, his tall, hard-muscled body taking easy, powerful strides across the sand, his long shaft at rest, surrounded with golden-brown curls. Leonie was no more ignorant of men's bodies than any woman who lived within the confines of a hall. Men made little effort to hide their bodies, nor did women pretend they did not see. Nor was she stranger to the tendrils of desire that sometimes arose in her when unusual sounds and movements of lovers came from some dark corner. Perhaps it was her Faerie blood, for she knew their kind was different in those ways, too, but she had at least the good sense not to make her desires known to others. But for the most part her glimpses of men showed little more than a stub of a shaft. One this large when at rest wouldn't be a mere stub when erect.

What would he be like as a lover? At the thought, her body took on a sudden, hot, longing ache. Leonie slunk back behind a tree. He was too much to look at without wanting. Still, she might never have such a man for a lover. No reason to squelch her dreams.

She peeked around the tree.

A tall wash of water splashed at the Peregrine, soaking his legs. He turned toward the hearty laughter and dived into the flowing river at the offender, catching him at the waist, and the two men threw each other about, slipping and wrestling, until at last the Peregrine got the upper hand, tossing his opponent beneath the water. The struggle ended. Evidently the winner was the man who went underwater last.

He stood in the beck and slung his long golden hair about, spraying a sparkling arc around him, then braced his fists on his hips as the vanquished knight came up sputtering. The other knights whooped, and the water erupted in tangles of body parts, each man seeking supremacy over those about him.

Her breath was tight in her chest. Her gaze was fixed on the Peregrine, and she couldn't break it. She shouldn't be watching, she knew, yet she couldn't make herself stop. She smirked. She had watched men at their play before. They were like that, every man she had ever met. Laughing and romping like small boys in their own company. All solemn and bowing and polite manners the moment a woman appeared in their midst.

She glanced back to the trail behind her, shuddering at the very thought of going back that way. She had hoped to walk upstream and take the long way home, but there was no way she could get past the knights without them seeing her.

The sun was dropping toward the horizon. One by one, the men began to leave the beck. They still laughed, but with less rough exuberance, almost as if they sighed with satisfaction.

The Peregrine ran a cloth over his hair, then combed back the water-darkened locks with his fingers. He ran the rough cloth over his body and reached for his tunic.

His body suddenly stiffened. A frown crossed his face, and he turned toward the forest, looking straight to where she stood in the dark shadows.

She ducked behind the tree. He couldn't have seen her! She hadn't made a sound. She was certain. Yet did he know somehow? Cautiously she peeked again.

He shrugged and went back to dressing.

If she stayed where she was, the knights would come straight for her as soon as they finished donning their garments. Which was worse?

She knew. She had only to imagine the look on Philippe le Peregrine's face when he caught her snooping. But the thing in the forest—

Nay, it was impossible. It was not there. It was just her imagination. She was very good at imagining things. Aunt Beatrice told her that almost every day.

From somewhere deep inside her, she gathered little bits of courage and pasted them together. Drawing her lower lip between her teeth, Leonie stepped back onto the path that led from the beck to the castle, making sure she stayed in the darkest shade so the knights would not see her. Her eyes scanning in all directions, she edged along, step by careful step. She could hear the knights along the beck as they gathered. She scurried faster, scolding herself for knowing her only courage came from an even greater fear, but soon the path broadened and she began to run. The sooner she could make it through the forest, the better.

She slowed as she approached the place beneath the huge old beech tree where Sigge had cut his foot on the sword, which was not a sword but nothing more than her imagination. She bit her lip and sidled slowly, her eyes darting both ways up and down the path, then back to the place where she had dug.

Not there. Not there. Nothing was there.

She drew closer, holding her breath, preparing herself for a mighty dash past the hole. Closer. Closer, until she could see beyond the surrounding brush to the base of the tree.

The ground was undisturbed. Dry leaves littered it just as they had before she had begun digging.

The sword was gone. And so was the skeleton. As if she had never dug.

Leonie gulped down a scream and ran through the forest, her skirts lifted high, her hair flying like a pennant in a stiff breeze, her long legs fleeing over the ground faster than she had ever run before. Her thoughts raced equally as fast.

It was God punishing her. It had to be. Punishing her with her own overwrought imagination for being so wayward and immodest. From now on she was going to be the most demure, obedient maiden Castle Brodin had ever seen.

CHAPTER TWO

THE TRESTLE TABLES WERE BEING SET UP IN THE HALL, AND Philippe could smell the taunting scents of freshly baked bread coming from the kitchen, mingling with those of juicy roasting oxen. His mouth watered so much he felt like he'd been starving for days.

The hall rang with the boisterous clamor of hungry knights. Philippe sat beside his host at the center table. Lady Beatrice took her seat in a chair across from them, with Philippe's two best men benched to either side of her. Other benches were pulled up to the two long lines of tables, filled with knights and the household retainers.

Philippe frowned, feeling oddly anxious. The two young ladies still had not come.

Then he saw them, coming through the kitchen door, the servants following in a processional, carrying trays and bowls, all with food in mountainous heaps.

The younger, Lady Claire, the daughter and heir of the household, was as petite as her cousin was tall and slim. Claire was the ideal woman, the perfect wife for most men, so properly demure in her blue kirtle and yellow veil. Behind her Lady Leonie towered over her, slim as a willow, her bushy golden curls flowing out beneath a nearly transparent veil. At least for once, she did not boldly look a man in the eye.

Claire reached her place, and all the knights stood to make room for her, giving him a full view of Leonie. No longer a tangled, bloody, and muddy mess. And still too much of everything to be beautiful like her cousin. Yet in spite of all, his hand fought him for the chance to slip within the mass of long, dangling curls, now caught up in narrow braids laced through with bright ribbons. Her eyes sparkled like huge, dark emeralds that drew him into their depths. Aye, too, too much of everything.

Leonie followed Claire, her gaze fixed firmly on the hem of her cousin's kirtle in her determination to behave like a proper maiden. Tonight she would, for once, not embarrass her uncle before his guests. Her awful hair was as controlled as it could be. In her favorite shade of green, trimmed in twining golden and crimson embroidered lions and cranes, she looked as decent as she could be made to look. She hadn't liked the way Ealga had set the veil on her head, but when she pulled it down farther to hide more of her hair and face, Ealga had whacked her with her comb.

She repeated the litany she had designed for herself for this night. *Smile sweetly. Speak only when spoken to. Look no man in the eye.* And every moment when not eating, fold her hands in her lap. Her eyes firmly focusing on the white linen tablecloth, she took her place. Heat blazed in her cheeks as she realized she was seated directly across from the man she least wanted to see. Gritting her teeth, she reaffirmed her vow. She would keep her eyes downcast if she had to count every bread crumb fallen from the trencher.

The Peregrine cleared his throat, and she jerked at the sound. "Lady Leonie," he said, "allow me to present to you my knight beside you, Hugh of Hatterie."

Jarred, Leonie blinked, absorbing the words, and nodded sideways to the knight. "So pleased, sir," she said.

"My pleasure," said the knight in a sweetly smooth voice. "Lady, will you permit me to cut your meat?"

Leonie smiled weakly. "How kind of you." She groaned. Of course it was kind of him. It was his duty as a gentleman. She didn't have to sound like he was the first man ever to deign to cut her meat for her.

"Hugh is heir to his uncle, Roland of Hatterie," Philippe said.

The knight chuckled. "He neglects to mention my uncle is young and newly wed. I vow I'll not be heir much longer." He laid a carefully trimmed slab of beef on Leonie's trencher and cut it into dainty pieces. "Alas, lady, I am but an impoverished knight, but I vow always to cut your meat finer than any man, for I shall be enslaved to your lovely green eyes all my life."

Lightning swift, her gaze flew up to meet his, and she was shocked by the man's male beauty. With dark brown curls dangling over his brow, lips that curved in elegant arches like a bow, and deep brown eyes, Hugh of Hatterie was a man any maid might dream of wedding. He gazed at her in utter adoration. God in Heaven, help her. She did not have the power of the gaze, but he talked as if she had entranced him. She had not even noticed him before now. What had she done? It must have been something.

The Peregrine cleared his throat again, loudly, startling her. She looked up at him before she could remember her vow, and caught a fire sparking in his dark eyes. With a twitch, she lowered her eyes, pretending fascination with her food. Hugh straightened and returned his attention to his own trencher.

Oh. He was just flattering her after all, like a good guest. Any polite knight knew to gaze adoringly at even the less-than-fair maidens of the household.

She renewed her litany of modest behavior. If it cost her every nerve and sinew in her body frozen into permanent rigidity, she would not look into the Peregrine's eyes again.

Uncle Geoffrey, moderate in his drinks but not in his meat, ate heartily, engaging Philippe in conversation as they ate, while Leonie managed a few agreeable words with Hugh. But the man's voice had become pleasant but distant. That was just as well. But it would be rather nice to really be adored by a fine-looking man such as he.

Oh no! Don't even think of it!

Leonie pleaded with God to never give her the power of the gaze and to help her keep her eyes off both men. But again and again she strayed, just a peek, and every time the Peregrine was watching her.

She was hopeless. She begged God instead to end the meal quickly so she could flee up the stairs to her chamber.

"Tell me, Philippe," said her uncle, swiping a linen cloth across his lips to signal he had finished with his meal. "What news from the king's court?"

"'Tis no secret, the Scots king is in England," the Peregrine replied.

"Aye, so we heard. We hear the Scots raid less when their king is not safely within their borders."

"He is safe enough here. Rufus will scrupulously honor his safe conduct. Unless Malcolm means mischief."

"When does he not?"

The Peregrine drew in a long breath that sounded thoughtful. "Now that he has come, he refuses to submit to the king's court. He denies he is Rufus's vassal, yet we all saw him bend the knee not a year ago. So Rufus ignores him. You know, of course, the Scots king's daughter, Edith, is at Wilton Abbey where her Aunt Christina is abbess. 'Twas only the week before Malcolm arrived that the Count of Richmond petitioned Rufus for Edith's hand."

He had? Leonie exchanged glances with her uncle, embarrassingly aware that the Peregrine observed them. Did he know that same Count of Richmond had been here at Brodin not three days ago seeking her uncle's blessing to ask the king for her hand in marriage? Thankfully, her uncle had refused. She could only hope the king would as well.

"That randy old goat?" said Uncle Geoffrey. Leonie held her breath, but her uncle said nothing more.

The Peregrine took such a deep sip from his cup that he must have drained it. "Rufus said if the girl was ready to wed, perhaps he'd marry her himself."

Someone near the far end of the table dropped a cup that clattered all the way to the floor. No one else moved. Even Leonie stared.

"Rufus? Marry?" A chorus of voices spoke together.

The Peregrine chuckled harshly. "Then the king took seven knights and rode to Wilton Abbey. Within two days, Rufus rode back and announced to all that with his own eyes he had seen the Scots princess take the veil, so she could not marry any man."

"Close call for Rufus," said a deep male voice.

A dark chuckle rumbled along the table. Even the ladies knew the scandalous stories about the king and his court, so strangely empty of women. None believed Rufus would ever take a bride.

"Then it was a bluff," Leonie said. She gasped. She'd forgotten herself again. And there she was, eye to eye with the Peregrine, his censure pouring through his eyes at her, while she could not force herself to look away.

He nodded politely. "Aye, lady, nor do you need fear for yourself. Even Rufus is shocked by the Count of Richmond, and he will let no decent woman fall into the man's hands. But more important, the Princess Edith will never marry if Rufus can prevent it."

"Is that not her father's choice?" she asked.

"Aye. But recall, the blood of Saxon kings also flows in her veins. To ally Scotland and the old Saxon kings with a Norman as powerful as Richmond—'tis far too dangerous."

Then what had the Count of Richmond wanted of her? But of course. If Richmond couldn't have the princess, Leonie at least would bring fine lands and a castle to a marriage.

"Mayhap," said Aunt Beatrice as she daintily dabbed her napkin to her lips, "Rufus has chosen a husband for our Leonie?"

Leonie sighed. It was Aunt Beatrice's favorite subject, and Rufus's delay was almost beyond explaining. Unless every man Rufus had chosen had argued the king out of it.

"I think not," replied the Peregrine. "If he had made a choice, he would have no need to send me to be castellan of Bosewood."

Leonie dropped her napkin. Her castle? The king had chosen Philippe le Peregrine?

Uncle Geoffrey frowned. "Yet he does not seek to ally you with the castle's heiress?"

"He knows I would not."

Hot shame turned Leonie's face brilliant crimson. He didn't have to say it so bluntly and publicly.

"The king honors my vow," he said, as blandly as if she were not present. "I do not wish to wed. When Rufus chooses a husband for the heiress, then I'll be free to wander again."

She wished she could pull her veil over her face. Not even to obtain the very castle and demesnes other men coveted would Philippe le Peregrine take her to wife. Her hands knotted together in her lap. Well. She did not want him, either. He was arrogant and rude. She did not doubt he would be heartless with any wife.

"Enough of talk about a court that is so far away," said Uncle Geoffrey, and his voice had a kind and gentle tone that she knew was directed at her. "Time for some gaiety. Let us clear the hall and enjoy some dancing."

The Peregrine reached out his arm, staying her uncle, who had just begun to rise from his chair. "I have another idea," he said. "A different sort of entertainment. Let us have a shooting match."

Uncle Geoffrey sputtered. "'Tis dark, Philippe."

"Let the bailey be lit by torches. I have a yen to redeem my damaged reputation."

Every muscle of Leonie's body tightened like a bowstring. Had he not humiliated her enough tonight?

"Sir knight, I do not wish. Perhaps the knights of Brodin might be a better match," she said.

He laughed, and something dark and hard changed his eyes. "Can any of them outshoot you, Lady Leonie? I think not. Perhaps you are afraid you might be bested?"

The heat of anger pulsed in her veins. "Do you think you can?" she asked, her words low and measured.

His eyes narrowed. "I'll split your arrows down their shafts."

"Mayhap she will split your shaft," said one of her uncle's knights. The howls of laughter from the Brodin knights echoed off the hall's stone walls.

Her glare surely shed sparks like a horseshoe striking stone. Ice and fire throbbed in her heart. "Very well, then," she said. "So shall it be. Forgive me, dear uncle, for disturbing your pleasure. I must fetch my bow and face Sir Braggart's pleasure instead."

"Leonie!" Aunt Beatrice gasped.

Leonie hardened herself and turned away from her aunt, whose horrified displeasure would shame Leonie too much.

A cheer went up from the Norman knights. Leonie gaped down the length of the trestle table. Had the cursed knight bragged to them about besting a woman? Did they also cheer for her coming defeat?

"Aye, lads!" said her nemesis, and he stood, clapping Uncle Geoffrey on the back. "I've promised them the best shooting in all England, and now we'll have it! Where are the butts? Still beside the quintain?"

Leonie fled the hall, her cheeks burning. He did mean to humiliate her!

With that thought, she halted so abruptly that if any man had been running behind her, he would have slammed into her hard enough to knock her down. Nay, Philippe le Peregrine would not shame her. She would shame him.

She could. If she handled it just right.

CHAPTER THREE

———◆———

LEONIE STOMPED UP THE STAIRS, THROUGH THE SOLAR, AND into the ladies' chamber, where Ealga stood, wringing her aged hands.

"Oh, must ye?"

"He baited me." Leonie strode to the corner where she kept the ivorywood bow and quiver of arrows her mother had left behind when she disappeared, long years ago.

"Ye shouldna rise to the bait, girl. 'Twill be your undoing."

"If it is so, then it is so." Her chin jutted as she picked up the soft leather quiver, and she paused a moment to finger the feathers of the arrows and slipped the quiver's strap over her shoulder.

Ealga moaned. Heavily etched wrinkles in her face became deep crevices, and Leonie ached at her beloved maid's distress. But she could not give in now. If Leonie knew anything about humans, it was that they saw what they wanted to see. One merely needed to be careful. After all this time, not even her beloved uncle knew Leonie's secret. He only thought her too much like her mysterious mother.

Leonie reached for the ivorywood bow, braced it between her legs, strung it, and slung it over her other shoulder.

"Have a care, lass," Ealga whined after her as Leonie marched down the stairs, through the hall, and across the inner bailey.

The glow of torches lit the lower bailey. There, her adversary awaited, his powerful legs standing wide, his bow propped at arm's length. Every inch of him, from his long, straight blond hair to his muscled arms, legs, and torso, proclaimed his arrogant maleness. She sneered. She had not thought a man could swagger while standing still.

His knights lined up on one side of the straw-stuffed manikin, opposite the knights of Castle Brodin. When men took sides like this, there was always wagering. Behind the knights, lining the stone steps and parapets, the folk of the castle milled and buzzed with excitement and cheered her approach. At least she knew she would please them.

Chin high and back straight, abrasively displaying her unusual height, Leonie strode to the Peregrine and stopped, looking him straight in the eye in the very way she had spent all evening trying to avoid. The man responded with a smirk.

He would not smirk long.

She scanned the line of Brodin's knights and found her favorite. "Gerard," she called.

Gerard stepped forth. "Your servant, lady."

She held out bow and quiver. Gerard bowed and took them. Then she whipped the veil off her head, twisted it into a rope, and bound back the wild hair that was always getting in her way.

"You may have the first shot, Philippe le Peregrine," she said.

"A lady always goes first."

"But not first before a guest."

He nodded warily and eyed the straw manikin dangling from the quintain post.

"One in the heart," he said.

The muscles in his arm bulged as he pulled his powerful bow. The arrow sang through the air.

An excellent shot. Nearly perfect.

"Ah, but that is not the location of a man's heart," she said.

She drew an arrow from the quiver. She caressed its stiff feathers, nocked it to the string, and drew the bowstring back as far as her earlobe.

Fly straight, sweet shaft, she sang in her heart to the arrow. The bowstring twanged dully as it was released, and Leonie silently steered it as it flew, to thud into the straw manikin's crotch.

A low moan coursed through the gathering of men. She didn't have to look to know more than one man clutched his nether parts.

She turned back to the Peregrine. "You said you would split my shaft, sir knight. I invite you to do it."

A deeper groan came from the men. Even Philippe le Peregrine looked a little ill. He narrowed his eyes.

"Your claws are showing again, little lioness," he replied. "You know little of a man's true heart. I shall split my own arrow instead."

And if he called her little lioness one more time, she feared she would kick him in the shin.

Nocking his next arrow, he paused and sent her a narrowed look. He drew back, took aim, and let it fly. It whizzed the distance to the manikin and thudded into the straw. Perhaps it shaved the arrow. But it did not split it.

Perfect—for her. She might have smiled. But she was of no mood to waste any pleasantry on him. Leonie pulled four arrows from the quiver, one at a time. Three of them she clutched between her third and fourth fingers, just beneath their fletchings, and the fourth she nocked into the string.

"What's she going to do?" said a voice said from the Peregrine's side of the shooting yard. "Shoot all four at once?"

She ignored them. And no one from Castle Brodin made a sound. For they knew.

Her mind singing the secret arrows' song, she drew, aimed, and released. In rapid succession her long fingers flipped the next arrow upward to nestle into shooting position, and it flew. Then the third, then the fourth, so quickly the knights had no time to exclaim between shots. Each arrow found its target: the Peregrine's first shot flayed, his second beside it split, the arrow lodged in the crotch of the manikin rent in two, and the last, aimed high.

Soar, sweet arrow. Find your mark.

It cut through the rope, and the straw manikin tumbled to the earth.

Leonie lowered her bow and looked around. Not a noise came from anyone. Their mouths hung open.

Then her stomach twisted into a huge knot as she realized her error. Their silence spoke as loudly as a thunderclap. *God in Heaven, help me. What have I done?* What she had done no man could do. Would they now begin to see her for what she really was—not human? Or worse, spawned of the devil, as Normans believed witches were?

She had to turn it around. Or stall until she thought of something. "Gerard, my arrows."

Gerard nodded solemnly and walked to the target to pull out the arrows, then returned.

"I am defeated," said the Peregrine, as softly as if he spoke in the nave of an empty, echoing cathedral.

Leonie swallowed her building fear, but she was well practiced in hiding her secret. She could do it.

"Do not disparage, sir knight," she said, her nostrils flaring above her honeyed smile. "The secret is in the bow."

Leonie held out her mother's ivorywood bow to the knight. She gestured to Gerard and his squire to set up the manikin against the quintain post.

Philippe frowned as he studied the bow's pale wood and the bronze bands above and below the handgrip. "What manner of wood is this?" he asked. "I've never seen the like."

"I do not know. I am told it is merely ash, treated in some unknown way. I call it ivorywood because it looks to me like ivory."

He pulled on the string, bouncing it easily. "This is no man's bow. It is too weak."

"Aye," she said. "Fit only for a woman."

The crowd chuckled lowly. He frowned in response.

"Try it, sir knight," she said. "Plant the arrow between the dummy's eyes."

It was an easy shot for him, but just in case, she sang silently to the arrow, and it hummed through the air to hit its target perfectly.

Leonie drew an arrow from her quiver and handed it to him.

"Now, split the shaft, Philippe le Peregrine."

The missile flew as straight as she sang it, as if it sought its soul mate. But like no soul mate God ever made, it hit squarely at the nock and split the wood down to the iron point.

"God's face," he whispered raggedly.

"Would you care to try again?" She grasped another arrow near its nock as if to pull it out of the quiver.

The way he shook his head was strange and slow, as if he were dazed. "Where did you get this bow?" he asked. "Who made it?"

"It belonged to my mother. 'Tis said she made it. I only know that it was among her possessions. But she is gone, so I cannot ask."

"I don't suppose you'd sell it. Haps, for the price of a king's ransom?"

She almost smiled. Almost laughed. "Nay. I have very little of her, and I would never part with it."

Then the urge came over her, wishing she could lay upon him a gaze so devastating it would bring him to his knees with overwhelming need to love her, just to make him suffer. She would have succumbed if it had only been in her power, for she wanted—what? Did she want him to suffer even more than the humiliation of a staggering defeat by a maid?

But it made no difference what she wished. It was not within her power.

A trembling coursed through her arms and hands. Lest it betray her, she bowed an immodestly low, mocking curtsy and spun away. Her heart pounded, rushing blood that clouded mind and vision, screaming at her to flee. Somehow she forced her steps to long, swaggering strides, back through the gate to the inner bailey, to the hall and through its doors.

CHAPTER FOUR

An oath clung to the tip of Philippe's tongue, but thankfully got no farther. His gaze was fixed on the twitch of arrogance in the lady's swaying hips. Even her tied-back rope of impossible curls swung back and forth to the rhythm of her steps.

"I told you," said the Brodin knight, Gerard. Smirking, he held out his palm.

Philippe fumbled a coin out of his pouch and plopped it into the knight's hand. The knight snickered.

"It must be magic," grumbled Michael, adding his coin to the growing pile in Gerard's hand.

"Nay," replied Philippe as he frowned, his nostrils flaring with the bitter remembrance. "It lacks the stench. Magic is always evil. This was talent. Did you not see how she handled those arrows? When I return, I vow I will force her to show me that trick."

Gerard laughed and tossed his newly plump purse to the Brodin knights to divide their booty. "Not magic, but she does deceive you. 'Tis skill and much practice, not the bow. Although it surely is the finest I have ever seen. I have pulled it myself, but it did nothing for me."

The Brodin knights burst into a guffaw.

"Naught could help you, Gerard," said one named Ivo. "'Tis a good thing you are a knight. Were you a huntsman, you would starve."

Philippe handed his bow to his squire and glanced back at where the straw dummy sprawled on the ground. A small shudder passed through him, remembering those shafts to the groin.

Geoffrey clapped a hand to his shoulder. "Do not take it to heart, my friend."

"She gulled me again. I should have known better. But I thought I could beat her this time."

"Nay, you gulled yourself." Geoffrey laughed. "She tried to avoid the contest. She does not like to be thought unwomanly, you see."

Philippe could not think of a woman more unwomanly. Yet she had an allure that grasped him by the heart. Or by the bollocks, to be more truthful. He counted four times now that he'd had a good view of her enticing backside.

He frowned. The girl was dangerous to him. He needed to get away from the little lioness of Brodin Castle as soon as he could.

"You do her no favors to allow her such freedom, Geoffrey. A husband might beat her for such audacity."

Geoffrey sighed as he started back up the slope to the upper bailey. "I fear it is in the blood. Her mother was the same, and it did not serve her well. The girl does try hard to please, though. I can only hope Rufus chooses her husband well."

"Yet who would he choose? I fear for her, Geoffrey."

"Fulk of Durham, mayhap."

Philippe's head jerked up. "Fulk, the Warrior of God? May God help her, then."

"You do not approve? He is a pious man."

"He is a mountain of righteous arrogance, and arrogance does not tolerate other arrogance. He will beat her. No man likes to be challenged, and he most of all."

"You sought out the challenge, did you not? Are there not other men who measure their worth by more than the strength of their arm?"

"Strength is what the world values."

"Is it? Fine knight though you are, you are replaceable, for more new knights grow to manhood every day. But your way of making peace is unequaled, and Rufus would be hard put to find a man with your wisdom at politics. Nor, if I were king, would I wish you anywhere but where you have been placed."

"At Bosewood? I did not choose it, nor want it. But I do my king's bidding."

"Aye, I know. He could have none more fiercely loyal than you. He values you most for that. You go to Bosewood next?"

"Not immediately. I'll send my knights ahead, but I have more of the king's business I must attend first. Business with the border."

"Truly, there will be trouble, then?"

"Truly. Malcolm will likely go from raiding to invading. But Rufus means to forestall him. If trouble comes, you will need to call your knights and soldiers to arms."

"I'll be ready."

Already the knights of the hall were enjoying another round of ale, toasting to their female champion. At least they approved what she did for their purses. Philippe suspected the servants would be very late in folding away the trestle tables this night. As for himself, he expected a merciless ragging from the king's knights.

He laughed to himself. Although he had thought he might win this time, he had many times bragged to his men it was a woman who was the finest archer in all England, perhaps in all Christendom. He just had not known she would drub him so badly.

Something about it made his soul tingle. Perhaps if he were not a man cursed.

But he was.

The stifling heat still lingered in the solar. Only a whiff of breeze passed through the lancet window, not even enough to stir the bed curtains, but out beyond the castle walls the black branches and leaves swayed quietly against the bright moonlit sky.

Beside her sleeping cousin, Leonie lay in her thin chemise atop her covers. She could not sleep. She could not shake the thoughts of the Peregrine from her head.

She rose so quietly the bed's ropes did not creak, and padded silently across the ladies' chamber. The door to the solar groaned on its massive metal hinges. She hesitated, but seeing Claire did not stir, Leonie skimmed through the solar and out its door into the night.

The cool shaft of night air lapped at her face and sent long, pale tendrils of hair dancing around her cheeks, relieving the stickiness beneath her chemise as she descended the steps. Even the stone felt cool to the bare soles of her feet. Soon she landed on the paving stones of the upper bailey, strangely deserted and nearly silent, save for an owl's hoot and the chittering of the night-jar. In the distance, the rush of water hissed over the rapids in the beck.

She had no destination, only a need that drove her through the dark gloom of the upper gatehouse to the lower bailey, lit by a moon so full her Fae sight was unneeded. The breeze tickled her skin, yet a hazy mist trailed at her feet like an eager litter of puppies. A September fog, though it was hot August. Wind and fog did not meet in such a way.

From the fog appeared the straw manikin, swinging from a rope at the quintain like a criminal hanged. An arrow protruded from its crotch like a limp shaft. Yet it was reversed, the triangular iron head dangling down.

The manikin was a man. The golden-haired Peregrine, his flesh silvered by the moonlight. The arrow shaft became erect, thick, long, and hard.

"You wound me, lady." She knew his voice, for its low rasp had spoken to her in many dreams.

"Nay. You are whole."

"Not whole."

The man stood before her, not hanging from the rope.

"You should not wander alone at night, lady."

"I am safe. It is my uncle's castle."

"You will never be safe."

That was true. It was why she would never run, but also why she would never say it.

"What is it you want, lady? Do you seek a forfeit?"

"You did not pay the last one. Why should I ask one of you this time?"

"Is that what you want, lady? A kiss?"

She felt the hot flush growing on her face, flooding her body, for she was of the Faeriekind and her blood ran hot. Only human women had to be taught to know man-pleasure.

She turned to face him and was lost in the dark honey depth of his eyes. His lips looked hard, yet soft, as they parted and revealed the white tips of his teeth.

She licked her own lips as she raised a finger to trace the artful curves of his mouth. His tongue touched to her fingertips. She closed her eyes and felt the touch of his lips to hers, like the light caress of a feather.

"What do you want, Leonie?" his ragged voice asked. "Do you want more?"

"Aye," she whispered.

Cool breeze and hot flesh tormented her shoulders as the loose chemise was pushed down. Roughened hands slid around her breasts, lifted them, and rubbed her virgin nipples between finger and thumb. *The heat in her body grew, like sharp tendrils coiling downward, jabbing like strokes of lightning at the ache of passion growing inside her.*

"Do you want more?" whispered the Peregrine.

"Aye."

The baggy chemise drifted past her thighs and vanished as if it melted into the air. Her moonlight-silver skin touched the Peregrine's sun-tinged flesh, felt the hardness beneath its surface, great corded muscles and the rippling male planes of his chest.

His hand slid between her legs and up, to find that strange nub that housed passion. It had no name as other body parts did, not like an arm or leg, nor even a shaft. But it was like a shaft, excited, swollen, aching, begging for the touch of his hand.

"You would be a man, but you would have a woman's pleasures? You are unseemly. You play the man and you play the whore. But you are neither, nor are you what you should be. Nay, lioness, you shall have no pleasure from me."

The Peregrine removed his hands from her body. He dropped a mocking bow and turned away.

And disappeared into the fog.

With a jerk, Philippe sat up and looked around him. The pallet where he had lain down was still beneath him, and he was still in the solar of his friend Geoffrey, his knights sleeping nearby. But his body said he had been somewhere else.

The heated ache in his shaft was more than a dream, for it stood hard and erect from the long fingers that had curled about it.

Nay, no fingers enclosed his shaft. He had dreamed. Yet he could feel them still, as real as any that had ever touched him.

Hugh rose up on one elbow, cocking his head in curiosity.

Philippe frowned back. "It is too hot," he said.

He rose from his pallet and went out the solar door, down the steps, and across the bailey. He dashed up the stone steps to the parapet, and the guard stopped his pacing to watch.

"Too hot," he said again. "It's cooler here."

"Aye," said the guard. "'Tis a fine summer night. Too soon it will be cold winter."

Philippe nodded and turned to walk along the wall. It was at least cool enough to dampen his ardor. He had been without a woman for a very long time, but he had made his vow and he meant to keep it. And, God's holy face, he was not about to let a wench seduce him in his own dreams.

"Leonie, wake up. Are you ill?"

"Nay."

"You're dreaming of him, aren't you?"

"Nay." Leonie sat up. She was not in the bailey. She was in her own bed, beside Claire. For once, she was where she ought to be. It was a dream.

"Aye, you are. You think me so innocent that I do not know? Where do you think he is, Leonie?"

"In the solar with his knights?" Aye, he must be there, for that was where such visitors always spent their nights.

It had all been a dream, then. She could not have walked through the solar, for it was full of knights. She would have never entered the bailey barefoot and clad only in a thin chemise. No mist could form near the ground while a breeze stirred the air. And never was there a time when no man kept watch from the parapets, night and day.

She had dreamed it all. Yet her body still tingled with need and excitement.

"Not in the solar," said Claire with a secret sort of smile. "He is still walking the parapet, long after the others sleep. You can see him from the window. Go look."

"Nay."

Claire tugged her hand, and Leonie followed. Out on the sentry walk, lit by the bright full moon, the Peregrine stood, arms folded, looking directly where she stood. He would know it was she by her shape in the shadows. No other was so long and thin as she.

He turned and walked away.

He would never forgive her for what she had done to him this night.

Leonie lingered at the narrow window, watching nothing, only feeling what little breeze penetrated into the chamber. The dream was not real, but it spoke the truth. She could never have him, nor should she want him, for he would never approve of her. She could never please him. He would never love her.

But yet, the dream was wrong. No one could deprive her of her dreams, and in her dreams, he could be the man she wanted him to be. And she would never tell anyone. She would do the king's bidding when he chose a husband for her, and never would anyone know it was the Peregrine who had taken her heart captive.

CHAPTER FIVE

Leonie stood near the lancet window in the solar as the king's knights prepared to leave. The Peregrine stood in the bailey, taking his last leave of her uncle. They talked and clasped shoulders. Then the Peregrine glanced up at the lancet window in the ladies' chamber, but he could not have known she watched from the solar, hiding in shadows instead.

She did her uncle no honor to not go down to see him off. The thought of it brought a flush of shame for the spiteful way she had humiliated him. Shame for the passion of her dreams, to feel such things for a man who thought so little of her.

What man could want a woman such as she? The Peregrine she dreamed about was right in that regard. She sighed. She was a grown woman now, but she'd behaved foolishly. There was naught to be done about what had happened, for it was like water in the beck flowing past the castle, and long gone. The only thing to do was to go on about her life.

If she did not have enough of the Fae blood to make her one of that kind, why couldn't she at least have enough human blood to make her a real woman?

That afternoon she watched from the village as another entourage rode in. Fulk of Durham and his knights and servants, in their liveries of red, black, and white. With a sigh, Leonie slipped away quietly through the back side of the village and returned to the castle by the sally port, then rushed across the upper bailey and up the steps to the ladies' chamber. She barely heard Ealga's nattering as she changed into more suitable garments.

But not the green kirtle. It belonged to that other time, the time of her great embarrassment.

Her lips stretched thin over her teeth. Haps what she really needed was a husband who would occupy her so completely she would have no time for silly, disturbing dreams.

As she entered the hall through the back passage, she saw the tall knight in red and black who had been so attentive to her only a few weeks before. Fulk had the dark coloring of Frankish blood and sported a closely trimmed beard and narrow mustache that added sharpness to his dark eyes and wide cheekbones. He was handsome. She'd always thought that.

When he spotted her, his pleasant smile warmed. "Ah, my lovely Lady Leonie," he said, and approached to take her hand and lift it to his lips. Instinctively her hand became stiff, but she corrected her response. If the man was to be her destiny, she'd best try to get off to a good start.

"Lord Fulk," she replied with a modest nod. From now on, she would make modesty the cornerstone of her demeanor.

"I have your uncle's permission to walk with you in the garden. Shall we go?"

She dipped a perfect curtsy as a reply, and he took her arm. A glance to the side revealed Aunt Beatrice's sweet round face and her chubby hands folded almost as if in prayer. But Uncle Geoffrey had a worried wrinkle to his brow.

Well, she would let destiny take her where it chose to go. It seemed she had spent most of her young life fighting it, all to no good purpose.

Outside the oak doors of the hall, she let him lead her into her aunt's little walled herb garden. In the shade of the wall she saw Claire and one of her aunt's ladies, busy at their mending and embroidery. She felt a certain comfort in knowing they were there.

"I have heard you sometimes take to gardening, Lady Leonie. Like your Aunt Beatrice."

"Aye, Lord Fulk," she said.

He moved his hand from her arm to take her hand. A shudder rippled through her. But she succeeded in not jerking her hand away.

"At Drogie Castle we have a much finer garden. A lady would find it very pleasurable. She need not dirty her hands, for there are four gardeners to do her bidding."

Leonie attempted a smile. It would not do to tell him half the pleasure of gardening was in the feel of the soil on her hands, even for her aunt, who in all other ways was the most ladylike of ladies. "Gardens are a great pleasure, I find," she replied.

"Of course, a lady must manage her household. But at Drogie, a lady would have all the servants she needs to do such things. There would be no need to fret over vats of dye or the garden vegetables. Or the baking of bread. A proper lady supervises her household. She should not have to do the work of peasants."

She clamped her teeth shut. All the things she and her aunt had so often enjoyed together. And she knew her aunt had been raised properly. Her mouth started to open, and she promptly shut it again before words could tumble out.

He is Lord Fulk, vassal to the Bishop of Durham, a pious knight who has been on pilgrimage to the Holy Land. He is called the Warrior of God. He is handsome and rich. He would make an excellent husband.

"Of course, Drogie is not my only holding. I have twenty-six manors and castles, all over England."

And I am heiress to twelve. I suspect you are thinking of that.

Time to change the subject. "Have you been to Bosewood, Lord Fulk?"

"Your father's castle? Of course, many times. It is much dilapidated, I am sorry to say. I was your father's very good friend, you know. He would have approved of our marriage, and said so many times."

A huge lump formed suddenly in her throat, almost causing her to cough. "Marriage? I know nothing of that. Surely the king would tell me if he had plans for me."

Fulk slid on a smooth smile, and his voice grew sweet and gentle. "But it would be a good match, I'm sure you realize. We are remarkably well suited. I have come to speak my intent to you before I approach the king, but I am certain the king will agree with us."

What was he up to? Something felt wrong. Aye, a man might speak to a lady first, but he had not asked, and merely informed her. Her fists were growing tighter and tighter.

"I have not agreed to anything, Lord Fulk. It is not my place. King William will decide my husband."

She watched the movement of his head, ever so smoothly rising then leaning left, then nodding deeply as his smile became even broader, as if he meant to bestow his great benevolence on her.

"You could choose no better than I, dear lady. Who else? Not the odious Alan Niger of Richmond, who has taken his own dead brother's mistress as his own. Aye, I know the handsome Philippe le Peregrine has only recently been to visit, but all know he will not marry. He is, I am sorry to tell you, more than a little like his licentious king in his preferences."

Leonie's nose wrinkled. That she didn't believe.

"You shall not marry outside England, for the king will never allow it. Who else could it be? Nay, dear lady, we shall wed, and our lands merge in most effective ways. We shall have heirs more powerful even than the Count of Richmond. Imagine such for your sons! Your father regretted always that he had no sons, but you may give him the progeny he dreamed of."

Leonie promised herself she would not dislike this man merely because he kept invoking her father's will. "I do not even remember my father, as I have not seen him since I was a baby."

"It is your duty to honor him with the marriage he wished."

I would honor Uncle Geoffrey. But not the man who sired me and cared nothing more for me.

"Of course you shall marry me," Fulk continued. "Surely you see the perfect sense in it. You have only to say it."

She sensed a snare closing in on her. "It is not for me to say, Lord Fulk," she repeated. "I shall marry as the king commands."

"And he will so command, my dear lady. So you will then agree, I am sure."

"I shall do as the king commands, but I cannot say what that should be."

"Then we are in agreement," he said, almost mumbling into the kiss he planted on her hand. "And now I shall go to the king in confidence."

More than ever, she wished she could jerk her hand away, and even to slap him with it, but she had sworn not to misbehave again. "You misunderstand me, Lord Fulk. I did not say that. I cannot. It would be appalling to presume upon the will of my king. That I will not do."

The Warrior of God propped one hand on the pommel of his sword, causing it to swing backward. She drew in a sharp breath, watching that hand where it rested against the chased silver snake that ran from the cross guard, winding around the grip to terminate in a ruby-eyed head at the pommel. But he released the sword and instead took her hand on his arm to lead her back to the hall.

"Fear not, dear lady. He will hear our plea and be pleased." Fulk merely continued the smile, which she began to see as oily. Leonie could feel her heart beating rapidly, as if she ran from a wild dog. What would she do if he told Uncle Geoffrey she had consented to be his wife? What had he told her uncle before she had arrived?

But all he said, once they returned to the hall, was how pleased he was with her, and that he could hope for a happy future for them. Leonie took her first chance to escape, wishing she could run and hide in the woods for the rest of her life.

How could she bow to such a fate? She had tried, so very hard, to be like other women. But never had she felt so unhuman as she did now. Yet what else could she do? Was there no man in England like her uncle, a decent and fair man, yet a suitable enough husband for her in the king's eyes?

If only she could find the way to the Summer Land and the Faeriekind, and leave behind this world where she would never fit.

Uncle Geoffrey did nothing to encourage Fulk and his entourage to stay the night, unlike the king's knights who had come the day before. But they stayed anyway. Leonie could not sleep, knowing the Warrior of God slept in the adjacent solar with his most trusted companions.

When in the darkest of night she heard subtle rustling and fumbling at the door, she was grateful for the heavy bolt thrown across it to bar access. Claire sat up at the sounds, her pretty blue eyes rounded with fear in the darkness of the chamber. Leonie quietly walked to the corner of the room where her bow and quiver leaned against the wall, strung the bow, and gathered the arrows in her hand, prepared to shoot them all if she must.

Claire took one arrow and held it like a dagger.

The noises ceased. After a few moments, Claire returned to the bed, but Leonie stayed near the far wall, waiting.

When the sun rose, the knights of the Warrior of God rode out, much as the Peregrine and his knights had done the morning before. All Leonie could think was that she wished she had not been so arrogant with Philippe le Peregrine. Even if he wouldn't choose to marry her.

As she had every day since Sigge had cut his foot, Leonie went to the modest blacksmith's quarters within the castle's lower bailey. And every day, right in front of both Sigge's parents, she had swiftly traced her thumb over the wound as if merely touching it.

Days before, Harald's wife had returned Leonie's veil, carefully soaked and cleaned of the last trace of blood, presenting it to her meekly, as if she had personally caused great harm to the lady's fine possession, and this day Leonie wore that same veil with pride. Leonie was as fond of Gerdrund and Harald as she was of Sigge.

"I can walk now, Leonie," Sigge said, his squeaky voice rising as if he pleaded.

His mother turned a beseeching look on Leonie.

"Nay," Leonie replied. "I said your foot is healing the way it should. I did not say it has healed. Perhaps tomorrow."

Sigge stuck out his lower lip and slumped into a wretched heap where he sat by the empty hearth. Only dire threats from his father kept him within the house, but that was where he needed to stay a bit longer.

Leonie kept herself busy in the castle, making up a new batch of green dye in various shades to color wool for embroidery. Green had become the castle's favorite color, not merely because it was Leonie's preferred color, but also because it was her best dye. She knew full well that if she could just find a way to make her scarlet more brilliant or her blue more like the bright summer sky, those colors would soon become the new favorites. As it was, the only way she could get the bright colors she wanted was to trade her green wool to peddlers.

Several days of rain that heralded the beginning of September also kept her within the castle, embroidering fanciful beasts along the neckline of a new kirtle for Claire. But as busy as she kept herself, the mystery that lay in the forest lingered in her mind.

Lingered. And made a shiver rumble down her spine. Twice she set out when the sun broke through the clouds, but both times she stopped at the forest's edge and turned away, thinking there was surely something else she needed to do instead.

At last she gave in to Sigge's pleas, for the wound was completely healed. And she needed a companion in the forest. If she did not return to the forest soon, fear would take over and she would lose her favorite place in all the world.

And soon she would be married. Who knew if her new husband would allow her the pleasure of walking among the trees, or of gathering leaves and moss for dying the wool? If Rufus chose Fulk, she suspected he would forbid even her experiments with dyes as being beneath her dignity.

Ha. She was a Faerie halfling—not a lady. She had no dignity.

Sigge danced about like a young puppy, circling and hopping as they crossed the meadow below the castle. As they came within the boundaries of the trees, he found a long, straight stick and began swinging it about, swishing, swiping, and jabbing into the air. "I'm a brave knight, Leonie!" he shouted, parrying his invisible opponent. "I'm the Peregrine, and I'm fighting the King of Scotland!"

Leonie found a pained smile. Why did it have to be Philippe the boy idolized? But she knew. All the boys wanted to grow up to be the legendary Peregrine.

"I wish I had a real sword," Sigge said. "One just like the Peregrine's with that big red stone on the pommel. And the falcon etched on the blade." He swung his play sword in wide arcs that would have cut through the brush if the sword had been real.

"You're too young for a sword. You'd probably cut off your other foot."

"Would not!" He shouted a battle cry and jabbed at an imaginary enemy.

"Don't you want to be a blacksmith like your father?"

The lad hung his head. Leonie knew how much he loved his father.

"Mayhap your father would let you become a monk so you could study, and learn to read and write. You are always so interested in everything."

"I don't want to be a monk. They never have any fun. And they have to shave their heads funny. And besides, my father wouldn't ever have any grandchildren and he wouldn't like that."

"You have two brothers and two sisters, Sigge."

"I know, but he still wouldn't like it."

"I suppose you'll have to be a blacksmith, then."

"I want to be a knight," Sigge replied. "I'd ride on a huge white charger to war like the Peregrine, and slay lots of enemies so the king would make me his favorite knight."

"His horse isn't white. It's grey."

"Mine would be white."

His dream tugged at her heart. She knew what it was like to have dreams that could never come true. "You know it is not likely, Sigge."

"That's what Papa said, too. A blacksmith's son is always a blacksmith's son. And then he's a blacksmith himself."

"'Tis an honorable heritage. And your father is Lord Geoffrey's armorer, not just any blacksmith."

"But he can't ever be a knight. So I can't be either. But my grandfather was a knight. Only he had to go be a traitor. I guess my father was lucky the king let him live."

So he was. Leonie had heard the story told in the hall when she was very young. Some even mentioned Emilien, the Norman given name Harald had disowned. But Harald was valued and honored in this household, so no one mentioned it anymore.

Today she had to smile. There was nothing wrong with Sigge's foot now besides an ugly red scar, and Sigge would be far less likely to get into trouble if he went with her.

"Can you show me how to find the good mushrooms, Leonie?" he asked as he bobbed along beside her.

"I don't know them, Sigge," she replied. "I always go get old nanny Brigid to look at them."

He swaggered a bit as he walked. "I know some of them."

"No, you don't. You only think you do. Only old nanny Brigid can always tell. When you are older, we will ask her to show us both."

"Aw." He kicked at a stone in their path. "Ow!"

Leonie smirked. Bright as the boy was, he seemed always to have to learn the hard way.

"We're looking for sumac leaves today. I want to see if they make better dyes when they first get their autumn color, or if it helps to wait till they fall. And while we're there, you can show me the piece of metal where you cut your foot."

"That's good," he said. "Can you make something really bright yellow, so I can have a tunic of it? I'm getting tired of green."

Leonie laughed. "I am too. Yellow is hard, though. Some of the leaves may work better this year, but most of them aren't very bright or the dye fades too quickly. I need a different mordant to set them, I think. The coneflowers were the best last year. I'll have you pick them from the herb garden when we return."

Sigge whistled as he danced along the path. Leonie began to feel the now familiar dread soaking into her, as it had all week, and she took a deep breath. She had taken to thumping her fingers against her palm as a way to remind herself not to become embroiled in ridiculous fears. Now she thumped her hand with increasing ferocity. If one had reason to be afraid, that was one thing. But not silly fancies. That was cowardly.

The first sumac was turning a brilliant scarlet, and Leonie picked some of the lower leaves from a climbing vine. She sent Sigge to find yellow ash leaves that had drifted to the ground near the forest's edge. Whenever he moved out of sight, she called him back and changed his task. The boy was too curious for his own good.

Toward the middle of the small forest, she edged closer and closer to the place where Sigge had cut his foot. She thought of calling to him but he was close enough for her to see him. So she exhaled hard and walked over the old leaf debris until she stood near the base of the big beech tree.

How strange it was that there was no sign that the decaying leaves had ever been disturbed. They had that greyed look of leaves dried out where they were exposed to air and filtered light. She picked up a dead branch and stirred up the leaves, revealing the dark humus beneath them. Gingerly, she scooted more leaves about, trying to make herself come up with the courage to bend down and dig with the small trowel she had brought along. Instead, she just kept stirring, as she might a dye pot.

"Leonie!"

The hairs on her nape spiked at the terror in Sigge's voice.

"Leonie, run!"

She whirled about. Her heart stopped cold.

The thing. Standing between her and the boy, tall as the tallest man. Grey bones hung with rotting rags, but its armor gleamed as if freshly sanded. Bloodred eyeballs fixed on her. The hand of bones raised a sword into the air.

"Run, Sigge! To the castle!" She spun back toward the path, stumbling on an old oak's roots, and dodged behind the tree, then scrambled through hazel bushes, heading for the beck.

The thing behind her roared.

Hazel bushes snagged her clothing. She tore free and sped through a gap.

"Run!" she screamed.

"I can't! I can't move! Help me, Leonie!"

It roared again. In front of her. It blocked her path. She had to get to Sigge. She turned back again. Now it was behind her. Another to the side. Another and another. Her heart pounded and raced as she gasped tiny, worthless breaths.

Four of them, all around her, leaves clinging to their rags. Leonie turned in a circle, moving slowly, looking for escape. The tree—could she climb it? Could they come up after her?

She jumped to grab the lowest branch, wrapped her legs around it, and swung herself on top of the branch. She grabbed the branch above it.

In a flash, long bones wrapped around her neck and jerked, crashing her to the ground on her back, knocking her breathless. She gasped, her lungs burning, fighting for air.

The monsters closed in. She pushed to her feet.

"Leonie!"

"Run!" she gasped. "Sigge, get help!"

"You!" said the thing, pointing its fleshless finger at the boy. "You cannot speak."

Sigge's mouth hung open, silent, as if he couldn't close it.

Bright stars flashed in her head, blinding pain, and she fell back to the ground, fighting as she faded.

The thing leaned down and touched its bone fingers to her forehead. Lightning sprang from the bare bones and streamed through her skull, pulsing and twisting like bright ribbons into her head.

"You," it said. "You cannot remember."

The monster became flesh and blood, clothed in fine silks. It was no monster that leaned over her, but the king's courtier.

Philippe.

He smiled as he caressed her cheek. The warmth in his Frankish honey-brown eyes gleamed and lit a reddish fire that turned to malice. He wrapped his hands around her throat and squeezed.

She clung to the light in the farthest corner of her mind, for it was her life, its circles of colored bands receding and merging with red, green, dull blue, each band smaller and smaller to a pinpoint, fading into an alien blue glow.

Philippe.

CHAPTER SIX

Philippe neared Castle Brodin as the late afternoon sun slanted long rays through the trees onto the beck's sparkling waters. The day was cool, unlike the sticky, hot day a few weeks before when he and his men had bathed here.

He frowned, remembering the prickly feeling of someone watching them as they bathed. He supposed, though, all manner of persons might find it interesting to watch formidable knights frolicking in the water like young boys. The dip had cooled and refreshed them all, and that was what mattered, and so he had let it drop. Then as they had approached the castle, still no more than half-dressed, he had seen the sprite-like Leonie fleeing across the meadow, long-legged and graceful as a leaping roe deer. Then he had known who was watching them. And now he laughed to himself. He hoped she liked what she had seen.

The weariness of the long ride had preyed on Philippe since early afternoon, but he had pressed onward, wanting to reach Brodin before nightfall. The king's courier had caught up with him and his knights only yesterday with word that Malcolm was on the move back to Scotland, spurred by rage, where it was suspected he meant to gather his army and invade. And Rufus was coming north to head him off. Philippe had immediately dispersed his men to spread the news to castles nearby and ridden alone to take the word to Brodin.

Now, as he snapped the reins and urged Tonerre through the shallow waters of the ford, a new sense of urgency filled him. The castle was only on the far side of the woods that lay on the other side of the beck. He had been looking forward to reaching the castle and throwing off the mail that chafed through his tunic, to drinking deep of the castle's fine ale. And a long night's sleep. In the morning, he would have to rise and leave before the castle folk broke their fast. But he would rest and eat with his old friends this night.

And the audacious Leonie. He chuckled aloud. Though she vexed him deeply, he would rue the day she married, for something in him was aroused to life by her untrammeled spirit. What would happen to her? If only Rufus could find a gentle man like the uncle who had raised her and doted on her too much. But men like Geoffrey or Hugh were hard to find and usually of modest means, or too mild of manner to become a marcher lord.

He frowned. Perhaps when Rufus came, he would plead for the girl—as long as Rufus didn't mistake his intentions.

The trail through the woods was narrow, meant only for walkers. But it was a shortcut, and he felt a longing to reach the castle that grew by the minute. He dismounted, leading Tonerre, but still had to dodge low-hanging branches. The path broadened and cleared as he reached a stand of ancient beeches. He walked easier, catching occasional glimpses of the meadow through the brush, but he was still too far to see the castle.

Across the path to his left, he spotted an odd patch of something about the color of hay, dappled by light sifting through the leaves. Odd, for a forest. It looked like someone had dropped a cloak of a dusky golden color. It reminded him of the impossible mane of curls on the little lioness's head. He drew closer, not taking his eyes off the splash of color.

It could not be an animal. He knew of none that color.

Quickly, the pale golden mass came into view, spread out at the base of a huge old oak among the beeches, amid a mass of old, dry leaves.

The reins fell from his hands. His heart stopped.

Leonie!

He dashed to the tree and knelt beside her where she sprawled nearly facedown, her wild hair flung over her face.

"Leonie!" he shouted, brushing away her hair.

Her skin was chilled. Blood caked on her scalp and splattered her clothes. He turned her ashen face upward and saw dark bruises on her throat.

"Leonie, wake up," he cried. He felt for a pulse at her neck but found none, nor at her wrist.

He leaned over her, his cheek to her face, and felt no hint of breath. It could not be! He'd warned Geoffrey something could happen to her. She was so vulnerable and didn't know it.

Like Joceline. God help him, he didn't want any woman murdered like Joceline!

He scooped her into his arms and sat among the thick roots of the tree, cradling her, rubbing his cheek against her matted hair. He should have made Geoffrey lock her up where she'd be safe. *Too late, too late. You've failed again. Someone evil has killed her and you could have stopped it.* Yet what could he have done? Something, surely. He had sworn never to let a woman go unprotected.

Did her hand move? Or had the shaking of his own body jostled it? He frowned, watching her fingers for any twitch.

Nothing.

It was too late. His throat ached with pain and he wanted to throw back his head and scream his rage to the sky. But he leaned his cheek against her face, waiting with patience strained to breaking. He thought—or was it a breath of breeze he felt? Did he merely fool himself?

There. Aye!

Quickly, he stretched her out again on the ground, placed his mouth to hers, and blew a breath into her. He sucked it out, took a deeper breath, and closed his mouth around hers to blow again. Over and over he did the same.

Her hand flopped. Again. Did he imagine it, or had he shaken it somehow? He breathed more air into her.

"Leonie, breathe. Come on, breathe." He blew some more.

And he could see, she was breathing. He found a faint pulse in her neck.

"Leonie, can you hear me?"

If she did, she gave no sign.

Philippe jumped to his feet with her in his arms and carried her to his horse, where he lifted and pushed her limp body over the saddle, facedown. He mounted behind the saddle, then shifted her into his arms as he worked himself into the saddle's seat. With spurs to the grey warhorse, he rode toward the edge of the wood. In the meadow beyond, he spurred the horse to a gallop over the meadow and up the slope to the road to the castle gate.

Villagers, soldiers, knights, all saw them. Cheers went up as they ran with them, but he ignored them, focusing on the open gatehouse. He galloped through the passage into the lower bailey, across it and up the slope to the stone-paved upper bailey, and didn't stop until he reached the wooden doors of the hall.

The knight Gerard ran out and reached up for Leonie. His heart still pounding, Philippe lowered her into the knight's arms. As he released her to the knight and dismounted from his horse, all his strength fell away, a black nothingness taking over. He thought he would collapse to the pavement, but he grasped Tonerre's stirrup.

As Gerard rushed into the hall, Geoffrey and Lady Beatrice ran to him, screaming and wringing hands. Gerard kept on going through the doors as if they were not there. The crowd cut in front of Philippe so he could soon no longer see.

"Come, Philippe." He turned to see tiny Claire, who took his arm despite the fear he saw in her eyes. "You look as weak as a new kitten. Into the hall, now."

It took him a breath's time to absorb what she was saying. He nodded. Just having her beside him seemed to restore his strength.

"Where did you find her?"

"In the forest. On the path from the ford."

She frowned, tilting her head to one side. "But the forest was searched. I was there, myself. It is her favorite place, so we went through it again and again."

He shrugged and shook his head. "This is all I know. She was lying beneath an oak tree amid a stand of beeches, off the path to my left. I could see her hair from the path. I thought at first it was a piece of cloth. But no other has hair like hers, so I knew."

"Who could have done this thing?"

"A fiend."

She nodded. "Is she alive?"

"Barely. How long has she gone missing?"

"Since yesterday. She went into the woods with Sigge, the blacksmith's son, to collect leaves for dying. Whatever happened, Sigge can't even talk, not even a sound. Whatever he has seen, he is struck dumb with terror."

"She has been brutalized," he said. "A blow to the head and bruises on her throat. I cannot say what else."

"Do you think—"

"I do not know. She should have never been let to roam the way she does."

"There was no stopping her, Philippe. Come inside."

A page held open the door for them. "I must leave you now. Mother becomes distraught at times like this. Father is not much better. Someone must take over and manage things." She gestured to a servant. "Leof, fetch water for the Peregrine, and food and wine. A place to lie down."

The thought of food roiled Philippe's stomach. "I'll just wash and drink some ale. I'll fast and go to the chapel to keep a vigil through the night."

"Say a prayer for her in my name too, sir knight. I fear I shall have a very long night."

"God bless you, Claire. Thank you for your kindness and your calm. Take care of her."

Claire licked her lower lip and bright moisture formed in her eyes, bringing tears to his own. She nodded, even attempted a smile, then hurried toward stone stairs at the far end of the hall.

"Claire," he called, and she turned back to look at him. "I nearly forgot my purpose. Your father will not forgive me if I fail to tell him Rufus is coming."

"When?"

"Likely in a day or two. Malcolm has seized his daughter from the convent and hastened back to Scotland. There may be war on the border."

"Do not fear, sir knight. I shall handle it."

Philippe nodded and found a hint of a smile for her. She surprised him. He had thought her a mere fragile petal of a rose, easily bruised.

He soon lost patience with the young servant Leof, who hovered over him, and he begged the boy to go be of help to the family. Then, freed of his mail and wiped reasonably clean, he entered the chapel.

It was cool and dark, quiet in a hollow kind of way. He approached the altar, which was draped in a cloth edged with Leonie's easily recognizable embroidery. He dropped to his knees. In his lonely silence, he prayed with no words, only offering up the ancient wound in his heart that had never healed.

The horror of Joceline's death revisited in the violence done to Leonie. Men could die horribly; that he could accept. But such a young, innocent girl? It should not be.

For hours, he stayed on his knees. Family and servants came and left, all finding a few moments to fall on their knees in prayer. And very late, even the distraught Geoffrey, whose tears became sobs. Philippe's heart was torn at the man's grief.

When Geoffrey had shed all his tears, he rose from his knees and touched Philippe's shoulder as he left the chapel. But Philippe had no other way of helping, so he kept his vigil.

At last, exhaustion from the nearly three nights he had gone without sleep claimed him. He prostrated himself on the cold stone floor before the altar.

Please, God, don't let her die. I am deserving of death. Take my life instead.

The sorcerer's cloak swirled like rising smoke as Philippe ran after him, and he caught but a glimpse of the prisoner. Joceline, his Joceline, captive of the evil Clodomir.

There they were, cornered in the tower chamber, as she begged him to save himself. But the sorcerer's spell bound Philippe like chains.

"Yield if you want to save her," shouted the demon from Satan. Philippe knew it was true. Joceline, his wife, given to him by the Conqueror. He would lose her if he didn't give Clodomir what he wanted. But to put his wife above his liege lord and king—to betray his king...

"Philippe, nay! Your soul! Your oath!" Joceline pleaded with him, her dark eyes round and huge, the whites glowing with terror.

He would do anything to save her. Anything. Defeated, he knelt at the feet of the sorcerer. He would become the weapon to destroy the Conqueror, the very man who had given him his beautiful wife.

She broke free of the sorcerer, ran across the chamber, and leaped to the window. Blue, jagged lightning streaked from Clodomir's extended fingers. Beautiful Joceline's dark, dark hair burst into dancing flames. Amid her screams, screams of fear and hideous pain, she tumbled through the air.

"Joceline!"

His magic fetters vanished, yet he did not think of them, for his heart was tearing from his soul as he ran to the window. But it was too late. Her last screams faded in the rush of flames engulfing the corpse below.

"Joceline!"

Anguish wrenched through him and turned to murderous rage. With one fierce move, he drew his sword and slashed through the sorcerer's neck. The head bounced and rolled across the chamber and came to a stop, sitting erect on the cleanly severed base of its neck.

The eyes still moved. The mouth opened. Philippe froze in shock, gaping at the impossible.

"I curse you!" said the head. "By my blood, I curse you, Philippe, spawn of Evraneaux. Never shall you love again, save she who you will slay by your own hand."

Rage turned his vision black. Philippe speared the head with his sword and flung it through the lancet window as far as it would go.

"Joceline, Joceline, it is my fault. You died because of my failure."

When he returned to the tower, the sorcerer's body was gone. And out in the bailey where he had flung the head, not even a drop of blood could be found.

The Peregrine rode, endlessly searching for the sorcerer Clodomir, to free the world from his evil. All over the known world he rode for two years, pursuing the vanished sorcerer, seeking clues and finding none. Defeated, he returned to Evraneaux.

The wandering Peregrine held the falcon seal of Evraneaux in his hand and passed it to his brother, Jean. His failure was bitter gall.

"You should not do this, brother."

But Philippe knew he must. His shame that he had ruined family and manor in his quest was more than he could bear. Jean could save them. Philippe would only destroy them.

"I must. Now I am the true Peregrine."

The seal of Evraneaux belonged to Jean now.

Only Philippe knew his great guilt. Only he knew why he would remain landless and penniless and penitent to the end of his days.

He rode and rode and rode, vowing never again to fail. Never again betray.

"Joceline."

"Philippe?"

Claire's soft voice echoed in the damp air of the chapel, stirring Philippe where he lay on the stone floor. He rose to his knees, then stood, his body stiff and aching. Around him others stood in the chapel or prayed on their knees. Had he fallen asleep? Or had the old vision come upon him once again as it had so many times, waking or sleeping?

"Aye," he answered, his hushed words echoing off the stone walls. He rubbed a hand over his face, then crossed himself before leaving the altar and exiting the chapel.

"I fear I failed in my vigil and fell asleep. How fares the lady?"

"You slept, but you did not fail. God has answered your prayers. She has wakened, and the priest has left, for it is apparent she is not in so much danger now. She asked for Sigge, the boy who was with her, but we only told her he was safe. And she called your name."

"Odd," he replied as they walked. "She was not conscious when I found her. She could not know it was I."

"But she might. If she has awakened since so easily, she might have stirred enough to know you were there. Now she is sleeping again. She is in much pain. I have left her with Ealga, who can manage my mother now. I shall take my turn to sleep."

"I must go soon. May I see her before I leave?"

"Haps peek in, but you should not wake her."

"I would not. Only to reassure myself."

She nodded. Philippe followed her through the hall and up the worn stone stairs to the solar. Beyond was the open door of the ladies' chamber and the bed. They slipped silently inside.

Leonie lay on the bed, curled up in a ball like a small child. The ashen color that had so terrified him had only slightly warmed.

Lady Beatrice glanced up at him and whimpered.

Ealga's grim smile folded into the wrinkles of her face as she beckoned him forward. "Lady," she said to Leonie, "can you wake? 'Tis the Peregrine, who has come to see how you fare."

The girl's eyes did not open, but she tossed fretfully.

"Lady?" Ealga called again.

"Nay!" Leonie said, curling tighter into her ball. "Don't let him—send him away."

Frowning, Ealga jostled the shoulder of the girl, who had not yet opened her eyes. "Nay, Lady, 'tis the Peregrine, he who rescued you. Can you not wake up for him?"

"Keep him away from me!" She pulled the blanket over her head.

Philippe sighed. "I think she is still dreaming, haps remembering whatever happened. But it is good to see she hears and moves.

I must go about the king's business now, but I'll return soon. I'll keep my vigil as I ride, for I hold all of you dear to my heart."

Old Ealga came around the bed and bowed before him. "I thank ye for saving her even though she cannot, kind knight."

"She is fortunate to have such a loving family. I am to meet Rufus here, so I shall return as soon as I can." With a sigh, he left the chamber and went down to the hall to collect his helm, mail, and sword.

"I am sorry," Claire said as she gave him a loaf for his journey. "She doesn't know what she says."

"It does not matter. I am reassured. Now you must rest, Claire."

"Aye. I can sleep now."

She waved after him as he rode away.

Philippe had rarely been as weary as when he returned to Castle Brodin. Dark clouds billowed at the horizon like a pack of wolves approaching their prey. Philippe's warrior's instinct pricked at the scent that always hung in the air when men ready for battle had passed through.

He spotted the king's crimson-and-gold pennon flapping in the wind, and relief flooded him. His mission was coming to an end, and he could rest.

As he rode through the village, scarcely even a child paused to look at him as they scurried about in the way people always did when a king was in residence. Lord Geoffrey would be calling upon every retainer he had to make the king's stay as fine as it could be.

Past the barbican, he could see the king's campaign tent pitched in the lower bailey. But Rufus would not be staying there.

The family would give over their private chambers and likely the entire hall, for although Rufus loved the rustic ways of a campaign or a hunt, he would take the comforts of a castle whenever he could.

Philippe's spirits rose as he rode up the road to the castle and into the bailey where the bustle became like bees swarming after clover in the meadow.

He stopped before the great hall door, and the young servant Leof came running. Philippe slapped his gauntlets into the boy's hand, then pulled off his helm, which had been tangling in his hair. He understood all too well why the old Normans shaved the backs of their heads, and wished sometimes Rufus's wild courtiers had never thought of the new style of hair flowing down to their shoulders. He would be equally as glad to get out of his mail, but that would have to wait.

"Where is the king?" he asked. "I must give him the news. And the Lady Leonie, how is she?"

"King William is in the solar with Lord Geoffrey," replied the page, "and he is anxious to see you. I last saw him heading for the stairs behind me. Lady Leonie is in her chamber. She is walking about now. She has broken her fast with the other ladies."

Philippe nodded. Now he could be more at ease. As the page held the door open for him, he strode into the cool, dark hall and saw Rufus approaching him. Philippe bent at the knee.

But Rufus seemed in no mood for formalities. He rushed up to Philippe, his short, stout body moving faster than it seemed such a man might go, and clasped Philippe by the arms.

"By the rood, man, I'm glad to see you! How goes it, Philippe?"

Philippe gave a weary smile, for he had a fondness for this man few people liked and most hated. "Your courier found us short of Bosewood and I sent him on to Durham with your message. I divided my knights, some to de Mowbray in Northumbria, some to Richmond, others to smaller holdings, and rode here alone. I appointed de Amiens to reinforce the border near Carlisle, but remain in readiness, should you send for him."

"Wise choices. By damn, you would have made a good commander, Philippe. You could have been Earl of Northumbria if you had just been willing."

"You said yourself there are things even a king must not do, Sire, and we agreed the wiser choice was to give de Mowbray back what was rightfully his."

"And now I wonder. Does he conspire with Malcolm against me?"

"I hope to find that out before it is too late, Sire. So far, I have heard no talk of conspiracies."

Rufus muttered and hummed as he thought. "He is a man nobody likes, but on that, I'm not one to talk. He's not as distasteful as Richmond, and at least he seems to believe in something, though I know not what. I almost think he meant it when he pledged to me."

"Who can say?"

"That is why I need you there, Philippe. I trust your assessment."

"What if I'm wrong?"

"You'd better not be. The crown could fall if you are. But come, I've given you no time to refresh yourself. Get rid of that mail and clean up. Then join us in the solar."

Philippe nodded and dipped a bow as Rufus turned away and in his frenetic way bobbed across the hall to the stairs leading to the solar.

Aye, he wanted the chafing mail off his body. It was good to have a king who knew for himself the rigors and discomforts of his knights. Philippe held out his arms, and the page and two other young men eased the jingling mail over his head.

He doused his face and hair in the bowl of cool water and finger-combed his hair, then started toward the stairs to follow

Rufus, who had stopped at the far end of the hall near the dais to talk to a knight.

At the foot of the stairs, Leonie stood, looking ashen but alive, her hand resting on her uncle's arm. For a moment his heart tripped an extra beat.

"Ah!" said Rufus, his beefy red face brightening in color. "Lady Leonie. Good to see you up and about. I have heard you had a very narrow escape. Come and tell me all about it."

"That is why she has come down the stairs, Sire," said Geoffrey, his face wearing the grimness of death. "She must make an accusation."

"Indeed, girl? Then who do you accuse?"

Leonie's green eyes darkened with fury. She pointed. "Philippe le Peregrine."

CHAPTER SEVEN

SILENCE HIT THE HALL BEFORE IT ERUPTED INTO GASPS AND A
wild gabble of shouts.

Fury surged in Leonie as she watched the Peregrine's honey-
brown eyes shift from the mask of caring and concern to astonishment. Had he merely assumed she would die, and no one
would learn the truth?

How well he fooled everyone else! How well he had once
fooled her! But no more.

The king's sharp eyes shifted from his knight envoy to her, to
her uncle, and then back again.

"We will hear this matter now," Rufus said. He flung gestures
about the hall and servants scurried to obey. The trestle table was
pushed to the back of the dais, leaving her uncle's elaborately
carved and padded chair, the closest thing to a throne the castle
possessed, for the king. Royal robes were hastily draped over it.
Rufus took his seat, and the crowd bowed and retreated a proper
distance.

"Now," said Rufus, adjusting his corpulent body in the
chair and resting his arms on the chair's carved armrests. "Lady
Leonie, explain. What is this about? Do you accuse Philippe le
Peregrine of attacking you?"

She dipped a reverent curtsy. He was her guardian and
avowed to protect her. But he called the Peregrine his friend. And
she had met Rufus only once before, when he was still a prince,

the second surviving son of the Conqueror. She could not call upon his loyalty as the Peregrine could. But she lifted her head proudly, her anger bracing her. "I do, Sire."

"Leonie, I am the one who brought you from the forest," cried the Peregrine.

Rufus raised his hand abruptly. All voices hushed again. He focused his sharp eyes on his knight, and Leonie could not tell what lay behind his thoughts. "I will hear everyone in this matter, but I will hear the accuser first."

Her heart pounded wildly. Did she dare hope to be treated fairly? What would Rufus do?

Rufus leaned forward, toward her. "Now, Lady Leonie, tell us. On what day did this happen?"

"Three days ago, Your Majesty, before the noon meal. I went to the forest to gather sumac leaves to make red dye for my wool."

"Yes, yes, I have heard about your embroidery. A nice skill for a lady. But what were you doing there alone?"

"The sumac turns very bright red this time of year, and I thought it might be the perfect time to pick it because I was told—"

Rufus waved a hand in a quick whirl. "Get on with it, girl. Tell us what happened."

"I only remember that I was hit hard on the head and nearly fell and fainted. But when I turned, there was Philippe le Peregrine holding me. Then his visage changed to evil, and he began to choke me. I fought, but then—then I remember nothing more."

"You are certain it was he?"

Her eyes closed as the memory returned, of Philippe's face, the one she had once thought so handsome, twisted in malice. "Aye, Your Majesty. It could be no other."

"Nay!" shouted Philippe. "Nay, Sire, I could not do such a thing!"

The king's eyes cut harshly to Philippe. His frown stopped the man from further protest. It gave her some hope that he might be made to pay for his crime.

The Peregrine stepped back. She saw one of the king's guards lay a hand on the brown sleeve of his tunic. A warning, she thought, yet there seemed something consoling in the guard's touch. Surely everyone in the king's household called the Peregrine friend. How could she hope to be believed above that?

"This is all you remember, Lady Leonie?"

"Aye, Sire."

"It was Philippe le Peregrine who brought you home, carrying you on his horse. Is it so?"

"So I have been told, Sire. I remember none of it."

"Then is it not possible you might have some memory of this, and confuse it with the assault?"

Something seemed to shimmer in her head, some distant coloring or fog, and she frowned, searching her mind for the missing pieces. Pain jabbed like a bolt of bright lightning, and she swayed but caught her uncle's arm. A breath or two. Now she was right again.

Nay, the memory she had was compelling. She saw his face clearly. Felt his malevolent hands at her throat, cutting off her breathing. "I remember his face when I was choked."

The hall flared up in shouts again, fists thrown into the air, demanding vengeance.

Once again Rufus raised his hand. Leonie drew a deep breath. She could see the king's great muscles bulging on his short arms. Rotund and small of stature though he was, his very body reeked of strength and power.

As the crowd calmed again, the king rose to his feet. Hands on his hips, he walked first to one side then back and to the other.

Seeing no one moving or making a sound, he returned to his makeshift throne.

"And who vouches for this girl?"

Gerard stepped forth. "I am Gerard, Your Majesty, knight and vassal to Lord Geoffrey of Castle Brodin, and I vouch that Lady Leonie has lived with her uncle since she was a babe. I have never known her to lie, nor heard from any other that she lies."

"Is she not known for having an unusual imagination?"

Gerard reddened in the cheeks. "Aye, I have heard so, but it was only childish things, Sire, and she is no longer a child."

"Do others vouch for her?"

Several knights stepped forward.

"Very well, then, we can say there are many who vouch for her. Now, Philippe le Peregrine, let us hear what you have to say."

"Sire, she has suffered an injury to the head. Surely it has made her remember wrongly."

"Possibly. We will hear everyone out. Continue."

"I came upon her in the wood, beneath a big oak tree near the trail. I could see only her green cloak and her hair, which fanned out so widely it even hid her face, and I thought her dead. She seemed to have neither breath nor pulse, and her face and neck were deeply bruised. But I breathed my breath into her mouth, and she began to move, so I hastened with her to the castle."

"I know you kept a vigil through the night. Do you know anything else?"

"Nay."

"No one around? No one suspicious?"

"Nothing, Sire."

"How long was the girl missing?"

"Overnight, Sire," said Uncle Geoffrey. "The blacksmith's son came running from the woods, but he has been so frightened he cannot talk. He had been with her."

"Then there is a witness. Bring this boy to me."

"But Sire, he has been struck dumb. No one can get anything out of him at all. When we ask him about it, his eyes become glazed and he becomes stiff as a corpse."

"Nothing at all? Perhaps, then, he has nothing to remember."

"Your Majesty," Leonie said, "Sigge was not with me. I do not remember him being in the woods."

Aunt Beatrice touched her arm. "But Leonie, dear, Harald says you came to his house to see the boy's foot and decided he was well enough to go with you when the boy begged you."

She had taken him with her? A strange pain jabbed through Leonie's head, like a stroke of lightning. The truth returned. "Nay, Aunt, I was alone."

"Lord Geoffrey, have you questioned the boy?"

"I have, Sire," Uncle Geoffrey replied. "And his parents. Though he did leave to go with Leonie, he can say nothing further, not even so much as a nod one way or another. Nor can I find anyone who saw them together. But we must say, something terrified him."

"Bring the boy to me anyway. Haps I can find another way to question him. If not, then mayhap we can learn something from him later. But we have not the time to wait, with the trouble on the border. Philippe, how is it you took so much time returning from Chauncy's castle?"

"The road is washed out in places, Sire."

"May I speak, Sire?" Claire stepped forward, gulping.

The king nodded.

"Philippe le Peregrine says he found my cousin beneath the big oak tree near the path through the woods. It is obscured but can be seen. I myself searched that place, for I know her favorite places in the forest. How could he have found her there?"

"Philippe?"

"I know not, Sire, only that's where she was. Haps she was returned to that spot."

"You have no other defense?"

"Only that I tell the truth and stand upon my honor. I would never willingly or knowingly harm this girl. She remembers wrongly."

The king rubbed his beard as he frowned. "A knock to the head is known to cause such a thing."

"You do not believe me, Sire?" Leonie asked.

"I believe you do not lie, Lady Leonie. But I myself must vouch for my knight, whom I have trusted above all others. There are two things he cannot do. He cannot be disloyal, and he cannot harm a woman. So, 'tis a great puzzle."

From the door to the hall, a commotion drew everyone's attention, and Leonie turned to see Sigge, wide-eyed and stiff, being brought into the king's presence. Her heart lurched to see her favorite child so frightened.

"Bring him," Rufus said.

Quickly, Sigge stood before the King of England, visibly gulping.

"Do you know how to behave before your king?" Rufus asked with a frown that would intimidate the bravest of knights.

Sigge dropped to his knees and bowed his head, but his eyes rolled upward as if expecting a blow.

"Well, I see your intelligence has not abandoned you, then." Rufus steepled his hands, placing them right at his lips. "Rise, boy—Sigge, is it not?" As soon as Sigge was on his feet, Rufus nodded his approval. "Now, tell me, boy, is there a person in this room, other than your family, of whom you are particularly fond?"

The boy glanced at Leonie, and his mouth opened, but then it seemed to lock in place.

"Point, then," the King said.

Sigge pointed at Leonie, then looked anxiously back at the king.

"Then," said Rufus, "is there anyone in this hall who frightens you?"

Sigge's eyes grew wider, if that were possible. He nodded his head and his shoulders hunched.

"Point."

The shoulders hunched more.

"You must answer truthfully, boy. No one will harm you for it."

Sigge's left hand rose very slowly and pointed to the king. A low murmur of chuckles passed through the people in the hall.

Rufus's reddish brows peaked above his eyes, and, nose rising high, he looked solemnly down at Sigge. "Afraid of your king, then? A smart lad. But not very afraid, am I right? You would come to your king's defense if you should ever be needed?"

Sigge straightened, surprised. He nodded vigorously.

"Good, good. Now, what about others? Do you fear anyone else present?"

The boy swiveled his head, studying everyone in the room. He shook his head.

"No one? Well then, you may go." Rufus gestured to Sigge's father, who then escorted the boy from the hall.

The king tapped his fingers on the arm of the chair, the only sound echoing through the long hall. Then he stood and paced along the edge of the dais, then back to the chair draped in his royal robes.

"There is another truth. Whatever has happened, the lady has been despoiled."

"Nay, Sire!" Nay, she knew that was not true.

"But you remember nothing after you lost consciousness. It may not be so, but the attack itself taints your honor. Who would marry you now? There can be only one answer. Philippe le Peregrine, you must marry the lady."

With a gasp, Aunt Beatrice swooned, and Geoffrey caught her.

"Nay, Sire!" Leonie gasped, backing away. "You would marry me to the man who means to murder me?"

"He will not. Though you marry and become his chattel, you will remain always under my protection."

"Sire! You gave me your word!" shouted Philippe.

Leonie lunged toward the king and threw herself at his feet. "Sire, I beg you, not this man. Any other. Let me take the veil, for I cannot bear to look upon such a vile man."

Rufus shook his head as if he pitied her. "I cannot, girl. You are an heiress, with a line of noble blood. Much is required of you."

"If it is my land he wants, then give it to him! Reward him for his evil deeds, but do not punish me for them."

"I do not punish you, Lady Leonie, and I cannot give away what is yours. It would set a dangerous and evil precedent. Nay, I command you to obey."

As Leonie stood, numbed and stunned, Rufus called to the hall. "There must be a wedding, and it must be today. We can blame that on the trouble on the border, but we have no time to waste, for Castle Bosewood is like a hole in a wine mazer that lets the wine splatter onto the table. All of England is not secure if the Peregrine does not go immediately to plug that hole. Lord Geoffrey, see to your womenfolk and prepare your castle. Philippe, you will walk with me in the bailey."

Leonie felt frozen, jaw agape. Was this the king's justice? Was she no more to him than chattel to be sold with her land?

"Come, Leonie," Claire said, taking her arm. "It will be all right. Perhaps Papa will let me go with you for a while. Let's dress you in your yellow kirtle with the green cotehardie."

Her mind raced so fast it made her aching head hurt even more. To spend her life with such a man? If he even let her live? Once they were married, the king would not notice her complaints.

Yet if she did not—but nay, there was no "do not." The king would force the wedding if she did not agree. A man would be set behind her to make her head nod if she would not assent on her own.

She hurried up the steps to the ladies' chamber, desperate to escape the stifling hall. Claire sped along beside her, with Uncle Geoffrey and old Ealga helping her shaken aunt up the stairs behind them.

If she could just get away—but to where? If only she could find the Summer Land. She knew her mother had to be alive, no matter what others said, and that was where she must be.

"If 'tis meant for ye to find the Summer Land, ye start walking and keep on going." It was Ealga who had told her those little snippets of her mysterious heritage, things Ealga herself had never seen.

"If 'tis meant to be, ye will find it. I cannot, but haps ye can, for ye have some of the blood."

But what if she didn't find it? Ealga had also reminded her she was but a halfling, and the Faeriekind did not see her as one of their own.

There was Scotland. It was far away, but if she could just find out where the Scottish king was now, she could throw herself on his mercy. She would promise him her lands if he would give her safe harbor. It was well known Malcolm possessed much land south of the border, promised to him by the many rebels and Saxons who had sought refuge from the Normans. Good enough reason to be disputing the border, so she had heard.

She was only half Norman. Leonie cared no more for Rufus's crown and Norman glory than those who had fled his father and crossed the border. Especially not now.

She looked about at those she loved, her aunt, uncle, cousin, and dear, crotchety old Ealga. If she escaped, she would have to do it without help. They must be entirely blameless when she left so they could not be accused of disobeying the king.

So be it, then. And if she were caught, she would not go to her fate with shame.

As she had done many times in her life, she put a false smile on her face. "Come, do not make so much over it," she said. "If there must be a wedding, then there is much to do. Go, Uncle and Aunt. Let it be done on the steps of the church in the village. Our chapel is too small. Go now, all of you."

"But we'll need to help you dress," said Claire.

"Nay, hurry to the church. I'll manage myself."

Rufus's eyes glowed fiercely as he turned and strode for the door. Philippe's anger seethed as ferociously, but he knew he'd better follow. Everyone in the bailey scurried away, even before Rufus swept his hand through the air to command them to leave. Almost in the very center of the bailey, with everyone else as far away as they could be, Rufus stopped and whirled on Philippe.

"I know what you mean to say, Philippe. You are not guilty of this and I do believe you. But this is the only solution."

"She lies."

"It does not matter. Whatever you may think of the girl, she did not violate herself, so her accusation stands. The situation is volatile and Geoffrey is furious. You can see he wants to challenge you. But he is getting old and could not win a combat even with God on his side."

"He has other knights to take his place. Gerard thinks the lady is beyond doing any wrong."

"Then likely I would lose two good knights, and I need both of you."

"Marry her to Gerard and give him Bosewood."

"He hasn't the wiliness. I chose you for Bosewood, and it will be lawfully yours if you marry its heiress. These northerners are a feisty lot, all but Scots themselves. They supported Theobald only because he married Herzeloyde, who was Saxon like them, and they will not contest you if you marry her daughter."

The king's betrayal seeped through Philippe, roiling his blood. He'd been a fool to believe Rufus would honor his promise. "Then you planned this all along."

Rufus's nostrils flared as his eyes widened, and his words became more carefully measured. "You were always the only choice I could make, but I did not see until now what must be done. You would wish to defend your honor, Philippe, but I wish to defend my kingdom. In the balance, the kingdom must come first."

"You throw away my life." Involuntarily, Philippe took a step back, stunned by his own defiance. Yet his anger surged in spite of himself.

"Do not think yourself above a king, Philippe," Rufus pronounced, low and soft, with a measured fury he rarely used. "You are not a free man. You are my vassal and are bound to my choice, whatever it might be. Not even I am so free as to follow my whims."

Fiercely, Philippe fought to contain his rage. All he had believed in, all his honor, everything, Rufus was destroying. To Rufus, it was as nothing.

But Rufus didn't know the real truth, and Philippe dared not tell him. Rufus was right: they were all pawns to necessity.

"Do you defy me?" Rufus demanded.

Philippe sucked in a heavy breath. He did not. Never would he betray his oath, no matter what his king did. He shut his eyes. "Nay, Sire. I am yours to command."

"Then kneel before your king, sir knight."

Philippe's blood throbbed in his veins. But he was honor bound, and that loyalty he owed at the cost of his life. He knelt on the stone, as cold as the anger in his heart. He bowed his head.

"Philippe le Peregrine, you shall marry the heiress Leonie of Bosewood, and take the castle of Bosewood as your fief held in my name. You shall defend it with your life and your strength. And on forfeit of your honor and your life, you will protect your wife, Leonie, with all your strength and courage, holding her life dearer than your own."

"I do so swear, Sire."

"Then rise and go to find the bride and bring her to the church steps for the wedding."

Rufus sighed as his knight backed the proper distance, then turned and walked away. Something almost like despair plummeted from his heart to his stomach. It was the look of betrayal in his knight's eyes that pained him most. The Peregrine would do as his king commanded, aye. But gone from his heart was the honor and trust that Rufus had treasured, and now had been obligated to throw away.

Rufus sighed. A king must have no heart. A king must have no friends.

The shadow on the stone wall beside Rufus shifted. Rufus drew his mouth thin. "Well, old woman, I hope you are satisfied."

The old woman in her rags formed from the mists, her image rippling like water in a pond when a stone is cast into it, then stilled as she took shape. "I am, Red King."

"I know it must be. Still, I hope they may find happiness."

"It will be what they make of it."

"Did you plan this?"

"I cannot foretell or make the future any more than you."

"Was it foreordained, then?"

"Nothing is foreordained, save death."

Rufus frowned. "But you said—"

"That you would find the opportunity? Aye. I know you, Red King. You will always find opportunity when you need it."

Her ragged laugh seemed to crack. The shadow shifted again.

"Wait! What about Malcolm? Where is the Scottish king? You told me—"

The shape that had been an old, haggard female shimmered as it came before the wall, then thinned. Rufus saw only shadows.

CHAPTER EIGHT

From the darkness of the woods, Leonie glanced back
at the castle and saw no great horde of men surging down the
hill after her. So far, so good. The castle had been buzzing with
the excitement of an unplanned wedding, and no one had even
noticed that the bride had chosen to absent herself. She had
walked brazenly out the postern gate, her bow and quiver slung
over her shoulder, and wearing a second cloak beneath her usual
one, her large gathering basket slung over her arm.

"Flowers," she'd said, smiling, and the guard had smiled
back benevolently. He hadn't even bothered to notice the basket
was full of things no maiden would ever need in gathering flowers for her wedding.

But she had no time to waste. Leonie wrapped the food and
supplies she'd brought in her inner cloak and tied its corners
around her waist, then tossed the now useless basket. They'd
know she would take the path, so she raced along it, making no
attempt to hide her trail.

She crossed the beck and made a show of entering the far side
woods. But she knew how to leave a trail and how not to. Quickly,
her tracks vanished onto rock.

Behind her, something crackled, and she crouched and
froze, her eyes searching the forest from behind the dense
undergrowth, her heart racing. A doe and her nearly grown fawn

moved cautiously through the brush. When Leonie stood again, they vanished in a flurry of rustling leaves.

She returned to the beck and walked along the bank where it was stony, and entered the water whenever necessary to avoid leaving tracks in mud or sand. She would regret her wet shoes and hose later in the night, but she could not afford any damage to her feet.

Where the beck turned to the east, she waded again until she reached a low waterfall. She had hoped for better luck, that the beck would take her farther north and east, for she had a long way to go before she reached Scotland.

Or, by chance, the Summer Land. And her mother. Perhaps her mother would at last take pity on her, for like her mother, she, too, had to escape a brutal man.

Why Herzeloyde had abandoned her daughter to be raised by mankind, Leonie didn't know. People often talked of the Fae as they did dragons, water horses, and the like, as if they knew of them yet did not quite believe they existed. They were not like men, she knew. But something in her heart remembered her mother's love, if not her face.

Yet how could any woman leave her baby daughter behind?

Leonie shook her head. Such thoughts were useless. If she didn't hurry, her escape would be fruitless. She was Rufus's ward, and he was not a king who brooked disobedience. His wrath would fall hard on her.

The beck tumbled over a jumble of boulders no higher than she was tall, and she climbed around it swiftly. She was hungry, but she could keep going, thanks to the Faerie sight that let her see through darkness better than a cat. Few men could follow her this night in the darkness of the new moon. She would gain many a mile while the Norman knights waited for dawn.

Except that they had horses.

Leonie shivered, noting the wind was picking up and turning chilly as the sun faded behind the horizon. She hoped the night did not turn cloudy, or she would have no stars to guide her. She tightened the knots that held the cloak full of her few possessions and fingered the knife at her waist cord. Now she headed away from the beck, bearing north into tall, rugged hills.

Clouds were coming in, as surely as the sun was setting. Darkness moved upon her rapidly. The terrain grew steeper and rockier, the forest denser.

Darker. She should be able to see better than this, for the ground at her feet was becoming greyer, indistinct, as if it faded into oblivion.

At the top of the hill, Leonie reached a stony outcrop and turned around to survey the valley behind her. Only a dim band of light separated the far horizon from the starless sky, and everything was dark below. She could see nothing but darkness. She turned back. The trees beyond the outcrop were barely visible, like dark lines against black. Something was wrong. Fear pounded in her veins. She could not see where she was. That pale sort of glow that had always illuminated her way in the dark—that secret advantage that ordinary people didn't have—

It was gone.

The darkness pressed down on her like a smothering blanket. It was like the inside of Hell, with its fires gone out.

She was lost.

Philippe stopped at the edge of the rocky streambed. It was nearly too dark to continue. It had been easy to determine her direction, which showed she headed for Scotland. When the hills grew rugged, there would be only a few ways she could go, and they all led to this point. He could easily cut her off by taking the road. She wouldn't know that, of course, for likely she had never traveled the road before. Nor would she have known how much the beck meandered in its journey from mountains to sea. Now it was too dark to track her, but fortunately, she would also have to stop in the dark.

He tethered the horses where they could both graze and drink and went back to the beck. Hands on hips, he studied the steep cliff across the beck. He could barely see the top, which was obscured by tall trees and encroaching night.

He saw a movement, but as he blinked, he was no longer certain he saw it. And the longer he scrutinized the spot, the more the something became nothing and disappeared into the gloaming.

Damn the girl! Why in God's Heaven had she come up with that lie? He'd always dismissed her interest in him as a young girl's silliness, but never had he thought she would resort to such a trap. Yet if she had meant to trap him, why had she fled? Had the rage on his face sent her fleeing?

Heat rose in his face. Now he dared not let anything happen to her. Rufus would excuse nothing, not even her running into the wilderness and being devoured by wild beasts. Maybe she'd just drop dead of some dread disease that even Rufus could not blame on Philippe.

He sighed. He didn't want her dead. He just wished she'd picked someone else to accuse so she could marry. But he was stuck with her now, and he had to make the best of it.

He grumbled unintelligible sounds that could not even be called words.

Philippe made a fireless camp and sat down on a boulder. Hungry though he was, he hardly appreciated the sausage and cheese for his supper. He rolled up in his cloak with his soft saddle as his pillow.

Taking the horses up that hill beyond the cliff would be hard.

No matter. He'd do it. He was charged with her life, and by God's grace, never mind hers, he'd see that she stayed alive. He'd be damned if he'd die dishonored because of a plaguey, lying female.

But that wasn't what worried him. He had to send her off to one of her estates in the south as soon as possible. Surely that would please her to no end.

Rufus had no idea how unsafe any woman would be as his wife. For if there was anything of which Philippe was certain, it was the power of Clodomir's curse. Philippe was the kind of man who loved, and if he began to love her, it would be his own hands that killed her.

He supposed, if nothing else, he could persuade her to remain disagreeable.

Leonie forced the tight curl out of her fists. If she'd just known it would be so hard to see, she would have picked a spot to spend the night before dusk. But it was too late for that now, and there was no sense in frightening herself.

First she secured her bow and quiver and her damp shoes in the safe branches of a scrubby oak, then she cleared a level spot to eat and sleep. The bread and hard cheese she'd stolen from the kitchen could never have been tastier. It ought to last three days, and by then, she could take time to hunt.

Her leftovers she bundled and stowed high up in the branches where they would be safe from predators, and then she lay down, wrapped up in her two cloaks.

She closed her eyes. Exhaustion flooded in. She didn't even care that her hose were still damp. Quickly a meandering reverie took over and led into sleep.

Something stirred. Leonie jumped awake.

Rustling leaves. Beneath the scrubby oaks on the hill. She stifled her shriek before it came out. Man? Beast? She could hear snuffling. A grunt.

A pig. No—a boar! She gasped.

The underbrush came alive. Leonie ducked behind the tree as the grunting creature charged. She grabbed a branch and swung up, hooked a leg over the branch, and scrambled upward, but fiery pain seared through her dangling ankle.

Screaming despite herself, she climbed higher while the wild boar below her pawed at the ground and butted the tree.

Her ankle throbbed with fierce pain, and her hose grew warm and wet with blood. Below, the enraged boar slammed against the tree, its grunts like growls. It must have scented the blood. She had to stop the bleeding and heal the ankle enough that she could walk on it in the morning.

Leonie gritted her teeth, forcing calm on herself, for the healing needed all her concentrated energy to work. She nestled herself into a safe position against the tree trunk, worked her hose down her leg to bare her skin, and cupped her palm over the wound. Her eyes closed, she focused every part of her being to the healing.

She could feel—

Nothing. Only the jabbing pain. The blood seeped onto her hand.

Haps a little less. Leonie squeezed her eyes closed again, furrowing her brow. Her palm pressed hard, forcing all her energy into the wound. She felt the familiar weakening. The pain seemed to lessen. Then it came back. Harder, she focused, forcing in the energy.

She frowned. It was not working.

It was not possible. Her healing energy never failed. Since she was a very young child, she had been able to close wounds. It had to work. But she could barely draw breath, and grew so weak she feared she might fall from the tree.

She tried her fingers on the gash again.

It still bled. What was wrong?

The only thing to do was bind the gash with her stocking.

The boar still roamed below. Every time she moved, it came back to the tree, grunting its ferocious threats. She could barely make out the boar's head and the pale eyes glaring malevolently up at her. She would never get out of this tree unless she killed it.

The boar discovered her bow, dangling from the short, broken branch where she had left it. The beast lunged as if it meant to knock it down to trample it or chew it to shreds. If it reached just a handspan higher, it would succeed. She had to get to it first.

Balancing on the injured foot despite the pain, she shifted down one limb, aware that the boar had noticed her movement. She reached as far as she could, but the oak's thick trunk was in the way. One more limb down and she would be within reach, but that limb slanted downward and her weight would bring it even closer to the ground, closer to the boar's savage tusks.

She'd have no chance at all if the boar got its brutal teeth on her bow.

Taking a breath to calm her racing pulse, she tucked the skirt of her kirtle into her waist cord, and she eased out onto the thick, low-hanging branch toward the bow. The boar lunged and grunted. She supposed it might be comical to watch an enormous, heavy animal trying to rear up on its hind legs, but from her viewpoint it was not particularly funny. When she realized she could feel its hot breath touching her leg, she almost screamed, jerking her leg back to the top of the branch, which was beginning to sag from her weight.

The bow was easy enough to grab. She inched along until the quiver's leather strap finally touched her fingers.

With a furious screech, the boar leaped. Leonie yelped and shied backward, all but losing her hold as she grabbed a smaller branch for balance. The boar was smarter than she thought. It meant to frighten her into just such a mistake.

Well, she wasn't going to cooperate. If it hadn't reached her so far, then it probably couldn't. She slipped both bow and quiver over her shoulder and backed up the sloping branch. Backing up was harder. Her foot slipped. Terror helped her get it back up before the boar caught it.

At last she reached the crotch of the branch and pulled herself to standing by holding on to small branches. But the moment she got the bow strung, the boar, apparently bored, wandered away from the tree into darkness.

No matter. As soon as it came within sight again, she could shoot it. In fact, she probably could kill it, just listening to its noises as it rooted around nearby, but she didn't want to waste arrows. And the last thing she wanted was to be stuck in a tree with a wounded boar somewhere in the area.

It hadn't forgotten her. It soon returned and sniffed out her shoes where they dangled, too far away for Leonie to reach. She'd never get far without shoes. No more time to waste.

She aimed her arrow at the eyes and shot, guiding it with her silent song.

The arrow thudded. The boar kept on rooting and grunting. Not even a squeal. She'd missed!

She shook so hard she almost dropped her bow. She never missed. With her ability to guide an arrow to its target, it was impossible!

But she had.

One piece at a time, Leonie forced her racing heart and shaking hands to calm. She could kill it with ordinary skills. All she had to do was wait for it to come close enough again, where even a child could not miss the shot. She just had to recapture its interest. What it wanted was her leg, and she was not of a mood to give that up.

Or her blood. The scent of her blood seemed to enrage it. There was plenty of that on her stocking.

Bracing herself, Leonie untied the bandage she had made of the blood-soaked stocking. She squealed like an injured piglet while she waved the stocking almost within the boar's reach. The boar turned and charged, banging head and hooves against the tree as if it could butt the entire oak to the ground.

She got a perfect view of its eyes and released her shot.

The boar's scream split the sky. It wallowed on the ground, rolling its mighty head, and screamed once more. Then lay still.

Was it dead?

Haps she'd wait awhile before testing it.

She leaned back against the oak's trunk, propped in the safety of its branches, to await the soon-coming dawn, still unwilling to let her legs dangle freely, too disturbed to sleep.

"If 'tis meant for ye to find the Summer Land, ye start walking and keep on going."

Now she knew why, despite walking all day into the wilderness, the way to the Summer Land had not come to her. She could not see in the dark, as the Faeriekind could, as she had been able to do all her life. She could not heal her own wounds, as she had always done. Her arrows would not go where she willed them. The awful truth descended on her with the crushing gloom of the dark night.

All about her that was Faerie—was lost.

CHAPTER NINE

"GOOD MORNING, PRECIOUS BRIDE."

Philippe!

Leonie jerked awake and grabbed a branch in time to keep from falling from her precarious perch. She glanced wildly about. He was alone, but she had no chance of getting past him. She was in a tree almost at the edge of a cliff, her injured leg burning with pain. And he held her shoes and bloody hose in one hand.

"You may come down now. The boar is slain."

"Only one of them," she grumbled. "I believe I prefer the fat one with the tusks."

His dark eyes blazed with an anger that belied his pleasant tone. He held up his hand to her. "Shall I assist you, my treasure?"

She had no choice but to depart the tree, but she didn't have to accept his help. "I can do it myself."

She laddered down through the branches, wincing at the pain shooting up her leg with each step. As she jumped to the ground, red waves of pain swamped her mind.

He glowered, focusing on her foot. "Let me see it."

Leonie backed up, but the oak tree was behind her, and the cliff altogether too close beyond that.

He dangled her shoes just out of her reach. "Sit down. Let me see it."

She probably wouldn't make it three steps if she tried to run. With a sigh, she sat, leaning her back against the oak.

Philippe knelt beside her and lifted her foot to examine it, turning it slightly. She winced. For the first time she saw how much damage had been done by the boar's tusk. A wide, bloody gash ran diagonally along her ankle. She knew he meant to be gentle with his touch, but his finger trailing alongside the gash set it afire with pain.

"Do you have any water?"

She nodded toward her bundle that sat in the fork of the lowest branch, and he retrieved the waterskin. As he wiped the dampened stocking over the wound, she sucked in a breath to keep from crying out.

"Not too deep," he said. "The muscle isn't torn. But it could turn putrid. I'll have to carry you down the hill."

"I can walk."

"No, you can't. I don't suppose you have a needle?"

She nodded again. A needle was an essential of life for her.

"Linen thread?"

"Only wool."

"Wool won't do." He unsheathed his knife and raised her kirtle to reveal the linen chemise beneath it. He cut a narrow swath, pulled several long threads from the weave, then rolled the fibers together. Leonie didn't have to be told to thread the needle with the newly made thread.

The first jab into her tender skin at the center of the gap made her jump, but she gritted her teeth so she wouldn't do it again.

"I suppose you've never been stitched before."

"Nay, but I can see you're going to do it crooked." She pushed him away and repositioned the torn flesh so it would line up better.

He frowned, but then he nodded and put the needle at the exact place she indicated. Slowly he pulled the wound together, knotted the stitch, and used his knife to cut it. Halfway up from there, he began another stitch, which she again corrected. He didn't really seem to have any notion of how much he stretched the skin on one side but let it sag on the other.

"If you sewed a seam like that, it would have an ugly pucker in it," she said.

"And of course a lady would not want puckered flesh on her leg. Well, then, precious bride, would you care to point out the next stitch?"

She ignored the sneer and directed the rest of the stitches. But by the time seven stitches held the wound together, she was dizzy from the pain.

"You're pale," he said. "Lie down for a moment."

"Nay."

"Drink some water. Then lie down."

She could hardly swallow the swig. But she rested against the tree as he laid out the bits of food from her pouch, until she thought she could eat.

While she picked at the cheese and bread, he walked over to the boar and removed the arrow from its head. "No sense in letting good meat go to waste," he said. He skinned the beast's haunch and carved a thick slab of meat.

He sat back and watched her, his brown eyes almost hooded by golden-brown-lashed lids. He seemed as detached as a man sitting in a hall drinking his ale with his knights, discussing politics and skirmishes. But his anger fairly radiated from him.

"You've never been in the wild at night, I'll wager," he said. "Else you would have never done such a foolish thing."

She paused to sneer, then broke off another piece of the dry bread. She would have been just fine if her Faerie skills had not betrayed her.

"Luck was with you, that you even escaped," he said. "I thought you were doomed when I heard your scream."

Leonie bit her lip to close off her retort.

"And fortunate it was a boar. You could not have escaped a pack of wolves."

She turned her head away. What was the point of his conversation?

"You could not have made it to Scotland alive. Even if you did, Rufus would consider you a traitor for giving your English lands to his enemy."

"What does it matter? He has already given away my inheritance. Rufus cares nothing for me, to wed me to a man who would murder me."

"Still the lie, precious bride?" His nostrils flared, and the harsh, gravelly tone returned to his voice. "Surely you realize I know better. But it makes no difference. I don't know why you've done this to me, but it is done, and you are as bound to this marriage as I am. I have promised Rufus to bring you back, safe and unharmed, and marry you, or my life and honor are forfeit. While I might throw away my life, my honor I will never sacrifice. You will return with me."

"And once you have won my inheritance, it will no longer matter what happens to me."

"I don't want your inheritance, but I have no choice. By law, it will be yours until you die, but a man must administer it. And Rufus has bound me by oath to you forever."

"Once married, it will not matter. Ah, I can hear it now. 'So sorry, Your Majesty, but she fell off the tower in a windstorm and broke her neck.' Then Rufus will sigh piteously. 'A shame about wives, how often they fall from towers.' You do not fool me, Peregrine. It's murder that's in your heart, and you'll be done with me soon enough."

His jaw tightened. "Let us make an agreement, then. I will cease thinking of murdering you if you will cease vexing me."

"Everything I do vexes you. If I breathe, I vex you, you bloodthirsty varlet."

"Alas. But your murder will have to wait. You're of more use alive. You're needed at Bosewood, you see. They're a rebellious lot in the north, Scots in their hearts and blood, and only English by virtue of a border. After your father died, two castellans also died suspiciously."

"A pike through the heart is too obvious to be suspicious."

"The question is whether it came from a Scot or a village man or even a Norman. Only one other Norman has had any success in Northumbria, that villain Robert de Mowbray. Who knows what interest he might have in Bosewood?"

"So Rufus uses you to spy on de Mowbray."

"I'll be the king's eyes in the North, aye. Rufus hopes I can do as well with Bosewood as de Mowbray has done with Northumbria, but it's more likely I will also meet a suspicious death. You, on the other hand, are your mother's child, and from what I hear, much like her, who the people loved. They will follow you, Leonie, but without you, they will descend into the chaos of war and face slaughter. They need you."

She sneered. "And you need me to keep yourself alive."

He sat back a distance, and the taut muscles of his jaw flexed, playing the morning light on the day's growth of beard.

"I'm no coward, and do not ever question my courage. You and I have a common purpose, whether we wish it or not. If I die in my duty, so be it. The same, I am sorry to say, is true for you. If you find that so onerous, then when the land is stable again, you may go live on any of your other properties. You have some estates in the South, I am told."

"Bosewood is mine." She leaned her hand against the scrubby oak at her back to help her stand. She winced, but the pain was not as bad as she had expected.

He nodded. "Then you may stay. But I cannot leave. I must keep the border safe for my king."

"I do not wish to be married to you. I do not wish for you to touch me."

"You need not fear that. There will be no heirs born of this marriage. That part of my vow I can keep. But be forewarned: do not place yourself above your husband, even less above your king. You are to be my bride, and if you do not know your place, I will show it to you."

She glared but said nothing.

He picked up her bundle, then reached a hand to her. "I loosed the horses so they could escape if the wolves came after them, but they might wander. We'd have a long walk without them. The slope on the far side is gentler, and I can carry you down that way."

"I can do it," she protested. But when she touched the ground with her foot, she was not so sure. Leonie steadied herself and took a step, then another. Near the cliff, she stared down at the valley below, where her brown palfrey grazed alongside his grey warhorse and a packhorse. "Haps you could bring the horses up here?"

He shook his head. "I have no doubt, wounded or no, you would not be here when I returned."

"I gave my word."

"You've said nothing. You've merely pretended to comply. That does not discount the fact that you, precious bride, are a liar. Come, I'll help you."

She flinched at his touch. Yet what could she do? Later, another chance might come. Perhaps the folk of Bosewood hated Normans enough to help her escape.

But what if they really did need her? Life had been hard for the folk of the North since the Normans had come. She could barely remember Bosewood, but she had to go, and he knew it.

Philippe took her arm over his shoulders so she could hobble along. The path she had taken going up looked so much steeper looking down.

"You climbed this in the dark?" she asked.

"I heard you scream. I had no choice. It will be easier now."

The path soon disintegrated into rough cobble where it steepened—likely it became a rivulet in a storm. Philippe went ahead of her and lifted her over each rough spot. They reached the last low cliff. Philippe lifted her by the waist, and she winced against his touch. Finally, they both stood beside the rushing beck.

Philippe frowned at the rippling water, foamy white in places. "It's shallower here," he said. "I'll carry you across."

"I can ford it."

"You will not. I do not want your wound in the water."

Before she could protest, he swept her up into his arms, stepped into the water, and started over the cobbly streambed. Leonie stiffened as if she might hold herself away from him.

He staggered for his footing, and Leonie stiffened again.

"You might make it easier, precious bride," he snarled.

"I am not resisting."

"I've held swords more pliable. At least hang on to my neck and lean closer so I can keep my balance, or we'll both end up sitting in the water."

She growled and slung her arms about his neck, leaning her body into his with her cheek against his mailed shoulder. Instantly the heady scent of maleness overwhelmed her, bringing back a sudden memory of that dream of the bailey in the foggy night, that vision of his magnificent, manly body and the way he touched her.

She shut down the image. It had been a false dream, a fantasy. He sought only his own interests. All that mattered to him was to please his king.

At last across the stream, he slowly released her legs to touch the sand. He let out a sigh. He must think her heavy as a cow. She sneered. It hadn't been her idea to be carried.

He whistled for his grey warhorse, and the three horses came running. She nuzzled her palfrey, but her smile faded away as she realized he had brought the animal because he had known he would find her.

Quickly he saddled the horses and strapped the bundles onto the packhorse. He lifted her to the stirrup, something she could have done perfectly well alone, despite her injury. Afoot, he led the train of animals away from the beck on an overgrown track so narrow it could barely accommodate Leonie when she ducked the low branches until they reached a rutted road that was little more than a pack trail.

"De Mowbray has an outpost between here and Bosewood," he said as he mounted. "We might be able to reach it by nightfall, but I suspect we will have to spend a night in the open."

"We should go back to Brodin."

He shook his head. "We are too far away now. Rufus has persuaded your uncle to send your dowry train directly to Bosewood. De Mowbray's outpost is on the way. There should be a track close by that meets the road to the outpost, and we may be able to intercept the train. Then we can send a man back to Brodin to let your uncle know you are safe."

"Already you have attached my dowry. I am impressed."

"Don't be. Rufus wants me at the castle with no delay."

Leonie's nostrils flared. And he always did as Rufus commanded. She was beginning to despise Rufus as much as the rest of the world did.

"A pity you'll miss the fine wedding your aunt arranged."

"And I thought you were in such a hurry to be married."

"Not I. But we have delayed too long already. Malcolm could have crossed into Scotland and started amassing his army against us. A wedding will have to wait until we reach the castle."

"I cannot spend the night with a man who is not my husband."

He snorted. "We are betrothed, my dearly beloved, by the king's command. That is all but the same and you know it. Worry not, though. I'll even allow you to sleep by yourself, wrapped up in your two cloaks to keep you warm."

Leonie jerked her gaze away from him and urged her horse onward. That, she knew, was true. There was not a man in all of England or Scotland who would not consider her the Peregrine's rightful property now. Not even Malcolm was likely to intervene. But one way or another, she'd break free of him after they reached Bosewood. There was still the Summer Land. She would find her way either there or to Scotland.

Or die trying. Another strong possibility.

For hours, Philippe had ridden beside her, largely in silence, and they stopped only to water the horses and to relieve themselves in nearby bushes. The last time they had stopped, Leonie had retrieved a bone comb from her bundle, and since then, as they rode, he had watched her unbraid her hair and comb strands around her fingers into impossibly long ringlets that hung past the saddle.

With each stroke, each long curl, he found himself thinking of nothing else. His fingers fretted with the need to be woven through that silken gold. He could not deny her hair was outrageously glorious. The rest of her might be odd, from those amazingly long legs that gave an enticing swing to her gait to the deep green eyes that made him squirm as if she invaded his very thoughts. But the golden hair was beyond compare.

It mattered not. He was in perfect control of himself. He would ignore her.

They rode on. She took up another long hank and combed through it, sleeking out the tangles, wrapping and combing it about her fingers, longer, longer, longer, all the way to the end, then tossing it back over her shoulder.

His hands knotted around Tonerre's reins.

She parted off another hank and began again.

"Cease this constant fiddling with your hair," he grumbled. "Put up your hood."

Her hands paused in the combing action. "Why?"

"I cannot abide your constant primping."

"I am not primping. I am combing out the tangles, as I have had no other chance today."

"Then braid it."

"It must first be combed out. There is little else to do while we ride."

"Braid it or pull up your hood."

Her lip curled. "If I do not?"

"You vex me, lady. Murder comes to mind."

He had meant it as a joke, a lame sort of sarcasm aimed at the absurdity of her accusations against him. But she jerked back. She stopped combing and flipped her wild hair back over her shoulders, and her haughty, narrow nose rode high.

Saints in Heaven and demons in Hell! She might fool everyone else on this earth, but surely she did not think she could persuade him of her lies and false acting.

Her long back was so rigid her tempting, round breasts jutted. Her eyes blazed as she focused her gaze straight ahead. She made no move either to braid the errant mop of curls or to hide it beneath her hood. And it was as enticing to him as if she had bared her breasts.

His jaw muscles worked with the ferocity and fervor of ropes hoisting great stone building blocks to build a curtain wall. What was going on in that head? Either she was angry at being caught in her scheme or she was demented. She gave every appearance of believing her own lies, even though it was nonsense.

Did she believe it? Damned if he knew. What if she really did?

Could she have another motive, not marriage? Vengeance for some imagined slight, perhaps his lack of interest in her? Maybe she had expected Rufus to draw and quarter him for daring to defile the king's ward, and instead found herself shackled for life with the very man she hated. That would make two of them bound together in hatred, when each would as soon hoist the other on a petard and sling him over a castle wall.

He hadn't thought of that before. Haps she was not besotted with him, but hated him instead.

Or perhaps it was fear she hid. He had seen too many men in battle not to know they covered fear with rage.

That changed everything.

CHAPTER TEN

"IT WAS A POOR JEST," HE SAID. "FORGIVE ME."

Leonie startled, then remembered she had made up her mind not to react to him. "Why would you think murder a jest? I see nothing funny about it."

"Agreed. It was not funny. But it was also not a threat."

She leaned back her head and rolled her eyes. "Odd that it sounded like one. No apology for assault or a forced marriage that deprives a woman of her property, but the man apologizes for a bad joke."

He rubbed his forehead and frowned. "We do disagree. Nonetheless, I ask your forgiveness."

She frowned. One ought to forgive when asked. But no one had ever done her such harm. The ache in her head still pounded from what he had done to her, barely days before, and he ignored that? How stupid did he think she was?

Leonie tossed her head, knowing it made her hair fly about and irritate him. "I cannot imagine why you think I should want you for a husband. What do you have, after all? Are you the powerful earl of some mighty demesne? I think not. Nor is it your great wealth."

"Aye. Hardly enough to incite greed. I have little more than a few estates in Normandy, enough only to support my needs. All else has been given over to my brother."

"Surely, then, I must be overwhelmed by your charm, kindness, generosity."

"You mock me, lady."

"Possibly so, since you possess none of those better qualities. I'll give it that you do have a handsome face, but I can't see what use that is. A detriment, in fact."

"Why is that?"

"What good is a handsome face to a wife? It cannot furnish food for the table nor a roof over her head. An ugly man could at least be put out to the field to scare away the crows."

His brown brows lifted in high arcs. "Or in defending the castle. He might add only a glower and a deep, throaty growl to chase away his enemies."

"There you have it. A handsome face is of no use at all. Therefore, Sir Philippe le Peregrine, you cannot give me a single reason I would have desired to marry you."

"Yet you went to so much trouble to force me into this marriage."

"You flatter yourself immensely."

From the corner of her eye she saw the sides of his mouth lift. She licked her dry lips and rode on, pretending she had not seen his smirk.

The forest grew dense and dark, and the hills steeper. The road they'd found was rutted and so narrow they almost could not ride side by side.

"Are we lost?" she asked, trying to sound unconcerned.

"Nay, but we might be farther west than I thought."

"You don't know this road?"

"I haven't been on it, but it has to be the road from Carlisle."

"You don't know."

"Of course not. But there aren't all that many roads from Carlisle. One, in fact."

"We're lost," she said.

"We are not lost, sweet bride," he snarled. "We only need to travel south and east to eventually reach our destination, and that is easy enough to determine by the sun."

"We're lost," she repeated.

"You do deliberately vex me."

"'Tis hardly a road," she said.

"Aye, more like a rut."

"Then how can it possibly be the road to Carlisle, which surely should be an important road?"

"If you knew anything about roads, lady, I would listen to you. But it is clear you are not a traveler. I doubt if you have ever journeyed beyond the bounds of your uncle's demesne. So I'll ignore your snarling."

"I was born at Bosewood."

"You left as a babe. That does not count. This may be little more than a path, but it is well used by traders and tinkers. We have passed two travelers' shelters this morning, and they would not be there if the road were not important."

Leonie tossed her head, throwing her long, unbound curls back over her shoulder, thinking that she must make it a new habit, considering how he glowered when she did. From then, they rode in silence along the shadowed, tunnellike road between the towering trees. Eventually, the trees became hills of heath, and Leonie could see a crossroads ahead.

"I suppose you think that is the road to Bosewood?" she asked.

"Likely."

Philippe spurred his mount, and her brown palfrey quickened its pace to race Tonerre to the crossroad. It was rutted and narrow, near a small meadow where they could stop to graze their horses. That, too, was disappointing, for it was so rocky, the grass was almost too sparse.

Philippe dismounted and crouched to study the disturbed track in the road.

He ran his hand above the churned-up dirt. "If this is their track, the dowry train has already been here."

"How can you tell?"

"Oxen, pulling carts. Two riding horses, likely guards. Others afoot. The tracks are fresh."

"Then we should catch them."

He shook his head. "Dusk comes soon. We can't risk being caught away from shelter. Wolves have a fondness for horseflesh."

"We should press on to the outpost."

"Too dangerous. Think of the horses, if not yourself."

"I do not wish to spend a night alone with you."

"So you have said." His jaw set hard. "We'll stop at the next shelter."

A shudder rippled up her spine.

"Don't fear me, lady. I swear to you I will not harm you."

"'Tis nothing to you, I vow," she said. "If I'd had no bruises, no doubt you would have persuaded everyone I imagined everything."

"You think I feel nothing? I still see the bruises on your throat and face. I saw the knot on your head. The blood ran down your hair and caked onto your face. It was a sight I'll never forget. I know how much your head must hurt still, no matter how you hide it."

Her chin jutted a little bit more. Now he thought his sympathy would soften her.

"No matter what you think, I did you no harm."

"I know what I remember."

"But is what you remember the truth? Could you have awakened briefly and seen me, and the two memories merged as one? Couldn't you try to remember?"

Her frown deepened. Nay, it could not be. She knew—yet she forced her thoughts back to that horror, searching—

Blinding light flashed. Pain splintered through her head. She cried out, clasping her temples as if her head might burst and spill out like blood—

"I have you." A murky voice coming from nowhere, wrapping around her.

She couldn't see. Everything blurred. She swirled, caught in a maelstrom, whirling and whirling as the hammer pounded her head. Sick, she was going to be sick—

"I have you, Leonie. You won't fall. You're safe."

She could hear his voice, far away as she floundered in the dark world that spun her and pummeled her—

The pain—she gasped—her throat filled with choking nausea.

The spinning slowed as the pounding eased. She gasped for her breath. She was on the brown palfrey, and Philippe held her in the saddle, his own horse pressing against the brown as he clenched her against his chest.

Her fingers probed the iron mail beneath his tabard. Taut, hard-muscled arms wrapped around her, supporting her. She could not fall. She had not realized she was falling, but now she was safe.

"That's good," he said, his voice soft and gentle. "Take deep breaths. It's passing."

What was passing? What had happened? She blinked and forced her eyes open, surprised to realize they had been closed. Or had they just not been able to see? The ferocious pain still swirled in purple bands inside her head, but slower, slower, fading.

She clutched his arms and forced her sharp, shallow breaths to slow, breathing deep. She rested her cheek against the mail, absorbing its iron bite as something precious. The brown palfrey danced a jittery step beneath her.

"You need to rest. We'll stop for a while," Philippe said. Odd, how soothing the throaty, rumbling words were.

The last of the attack, whatever it was, was fading away now. She pushed against his arms and straightened up in her saddle. "Nay," she said, taking in one more slow, deep breath. "Let us keep going. It cannot be much farther."

"It's too far," he replied. "It's almost dark."

"But soon after, surely."

He shook his head. "There'll be a stream in the next valley," he said. "Probably a traveler's shelter too."

"If not?"

"Then we'll go till we find one, but no farther. They aren't far apart. Travelers build these small stockades to keep their stock safe when they must stop for the night. It is a custom to leave them for other travelers, and each one who stops tries to leave the stockade better than he found it."

Leonie nodded, but even that slight motion hurt her head. And every time she glanced at him, she saw him watching her as if he thought she might faint again.

She would not. She would not let it happen again, ever.

Over the hill and down into the next valley they rode. As if at his command, the beck and little stockade appeared.

The ragged camp was set into the earth not far from the beck in a clearing, much like a stockade wall surrounding a wooden castle. Instead of huge logs set upright in the earth to protect the mound behind, the staves were tall, straight saplings, crudely bound together. It was well sited, with a good grazing meadow and a clear beck, but close enough to a stand of trees for firewood. The gate stood ajar, giving it an abandoned look, but it was stout enough. Some of the poles were so short Philippe could look over their tops, and a few well-aimed blows from an axe would bring it down, but he doubted any wolf could jump those spiked tips without impaling itself.

"Wait," he ordered, and he quickly dismounted and rushed to the palfrey's side to help her down. But when he tried to carry her, she brushed him off.

"My foot has rested all day," she announced. "It's time I try it again."

Oddly, it didn't hurt all that much as she hobbled down to the beck. She splashed her face with the mercifully cooling, soothing water and filled the waterskins while the horses drank. Philippe took the horses from the water and led them to graze until sundown, and Leonie hobbled back to the little stockade.

She had no choice but to comply with him. She hated it, but she was in no shape to escape now.

He told her to sit. She ignored him and went off to gather an armful of kindling and firewood. Like it or not, she was beginning to look forward to sitting by a hot fire and eating food that had been cooked. And she'd comb and braid her hair, not caring a whit if he liked it or not.

With her arms full of good, dry wood, she turned back toward the camp. She heard a hiss and stopped cold.

Something reared up before her, like a huge rope rising into the air.

Snake!

She screamed.

She stepped back. It dropped to the ground and slithered toward her. She retreated again, afraid to take her eyes off it. She'd never seen any snake like it, huge, long, and black. Enormous fangs showed when it opened its ashen white mouth and struck at her. She dodged, barely in time to escape the snake's lunge. Hissing, it fixed its slanted red eyes on her and swayed a strange dance.

She snatched a broken branch from the pile in her arms and threw it. The snake dodged sinuously, its lower coils moving forward as it swung its long body side to side, each move advancing on her. She threw more kindling and more, but the creature evaded each. All she was doing was slowing it down.

The last log gone, she grabbed a long branch for a club, but the branch snagged on the brush. She yanked it free, swinging it like a sword.

Behind the beast, Philippe called for her, and the brush and ground thrashed as he ran.

He wouldn't see it in time! Wild terror flooding into her, Leonie leaped toward the snake, shouting and flailing her weapon in furious strokes.

The snake dropped to the ground and slithered away beneath the brush. Leonie gawked at the great length that seemed to go and keep on going into the brush. Philippe leaped into the clearing just as the last of the malignant black creature disappeared.

"What?" he shouted. "What is it? Are you all right?"

"A snake. A big one." Leonie gasped for breath, her pulse still racing.

He stared at the firewood pitched around the glade. "You've scared it off. Adders are usually shy of men."

She shook her head. "It wasn't an adder. It was much too big. And black."

"There are some black adders."

"Not like this. Its head was wrong. It was round, sort of spoon-shaped, and it had huge fangs. And it was about as long as you are tall."

He looked at her like her brain was addled and shook his head. "There are no snakes like that in England. Only adders. It is getting very dark. You must have seen a vine or a fallen branch."

She couldn't blame him. It was impossible to believe. He was right, there couldn't be such a creature. Was it her imagination once more spinning out of control?

"Aye," she replied. "A branch. No doubt."

"Come back to the stockade now. The light's almost gone. I've brought the horses in and pulled some forage for them. We need to shut the gate."

She mumbled some sounds even she didn't understand and picked up the firewood she had thrown at the snake.

"Don't mind the firewood," he said. "I'll get it."

She shook her head and continued her gathering.

"I want you to go back to the stockade and lie down," he said. "Prop your foot up on my saddle. It's supposed to be good to keep an injured foot elevated."

"Only a few more minutes. And the more wood we have, the better our fire."

"And if your leg putrefies and falls off, Rufus will surely blame me and cut off my leg to match. You might want to spite me, but surely not enough to lose your leg."

"I might," she grumbled.

Philippe shrugged and helped pick up the remaining chunks of wood. Leonie hobbled back to the stockade with her arms full and let the pile in her arms roll off onto the stack Philippe had already begun. Once safely inside the stockade, she gave in and lay down on her cloak, her aching foot propped up on his saddle, while he whittled two sharp sticks and threaded long strips of the boar haunch back and forth. Her heart just kept pounding every time she thought of the evil gleam in the snake's eyes. Did snakes have red eyes?

"Do you know how to cook?" he asked.

"Of course."

"Can you roast the pork over the fire?"

She nodded.

"Then do your best to keep your foot propped up while you cook it. I'll see to the horses and our packs."

The last of the bread had dried, and Leonie cut it into two long halves to serve as trenchers while the meat was roasting in the flames. She turned the skewers several times, grimly laughing to herself at the impossibility of meeting Philippe's demands. Her foot didn't really hurt much. The leftover ache in her head was worse. She promised herself, as soon as she had time when he was not looking, she would make another attempt to heal the cut on her ankle.

She sighed. That was the worst of the entire situation. If her Faerie skills had not so suddenly deserted her, she might have been long gone through the night while he had slept. But if she regained them now and he saw her using them, he'd leap to the conclusion she was a witch.

Or was she going mad after all? He was right, there could be no such snake in all of England. She shuddered.

She watched him tending the horses, quietly currying, humming softly to them. He had not yet taken any time for his own needs, seeing to the animals. And to her.

So beautiful to have so much hidden malice. A body and face that put all other men to shame. What a waste it was! Why did no one else see the evil in him? Yet she knew why they did not, for just looking at him it was so hard even for her to believe. Even his face, that of a peacemaker, belied it.

She winced, remembering the dream she'd had the night he'd visited Brodin. She had not understood it for what it really was: feelings, wishes, desires for what could never be, because he was not the man he appeared to be.

"What is wrong?" he asked.

She looked up at him. "Nothing."

"Does your head hurt? Your leg?"

"Nay."

"Lie down. I will tend the meat."

"Nay." Frowning, she turned the handmade spits, noting the wild pork seemed done, for the drippings sizzled into the fire, tantalizing her nostrils with delicious smells.

She pulled the spits from the fire and used her knife to push them onto the trenchers she had made.

"Save some of it for morning, and we'll have it with the last of the cheese before setting out."

She nodded and set aside two chunks, which she wrapped in a cloth.

If he was evil, what good could there be in this world?

Yet—could he be telling the truth? What if he was right, and it was the injury to her head that caused her to disbelieve him? Was she imagining all these things? Like the creature she had dug up, but then when she returned, found nothing there, not even a disturbed leaf?

Yet she remembered—

"You cannot remember." No, don't remember. It hurts.

The door to memory slammed shut in her mind. Shut out the pain.

They ate in silence. For once, she had no trouble keeping her usually wayward gaze properly downcast. Everything was wrong now. What had happened to her Fae skills? Was she merely human now?

She had never minded that Rufus would choose her husband to suit his own purposes. That was the way of the world. It was her duty to accept the king's choice. But a man who, despite his denials, was secretly determined to rid himself of her—to kill her.

Her jaw clenched. She would escape. If she lived long enough. But she must appear to be compliant until then. Could she? True, she had been good at hiding her Fae heritage, but she was not so good at hiding her true feelings.

"What was it, do you think?" he asked.

"What? The snake?"

"Nay, there was no snake. The pain, the fainting. Is it the injury? Surely it must be."

She clenched her teeth. It was a snake. She knew it was. Yet it was so impossible. "It's nothing."

His brow arched. "Blows to the head can do strange things. I have seen big men develop the falling sickness from a blow, although it usually gets better. You will be better in a few days, I think."

"If it was not a snake, what could it have been?"

He sighed the sound of patience that was not patient. "The gloom of dusk can be deceiving. Things seem to move when it is only the fading light."

"It moved. It hissed. It rose up half its length off the ground, and it stood as tall as my shoulder."

His brow furrowed with a pained look. "I have heard tales from pilgrims that there are some enormous snakes in the Holy Land, but not here. Haps it was a dragon?"

She winced. Was he actually trying to be conciliatory? "I don't know what a dragon looks like. I've never seen one. Have you?"

"Some say they have seen them, but I haven't. There are many tales. Some say they have legs and wings, and breathe fire, or they are strange colors. I have seen drawings in the holy books. There are huge worms that are sometimes seen at sea. But I have never heard of their like on land."

"But it looked like a snake. It had no legs or wings. It had red eyes and long fangs."

And the look on his face told her he thought her daft. She sighed. She had said too much. But she knew whatever that creature was, it was evil. It had stalked her. A cold shiver ran down her spine. Something in her remembered feeling that way before. That day in the forest, she had been stalked.

By Philippe.

And now? Did the snake lurk beyond the stockade? Could it get beneath the poles that were buried into the earth? She glanced around the inside perimeter, noting heavy rocks that had been placed around it, meant to drop on wolves that tried to dig beneath it to reach their prey. But would that stop a snake? Could the snake squeeze between the occasional gaps between the poles?

If only she were really Faerie, she would know how to deal with creatures like that. If she were Faerie, like Herzeloyde, she could walk away from this enemy of hers, or fade against whatever was behind her, and he would never find her. She would raise her bow and kill whatever foe attacked her.

If she were Faerie. She was but a halfling, belonging in neither world. Perhaps her mother had left her behind because she was ashamed of a child so imperfect. Certainly her father had not wanted her.

Seeing that Philippe busied himself with the packs, she quietly unwound the bandage on her ankle and ran her fingers over the stitched wound. She placed her fingers on each side of the wound and squeezed her eyes closed to concentrate all her thoughts and power on the healing. She pictured the wound knitting together beneath her fingers, felt the warmth of healing flowing through her fingers and draining her of strength.

Hopefully, she lifted away her hand and looked.

Nothing. Her shoulders sagged. She had nothing to make her safe. A sudden terror surged through her.

She squared her shoulders, and her jaw and fists tightened in tune with her resolve. Then she would have to be human. Because that was what she had left. And with what she had left, she would find a way to change her life.

CHAPTER ELEVEN

W HICH WAS WORSE, THE DEVIL SHE KNEW OR THE DEVIL SHE didn't know? Never mind. She could deal with either. Leonie wrapped herself in the two cloaks she had brought and sat by the fire, her knees pulled up near her chin.

"You should sleep," he said.

She shook her head. "I'm not tired."

"You will be. You got little enough sleep last night, I'll vow, and this night will be shorter than you think."

She shook her head again. "I'll just watch the fire for a while. You may sleep if you wish."

From the dark night beyond the stockade fence, something barked. She jerked around. "Wolf?" she asked.

"Wolves don't usually bark. But a dog, perhaps?" Philippe rose to his feet and walked to the fence, his hand resting on his sword hilt.

Leonie dropped off her outer cloak and stood, picking up her bow and stringing it. "What would a dog be doing here?"

"Lost or a stray." Philippe stretched up so he could peer over a low gap in the fence.

"Or a moor hound. Be careful. They can enthrall you with their eyes."

"It's a dog," he said. "Moor hounds are huge and black and have red eyes. He's huge, but he's not black. And his tail is wagging."

"It could be a trick."

"Come, take a look."

Leonie edged closer to the stockade. She was tall, but not tall enough to see over it. Her curiosity forced her to accept Philippe's touch as he lifted her by the waist. Stretching her neck, she got a glimpse of the biggest dog she had ever seen, with a grey-brown shaggy coat and perked ears that flopped at their tips. Aye, it was a dog.

The dog yapped, leaping. Leonie jerked back. It sat, its long, shaggy tail all but pounding its sides as it wagged, then suddenly jumped up and ran to the fence, barking like a yapping puppy hungry for its dinner.

"It wants in," she said.

"Aye." Philippe set her down and watched the big animal as Leonie found a rock that stood high enough to give her a better look. "Sometimes dogs run with wolves. Could be he wants us to open up to let his friends in."

"Or if we leave him out there, the wolves might get him."

Philippe reassessed the shaggy creature. "He looks big enough to handle a wolf."

"He's big, but there's only one of him. Wolves roam in packs."

"Aye." Philippe's brown eyes were dusky in the depth of firelight and searched her eyes as if he meant for her to decide.

The big animal leaped against the fence, its deep bark seeming both friendly and menacing. It leaped so high she could see its head over the spiked fence top.

"Let him in," she said.

She could see the relief in Philippe's eyes as he hurried to the gate and removed the bar. With a brief glance back at her, he pulled the gate open.

The dog bounded in like a puppy, its great brush of a tail sweeping its hips to and fro. Leonie laughed as it raced up to her, but she let out a yelp as it leaped up on hind legs and swiped its huge, sloppily wet tongue over her face. She staggered back, averting her face unsuccessfully.

Philippe burst out laughing, but seeing her lose her balance, he glowered at the dog. "Down!" he ordered, pointing to the ground.

Whimpering, the dog dropped to all fours, and as Leonie steadied herself, it sidled up to Philippe and lay down on the ground in front of him.

He laughed again and squatted before the dog. "She's well mannered. Someone has trained her." He reached out and scratched behind the dog's ears. "I wonder if she's one of de Mowbray's dogs. I'm told he has a pack of big dogs he's trained to hunt wolves. She could have been lost when hunting."

"We could be the first people she's seen for a while. But she looks well fed." Leonie chewed on her lip.

"Aye, but hungry." Both dog and knight looked at her with soulful brown eyes.

"We could eat the cheese in the morning," she suggested.

"Give her the remains of the trenchers."

Leonie eyed the monster dog, who barked expectantly and whose tail wagged her body even as she sat. From what she knew about dogs, she suspected this one knew when her feeding was being discussed. She removed the old bread with its drippings and tossed pieces to the dog, who made a game of leaping after each one to catch it before it touched the ground, gobbling faster than Leonie could tear off hunks. With the last of the bread gone, the dog sat back on her haunches and wagged for more.

"There's the boar meat," Philippe said, frowning.

"I thought you liked the boar meat."

"I'll have it again. We won't go hungry. She shouldn't either. That old boar did us a favor, you know. We enjoyed its meat. And no doubt the wolves will be enjoying the feast we left behind and will be too busy to bother with us. The dog ought to have some too."

Leonie raised her brows at the interesting logic. Well, why not? She unwrapped the meat, which she had cut into smaller chunks, and held one out. The dog leaped, grabbed, and swallowed, then sat again so quickly Leonie almost wondered if she had imagined having the roasted pork in her hand.

She glanced at Philippe, who laughed as he watched. He nodded, and she threw the second piece, which the dog caught in the air and gulped down.

"No more," Philippe commanded the dog.

The dog whined, sitting and wagging her tail. He frowned and repeated himself. Leonie suspected the dog sensed Philippe's barely concealed mirth, but with a whimper, she turned and walked over to the fire, where she plopped down, head resting on her paws.

"Brute," she muttered under her breath, not liking the way his tenderness toward the dog warmed her heart.

"Give the animal your morning meal if you want," he muttered back. "I suspect you will anyway." He threw more wood on the fire, then wrapped in his cloak and lay down, his head resting on his saddle. "I'd suggest you sleep, but I doubt not you will do as you please."

For a moment, she just watched him. He'd had little sleep the night before, too, but men tended to need little. What would happen if she fell asleep? Did she dare?

She spread one cloak on the ground and wrapped in the other, pulling the excess fabric of the first one around her legs, and laid her head on the palfrey's flat saddle.

The dog made odd whuffing sounds and crawled close. Then when she did nothing to stop her, the dog moved again until she was snuggled up beside Leonie.

"I doubt you'll be cold tonight," Philippe said, shifting his weight for comfort.

The dog growled.

"I suspect you have your own watchdog as well. Easy, dog. I have no intention of bothering your new mistress."

The dog growled again, a low, short growl meant to warn rather than threaten.

"Smart dog," Leonie said, and laid an arm over the animal.

Philippe made a grunting sound of his own and turned his back to them.

Leonie drifted off, remembering nothing more after the dog snuggled up to her, until a strange tension in the night air roused her. She reached out and the dog was gone. Philippe rose, shouldering his scabbard belt, and picked up his bow. Catching her eye, he made a motion to her of drawing a bowstring.

Leonie rose quietly, strung her bow, and snatched up her quiver. The shaggy dog crouched near the edge of the stockade close to Philippe, low, long growls emanating from her throat.

Leonie tiptoed up to Philippe. "What?" she whispered.

"Don't know. Something the dog doesn't like."

The fire was almost out. "Shall I put some wood on the fire?"

"No. Bring me a burning fagot so I can see."

The dog suddenly leaped at the fence in a rage of growling and barking. Philippe stood, revealing himself to the outside, his bow aimed.

Leonie straightened, then stood atop a rock, barely able to aim over the top. "Animals?" she asked. "Men?"

"I don't see anything."

Something pale showed itself against the darkness of the forest. Leonie drew and aimed, but then slacked the bow. She had hoped her Faerie sight would return. But it was gone, and she saw only darkness. Likely, then, she could not count on her arrows hearing their guiding song.

"Don't waste the arrows," he whispered.

She nodded.

Beside her, the dog growled lowly, her agitation mounting, body tensing and twitching. Suddenly, the dog jerked to attention, her growl ferocious. The dog gathered her body, jumped twice at the fence, and then leaped. Leonie gaped as she watched the dog sail upward and clear the stockade's pointed top without touching it. Barking, growling, and tearing off into the trees, the shaggy hound attacked.

Screams punctuated the disturbed night, laced with the sounds of a predator ripping its prey apart. Wide-eyed, she looked to Philippe, who returned her astonishment.

"She leaped the wall!" Leonie said.

"I saw." Philippe squinted toward the forest as if somehow that would help him see the melee beyond. "Doesn't seem possible."

The battle, if one could call it that, began to subside. The screams became distant, and then were gone. Still, Leonie and Philippe watched.

Just as moonlight broke through the dense clouds, the dog loped into the clearing, carrying a long bone in her mouth. She stopped at the fence, sat, dropped the bone, and barked.

"What? You want us to open the gate?" Philippe said. "Didn't I just see you leap over the wall to get out?"

The dog barked again, then lolled its tongue as it grinned.

"Why don't you just leap back in?"

The shaggy beast picked up her bone, pranced around to the gate, and again sat and barked. Philippe folded his arms and frowned, to which the hound responded by dropping the bone, sitting and barking again, repeatedly.

"I do not think we will be sleeping more tonight if we don't open the gate," Leonie said.

Philippe shook his head, but it was clear he knew his cause was lost. He barely had the gate unlatched before the dog pushed her way in. He quickly barred the gate again, as the dog dropped the bone at his feet and sat back grinning.

"All right. Good dog," he said. He picked up the offered bone, frowning. "Human. Leg bone. But it's old, probably lain out in the weather for years. Sorry, girl, but you're not going to convince me this is a fresh kill."

The dog growled.

Suddenly remembering the skeleton she had dug up in the forest, Leonie shuddered. But it made no sense. Besides, she had to have imagined all that. Skeletons did not have bloodred eyes. Swords left buried rusted away, if such a valuable thing would have ever been left in the forest in the first place. Still, her heart raced faster. The brave mask she was trying to wear seemed to be turning to dust.

The dog took the bone back. She plopped down in her spot by the fire, her paws crossed over the bone.

"Do you think they are gone?" Leonie asked.

"The dog thinks it, and she knows more than we do. We have another problem now. We must leave in the morning, but if we do, they might set upon us. Haps if we dash for it early, before dawn, they may not be prepared. You sleep for a while, and I'll wake you as soon as I have everything ready."

"No." She shook her head. "I couldn't sleep."

"I'll watch. And the dog," he replied.

But all Leonie could do was wrap her cloak around herself and sit. Never in her life had she felt so vulnerable.

The night remained silent. Somehow she slipped away into sleep, waking every time the dog moved or made a sound, every time a harness or rope creaked. By the time the sky began to pale, she had begun to sleep more soundly. She awoke to Philippe's finger laid across her mouth to warn her to be silent. All three horses stood packed and ready. Within a minute, her bow was strung and she was in the palfrey's saddle.

The shaggy hound brought her bone and dropped it at Philippe's feet, then looked up at him expectantly. Philippe shrugged and crammed the desiccated bone into the packhorse's panniers.

Philippe swung open the fence gate and jumped into his saddle. With a hiss to the mounts, the horses burst through the gate into a full gallop down the road, splashed across the beck, and up the next hill. The dog kept pace, her floppy ears flying, tongue lolling. They rode with the wind blowing in their faces over several more hills to a long valley, and seeing no pursuers, they slowed to a walk to give their mounts a rest.

From a pouch, Philippe removed chunks of cheese and passed them to her, taking none for himself. Leonie accepted them with no acknowledgment, for they were, after all, hers. Occasionally she glanced warily at him, but he paid her little regard and instead kept his eyes searching all around them. She had to admit she was probably safer in his company than being alone, but that made her want to trust him. That icy shiver went down her spine again. She liked it better when they quarreled.

"I have figured it," she announced. For good measure, she lifted her chin and concentrated on the road ahead.

"What have you figured, lady?"

"Why you set upon me in the forest."

"I did not set upon you. I did not attack you, nor mean to kill you," he replied curtly.

"So you say."

"Aye, so do I say."

"There is the problem of certain bruises, and that no other man was about. As I said, I have figured it. You thought I would be given as a bride to some other man, and along with me, Bosewood, which you covet."

"I do not covet it."

She ignored that. "But if I were dead, the king would have to award Bosewood to someone, likely his favorite, that being you. Simple."

"Not so simple. If I had meant to kill you, you would be dead."

"Perhaps you thought you had and brought the murdered maiden back to Brodin and showed your own grief mingled with theirs. You cannot deny I seemed dead."

"By God's breath, woman, I did all I could to save you. If I so coveted your inheritance, and I am so much the king's favorite, why would I not simply ask him for your hand?"

"Mayhap you have a secret love tucked away somewhere."

"My love is dead." His jaw jutted in fury. "I'll have no other."

For a moment, she thought he meant it. 'Twas said the Peregrine clung to his dead love the way a wet glove clung to a hand. But that fit even more with her thoughts. "And so, with your dead love still ensconced so firmly in your heart and the lady of Bosewood dead, you have no need to marry her to gain her demesne."

"God's blood, you are the most vexing woman I have ever met. I am almost sorry what you say is not true."

"So you do mean me ill."

"I do not and never have."

But in her mind, his smiles and tenderness were for everyone else, even the shaggy dog, and he had only scowls for her. He might protect her simply because Rufus had demanded it. "The outpost cannot be much farther," Philippe said, his jaw clenched. "A good thing, for the horses are weary."

"A good thing indeed," she said. "But haps a bit too late."

She pointed ahead. Armed riders. Black silhouettes against a brightening sky.

"Behind me," he said, moving his horse between her and the warriors, or robbers, or whatever they were.

The dog yelped and barked and bounded away toward the oncoming riders, abandoning them. Leonie nocked an arrow in her bowstring, with three more ready. Philippe, bow in hand, had also shifted his sword for a quick draw if he needed it.

The warriors rode toward them, and the dog reached them just as they came close enough for recognition. The riders reined in and the dog joined in a frolic with a pack of similar dun-colored shaggy dogs.

"Robert de Mowbray," said Philippe. "The Black Earl of Northumbria." Yet she noticed he kept his arrow nocked.

The man was the biggest, darkest, hairiest man she had ever seen, both tall and brawny, and he had a beard as shaggy as the dog that sought his attention.

"Peregrine," said the huge man, and he reached down to scratch the dog behind her ears. "I see Ilse found you."

"You sent the dog after us?"

"More like she sent herself. Ilse has a way about her, like she has the second sight. And this one riding with you?"

Leonie threw back the hood of her cloak.

"Saints in Hades," de Mowbray said. "'Tis Herzeloyde returned."

CHAPTER TWELVE

PHILIPPE EDGED TONERRE AHEAD OF THE PALFREY, HIS WARY eye following every move the huge Earl of Northumbria made. Rufus might have forgiven the man publicly, but neither the king nor Philippe trusted him as far as they could throw a mountain. He was probably the only man of the North who had not petitioned the king for Leonie's hand, and that by itself made him suspicious. She would be a very good prize for a man who planned to change camps. Haps de Mowbray planned simply to steal her.

"I am Herzeloyde's daughter," Leonie said.

"Aye, lass, I see that," de Mowbray answered, even as his harsh voice softened with wonder. "You are her image entirely, save your hair is darker. Herzeloyde wears a mantle of hair like spun moonlight."

Suspicion stiffened Philippe even more, if he had not already been ready enough to do battle. A man would not make such a statement idly. Odd, too, that he spoke almost as if the woman were still alive.

"You knew my mother?" Leonie's bow hand lowered and she leaned forward almost imperceptibly.

"Aye, every northerner knew of her. Has this blackguard stolen you, lass?"

"Stolen? Nay, I—"

The man must have heard, unless the dowry train had not made it to his outpost. "We are betrothed, by the king's command," Philippe replied. "Though 'tis not by our wills, we obey."

"So I have heard. I've heard more than that. 'Tis said the lady fled from the Peregrine, who would do her evil, yet now I find her accompanying him to Castle Bosewood. I ask again, lass, are you this man's captive?"

Leonie cast her glance sideways but did not allow it to meet Philippe's. "Nay."

Philippe studied them both, glancing also at the earl's men, whose horses sidled about, as restless as their riders. Someone in the dowry train must have told him Philippe was suspect in the attack on Lady Leonie. So, had the Black Earl of Northumbria set out to find her? Did he mean to protect her? Help her in her flight over the border into Scotland? Or snatch her for himself before a wedding could take place?

"So, lass, daughter of Herzeloyde," said de Mowbray, "do you mean to say you are agreeing to marry this lackey that slavers after the Red King's dole?"

Leonie's chin went up. "Bosewood belongs to me, but if I do not wed him, I will lose it."

"You do not wish it? Are you afraid of him?"

"I fear no man."

"But you should, lass. Even a man should fear his enemies."

Philippe frowned. "She's loyal to Rufus, as am I. We will do as he commands."

The black mustache that was as shaggy as the man's dogs lifted in a sneer. "So I have also heard."

"And you will not?"

"I willna, unless I wish. And he knows it."

Oh, that Rufus did know. "Then are his borders safe in your hands?"

"I've sworn to defend the border, and that I'll do. But naught else. That, also, the Red King knows."

Philippe searched the black eyes, which seemed lit by some mysterious inner fire. The man no longer even talked like a Norman, but sounded more like the rough northern folk whose dialect was so similar to the Scots'. There was something unearthly about de Mowbray, something that went far beyond mere danger and treachery. Rufus was right in not trusting his back to this man. Philippe alone protected Leonie from this black demon's schemes. There was little Philippe could do at the moment if something should go awry, and one word from her would set it off. Yet she seemed to know it and kept her own counsel.

Warily, Philippe urged his mount forward, placing Leonie between him and the packhorse. De Mowbray reined his huge black warhorse to ride along Philippe's right, though it was clear he did not like it. Around them, de Mowbray's knights in their trappings of black and silver formed a shield with their mounts as they rode down the road.

Or a prison. Escape was as impossible as any attack from marauders. He had to remind himself that the outpost could not have been avoided in any case.

The day brightened to brilliant blue as the thick clouds left over from the night passed on. White puffs like tufts of wool already warned of thunderstorms later in the day. An open expanse of gorse-covered slopes spread out over the gentle hills and valleys all the way to the distant fells that rose abruptly like black tombstones. Ahead, Philippe spotted portions of the track as it wound up, down, and around toward the east. In the distance, perched on an isolated hill within a loop of the Wyfel River, sat the lonely outpost that marked the farthest reach of de Mowbray's demesne. The thought of it made Philippe's skin crawl beneath his mail.

"The dowry train arrived safely at your outpost?" Philippe asked as if he had no concern about the black giant who rode beside him.

"Aye, it arrived toward nightfall yesterday and was to be sent on its way to Bosewood this very morn. I'm thinking it's more than adequate for one such as you."

Philippe brushed off the needling. He'd never liked the man and wouldn't have minded a fair fight to slit his throat, but his goal was to protect his charge, and he would not allow himself to be distracted.

"I have not seen Bosewood in many a year," Philippe replied. "But I have been told its defenses and quarters are much neglected. I will not provide my lady with an unsafe place to live."

"Then you'll not like what you find," said the man. His voice had lost its sharpest edge, but still was a guttural growl. "If it were mine, I'd knock it down and start all over again."

"If we must. What word of Malcolm?"

"The Scots king has passed over the Tweed into Scotland, his nun of a daughter in tow. I saw him myself, passing by Alnwick in the distance. 'Tis said he's overbrewing with rage. Whatever it was Rufus said to him, it does not serve the North well."

"What about the bishop?"

"Durham?" De Mowbray spat on the ground. "And which way does the wind blow today?"

"That also does not bode well for Rufus."

De Mowbray chuckled, a low and menacing sound. "Does it not? The Scots king descending on his back and a bishop who's taken leave of his senses straddling the River Wear with a foot in each camp, and only the Black Earl of Northumbria standing between the king and Hell. Even the soddy Red King would quail at that. Aye, but I forget, he's got you, too, Peregrine. You'd best be spreading yourself very thin."

"I'd think you would be glad to have me here, then. Unless you mean to join the Scots."

De Mowbray jerked at his reins, whirling his mount toward Philippe, and his face twisted with sudden rage. "I am Northumbria!" he bellowed. "All that is north of the Humber is mine. I'll not bow to a damn Scot. You ask where I stand? I stand and die for Northumbria because it's mine, and if it means allying with Rufus to keep what's mine, I'll do it."

Philippe cocked one brow. Seemed pretty clear to him. If it meant turning on Rufus, de Mowbray would do that, too. But that was nothing Rufus didn't already know.

Philippe had been surprised to see the Black Earl of Northumbria riding toward them, although it was well known de Mowbray did not sit about idly in his finer castles, as others might. He was as wild and primitive as the remotest Viking Celt in the untamed Western Isles, and as suspicious and vigilant as the king himself. A man with no honor, consumed with his own importance, and yet blunt almost to the point of honesty. Save for the muffled clopping of hooves in the dirt and rough panting of the dust-colored dogs that ran alongside them, the trip was silent. Philippe kept his own counsel, now and then catching Leonie's wary gaze. Each time de Mowbray attempted to rein back, Philippe blocked his view of Leonie by doing the same. He ignored the man's dark glower.

Soon they reached the outpost, which except for its thick timber palisade was little different from the tiny stockade they had left that morning. Perched on a tall, conical hill flattened at the top, and surrounded by a deep earthen moat, it had a timber tower and outbuildings that Philippe estimated could hold no more than twenty men.

The river ford was shallow, although in winter it would probably be swift and deep. A crude drawbridge of roughly hewn planks lowered into place, and the party rode their horses across in single file. Philippe glanced about in every direction but saw nothing that led him to suspect de Mowbray had any nasty plans in store for them. He noted the tracks of wagons—the dowry train that likely had left for Bosewood this morning.

"You'll want to refresh," said de Mowbray as he dismounted and hurried up to assist Leonie down. Philippe gritted his teeth but let the man have that small win.

"Then," de Mowbray continued, taking Leonie's hand upon his arm for escort, "break your fast. Castle Bosewood is barely two hours' more ride. My men and I will make escort if the lady is so determined." De Mowbray's sharp black eyes glanced back briefly at Philippe.

"I am determined, Lord Northumbria," Leonie said. "Do not think so ill of it. Many a woman marries for the sake of duty or family."

De Mowbray meant to find a way to speak with Leonie privately. There was no stopping him. At first Philippe thought to bar him, but decided perhaps it would be better to let the man have his say. Still, he could not easily forget the stories that were told of the Black Earl. One of them was rape.

Still.

He'd give the man a few minutes. But not in a way that threatened the girl. She had already been through too much.

De Mowbray pointed Philippe toward the latrine and offered his solar to Leonie for her convenience. "'Tis not a solar at all. We have no womenfolk here, lady, and 'tis not fit for one such as you. But 'twill give you a bit of privacy."

Philippe narrowed his eyes but could find no justification for his suspicions. It was what any reasonable man would do in such primitive circumstances.

Leonie hastened to the tiny hall, following de Mowbray, while Philippe was given first seat in the latrine, followed by the knights who had ridden out that morning. Soon he, too, headed for the hall. But as he reached the corner of the timber hall, he heard voices.

"Say the word, lady, and I will take you to Scotland."

"You are kind. But it would brand you a traitor to Rufus, and he will not forgive you a second time. Nor would I be a traitor to my king."

"I do not cower from Rufus."

"I would not call you coward, Lord Northumbria, but that is not the point. I would not be the cause of a war for England, and you would most certainly be forced to side with Scotland. Why would you do this? You owe nothing to me."

"But to your lady mother, I do."

"Why? What is it you know about her?"

Philippe rounded the corner, startling the towering de Mowbray, who bent anxiously toward Leonie.

"It's not your mother's memory he honors, but his own gain," Philippe said as he stepped in front of the huge man. "He cares not to increase his holdings, like your other suitors. Your holdings lie within Northumbria's lands, but they are in the king's gift. This man cares more to decrease the king's power, not to increase his own. The moment you go off with him, you are ruined, Leonie. You would lose everything for the sake of the man who would claim to save you."

De Mowbray's face turned crimson, and his hands balled into massive fists. "Such a lady should not be forced to marry the man who brutalized her!"

"So says the man who led his men to rape an entire convent of nuns in Normandy."

"'Tis a lie! No man of mine touched any of them! 'Twas Robert Curthose's men that blamed us unfairly. And what would you, you cock-sucking whore to a sodomite? You say you want nothing, but here you stand, taking it all, and would have us believe it is the lady who lies!"

"She remembers wrong. Leonie, tell him I was not there. Think, girl, can you not remember?"

He watched in horror as the girl's face changed from anger to confusion, then pain. With a gasp, she held her head between her hands, trembling. "Can't—hurts my head—"

She arched and cried out, her head snapping back as if she had been hit. He lunged for her, catching her as her knees buckled and she went limp.

Philippe eased her to the floor and sat cross-legged, holding her in his arms, his mind flashing back to the evening he had found her in the forest with her bloody hair spread over her like a veil.

"Blazes in Heaven, is she ill?" asked de Mowbray, bending over. "What have you done to her?"

"Get some water. A wet rag," Philippe replied as he caressed her flaxen curls away from her brow. "Easy, Leonie," he said, stroking her hair and cheek. "I have you. You are safe."

De Mowbray handed Philippe the cup he had just been given, which Philippe held to Leonie for little sips. Then he took the wet cloth held out for him and wiped it tenderly over her brow, face, and neck, leaving it to rest on her forehead.

De Mowbray knelt on one knee beside them. "What is it?"

"I think the injury to her head. This happened yesterday as we were riding. And I think too in her uncle's hall before the king, barely three days after she was attacked." Philippe glanced at de Mowbray, whose evilly black eyes softened into concern. "But she gets better, don't you think? For a girl who was only a week ago thought to be on her deathbed?"

"Aye," de Mowbray responded, his words drawn out. "Aye, lass. You're a strong one. You'll be all right. Takes time to heal, you know."

Philippe thought she had been hit harder by the odd faint this time, but he dared not say so. She could not seem to lift her head from his shoulder.

"Hurts to think," she said. "Like someone stabbed me in the head. I can't think."

"Then don't." Philippe stroked her hair while something wrenched his heart. If he were wise he would not touch her for any reason. But all he could tell himself was perhaps he was not wise. "We won't talk about it anymore."

He stopped to wipe the cool, wet rag over her face again. "Just think about good things. Your family. Your cousin Claire. You're fond of her, aren't you?"

"She's like a sister."

"Aye. You should see them, de Mowbray, so different, yet both so beautiful as they walk together." Ah! What did he think he was doing, to say such flattering things? He did not think her beautiful!

"Hm," said the black-eyed earl. "Haps I'll be wanting to meet this Claire if she's as beautiful as our lady here." But as he stood, he signaled to his soldiers. One brought up a mazer of ale, and at the earl's direction offered it to Leonie.

Leonie frowned and brushed it away as she tried to raise her head. "Cease your overweening flattery, both of you. You can let me up now. I'm fine."

"Of course. But tarry a moment longer," Philippe said.

"I'm fine. Let me rise."

Nay, she was still weak and wobbly and too stubborn to admit it. Even her hand trembled. "A moment longer. It can do no harm. Think of that young boy who follows you about. You're fond of him, and he thinks you are the rising sun."

"Sigge," she replied, and with a sigh let her head lie back on his shoulder. "Aye."

"A smart fellow, isn't he?"

"He wants to learn everything."

"He'll become a cleric, then."

"Nay. He wants to be a knight. Always nattering about wishing he had a sword. But he'd surely cut his foot off with it."

"A blacksmith's boy become a knight? The world can be a harsh place for those who dream. 'Tis not his place."

"His grandfather was a knight. Severin de Brieuse."

"The traitor?" De Mowbray leaned back. "I remember William executed him and confiscated his lands. His widow died, they said, of starvation."

Leonie tried to nod, but it was a stiff movement, cut short by pain. But his fingertips resting on her neck told him her pulse was no longer pounding.

"A blacksmith took in de Brieuse's son as his apprentice, else he would have died, too," she said, and slowly leaned out of Philippe's arms to sit on her own. "Harald is Sigge's father. He took a Saxon name to honor the smith and turned his back on his father's memory. He doesn't want to be anything but a blacksmith, but Sigge is different. He says he wants to be like the Peregrine, except that he wants to ride a white horse instead of a grey one."

"Ah, lass, your heart is too soft," de Mowbray replied as he leaned forward, his hands propping on his bent knees. "You must not let it ache for those you cannot help. The other knights wouldn't accept the boy, nor would the king. 'Tis said a traitor's blood endures forever. 'Tis a rare thing even that a traitor's son survives."

Philippe released his arms to let her sit alone. "But if his father would allow it, we could bring him to Bosewood. We could find a use for him, surely."

She shook her head in a very slow motion. "He wouldn't leave his family."

This time when she tried to rise, Philippe allowed it. De Mowbray stood and took her hand to help her up. Philippe got to his feet and watched as the wounded girl became once again the strong and confident lady. He had been wrong. Now he knew that. She had not sought to trap him. Somewhere in her head, the real memories had gotten lost. He sighed as another new revelation seeped into his brain. He cared very much what she thought about him. That was the one thing, for her sake, that he should have never allowed to happen.

Like a noose tightening around his neck, he felt choked. He could protect her from everyone else. But how could he protect her from him?

Leonie straightened her back, and the long, lithe girl seemed to grow taller. A certain regal air came over her, which Philippe realized was a mask to hide her fears. "Lord Northumbria," she said, "it would please me if you would escort us to Bosewood and attend me at my wedding there."

De Mowbray's black eyes remained hooded beneath heavy lashes, but Philippe caught a rivalrous look flashed at him before the earl stepped back and bowed. "Your servant, lady," de Mowbray said. "My apologies that the meal I have set for you is scant. Your company wasn't expected."

As Leonie became more sure-footed, Philippe became aware of the huge, shaggy hound de Mowbray called Ilse nuzzling his hand and whining. He patted the dog's head, but she pulled away, then came back to nudge his hand again.

"She wants something you have," de Mowbray said. He fluffed the dog's long, shaggy ears. "What is't, Ilse? Show us."

Ilse bounced in a sideways leap and turned to run to Philippe's horse, then jumped repeatedly at the panniers behind the saddle.

"Oh, the bone," Philippe said. "She insisted I bring an old bone she found." He shrugged his shoulders and walked to Tonerre's side, where he removed the weathered bone and tossed it to the dog.

Ilse leaped into the air to catch it, then trotted to de Mowbray, who took the bone and examined it while the dog sat as her tail swished rapidly back and forth on the ground. The huge man turned the bone, studying it, frowning. "Where did she get it?" he asked.

"We don't know. Somewhere near the traveler's stockade where she found us. She brought it back after she leaped the fence and chased our attackers."

"These attackers, did you see them?"

"Nay. It was in the middle of the night. But we heard a tremendous fight, as if men were being attacked by wild wolves. But then she came back with this, which could hardly be the bone of a man recently killed. Yet she presented it like a trophy."

De Mowbray grunted. "'Tis one, of a sort. Well, Ilse, you know what to do with it."

Ilse took the bone and ran toward the drawbridge. Halfway across, she dropped it into the river. De Mowbray said nothing more and led them toward the crude wooden hall.

"What in the names of the saints is that about?" Philippe asked. "It's a human bone. You should bury it properly."

"Not a man. A gholin. Best to toss it into water so it can never reunite with its owner."

Philippe frowned. "Gholin? What's that?"

"Not sure," said the earl, and his wild black curls bounced with the vigorous shaking of his head. "They're like walking skeletons. Haps they're the bones of men who rest unquietly in their graves. Whatever they are, they're evil. Ilse hates them. She hunts them down. I've not seen them about for a long time. Till now."

His frown deepening, he looked back at Leonie, whose face had turned ashen again.

"Do they—have eyeballs?" she asked.

It was de Mowbray's turn to frown. "Aye, they might. You haven't seen them, have you, lass?"

"In the forest. Brodin woods. It was the day Philippe first came to Brodin, when a little boy cut his foot on something metal. I went back to find the metal but found that thing with a sword." She shuddered. "But when I had to pass the place again, there was no sign it had ever been there."

"Then might that have been what assaulted you in the wood?" Philippe asked.

She glared at him. "I know what I saw there, sir."

Philippe wouldn't let Leonie out of his sight as long as they remained within de Mowbray's walls. He had no doubt he owed his own life to her. Why, when she could easily have set de Mowbray against him with a mere nod? Philippe could possibly have taken the Black Earl in a fight, but not all of his men as well. And how strange that de Mowbray honored her requests when just as easily he could have forced her to his will. There was something. Philippe shook his head. He was imagining things. Everyone knew the Black Earl of Northumbria had the blackest of hearts.

After a crude meal of tough meats and havercakes, they set out again, accompanied by de Mowbray and his men. The road to Bosewood was broader, less rutted, and less full of possibilities for havoc, but until they set eyes on the castle's curtain wall Philippe did not mean to relax his guard.

CHAPTER THIRTEEN

IN THE BEGINNING OF THE NEXT LEG OF THEIR JOURNEY, LEONIE appreciated the protection the two men gave her, but the excessive vigilance soon began to wear thin. She felt like a prisoner with the two enormous men riding on either side of her, so close their leggings often brushed her skirt. They bickered about everything, from who should ride on which side of her to whether she should ride at all. Philippe thought the earl should send to Bosewood for a litter and his own troops to escort them. De Mowbray insisted Philippe was a bloody fool if he expected Bosewood to have such a civilized conveyance.

Every moment she spent with Philippe brought new questions, puzzles to her mind. He had held her so tenderly, cradling her like a mother with her sick child. Sometimes his tongue had been sharp, but he had only protected her. Was it simply because Rufus had commanded it? Something was wrong with that.

Yet the memory was so clear—

She stopped the thought before it could assault her again. It was like a hard wall in her mind that she could not penetrate, and her efforts only battered her mind till it was sore. She must not. Philippe must be right. Something was wrong with her. Very, very wrong.

And if that was so, she could not trust anything her mind told her.

But the men flattered her falsely. She knew she was not beautiful. If men stared when she walked with Claire, it was only to compare her lovely, tiny cousin with the gawky giantess walking beside her. Before, she had never really cared, being secure in the knowledge that her dowry was sufficient that the king would find her a suitable husband.

Then there had been Philippe.

De Mowbray reined in his great brown warhorse, and all the men behind him did the same. He pointed down the road. "There," he said. "That road turns north toward Bosewood, only a mile more. If you look, you can see its curtain wall where it sits on yonder hill, the River Wear winding at its feet."

Leonie frowned, shading her eyes from the afternoon sun. The hill rose above the trees and was easy to see, but she could not make out the castle.

"I see it," Philippe said. "Is the wall complete, then?"

De Mowbray gave a disgusted grimace. "They've done naught to finish it in several years. There are gaps at the back."

"A lack of funds? Rufus provided well to have a castle here."

"A lack of ambition. Theobald paid little attention to his obligations. He was obsessed in searching the woods for some sign of his lost wife."

"He looked for my mother?" Leonie asked. "I thought he hated her."

"He did. He hated Herzeloyde even more for escaping him. I don't doubt what would befall her if he ever found her."

"So she is alive," Leonie said.

"I didn't say that."

"Then what did happen to her?"

The earl's black eyes studied her solemnly. "She walked into the woods one day and was never seen again by the likes of man."

"That is a word puzzle," she said. "You say she was not seen, but not that she died. A woman would not likely survive long alone in the woods. But you do not say she stayed in the woods. Or is the puzzle with the word 'man'?"

"Clever lass." The black-eyed Black Earl focused on the narrow dirt road, refusing to look her way.

"Without a trace. It makes no sense. Even if she had been devoured by wild animals, something would have been found. So my father thought she was alive, too. And you know, don't you?"

The muscles in the man's dark face drew tight. "She's gone, lass."

Now she was sure. He was the key. "But you know, don't you?"

De Mowbray didn't answer. A strange thing for a man who otherwise talked so freely.

"Do you know where she is?"

"I do."

"Then can you not take me to her?"

"I know where she is, but not how to find her."

"Another game with words."

"Nay. I know the place, but one such as I cannot find it."

"Then would you if you could?"

"Nay. Let it go, lass. It is not for you to know."

"She's my mother."

He shook his head. "'Tis not for you to know. If it is meant to be, it will come to be."

"Your outrider comes," Philippe said.

"Aye," de Mowbray replied as they watched the dust kicked up on the road ahead. "Arm yourselves."

Leonie had kept her bow strung, though why she had felt the need among so many armed men she did not know. But she positioned her quiver forward near her waist so the arrows could easily be drawn.

The outrider was easy to distinguish, wearing de Mowbray's black-and-silver crest of battling wolf and dog. She watched the man race up to the master and turn. The horse whuffed heavily.

"'Tis Fulk," the rider said. "The bishop rides with him."

A shiver jolted her, remembering the last time she had seen Fulk. But they were all Normans, were they not? Surely he would be civil.

"Haps he brings news of Malcolm," replied Philippe.

"Malcolm it was who laid the cornerstone for Durham's new cathedral, not a month past. Do you think that makes him friend or foe?"

"Not a comforting thought," Philippe muttered.

"Aye. More like, he wants to know what Rufus is about, to tell to Malcolm. Best mind your words."

"There's no other route to the castle?"

"Nay, unless you mean to swim the river twice and scale its walls. 'Tis well sited, the river on three sides and the steep hill ahead of us. Look ahead. They approach now."

She guessed as she watched the oncoming riders that they outnumbered de Mowbray's men, but not by much, and if she must stake her life on the ferocity of warriors, her chances were probably better in her present company. But Fulk, facing her and riding in the fore with his great black horse emblazoned with his colors of red on black, was considered a mighty knight. She would not take anything for granted.

On the opposite corner, the Bishop of Durham, wearing a crimson cloak. Strange that he wore a miter when traveling, although this one, William of St. Calais, was well known for his pomp.

"Odd to have the bishop with him," Philippe said.

"Aye. It means something," the Black Earl replied in a low growl.

"He's there to give validity to something."

"Something they mean to do."

"Something they want the Church to back. Keep a close watch. I trust neither of them. Leonie, behind me."

"They will not harm me. I know Fulk. Haps I can talk—"

De Mowbray frowned. "'Tis for men to parley, lass. Stay out of the way."

She didn't like it, but they were right. She did know Fulk, and he had not listened to her the last time. He would not be different now.

Fulk's knights had a sameness to them, with their bright red tabards over their mail and mail coifs. She had seen them at Brodin. All of them wore the backs of their heads shaved in the same old-fashioned way as Fulk wore his.

The horses came to a halt a few lengths apart. The men called out their wary greetings.

"What brings you from Durham, Your Grace?" Philippe called out across the gap.

Glances shot back and forth between the bishop and his warrior.

"Turn over the Lady Leonie to us and your lives will be spared," said the bishop.

"For what purpose?"

"She is the lawful betrothed of Fulk of Durham, and you have taken her against her will. We have heard of your treatment of her, and we will not tolerate such shame to a lady. But all will be forgiven if you relinquish her to her rightful husband."

Leonie gasped. Could he have mistaken her so thoroughly? "You have misunderstood me, Lord Fulk," she said. "I gave you no promise. I told you instead the choice of my husband belonged to the king, my guardian, and I would abide by his choice."

"Nay, lady, you gave me your promise, if only the king would grant our wish," said Fulk, giving her an almost beatific smile. "We know you are coerced and cannot speak freely. I shall save you from these beasts who abuse you for their own purposes."

"You lie, Fulk," Philippe said. "Before I left the king at Castle Brodin, he told me he had rejected your suit. You already know he will not permit her to marry you."

Leonie's jaw dropped open. He had not said this. Fulk had come to Brodin with his suit after Philippe had left. Could Fulk have gone to the king in Gloucester after seeing her, then hurried back to Durham? It was possible. Or had Fulk lied to her, saying he was on his way to see the king, when he had already been there and been rejected? What would he gain by such deception? Rufus would call him traitor. But Fulk had the Bishop of Durham here as witness, and it was well known the Bishop of Durham did as he pleased, almost as if Durham were its own country.

The Earl of Northumbria guided his massive horse ahead of Philippe. "I have heard her pledge her troth to this man, Philippe le Peregrine," he said. "And that is as good as a marriage in the law. She belongs to the Peregrine."

"Nay," retorted the bishop, oddly agitated, his eyes strangely bright and wild, and his hands shaking. "It is not valid, for her promise was already given to Fulk, God's Warrior. She cannot give it again to another. We will take her for her own safety, or all of you will die, your souls consigned to Satan himself."

She caught the malice in Fulk's eye as he focused on Philippe, and she saw the plan. Fulk would first kill Philippe, then there would be no husband to contest him. He had the bishop here to lend sanctity to his scheme. If she didn't do something quickly, all the men who protected her were at risk. A shiver traversed her spine with the realization that Fulk was the most evil of all the men here, Warrior of God or no.

All of a piece, she raised her bow, the arrow already nocked in the string, with three more in her bow hand waiting. She drew and aimed, straight at Fulk's throat.

"Turn around!" she demanded. "Go back to Durham. You do not mean to rescue me, you mean to imprison me. I call you liar, Fulk of Durham, for I never gave you my troth. I have no such right, and so I told you clearly. The king and my uncle will both support me."

"Don't be absurd, girl," said the bishop. "Put down that silly weapon before you hurt someone."

"That is my intention. If you move so much as a hoof forward, I shall shoot."

"What little can you do with one arrow, lady?" said Fulk. "You cannot kill us all, and we outnumber you. They will all be dead."

"Ah. A pity. Then I shall have to settle for killing only you. Move back or my arrow will pierce your throat. Haps for good measure, one through your eye."

"I'd listen to her if I were you, Fulk," said Philippe. "You know her repute with a bow. One arrow will kill you before any of you can raise your sword. You have to kill all of us to win. We only have to kill you."

"This is nonsense," the bishop shouted.

Leonie pulled that last inch of bowstring, her ivorywood bow flexed to its limit. "So be it. I claim Fulk and the three men on his right. They are close enough, their mail will be of no use. Philippe, you may have the bishop's guards, and the bishop too, if he raises his hand in battle. My gift to you, my Lord Northumbria, and to your men, the remainder."

"My pleasure, lady," de Mowbray said with a growl. "We'll acquit ourselves as well as you."

All around her, she could hear the jingle and clopping of horses sensing the tension that rose before a battle, as eager to lunge forth as their riders.

"You, Lord Fulk, you will be the first to die," she added. "And then how will you force me to wed you?"

"You would not dare." Fury spun blackly in his eyes, but his hands did not move to his weapons.

"I will not give myself to you. I will happily die fighting."

Fulk's big black horse danced like a nervous spider as the knight pulled unevenly on his reins. Fulk had to know he could not move fast enough to save himself. He had moved too close, expecting a battle of swords, for no one shot a bow from horse-back. No one save Leonie of Bosewood, but he could never have expected that.

"You will burn in Hell for your perfidy, lady," Fulk said. With a jerk on the reins, he wheeled his horse and leaped into flight down the road, his men and the bishop's men turning and gal-loping after him.

"Since I have committed no such betrayal, I believe I'll leave that to God," she said. "In any event, I think I would find burn-ing in Hell a pleasanter experience than being married to him."

"By the devil and all the blessed saints!" said de Mowbray. "A battle fought without a shot, by one woman, and not a man to raise his weapon. I've never seen the like. What do you think you'll do with the likes of her, Peregrine?"

Philippe flashed a wary glance at her, but the odd upturned corner to his mouth betrayed something more. "Haps I'll have her train my archers."

Her heart still pounded, though she had not realized it before. Whence had this come, this sudden notion to play, nay, to be, the warrioress? It had just come. And something in her heart sang, that she had done something that pleased the Peregrine.

"Then," said de Mowbray, turning his massive warhorse toward the Castle of Bosewood, "if you mean to have a castle for archers to defend, you'd best hie there quickly. There'll be an army at your curtain wall before you can sneeze."

CHAPTER FOURTEEN

"I'T'S A PIGSTY!"

Leonie stared, her mouth hanging open. The tiny village surrounding the castle was pitifully neglected. It had been bad enough crossing the narrow drawbridge that looked flimsy enough to collapse from the weight of more than one horse, but this—

"A stinking, decrepit pigsty," Philippe added. "De Mowbray's right. Let's burn it." His mellow brown eyes turned harsh as he scanned the curtain wall from the inside. His knights, along with some of the king's, and villeins of all stations gathered around them as they dismounted.

Leonie followed his example, looking at the fortress from a warrior's eyes, and her heart sank. They would be in serious trouble if they faced an attack. The stone wall was nearly complete, but toward the upper slope of the ground, one large gap was blocked only by huge wooden pickets. The wooden parapets, from which men could defend the walls, were incomplete, leaving some places without protection.

"Lady! My lady!"

Leonie turned and saw Ealga running toward her. Her heart suddenly racing with joy, Leonie dismounted, ran to Ealga, and threw her arms around the woman who had been more mother than maid to her, as long as she had lived.

"I feared for you, my lady," said Ealga. She smoothed her hands over Leonie's high shoulders and tucked the wayward pale curls of her charge's hair back behind her ears.

When they separated again, Leonie spotted a hidden tear gleaming in the corner of the woman's eye. Ealga's lower lip quivered. "They said you had been found and were coming, but I was afeared."

"I am well. Only a small injury to my ankle, and I have already forgotten that."

"My lady, this place, 'tis filthy. We have been cleaning since we arrived, but 'tis no place for one gently born."

"Aye, so I see," Leonie replied. "'Tis no place for any of us. No matter. We shall make it fit."

"Leonie!" From the crumbling smithy, her favorite little boy came running.

"Sigge!" He landed in her arms with the colliding force of a big dog. She laughed. "You can speak now! How did you get here?"

"I can, Leonie, most times, that is. I came with my brother. The king said the Peregrine needed a blacksmith, and Lord Geoffrey didn't want to send Papa, so the king asked him for Modig and me. Only I've got to help in the forge, and it's a mess."

Leonie glanced at Philippe, who shrugged. Had he known about her attachment to the boy? If Sigge were here, and Ealga, it would be almost like home. "It looks like everything here is a mess, Sigge. We'll all have plenty to do to set things right."

"Now that we have the happy reunion out of the way, may I have a word with you, beloved bride?"

Leonie startled at Philippe's voice. She lifted her chin and narrowed her eyes at his folded arms and honey-brown eyes gone dark beneath glowering brows. Her chin went up as her back stiffened as straight as the lances his knights carried. "You wish to speak, esteemed lord?"

"Be sure, precious bride, you never again do what you did this afternoon."

"What was so foolish? Did Fulk not turn his tail?"

"You would have been killed in a melee. You were lucky. You will never put yourself at risk in such a way again. Do you understand?"

She sniffed. "You would be dead if I had not."

"I do not mean to say it did not work out well. But that matters not. I am a knight. As of this day, precious bride, you will begin conducting yourself in a wifely manner."

"And if I do not?" She gritted her teeth as her anger steamed her blood like water splashed into a fire.

"Do you wish for me to take that bow you value so much away from you? I'll do it if I must. You are not a warrior, nor a man. You will not act as if you are."

Fury heated her face and spread down her neck. If he ever dared.

But nay. She glanced around. All in the bailey—knights, soldiers, ladies, villeins—were as quiet as the dead. None of them would have sympathy for a lady who acted like a man, not even Ealga, who knew her secrets.

"If you are through, then, honorable lord, we ladies appear to have much scrubbing to do if we are to have a hall suitable for our delicate breeding." Before he could reply, she whirled away and stomped to the hall doors.

Hugh of Hatterie stepped ahead of her. "Haps, my lady, you might want to wait until—"

"Until what, sir? Until the rats have finished eating all the garbage? If I am to be a lady, I shall have a hall worthy of ladies. Step aside."

Wincing, Hugh pulled on the door, and Leonie saw that the upper hinge was broken. A death-dealing stench rolled out.

Leonie held her breath, forcing herself not to gag.

"Jesu and the saints," said Philippe behind her. "Let's tear it down and start over."

"You might tear it down, honored husband. I would clean it. Leave me to my task. You surely have plenty of manly tasks to perform."

She heard his grumbling, heard his footsteps, and knew he had turned and stomped away. Something in her heart sank.

Nay, *pigsty* did not begin to describe it.

She snapped off her veil and wrapped it around her face to dispel the foul odor. Seeing a rat scurry past her foot, she snatched a woman's broom and swung at it, but the act was futile, for the rat dived into the pile of refuse. She clenched her teeth and promised herself there would be no rats in her hall.

"Open the shutters and let some of this stench out."

"But lady," said one of the ladies sent by Aunt Beatrice, "Sir Hugh ordered them shut to keep the stench within."

"Open them," Leonie repeated. "I want the stench without. I shall have the keeping of the hall, not some lofty knight, and they will have more than bad smells in their bailey this day. We shall clean this place out if we must use shovels. Ealga, show me the solar. I hope it is better than this."

"It is not, lady," Ealga replied. "But come and see. Mayhap we'll soon have it fit to unload your dowry train, but I think not today."

Leonie signaled to the other women to continue their work on the hall and followed where Ealga led her to the solar, a chamber behind the hall. She lowered her hand from her nose to force herself to become accustomed to the wretched odors.

The solar was worse beyond belief, with strewn refuse occupying most of the floor. The bed was a mass of filthy rags and, she did not doubt, vermin. "Burn the mattress," she said. "Burn everything in the chamber, save the furnishing."

"Aye, 'twas my thought," Ealga responded. The old woman glanced over her shoulder, then began a whisper. "Lady, tell me true, are ye all right? Ye said ye were injured. Did ye heal it?"

Leonie shook her head. "All would have been well, and I would have evaded the Peregrine by walking through the night, but when night came, I discovered the sight was gone. I could see no better than anyone. I stopped to rest, but in the night a boar attacked me. I escaped into a tree, but he gored my ankle." She raised her skirt and showed the gash. "The Peregrine stitched it when he found me, else I would not have been able to walk. But it doesn't hurt now because it doesn't gape open."

"A boar? They dinna attack folk wi'out they are disturbed. Let me see."

Leonie propped her foot up on a stool, and Ealga bent to examine the wound. "'Tis not festered," she said in her assessing voice that sounded a bit like humming. "'Tis well stitched. But why did ye not heal it before he found ye?"

"It didn't work. Everything is strange, Ealga. I killed the boar, but my first shot missed. And on our way back here, I saw a giant snake. The Peregrine thought 'twas my imagination, or that I'm daft, but I tell you it was real. It was longer than a man is tall, with a huge head, red eyes, fangs, and a forked tongue, and black as night. When the Peregrine came running, the snake slithered into the brush. Then that night we were in a shelter and were attacked by people I couldn't see. We were warned because one of the Earl of Northumbria's dogs had found us and was in the stockade with us."

"I've heard of the earl's strange dogs," Ealga answered. She finished her assessment and dropped Leonie's skirt. "They say they are kin to the black dogs of Hell that roam the moors at night, but his dogs hunt the black dogs and other spirits. 'Tis all verra strange, lass. Do ye think ye lost your talents when ye were injured in the forest?"

Was that it? Had the injury to her head damaged her mind, then, and her Faerie ways were gone forever? "But that does not explain the snake or the boar. Nor how the earl's dog found us. Nor, for that matter, how the Peregrine found me so easily."

"And none of it explains why ye have decided to accept the marriage ye fought so hard against."

"How was I to fight him, Ealga? I could not even walk, and with my skills gone, I am but an ordinary woman now. How can an ordinary woman fight the king's will and one so sly as the Peregrine?"

"If ye are but ordinary now, can it be so bad? Is it not what ye always wanted?"

She had. She had so often said it. But now it did not look so good. "There's that," she replied. "None can call me witch now, can they? But I still find myself marrying a man who does not want me, who haps might kill me, and the only thing stopping him now is his promise to the king."

"Something he above all other men would honor, dinna ye see that? Haps ye are safe now, after all."

"And home, where I can help my people, as my mother did."

"Are you sure ye cannot close the wounds? It looks uncommon good for one naught but a few days past."

"I tried. I tried so hard, I nearly fell from the tree with the strain. But it did no good."

"Then test it."

Ealga seized Leonie's dagger from its sheath and slashed a gash across her own arm.

Leonie gasped. She grabbed the arm and clutched her hands around it, forcing herself into the flow of thought that had always worked before. Her mind began to spin in the maelstrom that was more emotion than thought, concentrating all her energy into the oozing wound. She could feel the blood seeping between her fingers and she tightened her grip, forced her thoughts deeper into her mind. Her body and her mind fought, and it was draining all her strength.

"Best to give up, lass," Ealga said with a sigh. "We'll just put a bandage on it. 'Tis not a deep cut, anyway, just a bloody one."

Leonie opened her eyes and stared at the seeping wound. It should have been completely closed, as if it had never existed. But it was no different from the moment she had grabbed the old woman's arm.

"So. I am to be ordinary after all," she said.

But she knew the Peregrine had always been right about her. She was arrogant, willful, wayward. Bold in ways no other maid would ever dare. She was not ordinary, nor was she superior to other humans. She was simply spoiled. And she had brought danger on herself because she had no humility.

Leonie of Bosewood, daughter of Herzeloyde, did not know how to be ordinary.

Through the gaping doorway came Maud, the lady maid her aunt had sent with the dowry train. The lady gasped at the blood.

"Ealga has cut herself," Leonie said. "But I do not think it is dangerous."

The lady's attention to the blood quickly faded, and she turned to Leonie. Leonie knew what was coming, for she had observed this whining woman many a time in her aunt's home. Perhaps Aunt Beatrice had simply grown tired of the woman, and she had taken her first opportunity to be rid of her. Perhaps she had grown equally weary of Leonie and her strident ways. Perhaps Aunt Beatrice would now have the peaceful household she had always sought. Claire was always the perfect daughter. Leonie had not appreciated enough the love and nurturance she had been given.

"Lady, surely you do not mean for us to suffer such labor," whined Maud. "Are there not villeins enough?"

Leonie's lips thinned, stretched over her teeth. Beyond Maud, she saw another lady who had served her aunt, Avis, who paused with broom in hand, quietly watching. The entire hall watched.

"The men have their own tasks, ensuring our safety," Leonie replied. "If I can sweep, you can sweep."

"Nay, lady, I offered to keep you company, not labor like a common woman. I shall appeal to your aunt."

Fury rose like hot blood, but Leonie remembered her sweet and gentle aunt. What would she do? And then she knew. What must be would be.

"Do that if you wish," she replied. "I'll gladly return you. In the meantime, if you do not wish to sweep, you may have another task. Go to the river and fetch a pail of sand so that you may scrub the trestle table clean for our dinner."

Maud's face paled, and she opened her mouth to protest, but Leonie cut her short.

"If the table is not clean enough for tonight's meal, you shall not eat. And if the hall is not clean enough for fresh straw tonight, you will sleep in the filth. You will not sleep nor eat with those who have done their part."

"I appeal to you, lady. I was gently born."

"None of us begged for this situation, yet here we are. And we shall only prosper if we all do our part. So you must choose, Maud. I leave it to you." For a brief moment, Leonie felt a pang of guilt, for Maud had likely never put her delicate hands around a broom handle before in her life. And yet—now she understood so much more.

Leonie stretched a grim smile over her face. Always she had quietly watched the ladies in her aunt's household jostling for power and position, but sweet Aunt Beatrice had in her own secret way been too strong for them. Maud might have thought to find better pickings in the household of a young and inexperienced bride, but Aunt Beatrice had not neglected her niece's education. Leonie caught Ealga's eye. They needed no words between them, and both of them began to sweep, turning their backs on Maud.

So the Peregrine thought her unwomanly, did he? Not a lady, was she? Haps he simply did not know what a true lady was, and it was a lot more than someone who sat in the solar and pushed a needle through a cloth.

"Don't you realize she saved your ugly hide?"

Philippe glared at de Mowbray. "She's a woman, de Mowbray. Is that something you don't know? It's not her place to be saving me. It's mine to protect her, even if it means forfeiting my life."

"You damn fool. I hope next time she lets you have your way. You would've been dead with the first blow. Fulk would have seen to it. And then how would you save her? My men could have taken them, but not in time to save either of you. She was the only one who could have done what she did. You can't let Fulk have her, lad."

Philippe frowned, fighting the ugly rage within him. Of course he knew that, but damned if he understood it. What kind of man would allow his wife to defend him? He couldn't imagine this braw and crude Earl of Northumbria ever letting a woman fight his battles. What was de Mowbray up to, then?

"You used to be the bishop's friend."

"Aye. But I tell you, William of St. Calais is not his own man now. He is lame in the head. And Fulk of Durham is not the man I once knew. 'Tis the Warrior of God they call him, but it's not God who gives him strength. I'd vow it."

"What do you mean?"

"I don't know. 'Tis something—and not a holy thing. Don't let him have the lass, if it means all our lives."

"Why? Why should I believe you?"

De Mowbray shook his head. "You must, lad. That I know."

Their eyes met in a steady gaze, Philippe searching the black eyes that seemed to blaze like the fires of Hell. Aye, they were hellish eyes, yet he read truth in them.

"The man lied," he replied, "and Leonie realized it. That's what provoked her, I think."

"Aye. She mistrusts him."

"But she mistrusts me too."

"Aye. She believes it was you who attacked her in the forest. The rumor of it has spread through all the northern folk." De Mowbray narrowed his eyes, quietly assessing Philippe as he tapped a blunt finger against the hard leather of his saddle. "But that's something else I know. I don't think she is right. It's something else—something I have seen, but I cannot put my finger on it."

The man rubbed a beefy hand over his thick, tangled black beard. "There are things in the North you'd never imagine, Peregrine. Some folks say 'tis best to keep your shutters closed at night. You cannot tell what the night air brings in."

"I don't suppose you might give me a hint. Do you mean witchcraft? Sorcery?"

"Haps. 'Tis not all. Many evils. The gholin bone Ilse brought. Bone demons, some call them, for they're mostly bones, but I do not think they are demons. Haps they are lost souls who are summoned from the grave by some awful power, and they cannot refuse."

"So you would know. Aye, I think you're right, the dog has a way about her. What about snakes? Dragons?"

De Mowbray shook his head. "I've seen no snakes. Nor dragons. But be you ware of black dogs with eyes of red. They'll steal your soul, should you find yourself alone on the moors at night, and there'll be no trace of you on the morrow."

Philippe pursed his mouth and rubbed his beard, which had grown rough since he had left Castle Brodin. Though he detested magic and its evil, still he'd hoped it might explain Leonie's sighting of the snake. But if anyone would know about it, de Mowbray would.

They turned and watched four women emerge from the hall, tugging sacks and tossing various things out the door. Leonie was in the midst of them, carrying what no lady ought to touch. She beckoned to a village man, who rushed up, tugging his forelock and bowing. Quickly the man called other villeins to haul away the garbage into a pile, which would likely be burned. A rat ran from the pile, and with a shriek of vengeance, Leonie took a broom to it, chasing it until it vanished again beneath the garbage. Unwomanly she might be, but he had to admire her ferocity. Remorse tugged at Philippe for his stern words to her. "I cannot deny she's tough enough for this wild land, de Mowbray."

"Aye. She's an uncommon one. She's what I'd expect of Herzeloyde's daughter."

"What is all this about Herzeloyde? Why is she so important here?"

"You'd have to know her. She's known and admired by all throughout the North for her kindness and generosity. But then, she was like them—not Norman. You don't know how fortunate you are, laddie."

Philippe's jaw clenched grimly. Oh nay, he was not fortunate. If the girl were plain and meek, a woman he could mostly ignore, he might have some hope. But already he could tell, Leonie of Bosewood was on her way to becoming as much a legend as her mysterious mother, and the more Philippe saw of Leonie, the more he comprehended the elusive Herzeloyde. There was something in Leonie that called to mind the Norse legends of Valkyries, and ancient Celtic stories of warrior women like Queen Boadicea, who led her people against the Romans. Something told him Leonie could be such a leader of men. He had to laugh at himself that only a few weeks before he had considered her little more than a child.

He watched her as she worked with the other women, women so common they might never have come close to a lady, yet she wielded her broom as deftly and purposefully as they. She was taller than every other woman he had ever seen, a full head and shoulders over any of these, slender as a reed, yet curved the way a comely woman ought to be. She was too busy now to remember to be haughty, but the way she strode made the hem of her kirtle wrap around her legs as she walked.

His shaft grew suddenly hard, and he had the sinking feeling she was a woman he would more than admire. But he must not. Somehow he must keep his heart in check or he would doom her. As well as his shaft, which he knew all too well would lead his heart astray.

He turned the conversation back to de Mowbray's last words and the question left unanswered.

"You can't convince me you don't know Herzeloyde lives. I hear it in your words even though that is not what you say."

"Is it? Haps it's a spirit that will not fade from men's hearts and minds. But don't you dwell on such things. You have another task. You must marry the lass quickly before Fulk finds another way to wrest her from you."

"Would it make a difference? He could simply kill me and make her a widow. Aye, we'll do it quickly. I promised Rufus. It's a shame, though, she cannot have at least a decent wedding feast. If we'd had the time to go to my manor in Sussex, or one of her properties, or even return to Brodin, there could have been a fine wedding and feast. But here we have nothing, and no time to get it."

"'Tis what must be."

"Aye. Still, I remember my first wife, Joceline, telling me it's every maiden's dream to have a wedding worth remembering. Leonie did not want this marriage, but that does not stop her from doing what she must for people she has not seen since she was a babe. She deserves at least a feast, but I cannot give her even that much."

"My lord," said Hugh's voice behind him. A grey-bearded man in a plain brown tunic approached in Hugh's company. From the looks of him, not a man of wealth, but one of some importance. Philippe summoned the man forward with a nod.

"Forgive me, my lord, I dinna mean to hear what is not mine to hear."

"This is Cyne, Peregrine," said de Mowbray. "Once a thane in times past, before we Normans came to make a fine mess of his life."

Philippe nodded his acceptance of the man, wary all the same. Very few of the old Saxon thanes had been allowed to live, even in poverty.

Cyne bowed low, and Philippe quickly formed his opinion. He did not seem to be a man who harbored a hatred for all Normans. But it was not wise to forget the fate of the two previous castellans of Bosewood.

"Lord," said the man, his eyes properly downcast, "our village is poor. We cannot give much, but we can give a wedding feast. We have food, though it is simple fare, and we can dance and sing to the pipes."

Philippe's mind leaped eagerly to the picture of the villagers caroling hand in hand, a long line weaving through the village to the sound of bagpipes, circling a bonfire against the dark sky, and all the way back up the hill to the castle. He'd seen it, and it was a thrilling sight.

He arched his brows. "Why would you do that?"

"'Tis your due, lord. 'Tis for Herzeloyde's daughter and her lord."

Philippe glanced at Hugh, whose eyebrows rose expectantly. He turned to de Mowbray, whose eyes gleamed in that way that made Philippe wonder if the man was from Hell or Heaven. Nay, though, not from Heaven. Of that much he was sure.

Philippe turned back to survey the incomplete stone curtain wall, judging the efforts Hugh and his men had made to bridge its gaps with timbers. "You've done well already, Hugh. Will the timber walls hold?"

"If we're lucky. Fire would bring it down."

"I have an idea on that. We'll turn the weakness into a trap. But we'll do that tomorrow. For now," he said, his thoughts going gleefully shrewd, "let us plan a wedding. And let us do one thing more—make it a surprise."

CHAPTER FIFTEEN

LEONIE GROANED AS SHE STOOD. SHE'D BEEN ON HER KNEES, chiseling some unknown substance off the flagstone floor, and her back must surely hurt more straightening it than it had being bent. At the *ching-ching* sound of mail, she looked up to see the Earl of Northumbria crossing the hall to where she stood.

"Lord Northumbria," she said with a small nod, for even her neck hurt.

"Lady Leonie," he said, almost with a smile, which she could tell only by the way his great black mustache broadened slightly. "'Tis the first time in years Bosewood's floor has been seen by the eyes of man. You'll make a fine hall of this yet."

She rubbed the small of her back, although the ache was already beginning to dull. "We have cleaned out the solar and unloaded the dowry wagons. Haps by tomorrow the odor will go away and the bed can be put back, with the feather bed my uncle had the fine foresight to send. At least the kitchen is usable. Naught but the table is salvageable in the hall, I'm afraid. Some of the benches are so rickety I would not dare to sit on them."

"Don't worry tonight, lass. 'Tis time to prepare yourself for your wedding. The Peregrine says he wishes you to wear your pretty green kirtle and have your hair done in long curls like you did at your uncle's feast at Brodin."

She sniffed. Now he wanted her hair in ringlets? "There's no time for that. There's too much to do if we are to have a table for our supper and a hall to bed down for the night."

"Nay, lass, the wedding's to be this day. You won't be safe from Fulk until you are wed."

"As if a wedding would stop him. Haps I'll just send an arrow to nail his randy shaft to his hide."

"'Twould not be a ladylike thing to do, lass."

"Indeed not. But then, have you men not already decided I am no lady?"

"Now, lass, you mustn't blame the man for worrying about your safety. You don't have much time, so go and dress. I'll be waiting here to take you to the church porch."

Leonie exhaled a long, hard sigh, and with a hurried motion at Ealga, walked to the solar.

Despite all their work, the smells of old sweat, smoke, and rotten food still permeated everything, even the walls. The Peregrine was right, they ought to burn it down. But she was not ready to give it up just yet.

A pail of clear water sat on a stool, and Leonie lavished the cool water over her face and body. It felt like the greatest luxury on earth. Tomorrow, she promised herself, she was going to wash her hair, an even greater pleasure, now that Ealga was here to help her.

In the packed goods, Ealga found a fresh chemise. She dressed Leonie in the green kirtle and a pale blue cotehardie, with a chain of gold and amber for her neck. Then she sat on a wobbly stool as Ealga unraveled the thick braid. Patiently, Ealga combed strands of Leonie's hair into long ropes of curls, then framed it all with two long, narrow braids crossing and loosely binding the curls like lacings around leggings. On her head, she set a fine, gauzy white veil, held down by a gold circlet.

She stood. 'Twas the best that could be done on such short notice. The Peregrine would have to take her as she was. In a manner of speaking only, since she didn't expect him to take her at all.

Leonie stifled a shudder. She was not sure which she minded more, that he might take her or might not. Confusion pounded like a rock banging around against her skull. He was evil. He was kind. She looked at him one time and felt only fear and revulsion. She looked again and felt trust, longing. Passion. And no matter what she believed, it changed nothing.

She walked through the doorway of the solar into the hall where the fearsome giant Black Earl of Northumbria awaited. Yet of a truth, she felt no fear of him. 'Twas only Philippe le Peregrine who made her heart tremble.

Reaching the earl, she dipped a very formal curtsy, and the man, completely cleaned and combed since she had last set eyes upon him, responded with a bow worthy of the court of the King of France. Even cleaned up, she could not call him handsome, but she could not help but think there was goodness in the man who was deemed by one and all to have a heart as black as the moonless night.

A sudden surge of longing for her family hit her, and she looked back over her shoulder as if she thought they might be there. But she was beginning a different life now. Many a woman, when she married, was lost to her kin for the rest of her life. But she would always know their love, no matter if she saw them again or not.

She took a deep breath as the hall door opened and they stepped out into the cooling air of late afternoon, still tinged with smoke from the burning refuse, yet fresher than the rotten air in the hall.

"There is no straw in the hall yet for sleeping tonight," she said.

"The sky is still clear," the earl replied. "Sir Hugh and his men have been sleeping outdoors, and 'twas good enough for the ladies last night at the outpost."

"But what about the supper?"

"You worry too much, lass."

She sighed as he patted her hand. Men always thought they knew best. Well, if these men who put themselves in such authority said she was not to worry, then let them find their supper where they might.

They walked down the steep path, across the lower bailey, and out through the barbican's thick wooden gate. The sounds of villagers grew as they collected about, their curious gazes on the passage of their new lady on the arm of the more familiar Earl of Northumbria. 'Twas an old church that sat at the foot of the castle, with walls cruck-built from the crotches of huge trees, a thatched roof reaching almost to the ground, and daubed walls almost bare of whitewash. Her uncle's church had been rebuilt in stone several years ago, but the one before it had been much like this.

At the church steps stood the Peregrine, broad-shouldered and massive in blue surplice trimmed in gold, embroidered with the emblem of Evraneaux, the black falcon in flight. His yellow hair, tossed in the air by the breeze, caught the golden light of the late-afternoon sun. Her heart leaped up into her throat and stuck there, fluttering like an injured sparrow in a trap. She didn't realize she was clenching the arm of the man who led her until he once again patted her hand.

"'Twill all be well," he said. "The lad will not harm you, or he'll answer to me. I give you my word, you can always come to me, and I will keep you safe."

She hardened herself from jaw through spine all the way to her toes. "I'm not afraid of him," she said through gritted teeth.

"Um-hum," said the earl. He led her up to the church steps.

Behind the Peregrine stood his men. Close by, her maids and ladies, and the villagers beyond them in a circle. And nearby, the priest, who stood beside an elderly bearded Saxon man she had seen in the bailey with Philippe.

She took the last step and stood face-to-face with the man who was to be her husband. Her heart raced even faster with the battle between it and her mind. Her heart could not win.

Their gazes locked, his brown eyes intense. She saw in them his resolve to honor his king's command.

"Do you come willingly, Leonie of Bosewood?" asked Philippe.

She nodded, though every part of her was as rigid as an old oak. She would not tremble. She would not be afraid. "Aye."

He nodded his own consent in return. "Robert de Mowbray, Earl of Northumbria, do you stand in the king's stead to give away the bride?"

"'Tis my duty and my pleasure," the earl responded.

Leonie frowned, confused. Had the man accepted the Peregrine, then? Trusted him? She had thought at least they stood at odds over their loyalties to Rufus. And it had not been many hours ago the man had offered to spirit her away to Scotland. If not to kill outright the man he now encouraged her to marry.

"Then call everyone to the chapel steps," Philippe said to the elderly man she had seen before. "Let us have all to witness this marriage. Have you a priest here?"

"Aye, lord," said another man, a Norman, but as filthy a Norman as she had ever seen. Not one of Philippe's men.

The throng began to buzz with noise. Leonie let back her veil and heard a common gasp as her mother's name echoed through the crowd, then her own.

So. She was home. At last. Her true family, she knew, were those who had cared for her, sheltered her through childhood, defended and protected her from her wild father's wrath. She would always honor them as her family. But something about this place had always drawn her.

It was her destiny.

Ealga stepped before Philippe, her face twisted in a knot of worry as she gave him a servant's curtsy.

He nodded, waiting.

"All is ready, lord," she said.

Leonie frowned. What was ready? Of course she was ready. What had he expected, that she would come to him adorned head to toe in gold coins?

"Then let us be on with it," he answered. "Lady, are you willing?"

"As I have said," she replied.

For a bare moment, her hand hovered as she hesitated. But there was no purpose in waiting. Let her strange mind think what it would. She gave her hand into his.

There were the words of the priest, Father Ivo, asking for the bride to be given away, and the low rumble of the Earl of Northumbria's voice as he stepped forward, said his words, then backed away.

Leonie had seen many weddings in her lifetime. Nothing was new, yet all of it was, for this time it was her life that was to be changed. She knelt, as did Philippe, the man who was both strange and familiar, each facing the other, hands held up, his encompassing hers, interlocked as if in prayer. The warmth of his palms shocked her. The priest wrapped his shawl around their hands.

The words she had heard so many times echoed in her head with the ringing of her ears as her heart pounded. So familiar, yet so strange, as this day had been.

"I, Philippe of Evraneaux, take Leonie of Bosewood."

She had not heard him called that, although she knew who he was. He had always been the Peregrine to her, the wandering falcon, the man who kept himself so aloof, the man who did not want her and now must have her. It was all so strange, like a faraway echo in the hills.

Now the turn was hers. She knew by the jostling at her elbow, for her mind had been playing tricks on her again.

She spoke her name and his, and added her vows. "As long as we both shall live." It was that last that frightened her so much. Was it marriage that had destroyed her parents? Would it do the same for her?

"So be it," said the priest. "Amen."

They stood, arms interlocked, and stepped out from under the church porch into the slanting rays of a bright sunset.

The solemn crowd exploded in cheers.

Pipes began to wail. Surprised, Leonie turned about, and the villagers leaped into a frenzied dance that became a long caroling line, singing a strange song in tune with the pipes and following alongside the newlyweds as they began their procession back up the hill. She had seen such a thing before, yet not quite like this.

Nor did they go uphill at all, but instead to a village green that was thick with lush grass and decked with tables of all sorts, laden with food, roasted fowl and pork, something that looked like a greyish gruel, and even a dark, round bread. And ale. Great wooden kegs of it.

"It's your bride ale," Philippe said. "The gift of the village, for Herzeloyde's daughter."

CHAPTER SIXTEEN

D ESPITE THE WARRING INSIDE HER, LEONIE COULDN'T RESIST smiling back at the delicious way Philippe's mouth crinkled at its corners. He smiled so seldom, always the darkly solemn knight with terrible dark secrets behind his calm face.

"Why?" she asked, still surveying the feast and dancing.

He shrugged. "Who knows? The common folk are not usually generous with any conquering Norman. And they didn't respect your father, so de Mowbray tells me. But the name Herzeloyde brings awe to their faces. I don't know why."

Leonie didn't know either. No one had ever been willing to talk about her mother. De Mowbray had told her little more than she had learned from Ealga.

"But come," Philippe said, leading her by the hand. "Let me introduce to you the villagers. This is Cyne, their elder, and once a powerful thane, so de Mowbray tells me."

Cyne bowed very low, showing to Leonie the balding top of a head of greying long hair. "'Tis my greatest pleasure, lady. Once I held a babe with a froth of hair so pale, 'twas like a crown of snow. Though your hair has grown long, I know you still by your look. 'Tis one a man can never forget."

Her heart had no doubts, and her smile warmed. He was kind. A man of honor. "I am at a loss, Cyne. I remember so little. Yet I know by the feel of it I have come home. I thank you for your kind welcome."

"Naught is too much for the daughter of Herzeloyde, though we have little, and the fare is poor."

Philippe shook his head at the old man. "Good food doesn't need elegance to please. We're very hungry. We've eaten little save boar meat and the rough fare of de Mowbray's outpost, and he does not have a cook worth praising."

"'Tis true, I vow," de Mowbray said, sadly shaking his head. "'Tis said the man boils rocks for stew."

Leonie snickered. She had not minded. "I'm as hungry now as I was then. It is a fine feast."

The whine of Celtic bagpipes began, and when the bags were filled, burst into a lively tune. A drum picked up the beat as villagers jumped up from their tables and joined hands to dance in a wide circle about their Norman lord and his bride. Other than the circling with joined hands, it was not like any dance Leonie remembered. Their brown kirtles and tunics, dun-colored leggings, with their dull plaids of brown and blue, were nothing like the vivid flashes of color she'd known in her uncle's hall. Yet the dancers kicked and swayed as if their lives were every bit as vibrant and rich, turning to each other, dancing in twos, then fours, and back to their ever-circling line. Voices both deep and high sang in northern words she could not recognize, to a tune she had never heard.

"Is this the way they treat all weddings?" she asked Cyne.

"Aye, lady. The song speaks of Adam and Eve on their wedding night, and all the things they shared with each other, save the apples on the tree, for they dinna dare. And for a sennight, they dinna think of apples, only each other. But then they saw the apples again, and Eve couldna resist the gift of an apple to her sweetheart. And that is how Adam came to fall from God's grace."

"It does not seem it would be a happy song, though," she said.

"Ah, but if she dinna, we wouldna have apples! And if ye'll taste the tarts, lady, forever ye'll be grateful to Mother Eve."

Leonie laughed and took a bite from the tart he gave her. She laughed again amid her hums of pleasure. "I've never tasted better."

Some of the Norman soldiers knew the steps of the dance and joined in. Others stumbled, clumsy from the ale, bringing laughs to all. Some found maidens among the village, but Leonie saw their behavior was carefully watched, and they minded their manners well enough. She resolved she would do her best to see they did not misuse the women and girls, although she had the feeling the great Black Earl and her noble husband had already seen to that. For now, they wanted peace, not dominance.

The caroling lines came to a halt at the end of the song, and the pipes droned on, depleting their bags. The common folk stood round, waiting expectantly as the pipes began to wail a new tune. De Mowbray left their lines and walked up, huffing as only a very large man can do. He placed his fisted hands on his wide hips, waiting along with the others who stood behind him.

"What is it?" she asked.

"'Tis the time for the bride to take her husband's hand for the marriage dance."

"But I don't know the steps. All I know are court dances. They do not suit with this music."

Philippe's deep laugh rumbled from his chest. "Nor do I know them. I've never seen such steps. The court dances I learned as a boy in Normandy. You know them too, de Mowbray, and you know the music and rhythm are not the same."

De Mowbray rubbed his black beard. "Hm, aye. They aren't the same at all, and of a truth, I don't know how to dance anyway.

I just jump around, and they don't seem to mind. But you must dance. The people expect it. If you don't—well, you must. Can't you make them fit?"

"Oh no, 'twould never work," she replied, shaking her head.

Philippe stood and held out his hand to her. "It could be done. Ignore the music, and count the steps to ourselves. Shall we give it a round or two, precious bride?"

She shook her head, imagining her feet stumbling over themselves.

His eyes took on that haughtily narrowed look she despised, half smile, half sneer. "Are you afraid, adored sweeting?"

At the taunt, her eyebrows shot upward. "I?" She lifted her chin. "I am afraid of nothing, esteemed husband. It simply cannot work."

A wicked smirk crinkled Philippe's face. "But if the piper can play our tune? What shall it be? The *danse real*?"

"He would not know it." How would a rough northern piper know the music of the royal French court?

With mischief gleaming in his eyes, he called out, "Piper! Can you play this?" Philippe hummed out a tune. The piper quickly picked it up.

Leonie felt a hitch in her breath. To dance with him. And later to lie in his bed.

She shook away the shudder. She had said she feared no man. And she had so promised herself. She could change nothing with fear, only with courage. So she must make it so.

"Slowly, piper. Ta dum, ta dum, tada dum, dum." Philippe waved his hands to match the beat he wanted. The piper slowed accordingly. He turned back to her, his head cocked at an enticing angle.

"Now, my sweetest bride?" he asked, thrusting his upward-turned hand toward her again. It was no question; it was a demand. She could see that in the way his eyes smoldered.

Well, then, she would match him. Dare for dare.

With a gimlet eye focused back on him, she took his hand and walked into the circle. Then they moved apart to the clearing's edge, the proper space for the *danse real*'s beginning. The fiery light of torches outlined his hard, lean body in his pale blue tabard, and a light gust of wind tossed his golden hair like strands of pure light.

Leonie's eyes met his, full on, demanding her own answers. *What are you, Peregrine? What do you mean for me, good or ill?*

His brown eyes threw challenge at her and the smirk twisted both corners of his mouth.

Her shoulders squared as she stood tall, resolve hardening like tempered iron in a forge. *So shall it be, then, Philippe le Peregrine, whatever you are. I will not be cowed. No matter what comes, it will not be said I have merely lain down and let my fate come to me.*

Did he read her meaning? As if he did, he tilted his head and the corner of his mouth turned up. Aye. Challenge met and accepted. Let the dance begin.

They stood several arm lengths apart, the farthest arc of the circle they would traverse, he facing one direction, she the other. Each sliding step would move them slowly closer to the center, winding round and round like wool on a spindle.

Philippe signaled to the piper, who began the dance, his wailing pipe making it sound like a dirge. Step-slide, step-slide, one-two-three, one-two-three, arms rigidly at her side, eyes straight ahead in the formal posture of the dance, Leonie matched her steps to the pipes, while a drum somewhere near the piper picked up the slow cadence. She could hear Philippe humming the tune as he circled on the opposite side of the spiral.

With the first repeat of the music, they continued around the circle, now with their faces turned toward each other, looking down along the arm each of them extended toward the circle's center. Step-slide, step-slide, the inward spiral began, subtly closing toward each other with each step, until at the end of the second refrain, their upraised fingertips barely touched.

With the next repeat, their hands clasped, zapping lightning between them. Leonie spun gracefully beneath his high-raised arm, and back to their upward-held clasped hands.

"He's playing faster," she whispered to Philippe.

"Aye." Danger sparked in his eyes. Or was it wild pleasure?

Her heart beat faster, in rhythm with her own excitement. It wasn't supposed to be this way. A *danse real* was a sedate dance! They should reel outward again, moving in and out, slowly, in exactly measured steps. But the piper played ever faster, ever faster. Philippe hooked his arm around her waist and spun her about in the wild way the villagers had done.

"Stop! I can't do that!"

"You just did." His low and throaty laugh mingled with the increasing pace of the pipes, a drum beating a barbaric, rattling rhythm that throbbed in her pulse. Her ribbons slipped, her confining braids failed, and her curls flung wild in the whirling exhilaration. Rapidly, wilder, they circled, her feet nearly flying. Whirling and whirling, the folk around them merged into a spinning blur of shouting and clapping with the piper's furious tune.

Philippe lifted her in the air, swinging. Her foot caught his leg. She shrieked as she lost balance, her flailing hand grabbing for his sleeve. With a flip, Philippe threw himself before her as they fell together, and she came down atop him.

She giggled between gasps for breath, looking at him beneath her. His eyes smoldered like embers. The crowd shrieked with glee. Her hands splayed over his hard, heaving chest, and she quickly curled them into tight balls. His smile was gone. His eyes were fierce. Then he chuckled and rolled with her, and then she was down and he was up. The crowd's murmur softened, like sweet music.

Philippe leaned over her, one muscular leg wrapping over her body. "I think I must kiss you now, my sweetest bride, else they will think me very strange."

Leonie tried her best to sneer but only managed a ridiculous flare of her nostrils. "Alas, most revered husband, they would be right."

Her last word was cut off as his lips touched hers. She closed her eyes against the raging storm that tormented his gaze. At first his mouth was hard against her lips as if he meant to punish her, but it softened to tenderness while the pads of his thumbs feathered over her cheeks. Her very flesh burned where his body touched hers, and she wished for once she had no Faerie blood in her to fan the flames of her desire. Always, always, he had provoked her to such unmaidenly fires. Always, she had hated him for that.

Abruptly, he pulled back from her. Ferocity, nay, perhaps anger, blazed in his eyes where sweet laughter and tenderness had been. Aye, she had forgotten, he hated her too. This was but a sham to please the villagers.

De Mowbray's raucous laugh cleared her mind soon enough.

"Come now, lad, if you're so anxious, we'll get on with the bedding now."

Philippe sat and rose sharply to his feet. He dusted himself off and reached down a hand for Leonie, but she was already rising.

As she stood, Leonie saw an old woman in a hooded dark cloak, standing alone between two crude cottages. She wondered if her Faerie vision was coming back, for she could tell the cloak was a deep mossy green. Strange and pale, the woman's eyes gleamed, as if they were not color but light, and her hair seemed as brittle as old, sun-bleached straw.

Philippe held out his hand to Leonie. "Old woman, come and join us," Philippe said, beckoning.

"There is a time for joining and a time for watching," the old woman replied in a voice that scratched its way through her throat. "My time has come to watch."

"Then come and eat," he replied.

The woman's light green eyes gleamed. "You please me, Norman lord," said the crackling voice. "Your heart is heavy, yet it is gentle. May many a blessing come to you and the daughter of Herzeloyde."

Leonie watched Philippe's face as it turned into a heavy frown, and his mouth opened, yet he did not reply.

"You do not believe," said the crone. She raised a long, gaunt finger and swayed it before them as if tracing a path that meandered toward the distant horizon. "Follow your heart, Norman lord. Where it leads, you will find your answer."

"Who are you?" Philippe asked. "What is your name?"

"I have no name."

"Everyone has a name. What is yours?"

The crone laughed, a ragged sound, but her solemn face did not change. Instead, she turned to Lord Northumbria. "You tarry too long, Black Earl."

The great hulk of a man rearranged himself into a reverent bow. "Aye. So I do. We will stay the night and hasten home with the dawn."

Pulling her dark hood over her straw-like hair, she turned and walked away through a mist that clung near the walls of the huts, until she disappeared into the darkness.

Silence descended on the villagers. Even the pipes had ceased their wailing. Among them, a whisper arose, and tucked within the low murmurs, Leonie heard a single word repeated.

Cailleach.

"Who was she?" Leonie asked the earl.

Northumbria gave her another of those rare smiles that was no more than the lifting of his black mustache, bushy once again, for he had been dancing as wildly as everyone else.

"Naught but an old woman who talks too much," he said. "Well, let's be on about the bedding now. The old woman's right, I've tarried too long."

Philippe glanced at her, frowning, and an angry rigidity overtook him. "There'll be no public bedding, de Mowbray."

The bushy black brows furrowed. "But ye must, lad."

"It is a heathen custom."

De Mowbray shrugged. "Aye. So?"

"It is our affair, not anyone else's."

"But lad, there must be witnesses. Especially this time."

"Then if any should ask of any man here, let him say Leonie of Bosewood and Philippe de Evraneaux, called the Peregrine, were betrothed by command of the king. They spent two nights alone in the wilderness, and the morning following their wedding, there was no virgin's blood found on the marriage sheets."

Leonie gasped, feeling the color drain from her face. How did he dare. She clenched her hands into tight fists, for if she let her wayward fingers have their way, they would claw his eyes out!

The earl rubbed his beard. "Well, you can't say I didn't warn you when Fulk comes to demand the lass. But it's your affair, as you say. So let's be caroling you back up the hill now, and I'll leave at dawn."

"Must you go so soon?" Leonie asked him, already feeling the loss.

"Aye, lass, I must. But don't you be forgetting, if he doesn't treat you right, you're to come to me for help."

Philippe offered his hand to the earl to shake. "I thank you for your help, but not your advice, de Mowbray."

The Black Earl bellowed a laugh as he clapped his other hand over their handshake.

"Strange man," said Philippe as they watched the earl disappear into the crowd.

The whine of bagpipes filling signaled to the dancers, who formed lines and burst into song. Philippe took Leonie's arm and the procession wound up the hill toward the castle gate.

Her cheeks were still hot with rage at him, but she gritted her teeth and played her role. Now she had only to think about sleeping in the solar where the odor of neglect still stank.

But instead of to the dilapidated hall, he led the procession to the wooden tower in the north corner of the castle, and to the ladder that led from the open base to the square tower room. She frowned at him. "I don't understand."

"Our bower," he replied. "Up." His hand circled in the air, making it clear climbing the ladder was what he wanted her to do.

She shrugged and climbed. She was, after all, trying very hard to be a reasonably obedient wife.

At the top of the ladder, she crawled through the square hole and onto the tower floor. Bright light from the newly risen moon flooded in the tower's windows, for the shutters were flung open wide. In one corner, the feather bed sent by her Uncle Geoffrey was covered in white sheets, with blankets and pillows aplenty.

"It's Ealga's gift to you," he said. "So you don't have to stay in the hall until the odor goes away. And saints preserve her for her thoughtfulness."

"But when did you talk with Ealga? She was with me since we arrived at Bosewood."

"There are ways."

She had not noticed, but now she thought of it, she had not seen Ealga since the wedding at the church steps. So she must have come here from the church.

"The night will be cool, but I think, no rain, and we have plenty of blankets to keep us warm."

Confusion began to hammer at her mind. What kind of man was he? One moment crassly lying and humiliating her in front of de Mowbray and the entire village, and the next, planning a fine feast, even to the point of making a place for her to sleep in comfort. He did not fool her to claim it was all the doing of others.

Did he mean to break his oath and take her after all? What could she do about it if he did? Not a man or woman below would understand a wife refusing her husband.

She thought she would never understand him.

"Did you have to say that about the sheets?" she asked.

He pulled his blue tunic over his head. "Aye."

"I don't see why."

"You did say you do not want to be bedded. And I wish to keep my vow. But they would have forced us, all of them meaning well. It was the only way to stop a public bedding, my precious, to persuade them there was no point in it. De Mowbray especially, the randy old dog."

He held out his hand to her. She took a step back.

"Do you not wish to lie down with me? I'll make myself a pallet by the wall, and in the morning I will see that I am found beside you, so none will suspect our lie."

Even now her mind screamed fear for his perfidious deed, for the terrifying dream that kept returning every time she closed her eyes. Yet her body thrummed the rhythm of excitement at the very scent of his presence. Even the hairs on her arms seemed to stand alert when he was near. And all the while her heart called out, *This is Philippe.* This Philippe was the man to whom she had foolishly and secretly given her heart when she was little more than a child, when he had brusquely tossed it away.

And he did not want her now. He wanted only to please his king.

She did not want to lie down with him. Even in pretense. But she drew in a long breath. She was Leonie of Bosewood, who would fear no man, fear no fate.

"We shall sleep together," she said.

He nodded silently and turned away as he stripped the last garments from his body. Perhaps, she thought, he was ashamed that he did not want her.

"Leave on your chemise," he said. "It would not be unseemly for a new bride. But if I am clothed, then our lie will not be believed."

She nodded.

"Your foot," he said. "I forgot it. Let me see it."

"It is fine. Ealga tended it earlier."

"It could not be, not so soon, and I made you dance on it. Forgive me."

"Nay, I tell you, I did not notice myself. Do not fuss over it. There is no pus, no pain. But there will be a scar."

He frowned. "Show me."

With huff, Leonie sat on the bedding and stretched out her foot, and he unwrapped the cloth to see for himself she did not lie.

"Still, I should not have made you dance."

"It was a good dance. A good reason to laugh."

In the darkness, he slipped beneath the sheets and turned his back to her. Now she had no doubt he would keep his promise not to molest her. And something in her felt the hurt as deeply as if it stabbed, knifelike, through her heart. As it always had.

Shafts of moonlight fell upon him where he lay, and her eyes could trace the fine curve of his spine. Her hands wanted to touch, to follow the beauty of the curve. There was no denying he was as well made as any man might ever be.

She had not expected love from a husband. She had always known better than to believe that, for women of her sort who inherited great properties would never be allowed husbands chosen by their hearts. But that was the irony of it all. For some reason she would never comprehend, she had been given the husband of her dreams, only to face his abhorrence of her. And that would be true even if the wild and frightening thoughts in her mind turned out to be false.

If they were fortunate, she could just go on living, doing what she must, and he could do what he must, and someday they might forget that they did not belong together. Or she might go away, as he had said, and he would forget her entirely.

"Philippe?" she said tentatively, in case he might still be awake. He had slept little if at all in the last few days.

"Umm?" It was the sound of a man already lodged in the world of dreams.

"Do you think Fulk will give up now?"

"Nay."

"Then what will they do next?"

Philippe rolled to his back. She could see the tired lines in his brow and wished she had let him sleep.

"The Bishop of Durham will complain to Archbishop Anselm that Rufus has given a promised maid in marriage to another man, and the archbishop will take the complaint to Rufus. Rufus and Anselm are at odds these days, though Rufus does listen to him. But it will not matter. Rufus knows the real truth and will know Fulk has lied to his bishop. Durham and Fulk may not realize it, but their very complaint will tell Rufus of their real intentions."

"How?"

"Rufus can read people better than the archbishop can read his Latin treatises. I have sent word to the king of today's affairs, but my messenger must pass through Durham's lands to reach the king. De Mowbray sent his own man, west through Westmoreland. Mayhap one of the messengers will get through. If not, Rufus will know when he does not hear from me that something is amiss. Rufus told me he had already turned down Fulk's suit before Fulk ever went to Brodin. Yet the fool still went to Brodin to stake his claim. So from all this, Rufus will deduce that Durham means to join Malcolm in war against the king."

"Rufus will see all that?"

Philippe smiled. "Did you not realize it too? I think you did. Whether Fulk means to or not, he will deliver my message to Rufus for me."

Leonie wrinkled her brow for a minute as she absorbed all that. Philippe rolled back to his side, away from her. She ought to let him sleep now.

A new thought hit. A more frightening one.

"Philippe," she said.

"Aye?" It sounded almost like a sigh.

"How did Fulk know where we were?"

As he turned onto his back again, shafts of moonlight illuminated his chest and the sprinkling of dark hairs on it, every single one of them calling to her to run her fingers over them. She quietly clenched her fingers into fists to remind them to behave.

"Mayhap he had heard you were lost and went in search, as de Mowbray did."

"Bringing the bishop? That seems odd. The bishop was not clad for a journey."

Philippe propped himself up on one elbow. "Hm, true. The Bishop of Durham is a man who loves his comfort. Ah, you are right. His only purpose was to give authority to Fulk's deed."

"But how did they know where to find us? He said he had come to rescue me from you, so he meant to find both of us. But how could they have learned?"

"De Mowbray sent word ahead to Bosewood. They must have learned from that."

"But nobody at the outpost knew you had found me until after dawn, and we set out for Bosewood shortly after. No messenger could possibly have reached Durham, for them to reach the crossroads when we did."

He propped up on his elbow, studying her, exposing the deeply shadowed muscular planes of his chest, causing her to catch her breath, lest she betray her thoughts about him.

"They could not," he said. "Yet they did know."

"How?"

Philippe returned to his back, his hands folded behind his head. "Not de Mowbray. He did not know before he found us, and he has been with us since then. His dog surely did not tell."

She snickered at the image of Ilse trying to tell a secret. "Though I do think she's smart enough, she does not speak the language well."

He chuckled. "But someone knew. Were we followed? Or mayhap they found where we camped?"

"Why would anyone do that? Who could have moved so swiftly?"

"I don't know. But aye, it was no accident that they came upon us. And it means, precious bride, that there is far more at stake here than appears on the surface. They want you badly."

"Ha. They want my land."

"Which is easier to control if they have you."

"More than that. I saw what was in Fulk's eyes," she said. "He means to kill you."

"Haps he will."

"It would be easier to claim the bride after dispensing of the husband than to go through archbishops and kings for an awkward annulment."

"They will do that anyway, for effect, to make themselves look blameless."

"Then what will you do?"

"Fight them. I will not let them take you."

"Even though they will kill you."

"Now they must kill me if they wish to gain their ends. But it doesn't mean they will succeed. Leonie, promise me two things."

"What?"

"First, if anything happens to me, you must escape to de Mowbray."

"You trust him? I thought you didn't."

"I can't say I do. It is natural that we would be at odds, for I support Rufus, the very king our Black Earl detests. But the man is blunt and speaks his mind. For now, I think I believe him. He must choose and knows Rufus is a better choice than the Scottish king, who would never let him keep Northumbria if the battle goes to the Scots. But more than that, he has some reason he has not told us that he will protect you. I know it, somehow. So you must turn to him. Promise me."

"But if you are wrong?"

"Do you not trust him?"

"Trust him? Five men: you, Fulk, the bishop, Rufus, and de Mowbray. I trust none of you. But haps I trust Robert de Mowbray a little bit."

He quirked his mouth in a half smile. "That will do. And now, the other thing. If ever I tell you, 'Do as I say,' in those words, you must do it, instantly. I promise I will never say exactly those words unless the circumstance is dire, but I must know, if I do, you will obey immediately, without questioning me."

"Why?"

"You see? You always question me. If I ever I say that, it will be a time when even a moment's hesitation will bring you danger or death. I must know you will do this for me. Promise me."

She couldn't help sighing. None of this was the way she had imagined her wedding night.

"Promise me."

"All right. I promise."

With a smile, he lay back down on his back, raising an arm to press against his forehead. "You will be safe. I promise you. You will never know all that is done, but what must be done will be done. And now, precious bride, I am more than a little tired. Give out a little squeal and moan, will you? That will please them, and then we may both get some sleep."

"Do your own moaning."

He chuckled and rolled on his side away from her. Almost instantly, she heard the funny rattly, whistling sound she had so often heard among the snores of sleeping men in her uncle's hall.

Deep and hard the night wind blew, like dark, frosty fingers lacing into his hair. Armorless, he rode, swiftly as his great grey warhorse would take him. The road beneath the hooves turned to dust, to mist, to heather-strewn rock, and fell away behind them.

Fly, my Tonerre, fly like the eagles!

"Help me! Philippe, save me!" She struggled against her captor, who would force himself on her to obtain her land.

"I charge you with her life, Peregrine," said Rufus. "Do not fail me."

He was the king's man. The woman was his. His heart throbbed with fear for her and ached at the thought of losing her. Calling to her, he rode hard, forcing his stallion to greater speed over the countryside after the fleeing villains.

The grey horse rose into the air and sped past clouds and moon, chasing the brigand knights on their ghostly mounts as they raced across the moors and valleys toward the spires of Durham, sitting on its hill above the sharp curve of the river.

He sliced and stabbed his way through the dark knights, parrying their blows, his sword swinging wide and deadly arcs until he reached the leader, who clenched Philippe's struggling wife with one arm and the hilt of his gleaming steel sword in the other hand. Fulk. Hot rage surged power into Philippe's arm. With a mighty swing, his sword took off the villain's head. The head flew through the air and landed among the rocks, bouncing and bouncing, and came to rest in a trail of its own gore.

The head of Fulk glared in frozen hatred, the mouth gaping and still. But nay, it was not Fulk. 'Twas Clodomir, the sorcerer. And this time, dead. His enemy, and hers, both dead, gone. She was safe now. Even from the sorcerer's curse.

Philippe's wife. Leonie, his wife. She stood before him, still and beckoning amid the bloody battlefield, her strange, compelling green eyes seeking her mate in him.

They'd had clothes, but now the garments were gone. It had been so long; weeks, months, and years had passed since he had taken a woman, and each day his bollocks had grown harder with need, their hunger unsatisfied. Now he had a wife again, one with sleek curves and long, long legs to wrap around him while he embedded himself deeply inside her, all the way to his hilt.

"You must not." Nay, it was Joceline who spoke to him, but Joceline was dead. Had died because of him.

"You cannot kill another," said the voice he could never forget. "You are cursed. Let me be the only one."

Nay, said his heart. The sorcerer is dead, the curse ended. It will be all right. She will be safe. And I will not let myself love her, just make love.

"I want you," said his voice to his wife, its rough, low sound betraying his raw hunger.

"You want me. I am here. Take me, Peregrine." She trailed the tips of her fingers down her chest between her breasts, over her navel, down to touch the rusty-blonde curls she wore like an indiscreet garment.

Through his hungry, slitted eyes, he saw her differently. His hands pursued the curves that had danced in his imagination for longer than he had allowed himself to know. His tongue grew thick, trying to form the words to tell her what he wanted, words he thought a virgin would understand. But his cock grew thicker, harder with the effort, for it was not a virgin's lovemaking he wanted from her, and virgin she might not be, but he didn't care. He only cared that she was here, and he craved her.

He thought to lay her down in the mossy grass to make love, but lifted her in his arms, and her long, long legs wrapped around him, trapping his hard shaft between her body and his. And then he was on his back, her knees spread out on either side of him, nestling herself but a tickle away from his wildly springing cock. The heady, musky scent of sex swirled about them against the sweetness of the night air, her scent and his, mingling.

"Take me, Peregrine," she said. "Make me scream. Make me soar into the sky with you."

His mind descended into an idiot's haze, heavy with a man's greatest hunger as he rolled her over, and came atop her, trapping her heat and moisture.

"Take me. Take me."

Mindless, he eased into her, tight yet slick, her hands clasping his shoulders with a silken-padded grip in a pleasure so exotic it was nearly pain, driving him into the madness of need.

"Take me, Peregrine! Take me to the skies with you."

He could do naught but obey, in the taking roughly going deeper and deeper, burying himself until his tip touched her womb. Her whimpers became moans, his gasps turned harsh. His balls turned hard as rocks and still he slammed into her as she thrashed beneath him.

"More! Give me more!" she gasped, and her hips rotated and bucked against him, driving him so deeply he thought he'd shout.

The grip on his shaft came upon her suddenly, a savage pulsating clench as she arched into him. God help him, what exquisite madness! In furiously pulsing thrusts, the Peregrine burst into his climax.

The Peregrine soared freely into the skies and reached the clouds, his heart singing with passion released, and then in swirling spirals descended and became once more the man. He rested his head against her breast, listening to her heart beat a rhythm that gradually slowed and quieted. His passion was spent, but he knew it would return quickly. He knew he was lost. He would never stop wanting her.

"By your own hand, Peregrine," said the head.

The head. It was the head of Clodomir, its lips dripping with blood, eyes staring evilly. Alive again. Refusing to die.

Of its own, yet still in his hand, his sword slid forward, easing like a knife through soft butter, into her flesh, through her belly.

His mind screamed, "Nay!" His muscles strained, fighting the thrust that moved still forward. Unstoppable.

"By your own hand, Peregrine, you shall love none, save she who shall be slain by your own hand."

Clutching her belly, blood flowing, spurting, and he could only watch, helplessly, in horror. She screamed.

She screamed.

Philippe jerked awake. A dream. His heart pounded a screaming pace.

His bride sat on the feather bed, clutching her belly. Nay, it could not be! It was a dream. 'Twas not real!

"You stabbed me!" she gasped, her eyes wide in horror and pain as she edged back against the wooden tower wall as far away from him as she could get.

But there was no blood.

It had been his dream. Had she dreamed the same? People did not share dreams.

But they had.

CHAPTER SEVENTEEN

Dawn brightened quickly as the brutal pain in Leonie's stomach faded. She stared at her hands, which less than a moment ago she had known for a certainty were soaked in her own blood. There was no trace of it.

The Peregrine fell to his knees on the feather bed, fully nude, his face contorted in horror as he reached out to her. She shrank back, terror racing her heart, her breath hard in coming.

Yet—she was not harmed. No wound, no blood.

"It's a dream, Leonie," he said, dropping his hands to his sides, for he must have sensed his very hands threatened her. "You are all right. Wake up. It's just a dream."

She blinked, shaking her head, trying to dislodge the terror. Again, she searched her hands to persuade herself. But the searing pain clung tightly in the lingering shards of the dream.

"Forgive me," she said, still shaking, still unsure. "Aye, just a dream. I've accused you unfairly."

"Nay, you need no forgiveness, lady." His eyes swam with anguish and guilt. "In our dreams, we cannot control what happens. You have been through too much these last few days. You were tired, and slept deeply. Breathe now and let the dream pass."

"Aye," she said, and nodded to emphasize her word. "It was so real, I could feel the pain even after I woke. And the blood on my hands, I could feel it too."

"But there is none. You are all right now, Leonie. I know it is a hard thing for you to believe, but I will never harm you. Never."

Yet his warm brown eyes were hooded beneath their lids as if they sheltered some frightful secret. He looked so guilty, yet she knew he had done nothing wrong. She shook her head to clear it of her confusion.

As she rose to her feet, her brow knitted and she rubbed her forehead, once more trying to focus her mind on that moment when she had seen Philippe tighten his hands around her throat. How could this man have attacked her? What had really happened? It must be somewhere in her memory. It had to be.

Knifelike pain stabbed through her head, violent as lightning striking. She grabbed her head as pain pounded and swirled like a whirlpool. She was going to be sick.

Dark.

Philippe dived to catch her as she spiraled downward. Anguish twisted through him as he lowered her to the mattress on the tower's rough wooden floor, cradling her head against his chest.

At the same time, he heard shouts from below and noises coming from the ladder.

De Mowbray burst through the hatch. His battle cry thundered into the cool air as his hand lunged for his sword.

"Stop! She's ill!" Philippe shouted. He rocked Leonie's limp body in his arms.

"What did you do to her?"

"Nothing!" Yet he lied, for it was his dream that had assaulted her. "She's fainted again. She had a dream. She stood, and she was in pain. It must be the blow to her head."

The Black Earl's great black brow frowned warily as his huge black eyes roamed swiftly over Philippe's face, and the man knelt beside Leonie, then scanned her for new injury. Leonie began to moan and struggle to rise.

"Not yet, sweet bride," Philippe said. "Rest a moment. You've fainted again."

"The dream—"

He ached for her—her pain, her confusion. He pressed his cheek against her mussed-up hair. "The dream is over. You will be all right. No one will hurt you."

"Aye, lass," said de Mowbray. "I'll see to it."

Philippe glanced at de Mowbray as Leonie fidgeted, and he knew she was recovering. He let her free herself from his embrace.

"Call for Ealga to come up and help her dress," he told the earl.

"Nay—nay, I can do it."

"Nay, lady," de Mowbray said, frowning. "You are the lady of the manor now. The servants would feel slighted if you do not let them perform their duties."

Philippe repressed a grin. He wished he'd thought of that. "Aye," he said. "Allow your maid to help you comb your hair."

"Does it look bad?"

"It's beautiful," he replied, "though wild as a winter storm."

"Aye," de Mowbray said with a chuckle. "It puts me in mind of your mother, though hers was more the shade of pale moon-light."

Her brows knitted together as she looked from one of them to the other. Philippe wondered if anyone had ever told her how captivating her wild hair was, for it was not the sort of hair that was thought to be beautiful. Yet he could not resist touching it whenever he could. And he dared not stare at it for long, lest he find his nether parts growing hard as rocks as he imagined the long, long curls dangling over her shoulders onto his chest.

Philippe squeezed his eyes tightly closed. That was one thought he dared not pursue. Abruptly, he turned away in an effort to grab up his garments, but not so quickly that de Mowbray could not see the arousal he tried to hide. He heard the man's throaty chuckle behind his back as Philippe pulled his blue tunic over his head.

"Well, then," de Mowbray said, "I'll be on my way. 'Tis past time I get on to Alnwick. A message has come this morning. There's mischief from the Scots there."

"You must allow us to feed you and your men before you leave," Leonie replied.

"Nay, lass, as the old woman said, I've tarried far too long, and it's a long ride from here to the sea."

"Then you must not leave until we can come down and properly say you farewell."

"You'd best promise her," Philippe said as he fastened his braies beneath the tabard, an awkward task, usually not done in that order, and he knew de Mowbray noticed. But the tabard had more quickly covered his raging shaft. That embarrassment was beginning to subside, now that it was out of view.

The two men hurried down the ladder and sent Ealga up to attend her lady before they started across the bailey toward the garderobe. Once inside the crude structure, the two men squatted over the trench. De Mowbray waited until no one else was in hearing distance to say more.

"So you haven't bedded her, eh, Peregrine?"

Philippe supposed such a thing was obvious to a worldly man like de Mowbray, whose reputation for wildness in his youth still remained unsurpassed. "Say nothing to anyone, de Mowbray, or I'll have your tongue on a spit to break my fast."

"Aye, it will not come from me. But why? She's a comely lass, and I can see you know that too. Is it that foolish vow of yours?"

"It's not foolishness. The girl is still afraid of me. She still believes I attacked and nearly killed her in the wood at Brodin, though I swear to you I didn't."

"I know, lad. It's odd that she still thinks it. Is she addled in the head, then, do you think?"

"You know how head wounds are."

"It's not the falling sickness?"

Philippe shook his head. "The pain is obvious. That's not so with the falling sickness. She just needs time." The men finished their ablutions and returned to the bailey and the brightening morning.

"The old woman might know what to do, but she is gone again," de Mowbray said, hands upon his hips as he breathed in the fresh morning air with more delight than an ordinary man might take. Philippe added that to his growing belief that there was something unusual about the man, something perhaps other men did not see.

"The old woman who was at the bride ale last night?" Philippe asked. "Doesn't she live in the village?"

"She lives where she lives. No one knows where but her."

"That's odd."

"Aye. It is. But she honored you, to come."

"Who is she? She said she has no name; I can't believe that."

"Haps she did once. None know it now."

"Ah. I heard someone call her Cailleach. Do they think her a goddess?"

"Aye, they call her that. It's not a goddess, yet 'tis. In the Gaelic tongue the word just means old woman, or hag. But the Cailleach is more than that. They say she makes mountains, and herds the deer, and meddles now and then in the affairs of man. The Cailleach lives a long time, they say, the span of many lives of men. She knows things—curses, cures, strange things no living man can know. 'Tis not always a good thing. But others say the Cailleach has blue skin and only one eye. That can't be our old woman."

"She knows of curses?"

"Aye. Many things she has told me about them."

"Do you believe in curses?"

De Mowbray hesitated. "Do you not?"

Philippe shuddered. He knew far more than most men of the power of curses, but he dared not say how. Now they even came to him in his dreams, and Leonie could feel them with him. How that could happen was even more baffling, but he dared not let the Black Earl know that, either.

"Aye, I do," he answered, glad for his years as Rufus's envoy that taught him how to keep his own counsel. He smiled benignly. "Did she tell you how to break a curse?"

The Black Earl stared off into the distance, somewhere down into the lower bailey. Philippe surmised the man must have secrets equally as dark as his own.

"Curses, she told me, are only worth the strength of the man who makes them," the earl said. "It's a tricky thing. It must be said exactly right, or it will come to naught."

"Then how can a man know whether a curse will affect him?"

"Aye, there's the rub, now, isn't it? All you can do is ask the old woman. If you can find her."

"Can she break a curse, then?"

"Nay," said de Mowbray, his jaw set so hard Philippe noticed the thick black beard jutted. "There's a trick, though, in the words. The clue to unbinding must be in the words, or it will not hold. There's always a way, if the man can find it. Why do you ask?"

"I'm a curious man, de Mowbray," Philippe said, though he doubted de Mowbray would believe it was no more than that. "I want to know things. You say she knows about cures, too? If so, then I must find her. Leonie needs her help."

For all that de Mowbray looked like a wild hermit of the mountains, he softened, looking almost wistful. "Aye," he said. "And here comes your pretty bride. She looks well enough now."

She did. Her cheeks had regained their pinkness. Her butter hair was combed out in its wild, bushy way, reminding him of their journey when she had patiently made one long ringlet after another as they rode, and he had lost his patience rather than admit how the sight of it aroused him.

She smiled at the Black Earl, the man who had been the scourge of all civilized Normandy. But she had no smile for her husband.

He could tell her not to fear him over and over, but perhaps it was better if she did. Because she was right to. The dream was a warning. He might control his actions when awake, but who knew what he would do when dreaming?

With every passing hour he was sliding down the steep slope into his own special Hell. If he couldn't find a way to separate from her, he knew what was coming could not be stopped.

He was going to love her.

And if he didn't find a way to break the curse, she was going to die. By his hand.

CHAPTER EIGHTEEN

ALTHOUGH THE PAIN FROM THE DREAM HAD FADED ALMOST immediately, its memory lingered in Leonie's mind. She shuddered, recalling the horror and guilt on Philippe's face. But he was not guilty. He had done nothing wrong. It had all come from her nightmare. Somehow she must put the dream aside until she could be calm about it, and then perhaps talk with him. She must make him understand she did not blame him. But for now, she had to think of something else.

As she watched the Earl of Northumbria ride away with his knights, Leonie chewed her lip. He was indeed a strange man. But that was not what concerned her. Why would a man who was said to have a heart as black as the inside of darkness care about her? What did he know about her mother that he would not say? Why?

She sighed and returned to her work in the old hall. Though Philippe might wonder why she meant to clean it so thoroughly when he hoped to dismantle it as soon as he was able, she knew preparing for war must be most important for him now. She would live in a primitive hut if she must, but she would not live in a pigsty.

Although the stink in the hall was much improved, it wasn't gone. Eventually, like all the women who scrubbed so furiously, she had to seek the relief of fresh air. She headed for the open kitchen to see how the meals were coming along.

As she stepped outside, she shielded her eyes against the bright day and followed the noise of the upper bailey to the uphill side. The villeins were raising an extra row of tall poles into a deep trench on the unfinished section of the curtain wall. She frowned at the curious structure, set back some ten paces behind the old wooden palisade that was probably the last of the original wooden wall. Men's business, she understood, but she would make a point of knowing its purpose before the day was out. Someday she might be forced to lead the defense here, and she would be ready if she could. She would not be the first wife to do so.

Throwing her green cloak over her shoulders against the day's chill, she started down the hill to the lower bailey and passed through the stone barbican, following the lane that meandered down to the village. Only last night the village had caroled them down, then back up. Now she looked forward to meeting her people, who had been so long separated from her.

Thatched huts stood around a common green, the place where the night before they had danced so merrily. She smiled, remembering. It had been a good bride ale, and no matter what came, she would always have that night to make her smile.

"Out for a stroll, sweet bride?"

Leonie made a grumbling noise. "You seemed busy enough," she replied. "I thought it polite to visit among the people."

"So it is, but I do not like for you to roam about so freely. This is very dangerous country."

"It is my home, glorious husband."

"Aye, it is. But no one knows you yet, angelic wife."

Leonie snickered. "Angelic wife? I have never been that."

"I do not recall ever being glorious, either."

That surge of warmth plowed through her again. Oh, he was. Their jests were usually lies, but that one wasn't. She sought a different topic. "Don't you have a curtain wall to build?"

"The men can manage it. I have a curiosity or two about the people myself. Haps we can meet them together."

Leonie waggled her brow in some sort of statement, which she supposed meant she might as well. It was probably a good thing for them to appear together in the village.

They passed a sprinkling of thatched cottages that became closer together as the path wound down the steep hill on which the castle sat. Near the center of the village, they reached the fading green where a dozen or so cows grazed, oblivious of the clangor and bustle of the village. No signs of last night's lavish feast remained.

"I have a yen to find the old woman," Philippe said.

"Why?" She darted a glance at him, wondering at the casual way he spoke the words. Nothing in his face said otherwise, yet she thought something was the slightest bit askew.

"I found her intriguing. De Mowbray tells me she has great knowledge of things like cures and curses."

"Why would that interest you?"

He shrugged. "Everything interests me. Who can tell when such knowledge will be useful?"

She drew her lips in tightly. Why would a great knight care about cures and curses? One more thing about the enigmatic Peregrine to puzzle her.

But they wandered through the village, meeting children and women. Most of the men who were not at the castle were in the fields collecting chaff for fodder.

Cyne left the men in the field to approach them, his aging body showing the weariness of a hard day's labor. She had thought him too old to still work in the fields, yet here he came. He bowed low, and she could see sweat darkening his grey hair and trailing down his gaunt cheeks. She soon excused herself to talk with the old man's wife, with one ear listening to Philippe's questions.

The blare of a horn, three blasts then a long, hard blow, startled them.

Philippe's eyebrows shot up. He grabbed her arm. "Back to the castle," he said. "Now."

"Why?"

"Unwelcome visitors. Hurry."

They dashed out of the cottage. Farther down the road, a huge dust cloud rose toward the sky. Riders! But who? De Mowbray was gone, and not in that direction.

The horn blasted again, its sound even more urgent.

"Fulk, I'll wager," Philippe said. "Riding too fast. We can't make it back before they arrive."

"Come, Lord," said Cyne, running back behind his cottage. "The sally port gate on the north. I'll show you the way through the woods."

For an old man he ran spryly, dodging through the trees along a slender path, Leonie behind him and Philippe bringing up the rear, his hand ready on the sword hilt.

As they reached the clearing circling the castle, the old man's strength flagged, his steps less sure and his breathing ragged.

"Go, lord, hurry," Cyne said, his eyes wobbling a bit in his head. "Leave me."

Leonie looked down the open field toward the main castle entrance to see the knights of Durham riding into the clearing, heading toward the barbican. They stopped, spotting the runners. One man, Fulk, she was sure, pointed at them. He would know them by their garments, and that they would need to cross the dry moat and climb the steep, narrow steps snaking up to the sally port, a route accessible only by foot.

Two riders dismounted to run over the uneven terrain into the dry moat to cut off their prey at the steps.

Philippe grabbed the exhausted old man and threw him over his shoulder. "Run, Leonie! Stretch those long legs like they've never been stretched before!"

"Not without you!" Why, oh why had this been the one day she had left her bow behind? Wanting to appear more womanly to her villagers was a foolish reason. Now she could not even defend herself and the husband who was burdened with the body of the old man.

"Do as I say! I'm right behind you."

She'd promised. She would do it. Leonie sped across the field, up the berm, down the dry moat, then up the slope leading to the steps and castle wall. Philippe's footsteps pounded the ground right behind her. Thanks to Heaven, he was such a strong man. But Fulk's men ran easily along the moat bottom, not climbing a slope as she and Philippe did. Four archers followed close behind.

She reached the steps just before the knights and dashed up. Philippe set Cyne on his feet to climb the steps, then whirled, sword drawn.

Her heart sank into her stomach. He did not wear his mail. He could battle the knights with his sword, but he was defenseless against archers. The moment he moved up the steps, the archers would have a direct shot. He would be doomed.

"Go, Leonie!" Philippe shouted.

The Durham knights attacked. Philippe parried their blows, his back against the stone wall as he moved up a few steps.

"Leonie!" The shout from above was Sigge. Fear hit her like a blow. He was running down the steps.

But he had her bow! She dashed up the steps and grabbed her bow and quiver. "Get out of here! Get the old man up to the gate!"

She grabbed a fistful of arrows, dropping the quiver on the steps as she nocked an arrow and pulled.

Fly, sweet shaft, she sang, though she needed no Faerie skills this time. The string twanged. Knowing the shaft struck home, pinning the archer's hand to his bow, she nocked the second from her fist, drew, and released. It struck the second archer's hand while she shot the third arrow and sang to it as it sped through the air.

The fourth bowman, seeing his three injured comrades, dropped his bow and threw his hands up. Leonie pointed the tip of her ivorywood bow toward the Durham knights at the barbican, and he fled, followed by the three others clutching their broken hands.

She aimed at the swordsmen. Two were down, but one still threatened Philippe, who backed up the steps toward her.

"Shall I finish him?" she called.

With one fierce stroke that nearly unbalanced him from the precarious steps, Philippe cut into the knight's vulnerable armpit, and the knight toppled backward, blood spraying.

"No need," he replied. A fierce scowl splayed across his sweat-soaked face, and his golden hair straggled before his eyes. Yet he barely breathed hard beneath the bloodstained blue tunic.

God in Heaven, but he was a magnificent man!

He frowned and waved his sword at her. "Go on, sweetly obedient wife. Do you mean to wait till they send an army for you?"

Leonie tossed her chin in the air, beginning to realize sweat soaked her scalp too. "I expect you to slay them for me," she said.

And just to please him, she rushed up the steep steps and through the sally port.

Sigge ran up, shouting, and threw his bony little arms around her. "Leonie! You're safe!"

"Aye," she said, hugging him back. "You were sent from God, Sigge!"

"No, I wasn't. I heard the horns and I knew you didn't have your bow with you so I ran for it, and then I knew you were coming up to the sally port because they were cheering for you from the wall, so I ran that way. And then the guard didn't want to let me go but I kicked him in the shin because I knew you'd need your bow."

"All things come from God, Sigge." Philippe joined them. "'Tis God who gave you the wits to know what to do and the swift feet and courage to do it. But I'll see you thrashed if you take such a chance again."

Leonie beamed along with Sigge, who stared in awe at his hero.

"And you!" Philippe whirled on her, his fury all but turning his sweat to steam. "Don't you ever dare disobey me. If you take such a chance again, I will chain you to your bed."

She almost flinched and stepped back, but caught herself, stiffened her spine, and glared back. "Aye, my ever gracious lord, next time I will obey. And leave you to them to be killed."

"Do you think I need a woman to protect me?" His face flushed red as Rufus in a rage.

Leonie lifted her chin high, as if she might look down her nose at the man who stood a head taller than her. "You did this time. I do not think your hide is so tough it can ward off arrows."

"That is not your concern. Shoot your arrows from behind stone walls, or not at all."

Hugh sped up to them. "Fulk and the Bishop of Durham are drawn up before the barbican gate," he said. "They're demanding to talk with you, Philippe."

"Not surprising, since they've been bested at their game of guile." At that, Philippe stalked away, soon picked up speed, and ran through the gate between the upper and lower bailey and down the hill, then up the wooden stairs aside the curtain wall to the parapet. Leonie hurried after him, with Sigge at her heels.

On the far side of the moat outside the barbican, both the bishop and Fulk, fully armed and clad in mail, sat on their dust-covered warhorses.

Leonie raised her bow. She had two arrows left. That was all she needed.

"Nay," said Philippe, his hand coming out to stop her. His voice had lost its fury, and he touched her almost gently. He turned back to the problem below. "What do you want, Durham?" he shouted down at the armed men below.

The bishop sidled his horse away from his warriors and rode forward with Fulk at his side.

"My apologies for my overeager soldiers, Peregrine," shouted the bishop. "I fear they misunderstood their orders."

"My condolences on the poor quality of your vassals," Philippe answered. "Again I ask, what do you want, that you come at us prepared for battle? Have you forgotten the king's command that forbids any Norman to take up arms against another Norman castle?"

"You misread me, Peregrine. We only come prepared, for these are troubled times. Mayhap you would show us the hospitality of your walls, where I can explain our visit more easily."

"I think not. I say again, Durham, what do you want?"

The bishop turned in his saddle to face Fulk, and they exchanged words Leonie could not hear.

"What, are you after my fair bride again, Fulk? You are too late. We said our vows yesterday and the bride ale was celebrated by the entire village. 'Tis best you go find yourself another bride. If you wait for this one, you will be greyer than your bishop beside you."

"I come only to talk with her, Philippe le Peregrine," the bishop answered. "You must let me in, for it is her soul that is at stake."

Leonie leaned over the parapet. "I confessed my sins only yesterday, Your Grace," she said. "I believe my soul is safe for now."

"Lovely Lady Leonie, only allow me a few minutes to talk with you. I must be satisfied. I could not allow you to condemn yourself by your ignorance."

"I think I could fight him off," she said to Philippe in a voice she was sure could not be heard below.

"You will not. He's a bishop, and no young man, but he is a fine warrior."

"We cannot refuse him. He will excommunicate you for it."

"He will do that anyway, but God will side with right. I will not risk you."

"Philippe, I know you can protect me from him. You have made that clear. Let us make it so there is no danger, and if we can speak to him away from Fulk, we might change his mind. He would not desecrate the chapel, so let him meet with me there."

Philippe's eyes darkened beneath his frowning brow as he regarded her. Whether he sighed or his exhale was more of a snort of disgust, she could not say. But he turned back to the wall and looked down at the Norman knights near the gate.

"The bishop may dismount and give over all his weapons and his helm to his squire. All others will ride down the hill to the far side of the village and stay within our sight, and then the wicket gate will be unbarred. The bishop will be granted entry through it."

Durham stiffened in his saddle. "You cannot expect me to abide by such demeaning terms, Peregrine. We will ride through your gate."

"You will not. You will face Lady Leonie of Bosewood with your hands bare of weapons and your head as free to the air as our Lord God made it, or you will not face her at all."

"And who will protect me from such brigands as Philippe le Peregrine?"

"God will protect you if you are in the right," Philippe sneered back. "And I will defend you from brigands myself if God will not."

Passing instructions to his knights to shoot any who made an attempt to follow the bishop through the small wicket within the heavy wooden gate, Philippe shuffled rapidly down the steps, Leonie following, to await the meeting of their terms and greet the bishop as he stepped through the tiny wicket gate beneath the barbican.

"Whatever you do, don't let him into the upper bailey, Leonie. I don't want him to see our new wall."

Leonie nodded and stepped forward, snuggling her bow into its place on her shoulder. One look at the man's sharpened gaze reminded her of his fury moments before. She hastened to the tiny stone chapel and found her place inside its cool darkness, close to the small door near the altar. She waited.

Soon the paired doors parted and the bishop stepped from the bright light into the dim chapel, Philippe behind him.

She dropped a quick but proper curtsy to the bishop, who turned to glare at Philippe. Philippe folded his arms and planted his feet in a battle stance.

"Come near to the altar, Lady Leonie, that we may speak in private," the bishop said.

Leonie sidestepped his attempt to grasp her arm. "It is not necessary, Your Grace," she said. "I have no fear of anyone here."

"Yet, dear girl, did you not say this very man who has forced you into marriage assaulted you brutally in Brodin Forest?"

She drew in a thick breath. She had been afraid he would bring that up. Yet she wondered how he could have known. How could even his spies have reached him with that information so quickly?

"My mind was muddled by the blow to my head, Your Grace, but it is clear now. Philippe le Peregrine did not harm me."

The bishop's jaw dropped open. "It cannot be," he said. But he composed himself again. "Women can be so easily influenced and misled. They have not the sense to see such things clearly. Come with me, girl, and I will see you protected, else he will surely kill you." He reached for her again.

Instinctively, Leonie dodged away and stepped behind the altar rail. "He is my husband now, and is so by the king's command, Your Grace. I would do his bidding even if I did not wish it, but I do."

"You say this because he is so close. He must leave."

"Nay."

"'Tis not a legal marriage, and you are living in sin. Your very soul is in danger. You did make your promise, and in God's eyes, that is binding."

"I made no such promise."

"Dare you contest the word of the saintliest warrior in all Christendom, lady? Dare you call him a liar?"

"I only say he is most mistaken. He listened poorly. I said nothing that could be construed as a promise. My cousin and my aunt's ladies were within hearing, and they will vouch that I tell you the truth."

"You said you would marry him if the king gave his consent."

"I did not. I said only I would marry whoever the king chose for me. I have no choice in the matter. I said it then just as I say it now. Surely both you and he know that to be so, so why would I make any promise I could not keep?"

The bishop's eyes gleamed strangely and he stared so hard at her eyes she felt the urge to turn and run. "You encouraged him to make his plea to the king."

She fixed her own gaze back on him and stood tall, for she was tall enough to look him squarely in the eye. "Nay, Your Grace, I did not even say that much. I said very little, in fact, as Fulk talked and I merely listened."

"You nodded your agreement."

Leonie took a deep breath, remembering Fulk's strange persistence. So this was the impression he meant to give, to support the claim he made now. "I shall be blunt, Your Grace. Not even a nod. I did not wish to marry Fulk then and did not want him to go to the king. And I do not wish to be married to him now."

The bishop continued his fierce stare as if he could drill his words into her. "Your mind has gone daft, lady. Aye, you cannot remember the very accusation you made against this despicable man, who only a greedy and uncaring guardian would ever choose for you. I must fight for your soul, for you cannot."

Nay, it was the bishop who was daft. Why? Would he say whatever would please his vassal? Was the knight the bishop's vassal, or was it reversed?

"I beg you, do not," she said. "I am content."

"This is an unholy alliance. I will complain to the Archbishops of York and Canterbury and have the marriage declared invalid."

"If you do so, Your Grace, you do it without my consent and against my will. This conversation has come to an end."

For a moment as he stared at her, she thought he looked as if he might finally have heard her. But then his face turned angelically cajoling. Too much so. It didn't fit.

"Walk with me to the gate, then, lady," he said sweetly, his voice softened and quiet. "'Twould be only mannerly to do so."

"She will not walk anywhere with you," Philippe responded, dashing up from the back of the chapel.

Leonie blinked. It seemed this husband of hers had unusually good hearing, to understand such low-spoken words.

The bishop grabbed her wrists. "I'll not leave her here!"

"Then you're a dead man."

Leonie launched her knee upward to the man's groin, and the surprised bishop yelled and lost his grip. She dodged and slipped sideways before the bishop could recover. Philippe stepped between them and shoved the bishop across the chapel and through the doors. Leonie held back, following cautiously out of the bishop's reach.

Once out in the bailey, Philippe drew his sword and forced the bishop toward the barbican. "If you touch her again, Durham, I will count you the aggressor, committing an act of war against me and my property. Hugh!"

Hugh's men surrounded the bishop. Philippe didn't even have to give his order, for the men pressed forward, leaving a path only in the direction of the wicket gate.

"You will all burn in Hell for this! You, Leonie of Bosewood! Repent or I shall see you both excommunicated!" The bishop kept walking, his arms waving wildly, and with each step, Hugh's men filled the gap behind him, forcing him ever forward.

"I think not," Philippe replied, all but growling. "But if you think you can, do what you will."

The bishop was still screaming as he stepped through the tiny wicket gate within the bigger gate, and could be heard even as it was bolted behind him. Leonie breathed easier.

"Do you expect them to attack?" Leonie asked Philippe.

"Part of his purpose was to test our defenses. That's why I did not want him to see the double wall we built in the upper bailey. He already knew we're severely undermanned and under-armed, which is why he held off until he knew de Mowbray was gone."

He turned to his lieutenant. "Hugh," he said, "send a man to de Mowbray. We'll hope he can get through. Set men to arming the parapets. Finish that second wall quickly. That will save us if anything does."

"I'll gather the women to help with making arrows," Leonie suggested.

"Nay, prepare the stores for a siege. We'll have to take in all the villagers, so they must learn how to fight a siege. Have them bring all their stores and animals, or all of us will starve."

"They are still cutting the chaff," said Hugh. That could mean they wouldn't have enough fodder to keep the stock alive.

"Aye." Philippe sounded so grave she wondered just how serious he thought their situation was. "You must not leave these walls, even with a guard," he said. As she opened her mouth to protest, he touched his finger along her lips. "Listen to me. Not even for a moment. Not at all."

He turned away, for he had more than enough to do to prepare for a siege on such short notice. If she did anything but help him, she could be destroying all of them. Quickly she passed his orders to Cyne and the others.

She had decided the bishop was insane. That was the only thing that explained his strange behavior. Or could he be perfectly sane, but had something to gain and needed this insane justification for it? What could possibly be so important that he would take such steps? Although she had inherited a handsome demesne, she herself was not all that valuable. Was it the siting of this castle? Philippe had said the river pass it guarded was vital to the defense of the North from the Scots. But Malcolm had twice taken his army down the eastern coast through Alnwick, even to Durham. Why would he bother going through the mountains?

Leonie closed her eyes, imagining armies marching, one through the mountains, another other along the coast. A third, the king's Normans, coming up from the south.

Caught in the prongs between the two from the north. Rufus would be trapped. So Durham really was aligning with the Scots.

CHAPTER NINETEEN

Bosewood was not a large castle, but it was what they had, and Leonie was grateful for it. For the remainder of the day, the women of the village brought their stores and necessities into the castle, preparing for a siege. The men remained in the village to complete the harvesting. They might need every bit of it to survive. Hugh's and Philippe's foot soldiers continued their work on the second palisade hidden behind the original one.

The women went into the woods and cut fine, straight branches from the pollarded trees for arrows, while the children gathered round rocks from the riverbed for slings. The forge fires burned night and day, making new arrowheads. Many a fine chicken would soon be losing its preening feathers to fletch arrows.

Leonie did as she was told and stayed within the castle. Truth to tell, she could not have left, for every minute of the day the Peregrine knew exactly where she was. In a time of lesser danger, she might have rebelled, but she'd had her taste of the dangerous knights of Durham and knew Philippe would be the one they would kill if they could. At least they wanted her alive. And more and more, she was beginning to believe Philippe would willingly die to protect her.

Where was the man whose hands had closed about her throat while his brown eyes gleamed with such evil pleasure?

She must not think of it. It would only bring on the pain. She was resolved. She'd had the sense knocked out of her and had her mind scrambled.

At the end of the day, the villagers trudged home, for they had no wish to remain within the walls of a Norman castle unless they must. Not even the most vulnerable, the aged, infirm, and mothers with tiny babes, would stay.

Yet, Cyne had said, they felt secure in knowing as much of their harvest and foodstuffs as possible were stored safely behind the gates, lest raiders scour the countryside and burn whatever they could not steal. How odd it was that the common folk trusted their fate so greatly to their Norman lord, this man who was now her husband, who had vowed to protect the villagers as much as his own men. And they had seen Philippe risk his life to protect Cyne as well as her.

At the long trestle table set up for supper, Philippe carved slim slices of pork and lamb and laid them neatly on her trencher. The aroma of the delicious juices drifted into her face, making her salivate. She could not remember ever being so hungry. Or so tired. She watched impatiently as he trimmed the meat into delicate strips. She was no delicate maiden who needed her food minced for her. Yet she was so tired, she almost wished he would chew it for her as well. Even do the swallowing.

"You have worked hard today," said Philippe. "A lady should not have to do more than ply her needle in her solar."

"It's my nature," she answered, and thought she sounded a bit too gruff. "I'm fond of my needlework, but restlessness overtakes me. And this is no time for maidenly airs."

She saw a smirk play on his lips, and he looked down at the meat he had carved so carefully. "Such maidenly airs would play you false, my long-legged wife."

Her face filled with a fiery flush. "You thought my long legs fine enough this afternoon, kind, handsome husband."

The sudden flash of his startled brown eyes as he stared at her took her by surprise as well. Quickly, she averted her gaze and began to pick at the slender strips of mutton, though now she had no appetite for them.

"Aye," he said, "I did. And I do still. I would not have you turn delicate and squeamish now. If I must ever leave my castle in your hands, I must know you have both body and mind to protect it, and yourself."

"Your castle, is it now?"

"You know it is. Though I did not wish it any more than you."

"So you say, esteemed knight and revered vassal of the king."

His jaw jutted into a hard line, for he had not missed the sharp edge of her jab. "You speak rightly," he replied, drawing out the words into carefully measured syllables. He added, "Lovely lady."

Abnormal silence fell upon the diners, and only faint clinks and clunks could be heard. To a man, the knights studied their trenchers with unusual interest. Leonie felt the flush pervade her entire body. It was not one of embarrassment, but one of shame. She had spoken harshly to her husband in front of his knights. If he were a brutal, violent man, she knew his hand could fly at her mouth faster than she could flinch away, and none would fault him. Instead he admonished her with a compliment. He did not think her lovely, nor ladylike, but all the same, he had given the compliment, not a vicious slap. He had not spoken ill of her before others. As she had of him.

Well, he had begun it.

Well, a good wife never derided her husband. And there was only one thing to do.

"Your pardon, lord husband. I mistook your meaning."

"Aye, haps you did. Methinks you know not your own charm." The tip of his tongue glossed his lower lip with enticing moisture. "Sweet bride."

Muffled chuckles floated about the room, coming from who-knew-which mouths.

"Gracious and well-favored lord," she mumbled back.

Eyes full of curious twinkling peered fleetingly from the knights about the table, then as swiftly darted back beneath their hooded lids.

"Lovely, gentle, demure lady," he answered.

Leonie choked on her drink. Dark wine sprayed on the white linen. The deathly silence as she coughed told her the knights were frozen as they sat, and Philippe slapped carefully on her back. She waved him off as she caught her breath, and finally sat back, leaning back her head and breathing a loud sigh of relief.

"If he continues to flatter her, haps she'll need to use the wine to dye all the tablecloths," Hugh said.

The chuckles about the table had an oddly tenuous sound to them, but Leonie broke into a new burst of laughter.

"They say you do not lie, Philippe le Peregrine," she said, still catching the odd cough in her throat between her words. "They say you seek peace through sleek words of truth, so that all believe you and fall under your spell. But I say to all, I am none of those things you call me. Though I was born a lady, I am my aunt's bane, for I never remember to be one."

Around the long trestle table, the knights roared their approval and pounded their crude metal tankards and wooden mazers to the rhythm of their cheers.

Hugh rose from the bench, lifting his wooden mazer high. "I say the lady speaks the truth, for never have we seen one like her. Yet I say our lord does not lie, for he has been enchanted by her wondrous spell. *Lovely* is not quite the word, yet I do not know what it might be, for we would not have you be any other than what you are, my lady. Cheers, then, to the lady's long legs that saved the day!"

"*Holá! Holá!*" the soldiers cheered, and pounded their tankards on the table again.

"And to her long arms that shoot an arrow so straight, Durham's archers flee in fear," shouted another knight.

"Our warrior lady," quipped Philippe quietly.

She thinned her lips at his remark. That was what she was to him. Something no woman wished a man to think of her. But she could not blame him, for he had wished for none of this. At least he had some respect for her, if not as a woman. She could not remember any time when she had blushed in so maidenly a fashion, and oddly, too, for such an unmaidenly act.

"You forget the boy," Leonie said, for she had to say something. "It was his quick thinking that saved us."

"Aye, to Sigge," Philippe said, lifting his cup. "He has a knight's heart. I shall make him your page when this war is ended. For now, I cannot spare him from the forge."

Leonie sidled a glance at Sigge where he sat beside his brother, and watched his face fall and shoulders droop. She sighed, knowing Sigge's dream. He did not want to be a lady's page. Even in this small gathering, his place at the supper table far below the salt signified to all that the blacksmith's son could never achieve knighthood.

"But enough for now," Philippe said, rising. "We must rest. Tomorrow is like to be troublesome."

"Aye, lord," replied Hugh, wiping his chin as he also stood. "Have you heard from Rufus?"

"None of our couriers has returned. I hoped to hear from Northumbria, but that man also has not returned. We have been isolated, my brave knights. The battles will soon begin. Set the watch with frequent reliefs. We shall all rise before cock's crow on the morrow, and very quietly. We do not wish to signal our readiness to the enemy."

The knights became solemn. All mumbled quietly. Leonie took Philippe's arm as he led her to the small, primitive solar behind the hall.

"Your little friend was not as happy as I expected."

"He would rather be your page than mine, gracious lord."

He shook his head. "It cannot be. The king would never allow it. A knight's page must be one who could become a knight himself."

"Was there never a tanner's grandson who rose to become a king?"

He kept his gaze fixed ahead, but Leonie spied the telltale jutting of his jaw that said he would become stubborn about this. "Do not compare him to the Conqueror. Never has there been one like him. Sigge is the grandson of a traitor. That is what condemns him."

Well, she was stubborn too. But she was learning to be less strident in her requests. "The Conqueror was known to be generous to his foes. His son has many times been forgiving, also. Did he not forgive de Mowbray and his uncle, the Bishop of Coutances?"

"It cannot be, Leonie. Can you not understand that? Some things a king will never forgive, and betrayal is one of them. Whatever was the enmity between the Conqueror and Severin de Brieuse, we know little. But the Conqueror considered himself generous in allowing the son to be raised by a blacksmith instead of putting him to death with his father. Do not open old wounds. Rufus would not be pleased."

They reached the doorway to the solar, and he pulled back the draping tapestry, one that she sorely wished to replace when she was able to make a new one. His voice turned gentle as he guided her, and she allowed it, for at least that was recognition of her womanliness. "Come now," he said, "you are very tired. I like it not that you must work so hard. But at least you are strong and capable. Let us get our rest now."

"Surely you are very tired too."

"Aye. We must sleep while we can."

Philippe pulled his tunic over his head and unbound his hose. Leonie quietly turned her back. It was an empty, hungry feeling to see his beautiful, lean body and know there would be nothing between them but dreams. She blew out the tallow candle stub he had carried into the chamber, then unbound her hair from its ribbons. This was such a primitive place, with no chests or tables other than those brought in her dowry train.

"What worries you, wife?"

"Nothing," she said.

"Come to bed, then."

"I must comb my hair. If I do not, tomorrow I will sorely regret it."

He made some sort of rough grunt, and the bed ropes groaned as he rolled over. She glanced over her shoulder and saw that he had turned his back to her.

Leonie picked up her ivory comb and tiptoed to the roughly cut window, wondering as she had so many times since coming here why her father had made no effort in his years at Bosewood to build a decent stone tower. She looked out over the quiet, moonlight-bathed upper bailey at all the unfinished work. Only the lord who already made the noises of sleep stood between the Scots and the survival of England, and now he must face Durham's assault with only this tumbledown castle.

Hank by hank, she combed her long curls. Not a person stirred, other than those walking along the parapet of the stone wall. Slowly as she eased the tangles, combing first the tips in a small section, then moving higher up until she could run the comb smoothly from scalp to tip, she went through one strand after another. When at last she had completed her task she parted her hair into three sections to braid it. She looked back to the bed to her sleeping husband.

Except that he was not asleep. He lay on the bed, propped on one elbow, watching. His eyes grew hazy, seeming like smoke in the darkness. She knew that look. She was one of the Faeriekind in that way, that the gaze of a man whose thoughts were fixed on sexual desire was never a secret. Could it be that he wanted her, though he denied it so completely? But all men were that way, she knew for a fact. They were not discriminate creatures when it came to their desires. What was close was good enough.

She would have turned away, except she could not. The very look of his eyes compelled her. Her heart began to speed, pounding, and something hungry inside her clawed at her insides, wanting to be released. She gathered her hair at her neck, slowly shifting it over her shoulder to cascade in thick waves to her knees. His steamy eyes followed every movement, as if they touched her skin and were like fingers playing through her hair. Her lips went dry, and she wet them with her tongue, aware that the bright moonlight played over her face, betraying her every move.

His back straightened abruptly as he sat up in bed. She held her breath, her skin tingling as she watched him rise in the dark, fully nude, with his shaft hard and huge, as it had been in her dreams, and she could imagine its heat throbbing in her hands. She bit her lip.

He was all bulging thighs and arms, with the magnificent curves only a huge, muscular man could have, broad shoulders and expansive chest tapering to tight muscles that rippled over his abdomen. And he was slowly, very slowly, moving forward, his eyes fixed on her, a rumpled frown on his brow.

She froze where she stood, sudden terror lacing through her like lightning. Was it anger? The erect state of his shaft, the focused, yet perversely hazy predatory gaze as he approached, said something else. Had she been wrong when she had begun to doubt his guilt of the crime against her in the woods? Did he mean now to put an end to this farcical marriage?

Nay. She let the shiver pass down her spine and fade away. She had made her decision, and she would not back down. Her resolution once more hardened as she awaited whatever was to be her fate.

He moved to the narrow window, standing before her. The bright light of the full moon silvered his hard flesh, outlining the heavy veins beneath his bare skin where they meandered over his muscular arms. The deep furrow in his brow shifted oddly as his hand touched the thick hank of her hair that fell over her shoulder, and he lifted it into the light.

Her own brow wrinkled in confusion, and then she saw it was not a frown of anger, but the strain of some deep sadness, a hungry yearning left suddenly bare and visible. She caught her breath at the starkness of his pain. Nay, not anger at all.

What is it that gnaws at your soul, Peregrine? It's more than the wife you lost. What is it?

But she dared not ask aloud. She knew in her heart he could not share it with her.

He released a deep sigh. Still fondling her long curl, he said, "Turn around. I will braid it for you."

She opened her mouth to protest, then closed it and did as he requested. Perhaps he could not look in her eyes any longer. He had shared, but just for a moment, and all she saw was his pain. But she knew as well he could not go further with it.

Behind her back, he gathered her hair into a bunch at the back of her neck. With each grazing of his fingers as they plaited her hair, touch and touch, stopping to comb through the strand, then braid again, tiny caresses set her afire again and again. As he reached her waist, she swooped her hand behind her neck to lift the braid higher, the way she'd always done for Ealga. 'Twas a practical thing to do, but she knew she did it so his hands would not stop touching her.

It could not last forever, though, and at last he came to the end of the braid, and reached for the ribbon to tie it. She mumbled her gratitude, knowing for these few moments they had both been liars, pretending they did not want, nay, hunger for each other.

"Get some sleep," he said, and turned his back to her. He removed his tunic from the carefully folded garments and pulled it over his head.

"Where are you going?"

"Go to bed. I must check the wall."

She knew better. His men were competent. He needed to leave, and that she understood. Perhaps it was best. She watched him buckle on his sword over his tunic, but he left the solar with bare legs and feet. Leonie lay on the featherbed and pulled the blanket over her against the cooling of the night, and turned her back to the door. She would pretend she didn't care, and mayhap some day it would be true.

She saw the Peregrine standing atop the mountain, wild wind tossing his golden hair in a frenzy with his deep blue mantle, his massive legs widely placed, arms spread out, sword in his hand, glowering down at the world.

"What is it you would have, Peregrine? You only need ask."

She was Faerie. She knew in her heart what he wanted. He longed for her. That was what a man always wanted of a woman. She faced him, unafraid, unwilling to be afraid. She had decided. She would never give in to fear again.

"You know."

"Aye."

But he did not ask. He only raked his honey-colored eyes over the length of her body. Why would he not take what was his right to take?

"'Tis yours, Peregrine."

"You do not know."

"'Tis a fact. I do not." The Faerie slid her willing hand down his chest and moved the cloak from his shoulders, so that he stood before her unclothed. She had known forever the feel, the look of his body, the smoothness of taut skin over hard muscle, the crispness of hair that clustered on his chest and around his shaft. She slid her hand over the heated flesh, feeling her own heat grow within, a mountain of wanting. She was Faerie. She knew wanting in the way no poor human maid could know.

"Is this what you want?"

"Nay."

"Say it."

"Nay. I must not."

"Are you a monk, Peregrine, that you have such monkish ways?"

"Nay."

The Peregrine pulled her into his embrace. He kissed her lips roughly.

They lay together on a verdant carpet of grass, their bodies touching, their hands exploring, fondling where they might. He found the crevice between her legs and explored. 'Twas a touch she had not known.

"What is it you would have, Peregrine?"

"Nothing. I want naught from you. Leave me, Faerie."

Leonie woke from the dream, feeling a tear sliding down her cheek. She brushed it away and lay back down.

Silent as a slinking wolf the Peregrine came into the chamber and slipped into the bed, naked. Lying down, he nestled himself against the lady's back. His arm lay over her waist, barely touching. The hardness of an erection came upon him quickly, but he had come to accept its ever-present state and shoved its demands to the back of his mind.

He slept.

Beneath his hand, the warmth of her flesh goaded his desire. He skimmed the silken flesh with light caresses. Desire would never go away, and somehow it felt better to torment himself with its exquisite pain as his balls grew hard, furiously, achingly hard.

Still he slept, he dreamed. The aching of his flesh propelled him into flights of color and cloud. He flew through the lovely torture.

Confusion stirred in her. Leonie shifted, feeling sleep part like a veil. It was a dream again, that deliciously frightening, enticingly sad dream. But her dream had become his.

Nay, she was wrong. He really was touching her, with strokes that sent heat flowing through her veins. Reaching up, she felt his hand where it rested on her belly in its lightly caressing strokes. Did he sleep? She thought he did. Else, would he so willingly touch her?

Aye, his dream, not hers. She had heard it, seen it in her mind, but it came from him. She could feel his torment, wanting, yet refusing himself, and she did not have to know why, only that his pain was deep. But in the dream, he could do as he wanted. If she closed her eyes again, would the dream come back to her?

She closed her eyes, relaxed against him, soaking in the sensuousness of his touch, to let the dream overtake her. 'Twas the curse of Faeriekind, Ealga had said, that they were forever bound to one love. But she was only half Faerie, or perhaps not even that much now. Would she be so bound? And her love was merely human, so he was not bound. If she were so cursed, she did not care. Shifting, she rolled partly to her back and moved her upper leg over his. His hand slid into the curls of her opened crotch. She hummed at the pleasant tingling. One broad finger slid into the cleft to rub against the excited nub inside. A jolt of passion shot through her like lightning, and involuntarily her back arched with a fierce shudder.

Jerking awake again, she glanced over her shoulder. He still slept, yet his careful, insistent strokes continued. Well, who was she to wake him when he seemed to be having such pleasure? Furtively, she wiggled her hips to open herself wider to his strokes. Reaching between her legs past his hand, she ran her fingers down the length of his hot, hard, moist shaft, wildness turned loose inside her as if it spun through her body like a whirlwind.

His moan was sharp. He lunged his body up off the coarse sheets, his eyes dark and wide, vacant of all except sudden, shocked lust. In one quick, fierce movement, he was atop her, his hands splaying fingers over her hair, his mouth pressed against hers, forcing against her, demanding. Eagerly, she opened to his kiss and the deep thrusting of his tongue that set her ablaze.

"Damn you," he said, breaking the kiss, then just as quickly pressing into another as she ran her fingers into his hair.

She rocked against his body, he against hers. Her legs wrapped around to his back, locking him tightly to her, feeding her craving to have him inside her. She was Faerie. Aye, she had never known that as much as now, in her yearning for completion. This she would beg from him, if she must.

His shaft fit against her as if made for her, and then began to push, sliding into the slick heat that had become everything. The murky haze of passion encompassed her like a thick fog, and her hips rocked, urging his invasion in every way she could, deeper and deeper, the most exquisite thing she had ever felt. No dream had ever been like this.

For a moment he stopped, his forehead resting on her head. She felt the exhale of his breath and a tense trembling of his limbs. His heart pounded in his chest, palpable against her skin. "Damn you," he whispered again, the words grating out.

Then, pinning her arms, he lifted himself and began thrusting into her with fearful ferocity. She should be afraid, for he was angry enough. But she didn't care. The harder he stroked the better it was. She bucked against him, forcing him into the places she most needed him, the ones that begged for more, for something that she knew could only come through her own release.

She met him with the same ferocity. Feeling him move slightly to one side, she moved quickly, dumping him over, then rolling atop him. Just as suddenly, she moved her knees, straddling him, answering his shocked look with a wicked smile.

She came down on him, burying him deeply inside her, and let her instinct, that Faerie part of her, have full rein. She could see the passion taking over his face as shock faded away and that ecstatic pain flooded his thinking mind and drowned it in the red haze. She wanted that.

Aye. Let it be.

Leonie threw back her head, eyes closed. Deep inside where his swollen shaft fought its battle, she let loose the muscles that tightened around it, relaxed, then tightened, harder, pulsed and pulsed, again, again. She moaned, shifting her hips to take in everything, repeating because she must. Her parts swollen against his, meant to fit, driving her need with such force, she thought she would die from it. Yet, nay, she must have it.

"Ride me!" he said angrily. "Ride me, woman!"

Aye—nay, she was not done yet. Instead, she contracted her muscles so tightly she thought she would scream.

He roared. Loud and rough, like a berserker.

Aye, my berserker, roar for me! Her breath like ragged northern winds, she leaned back and forth, feeling everything as deeply as she could, and then the violence of her completion convulsed through her, and she vanished into the hazy fog as her body found its rhythm.

Gasping for breath, she fell against him. 'Twas done.

But it was not. Even more fiercely than she, he rolled with her, landing her on her back, and in wild strokes drove deeply, deeply, over and over. With the rage of a bull, he thrust, bellowing, his body in the hard spasms of his release.

He fell against her, breathing hard. She felt his racing heart finally slowing, quieting as at last he came to stillness.

"Damn you," he said once more, still not moving from his rest.

Aye, she would be damned now. And she didn't care. Perhaps Ealga had told the truth about the curse. And if that love be human male, they were doubly cursed. She smiled, a tiny smile known only to her. If so, then she welcomed it.

CHAPTER TWENTY

Lying on his back, Philippe fought away the fog and lethargy that engulfed him. Nearly seven years he had remained celibate, had successfully fought off his most violently hungry urges, at all costs resisting needs to which any normal man would have yielded.

What had he done? How had she tricked him? Had she drugged him? He couldn't remember, only that there had been the dream, and his eyes had popped open to find her leaning over him, caressing him intimately, and he was beyond the point of turning back. Had he been awake, he knew he could have resisted. He had withstood so much for so long.

Forcing strength back into muscles and bones as limp as rags, he moved, and the more he moved, the more he regained his wobbly mind. He sat on the bed for a mere fragment of a moment, then leaped to his feet. Anger forced its way through the lethargy that fogged his brain. Briefly he wondered if he might have dreamed the entire thing. He often had such lurid dreams about her that they seemed real when he awoke. But then he looked down and saw that one limp part of his body sagging like a dead snake, and he knew exactly why.

How dare she? They'd had an agreement. Rage at the betrayal surged like red heat through him, bringing potency to his limbs.

"Witch," he ground out like a curse, and he snatched up his tunic to pull over his head and cover himself from her leering stare. From the corner of his eye, he caught her movement and quickly turned his back to her.

"I am no witch." A tinge of fear lurked in her voice.

"Then what are you, to turn me against my vows? You are no loyal wife."

"I? I only obeyed. I did no more than you asked—nay, commanded, of me."

"I commanded nothing of you." Not even taking the time to put on his braies and hose, he snagged his sword belt and strapped it about his hips.

"Are you so sure?" The temptress's voice turned sultry as she padded almost silently across the rammed earth floor and stood behind him. Instantly his nether parts twitched. He froze where he stood.

Damn her, didn't she realize the damage she had wrought? But then, why would she, since he had never shared his hideous secret with her?

He couldn't. Never could he tell her. Yet her very life was endangered by what she had done. Only anger could defend him from worsening his mistake.

She slid around to face him, her body starkly nude, and in spite of every oath he made to himself, his entire body sprang to life, readying for another go at it. Worse, he relived that exquisite torture in his mind in one wild, instant flash. He was doomed. And she, more so. God and Jesu help them both!

She raised one finger to his chest and let it fall between the unlaced split in his tunic, right above the breastbone. "Did you dream this night, Peregrine?" she said.

His breath froze in his lungs. Aye, he had dreamed.

"So did I," said the voice, twining about him and curling into his ears like a liquid smoke. Now she also knew they shared those lurid dreams. It could not be. Yet it was.

Her pure green eyes with their sharply haughty gaze ripped through him like a falcon's talons, then softened as if turning to smoke, and raked down his chest to that bedamned betraying instrument of his destruction poking upward through his garment. Her lips slowly widened into a smile as lethal as a sword stroke.

"Go if you wish, Peregrine. Be gone forever if that is your desire. Beat me, strangle me, truss me, and burn me at the stake. But never again will you convince me you do not want me."

He found the fury he desperately sought, swirling in streaks of darkly furious colors around him and girding him like the hard leather of his sword belt. He swung on his cloak to go back out into the night. The cock, the feathered kind, would soon crow. Night might belong to woman, but day belonged to man.

Turning toward the door, his ears pricked to a faint sound. An odd one, not belonging to this castle. Beyond the walls. He focused on it, straining his ears toward it.

"God's face," he hissed. "They're here."

"What?"

"Stay here, woman. This is man's work."

As silently as he could, he hurried through the hall, waking Hugh and gesturing to him to be quiet. With hand motions, he signaled his guess that a battle was about to begin.

Ignoring his command, Leonie rushed down the aisle, waking men as she went. At least she'd had the decency to pull on her chemise and kirtle.

Leaving the soldiers and knights to Hugh's supervision, he ran across the bailey toward the wall where he had heard the noise and dashed up the steps to the wall walk. He shushed the sentry before he could speak and leaned through the crenel toward the deep gloom beyond.

"Are they out there?" Devil's gore, it was her.

He hissed at her to be quiet. "If you're so determined to be a woman, go back to the solar and cringe behind the tapestries. The men will defend the castle."

"I cringe for no man. What do you hear?"

"Aye, lord, what shall we do?" the sentry asked.

"Wait. I can't see where they are. But I hear them."

"I hear nothing," the man said.

"They are there. Wait. Dawn will soon be coming. Be very still and make sure everyone is ready for them. They may attempt to distract us here, but then storm the gate."

The chilly air was cooling his heat. He had to admit he could hear what others could not, but it did them little good.

"There. By that huge oak. Almost behind it," she said.

He saw it too. "They lace the edge of the forest. I suspect more beyond. But not an army, unless they are unusually quiet. A troop to storm at our weakest point, before dawn. Haps we'll let them."

Around him, his contingent of archers gathered. Hugh spread them out along the parapet, two to a crenel.

"Two volleys, aimed high, as they approach," Philippe said. "The second behind the first. And you, lady, off the wall."

"You need me."

"In the bailey managing the stores and keeping order. Go. I want buckets of water to keep the barrels full."

Her lips drew tight over her teeth in what no one would call a smile. Acknowledging nothing, she walked past the string of archers along the parapet and down the parapet stairway to the bailey. He turned back to his business, knowing she understood her true duty and place in a siege and would do it. As would he.

With the first crow of the cock, the hidden enemy sprang into action. Fire arrows broke the darkness even before the dawn and littered the surface of the wooden stockade wall. The old wood caught fire, as they had expected. Barrels of water on the palisade and a line of full buckets were splashed down on the burning wood. But it was too dry and kept burning. More water was brought up to the barrels to extinguish the blaze. The enemy remained within the security of the trees.

Archers let loose a volley, the shafts flying like a swarm of bees in a shallow arc to their target. Screams filled the air. Then on Hugh's command, the second volley flew, and more men cried out. But fewer of them.

"Could be there are not very many of them, not more than a score," Hugh said.

"Enough to scale the palisade in the dark and overwhelm us in our sleep. Or the army could be holding back, awaiting their success. If they get through to open the gates, we would be doomed. We'll see what comes next."

Another volley of fire arrows hit the wall. They couldn't refill the barrels fast enough, so they knew the wall would soon burn through. Philippe held back on his signal to light the trash just inside the outer wall, and they watched as more and more of the wall was consumed. He could see Durham's soldiers now and knew they would soon rush the gap. They waited.

When the gap was nearly burned through, Durham's shouting soldiers burst from the woods into the clearing, across the drying grass, and through the moat, which was shallow at this point. Hugh directed his archers to fire two volleys. But more soldiers came from the woods to replace the wounded and dead. Even more took their place at the edge of the wood.

"Closer to five score than one," he said. Hugh nodded back.

A messenger ran up to say Durham soldiers had been spotted near the barbican and the sally port. "So they'll rush the main gate when someone gets through and forces the gate open. Light the rubbish."

The waiting firebrand was tossed down to the rubbish below, which burst into flames. The enemy soldiers who made it past the barrage of arrows jumped through the burned gaps, and there they saw their surprise. Behind the burning rubbish was a second wall. They were caught in a trap. Archers on the parapet picked them off, one by one. Those coming forward soon realized the trap and turned and ran to the safety of the trees.

"We've won," said Hugh. Around him the soldiers cheered.

"Not yet," Philippe replied. "Our barbican gate and the sally port are weak, and we don't know how large their army is. If they've brought all of Durham's forces, they can eventually overwhelm us. So hoard your arrows, but if you know you can pick them, do so."

One cheeky fellow drew his bow and fired. A solitary scream came from the woods. "Easy shot," said the archer.

"What now?" Hugh asked.

"We wait."

But nothing came next. From the parapet the moans of men and sounds of moving troops receded. The assailants were withdrawing. As the morning brightened, Philippe caught an occasional glimpse of armor reflecting the sun's rays, and on the far hill among the trees the big black stallion that was Fulk of Durham's favorite steed then disappeared.

At the river's ford, riders and foot soldiers hastened across, and he counted their numbers. Philippe ran down the wooden stairs and across to the far wall.

"Not enough."

"Lord?"

"Either we killed far more of them than the number of arrows we launched, or they mean to trick us into believing they are retreating."

"Then they are still out there?"

"If so, they lie back, deep in the forest. Keep watch, Hugh. Keep the men alert. I think they are not done with us yet."

The exodus across the ford suddenly expanded, moving with frenetic speed, enough that Philippe might have believed Durham's soldiers that had occupied the countryside near Castle Bosewood were also leaving. But he did not fool himself to think a ruse was not involved. Still, it seemed odd that a gap in time lay between the running invaders who would have scaled his walls and the quick withdrawal of a force that he reckoned to be at least half of Durham's power. They moved swiftly, the knights almost in a racing pace on their great horses, stirring up a thick cloud of dust and leaving their foot soldiers to fend for themselves.

"They behave like cowards," he said to Hugh. "It makes no sense. If we know anything about Fulk and his minions, we know they do not run in fear."

Hugh responded with a silent nod.

Toward noon, Philippe took a troop of riders out through the gate to scour the countryside for clues. They rode up the high, rugged hills behind the castle and searched for signs of the enemy's assault. Fulk had left so quickly that many dead remained, and Philippe would have to send laborers to bury them. Signs were also there that many wounded had made their escape. They rode along the river and traced the path of the knights and larger army. And all he saw told him that their guesses about the assault were correct. Fulk had intended to have the gates of Bosewood opened to them.

"'Tis a good thing we spotted them," Hugh said. "But I was on the wall, Philippe. I could not hear them."

"And I could not see them." That was not all, but he said no more. He refused to let himself think of the night before, and so kept himself busy on the hunt for any Durham men he could question.

But now, as the crisis faded, he could no longer shove the problem away. He had to find an answer and fast. No longer was the curse merely a heavy burden on him. Now it wrapped his heart in a tight band of terror.

"By your own hand, Peregrine." Clodomir's chilling voice rang in his mind again and again.

They rode back through Cyne's village, where the people were beginning to return from the forest where they had escaped to avoid the ravaging of war. He was glad he had made the decision to house their stores inside the castle's walls where they would be safe. But the villagers were not safe. And if Durham renewed his hostilities, which he was sure would happen, those who were caught outside the castle would be doomed either to violence or starvation. He had to persuade them to stay inside the walls for now, at least.

And he had to find the old woman. He stopped at Cyne's cottage and directed Hugh to return to the castle with the rest of his riders.

Cyne stood before his weathered door and bowed to his Norman lord as Philippe dismounted.

"Is everyone safe, Cyne?" he asked.

"Aye, lord." A sly smile twitched on the old man's face. "They did not harm us for fear we would raise the alarm, I think. Forgive me, lord, for we heard them not until they departed."

"It seems odd," Philippe answered. "They were not so damaged by our volleys that they should so easily give up the siege."

"Save for what my youngest son overheard, lord."

Philippe cocked his head, noting the sparkling amusement in the old man's grey eyes.

"Rufus comes."

Philippe's eyes rounded. Then he burst into a guffaw. "So they scattered like fleas from a drowning dog! Ah, it would have been a fair thing to see, my friend, if Rufus had caught them in the very act of disobedience. Save, the cost would have been too great. Then did you hear how close the king is to us?"

"Nay, lord. Just those words."

"I will send out a contingent to meet him, then. But I have another request of you now."

"I owe ye much already, lord. Ask."

"The old woman who appeared at the bride ale. Where can I find her?"

Cyne's dusky eyes narrowed. "For what do ye want her, lord?"

"I have heard she is a wise woman. I need her help. Is she in the village?"

Cyne shook his head. "She is not of this village. She cannot be found, save when she wishes it."

"Then how can anyone find her? Who is she? Is she a seer? A healer? I saw by the looks on the people's faces she is revered."

"She has no name, lord, as she said."

"But everyone has a name."

Philippe caught a twinkle in the old man's eyes, framed within wrinkled, sagging eyelids. "I only want to know about curses and cures. I have heard she knows such things. If there are old women who bring on the winter snow—" he shrugged. "How can I say?"

Cyne feigned a shrug in return.

"Then can a message be sent to her? My need is important, Cyne. 'Tis not for me, but my wife."

"Why do you call me, Norman lord?"

Philippe whirled around at the sound of the raspy voice behind him and saw the old woman standing in the shadow by the wall, clothed in a rough cloak of green almost as dark as night. Had she been there all along but he hadn't seen her? If she had come in, he had not heard her, and he knew his hearing to be very sharp.

The hag chortled but had no smile. Her sharp, pale eyes focused on Cyne. "Your garden goes untended, old man."

"Aye," Cyne replied. "My turnips have need of me." He shuffled to the doorway and bent his tall frame beneath the sill as he went out. He pulled the door shut by its leather strap.

The hag faced him, silent, her eyes piercing.

"There are things I must ask you," he said. "Things I must know."

She lowered the hood of her cloak, revealing thin, pale hair that had the stiffness of dry straw. "You will not find them from me. You have the answers in yourself."

"Nay, I know nothing. I must find out how to break a curse."

"You have the answer."

"I do not, but I have been told by the Earl of Northumbria you have some knowledge about such things."

"There are more things in this world than you know, Norman. You cannot see what is before you, yet you must. If you do not see, there is much that will be lost."

Philippe forced himself to draw a long, slow breath, reminding himself of the patience for which he was renowned in negotiations. "What do you mean, old woman? Speak plainly, not in double meanings."

"Close your eyes and open your mind. See what is in your heart."

"I do not need riddles. I must know how to end a curse, or terrible things will happen to someone I—to someone."

"Only you have your answer. You must lose your war if you hope to win it. Your king comes soon. You must find your path soon."

"You spoke of a path before. I do not know how to find my path. I have been seeking for many years. Old woman, hear me, my wife will die if I cannot rid myself of this curse."

"Do you care? Would it not please you to be free of her, yet possess what she leaves to you?"

"It would not! Let me die in her stead. You must help me. I can't send her away to safety, for she would fall into evil hands as soon as she left the castle. But I cannot keep her near to me. I am her greatest danger, old woman."

"Aye, you are, Norman lord. Her destruction is your salvation."

"Then I do not want to be saved. I do not want to love her and lose her because of it."

"Do you mean to say you love her, then?"

"I do not. I must not. But I know it will come. Had I known it, I would never have allowed the king to force the marriage."

"Did you perhaps forget to tell him something?"

The keen eyes stared at him with an intensity that sliced through him. He swallowed hard, wondering if she knew. How could she know what even Rufus did not know?

"I did not tell him," he replied. "For my own reasons. I thought myself adequate to the task he gave me."

"Perhaps that is your error."

"I cannot tell him."

"Then you will fail."

"All men make mistakes, old woman, you must know that. It is not something the king can be told. There are some things kings never forgive."

"A pity. You will not find your answer. You will not be what you were meant to be."

The old woman's head lowered, and her straw-like hair slid to cover her face. She turned away from him, pulling up the hood.

"Wait!" he called.

In two steps the hag began to fade. For a moment, he thought he saw long, pale hair that glowed as if struck by moonbeams. But he was wrong. He blinked once and saw only the wattle of the cottage wall.

CHAPTER TWENTY-ONE

HER HUSBAND HAD NOT SPOKEN TO HER BEFORE RIDING OUT with his knights. He had not even looked at her from the time he ordered her off the wall. Instead, he had given all his instructions to Hugh, then mounted and ridden away as if she were not even there. Leonie supposed she should not be surprised, nor even disappointed. He was angry, and as she recalled from many observations over her fairly short life, this was the way an angry man dealt with a woman.

It could have been much worse. For all his anger, Philippe le Peregrine had not so much as lifted a hand against her. But still in her mind was the evil image from Brodin Forest. Why? What had really happened? She had to know. Why did she remember—

The pain slammed like a hammer against her head. She gasped, grabbing her head as light flared and pain swarmed her head, violently pounding—

Holy Mary, but she was tired of this! *Nay! I will not let*—She fell to her knees, trying to hold her bursting head together.

Don't think. Don't think. Make it go away. Don't think.

"Lady! Are you all right? Are you ill?"

It was Hugh, his voice as distant as the clouds, yet his hands touched her shoulders. She forced herself to breathe deep, breathe again.

"Aye, Hugh." She took another deep breath. "I fear I have not yet completely banished the pain."

"Rest a moment," he said, kneeling beside her. Aye, she had fallen to the ground.

"Nay, I shall be fine." She looked up into his kind eyes and tried to smile. But this had happened too many times, and it was too strange. She needed to think. She tried harder with the smile, but knew it was unconvincing. She needed to be where she was alone and try to think. "I think I should rest in the solar for a while, if you will give me your hand."

"Wait a moment until you are steady."

Leonie rubbed her face, her painful temples, opened her eyes and quickly closed them again, for the bright blue autumn day enhanced the jabs of pain. There was something very wrong that every time she tried to remember, her head felt shot through with arrows. But what? Why? Was she going to die?

Or was it something else entirely? Was she demon possessed? What if she was? What would she do? She had to find out. Now.

"Hugh, help me up. Escort me if you would, please. None of us have had much sleep these days. It must be that."

"You are not well, my lady. You should lie down."

That was a good idea. Lie down where she could not fall. She could try to think out what was blocking her mind. Nay, she would not think of it until she reached her bed.

Do not think! Leonie chopped off the thoughts. "Aye, Hugh, escort me to the solar. I'll just lie down for a while. But tell no one, please."

"Save Philippe when he returns."

"No one, Hugh."

She managed to look into his eyes, and she knew he would not obey. But she accepted his arm to support her, and they walked through the hall and to the solar behind it. A bed had never looked so inviting. She sat on its edge.

"I wish to be undisturbed, Hugh. Give me a few hours to rest and all will be fine. I am sure."

"Perhaps a woman to stay with you?"

"No one. Let me rest."

Her hands gripping the edge of the feather bed, she listened to the voices beyond the tapestry draping the doorway until Hugh had calmed the last of them and silence reigned again.

She climbed onto the low bed and seated herself cross-legged in the middle. If she fell, and she suspected that was a strong possibility, she could not hurt herself. With closed eyes and hands folded in her lap, she led her mind back to the day in the forest.

She started with something easy. Sigge. They said she had been with him. But she didn't remember him. She was sure she had been alone. Tentatively, she probed the question, letting herself roam about in the corners of her memory, not thinking of words, but seeking to see the day.

It had been one of those rare but almost unbearably scorching hot days. She could feel the sweat forming on her face, then between her breasts and trickling down inside her kirtle. Even inside the forest, where the leaves were still green and the shade heavy, the air was still and sultry. But it was one reason she loved going into the woods. They had been searching for sumac and other red things, for she had been hoping to improve her red colors for dying wool.

They.

Sigge, where are you?

Nay, she could not find him. Had he been there? Something told her he had, but nothing came to her.

She wandered along the path, ambling off when she spotted the brilliant patches of crimson, the sumac she had come to find. She had been right; the leaves had just turned, quite suddenly, for they had not been red at all the day before.

But what about Philippe? What had happened?

Hammer blows of pain pounded her head. She gasped. It was worse than before, blow after blow landing on her head, sending her brain pounding against the walls of her skull.

She gripped her fists and squeezed her eyes tight. *Nay! I'll not quit! I will know! What happened? I will know!*

Like a whirlwind, pain spun her, tightening like a dizzying band of iron about her head, and she thought her head would explode.

"Give up! Give up! The pain will kill you!"

I will not give up! Give me back my mind. What happened? I will know. I will not give up.

"Give up. You will die."

You cannot kill me. What are you? Fiercely, she gritted her teeth. *I command you. I will have the truth of you.*

Like a swarm of bees homing in on a hapless creature, something attacked, clawing, scraping gritty, bloody trails. Blood poured from open wounds and swirled, drowning her in their rising floodwaters. She couldn't breathe.

Oh, no it isn't! This is not real!

Leonie focused against the violence in her, picturing herself pushing back at the dark and bright force, back, back, teeth clenched, fists clenched, back, she forced it, back away from her brain.

The thing burst free, spinning around and around, a creature, a skeleton, a fleshed being—nay, a skeleton again. It swam in the air before her, evil talons glistening like shining steel as they lashed out, flaying her skin.

"Yield!" It screamed. *"Yield!"*

A demon! Chills ran through her. Her blood pounded like drums in her head.

Nay! Fight! She envisioned a sword in her hand and swung, slicing through the demon. *Get out!*

"Yield to me! You cannot win! I have you!"

Never! Get out! Leonie called up a warrior's strength and swung with all her being. The demon split in half. It grew back.

"You cannot defeat me!" The demon took shape, empty bones clothed in hanging rags, a bare skull, yet eyes luminous and glowing red. In its hand of bones, a long, broad sword raised to parry her blows.

She swallowed hard, her hands trembling. The creature in the forest. She'd dug it up. What evil had she let loose on the world? Her fear doubling, the creature formed flesh and smiled. It had her, and it knew it could win.

Nay! It fed on her fear! She would not cower before this thing. Win or lose, she would not give up. She'd forced it to reveal itself. She'd fight with everything she had.

Renewed, she lunged, sword viciously swinging, slicing, swinging, slicing. *I am Leonie of Bosewood! You shall not have me! Get out! This is my mind! Get out!* Her fury strengthened, it propelled her swings and thrusts, carving the demon faster than it could reunite. Its flesh fell away and vanished. She'd destroy it or die trying. *Out! Out! I demand it!*

The demon backed away, edging into the dark corridors, too dark for her to see. If only her Faerie sight had not deserted her! But she hastened after it, into the darkness.

The demon's eyes glowed like a swamp plume, and the skull became a face, grey and stretched. It shifted again, becoming amorphous, then re-formed. A mouth, smiling. Honey-brown eyes.

Philippe!

Terror knocked away her breath. It was Philippe! The creature was Philippe! She was doomed.

Sensing her fear, the creature that was her husband advanced on her, and she backed away, her heart thundering.

It couldn't be. Her heart knew it.

"You lie! You're not Philippe! Get out!"

"But I am. I am your own true love. Come to me, my darling."

Again and again she swung the sword at the creature, chopping it. "Get out!" Her mighty blows rained down. "Get out! Get out!"

The whirlwind began again, spinning inside her head so fast she was getting dizzy as it forced its way into her head again. But she knew now. She clenched her teeth, let loose her own screaming voices and rigidly fought off the sickening spinning.

"Out! Out! Out!" Brandishing the sword of her thoughts, she chased the demon as it shed its fake skin and became once more bones, "Out, out, out."

Hideously screaming, it flung itself out of her head, rolled in a cloud of dust and smoke. It fell to the floor, motionless. Leonie stared, her jaw hanging open. It really was a demon. And she had forced it out of her. Killed it.

The cloud of smoke rose up, spinning. It was not dead! At its core, something else formed, tightened, rising and rising, taking on a dusky purple color, then darkened to black, long and thin, dropped and coiled on the floor, then rising again. At its top, the coil grew denser, bending forward.

The snake!

But even bigger, dull black, with its pale yellow underbelly. Its huge head, eyes like glowing red coals, aimed itself at her. The massive jaw gaped like a chasm, showing giant fangs.

Leonie's hand shot up above her head. Her arrows flew from her quiver into her hand. She flung them; all six slammed the snake with deadly force, severing the huge, ugly head. She stared in shock as she watched the serpent collapse to the floor, to writhe and turn belly up.

How had she done that? The arrows had simply appeared in her hand. She hadn't even thought of it. She'd raised her hand, and they had come to her.

She peered around the primitive solar, into its dark corners. The soft glow of her lost Faerie vision had returned.

"Face of Jesu! What is going on in here?"

Leonie whirled around at the voice.

Philippe! The real Philippe! And she'd never seen a man so enraged.

CHAPTER TWENTY-TWO

"THE SNAKE—I KILLED IT," SHE STAMMERED, POINTING toward the dead creature while keeping her eyes focused on the angry man descending on her.

"What snake? You turned it to powder!" He clenched both fists. "What are you doing?"

She glanced to the floor beyond the bed. She gaped. Only a dark, powdery dust in a convoluted line, with her arrows scattered on the floor where they had fallen. "It's gone!"

Philippe moved closer to the far side of the bed, horror distorting his face. "What is this? Witchcraft? I saw those arrows fly to you. I thought you were daft, but you're not! You're a witch!"

He closed in on her. Cold fear chilled her soul. She backed away, her fingers icy, eyes darting, with an eye on him and another for the great serpent in case it came back. Philippe closed in. She sidled to her right. He blocked her.

"Nay, Philippe, I swear to you. It was a demon, and I forced it out of my head."

She slammed her mouth shut. This was sounding worse by the word. She'd never before done or seen anything like what had happened here.

"Demons, now? Did you call them up? Or maybe you're a demon. Did you use demons to trap me into this marriage? How did you make it look like you were attacked, and only I could find you? You were there all along. Just how did you do that?"

Her blood turned cold as his fury grew. He'd kill her now, burned or stoned. Or with his bare hands. She backed against the wall as he caged her with his arms.

His eyes suddenly widened as he retreated a pace. "What! God's face, what, where? Where did you go? Leonie!" He whirled around, stepping back, looking all about the chamber, then back to the wall.

He couldn't see her. But here she was. Had she faded, like a real Faerie? That wasn't possible. She'd never been able to do it before. She could see her arms, but he couldn't. For how long? She didn't even know how she had done it. She edged sideways along the wall.

He reached toward her, almost as if something told him she was there. Haps his sharp ears had heard her breathe. She squatted and waddled closer to the window, as close to the wattle wall as she could manage. If Ealga was right, that was the trick, to stay against a background like a wall, where her Faerie sense could imitate what was behind her so closely an ordinary human couldn't tell the difference. She held her breath.

"God and the saints," he hissed between his teeth. He ran toward the doorway, tossed the tapestry back, and disappeared to the right. "You won't escape me, witch!"

He must have thought she'd gone through the wall. Ealga had said fading looked like that. So he'd be looking for her on the other side.

She had to get out of here, quickly, before her fading wore off, however long that was. She'd have to go out of the hall, where he was going. But to stay here was certain death, and she didn't feel as brave about facing death as she had a few nights before. Especially not at his hands.

Now she realized a demon had mimicked Philippe to delude her, but it was too late. Philippe had never hurt her after all, but this time he would, for no one despised witches and sorcerers more than the Peregrine.

All she'd done was raise her hand above her head. She tried it again. The arrows that had slain the black snake came to her. It was like the silent singing commands to her arrows she'd used all her life. She called the quiver and bow as easily, straight to her hands. With bow and quiver slung over her shoulder, she beckoned to her cloak hanging on a wall peg, but it did not so much as stir a corner of the fabric. Weapons only, then. She shrugged, snatched the cloak, and tossed it over her shoulders.

Holding her breath for silence, she slipped past the doorway tapestry and edged along the wall. Two men answering Philippe's calls ran past her as if she were not there. From hall, solar, and bailey, she could hear anxious voices. They might think Philippe was the mad one, but soon they would see she was missing. Then she would become a witch, whether she was one or not.

As she scooted along, back to the wattle wall, she planned her escape. Ahead of her was a small door leading from the hall out to the upper bailey. Not far from that was the temporary open kitchen. The upper bailey had numerous small buildings, but there was no route where she could stay against a wall all the time. And she'd have to leave the walls of the inner buildings to dash for the curtain wall.

By the time she sneaked into the upper bailey, it was alive with commotion, everyone running toward the lower bailey. She caught a glimpse of Philippe dashing for the rampart stairs, where he would have an excellent view of the entire courtyard. Would he see her, then, if she was not plastered as close as whitewash to whatever was behind her?

Time for another deep breath. She sidled along the outside of the hall as the upper bailey emptied. Seeing no one close, she rushed across the open space to follow the outer kitchen wall. Beyond that, some tumbledown lodgings, then to the smithy, where the open-air forge blazed as Harald's oldest son pounded on glowing metal. The blacksmith could little afford to drop his work until it was done. She couldn't move past him. She was exposed.

Haps if she crawled.

Aye, if she could not be seen against a wall, then she might not be seen against the ground if she crawled very low. Nothing to be gained by waiting. She dropped to her hands and knees.

She was about to begin creeping when the sound of trumpets blared in the distance. Everyone in the castle stopped and listened. Her pulse began its rapid race through her veins again.

The king! The king's heralds sounded like no other.

She'd heard Rufus was coming. The speculation of his arrival had been what had chased Fulk from the walls of Bosewood. Thank you, Rufus! But a king was no more likely to side with a perceived witch than anyone else.

The eerie hush only lasted until the trumpet blasts ceased, and the entire bailey burst into an uproar. Shouts and massive scurrying, the whole of the population of the castle had been caught unsuspecting with their king almost upon them.

Leonie would have laughed, but that wasn't safe. She crawled along the ground past the smithy to the outbuilding beyond, hoping to make the postern gate while everyone else was distracted.

A small whirlwind of a boy roared around the corner of the forge and stumbled, rolling over the top of her onto the ground. Sigge.

"Ow!" The boy rolled to sit, staring at the air.

Leonie sat up, watching the boy's blue eyes widen so that the whites showed as she leaned away from the low wall.

"Wow, how'd you do that?" Sigge said.

"Never mind. I have to get out of here, Sigge. They think I'm a witch."

"But you're not, Leonie. I know you're not."

"Nay, I'm not. But I'm not like other people, Sigge. You can see why I can't let them know that. They don't understand things like this." She leaned back and crouched to hide again.

His big blue eyes got even bigger. "I don't think I understand either. How come I can't see you?"

"I don't understand all that well myself. But it has something to do with my mother. She was Faerie, and I guess I am too. Promise you won't tell anyone."

Sigge shook his head rapidly, still staring as if he'd found himself talking to a ghost.

CHAPTER TWENTY-THREE

"RUFUS!" PHILIPPE STARED OUT OVER THE CURTAIN WALL AT the royal banner appearing from the dust beyond the river. "Why now?"

Even from this burned-out palisade at the back of the castle, Philippe could see that Rufus and his guard were outpacing his army, already descending into the valley to cross the river.

What was he going to do? He had to find Leonie. What the devil had happened, he couldn't grasp. Something was very wrong. Was she really a witch? He couldn't believe it, yet how else could he explain it?

A demon. She'd said it was a demon. What if it was? Had she been possessed all this time? What if she still was?

He shuddered. That could be worse than being a witch. If anything could be worse than witchcraft. But she had cast out her demon and killed it—so she'd said. God help him. And her.

Beside him, Hugh squinted into the afternoon sun. "Rufus is in a hurry. He'll want to see you right now or he wouldn't be racing so."

"I have to find her first, Hugh. Explain to Rufus for me."

Hugh put his hand to Philippe's arm. "You know better than to slight the king. You've already looked everywhere, Philippe, and you have no idea where she is. You'll have to tell him the truth."

Philippe shook his head. "I have to find her, Hugh." But he couldn't tell even Hugh why. He couldn't accuse her. He knew what would happen to her. He had to be wrong.

Yet he knew what he'd seen. It was beyond imagination that anyone short of a sorcerer could have done what she did. And if there was a demon involved, how could it be anything but the devil's work?

"Ride out to meet him, Philippe. I'll stay here to watch for her. She has to be within the castle walls."

Philippe swiped his dangling hair out of his eyes. He had no choice. With a frustrated sigh, he signaled his squire for his horse and walked down the slope, through the bailey gate, toward the stable near the barbican. Haps he could persuade Rufus to join in the search. The king at least understood the lady was a bit dotty.

"I have to escape the castle, Sigge," Leonie said. "If they think I'm a witch, bad things could happen. I need to get through the postern gate while they're all going to meet the king."

"You can't. The lord had all the gates blocked on account of he didn't want you to get away. Can't you just go through the walls?"

"It only looks like that. I can only disappear against them. It's called fading, but I could never do it before today. But you mustn't tell anyone. I'm afraid, and I've got to get out of the castle."

"I want to go with you, Leonie."

"Nay, you can't. I can't make you vanish too, just me—I think. They'd see you and then who knows what would happen to both of us?"

Sigge's bright blue eyes narrowed down and matched with a sly grin. "I can stand watch for you," he said.

"Only if no one ever knows. I don't want anything to happen to you. You'd be a traitor if you helped me, don't you see? You could never be a knight then. All your dreams would be gone."

The boy hung his head. "Doesn't matter. They won't ever let me anyway. I can tell."

"Oh, Sigge, don't give up."

"But I can help you and they won't ever know." He stood up and peered around the corner of the forge. "There's no one in the whole upper bailey now. They've all run down to the barbican."

"Including Philippe?"

"He's down there with his horse."

"Then he'll ride out to meet the king. And that's the only way out of the castle."

"You can't go that way. They'll see you."

"Or they might not. I'm not sure how this fading thing works, but if I walk along the wall, and you walk a little ways away, you can raise your eyebrows if I start to become visible, all right?"

"You mean you'll go right through the gate?"

"If it's the only way out."

She could tell by the way the boy swallowed her plan frightened him. But if she could just make it outside the main gate, she could follow the wall outside to the back of the castle, then disappear into the woods. What came after that, she had no idea.

"Sigge, one thing you can do. Do you remember anything from the forest?"

His eyes grew to boulder size, pupils suddenly tiny. His jaw locked.

"You remember but you can't talk?"

He blinked rapidly. So whatever it was, it still bound the boy.

"Sigge, somehow you must find a way to let Rufus find the truth. If not words, some other way. You've got to let him know Philippe is innocent."

The boy nodded rapidly.

"But I think you know that, don't you? Otherwise you would have been afraid of him, yet you told the king you weren't."

Again, Sigge nodded, and his jaw tried futilely to work.

"Oh, poor Sigge," she said. "Try to think of something else, like maybe hunting mushrooms."

The boy struggled, sending his eyes darting side to side, until his lips began to move again. "Swords," he said. "I always liked swords. Peregrine's has a big red stone on the pommel, and there's a falcon carved in the blade."

Leonie's jaw dropped open. She would have never thought of that. "And the thing that looked like Philippe had a different sword."

Sigge could only nod. But it was enough.

"Then find a way to tell the king."

"What about you?"

"We'll work on that. Just help me get out of here."

Her heart raced again, for now she remembered those skeleton creatures. Four of them, not just the single one she had seen when Sigge cut his foot. They had attacked her. They'd come for her twice. So they would again.

One thing at a time.

Sigge nodded and walked with an exaggerated lanky gait to the corner of the forge where he could survey the entire bailey, and he nodded to tell her it was clear. She blessed her long legs as she dashed to the curtain wall and flattened herself against it, then, moving faster than she dared think would protect her, she ran along the perimeter, completing the arc that took her to the gate between the two baileys.

She looked in all directions but now saw no signs of Sigge. Had he gotten scared? Or been stopped? Then he popped out of the kitchen with something in his hands in a cloth. He ran toward the bailey gate and glanced around, then laid the bundle on the ground next to the gate. The boy turned away, pretending to peer down into the lower bailey that was now the scene of all the commotion.

Of course. She'd forgotten. He had no idea where she was now. She bent down and picked up the bundle, hoping it also disappeared when she held it beneath her cloak.

A fleeting grin flashed across the boy's face, and he returned his attention to the gathering of horsemen below. Leonie smiled. If she hurried along, she'd be able to walk out the front gate right beside Philippe as he rode out. A stupid idea, but one that pleased her.

As Philippe waited for his squire to fasten the girth on Tonerre's saddle, his eyes scanned the bailey for any signs of Leonie. She wasn't anywhere inside the castle, yet she had to be. *Unless she really could pass through solid walls.* Yet there was something.

It was almost as if he could feel her presence, close to him. The hairs on his arms bristled as they might in a sudden cool breeze.

He'd had that sense before and been right. He turned in a full circle, letting his senses feel whatever it was they were feeling. There was nothing to be seen. Yet something was there. It was the same sense that had led him the day she had run away from Castle Brodin. Although he hadn't recognized it then, he'd known she'd been too easy to find. He'd followed that elusive sense once before. He could do it now.

Aye. She was here. Close. The feeling grew stronger and stronger until the very hairs on his neck and arms tingled with it.

Whoever she was, it was as if she'd grabbed his heart and ripped it from his chest.

"Go on, Philippe," Hugh urged. "You know it must be you who greets the king. I'll keep watch."

But Hugh wouldn't have that sense, whatever it was, to guide him.

I'll find you, Leonie.

Reluctantly, he mounted Tonerre and rode out through the barbican with his knights. The presence was close. Very close. He wished he could tell her—

What? What could he tell her?

That he didn't want to lose her.

"By your own hand, Peregrine."

The hideous shudder rippled through him yet again. But losing her might be the only way to save her. Or was her end to be soon and horrible? Nay, even if she were a witch, he would not allow the accusation. She had not really done him harm, and he must somehow stop anyone from hurting her.

He had to find her. And then get her away from him, where she'd be safe.

But what would he tell Rufus?

"Did you perhaps forget to tell him something?"

As he rode with his knights down the steep slope of the motte, he could see Rufus and his guard already splashing into the water at the ford where only hours ago the troops of Durham had made their hasty exit. Rufus spotted them and dashed ahead of all the others, for although the king had great respect for his own rank and demanded the same of all his minions, even those with whom he claimed friendship, in his heart he had the exuberance of a young boy.

Philippe was fond of the king, a man many others detested. He could not truly call him friend, for there was something in friendship that demanded equality, and Rufus never forgot he had no equals. Rufus was England. For all his self-interest, he held the kingdom above himself, but few besides Philippe understood that.

Philippe goaded his grey to a gallop and reached the river just as Rufus and his guard emerged from the ford. He couldn't help but return the king's broad smile, and they leaned across saddles to clasp arms.

"Ah, Philippe, I see I find you well. I hear you have chased Durham's lackey back to his lair this very day."

"Aye," Philippe replied. "Or it could be said you did, Sire. They heard you were coming."

Rufus let out an evil-sounding chuckle. "And de Mowbray, what do you think of him?"

"It's all odd. The Bishop of Durham claims to back you, and de Mowbray grumbles about all alliances. But when it comes to a battle with the Scottish king, I'll wager it'll be de Mowbray who will side with you while Durham will defect."

"And your lovely wife? I'll wager you are finding marriage more agreeable now?"

Philippe felt color draining from his face. "*Beau Sire*, might we talk of it in private?"

As heartily jolly as he had been before, Rufus's face dropped to deadly seriousness. "What has happened?"

"She—" What could he say? The words choked as he remembered his vow to protect her with his own life. "She has gone missing, Sire, just this last hour."

"Missing? How?"

"I cannot say, Sire. She—cannot be seen anywhere."

"From the castle? Then Fulk has found a way to capture her out from beneath your very nose."

Philippe watched tensely as Rufus's ruddy face darkened. "Nay, I do not think so."

"Well then, what else could it be? You did ride after Fulk, did you not? And while you rode out to be sure he was gone, somehow his men entered and captured her. Were your gates not secured?"

"All was secured. I had stopped in the village while Hugh held the castle. She had felt ill, so Hugh escorted her to the solar himself. I myself saw her there when I returned."

Rufus's eyes narrowed. "Ill?"

"There are pains in her head and she faints. I think from the injuries she suffered at Brodin. I have seen it several times, but I don't know what to do for her."

The king nodded, his body rocking with the movement as he absorbed the information. "But then she disappeared? Philippe, we cannot lose her. She is the key to everything, and she is in grave danger. Surely it is the Bishop of Durham who is behind this."

"My king, I beg you, release me now to continue my search."

"Aye, but let us go for the castle first. Haps we can add something to your search. A woman cannot simply disappear into the air."

Philippe felt the blood draining from his face. That was exactly what she had done. Somehow. Philippe feigned a smile that was grim at its best and joined in the ride up the high motte toward Bosewood. The last thing he wanted was to be subject to Rufus's intense interrogation, which he knew was coming. But all he could do was to be patient until the king finally released him, or he would provoke his suspicion. Philippe had no idea what Rufus's response would be, but he dared not take the chance.

"Did you perhaps forget to tell him something?"

"By your own hand, Peregrine."

He felt a chill. What could the two possibly have in common? Was the curse somehow tied in with his secret, which he suspected the old woman knew?

They rode up the hill with Philippe relating to the king the details of Fulk's attack and de Mowbray's visit. But the king very carefully avoided any further questioning that involved Leonie, and frequently looked about him. Philippe knew the motive, which was to move out of hearing range. Just as he had at Brodin.

Once reaching the upper bailey, Rufus spotted the second palisade and laughed. "Clever man, you are, Philippe. So you tricked them into burning one wall, to be trapped by another."

Philippe nodded.

"Now show me the hall." Rufus waved his hand backward, and that was enough to inform everyone present not to follow.

Inside, Rufus's nose wrinkled, nostrils flaring.

"We cannot get rid of the stink," Philippe said.

"Tear it down. This hill can support a strong stone hall." Philippe had no time to answer before Rufus dashed off toward the solar, his thick, compact body moving rapidly and his ruddy face growing deeper red with the exertion. With quick flips of his hands, he sent everyone scurrying out the doors.

The king's pale eyes flashed in all directions, and he passed through the doorway, throwing the tapestry aside.

"Now, Philippe, you are hiding something from me. I will have the truth. All of it. If Durham did not arrange her disappearance, then who did? How? Why?"

"I fear I frightened her, Sire."

"How? Why? Then she left of her own accord? She is hardly the sort of woman to flee without some cause."

"You must blame me, not her. I was annoyed."

"Speak the truth."

"Sire, she is not—she is very different, Sire. She can do things—"

"What things? Other than outshoot any man in England. How could she get out of here without anyone seeing her?" Rufus walked around the solar studying every corner of the walls, as if he sought a clue there. He suddenly stiffened and spun around, his sharp eyes and bushy blond brows forming a menacing kingly frown, yet something like horror or fear lurked in their depths. "Philippe, tell me true. Have you by chance seen her walk through walls?"

Philippe's throat turned instantly dry.

"Sweet robes of Christ!" Rufus said. "And have you seen an old woman around here, a very old hag?"

He had, just this morning in the village. He licked his dry lips, remembering the strange old woman. She had disappeared in exactly the same way. All he could do was nod.

"And she walks through walls too. Herzeloyde. I should have known."

"Nay, Sire, the old woman I saw could not be Leonie's mother. She is far too old."

With his small eyes still flared wide, Rufus tapped his pursed fingers rapidly against his thumbs the way he did when he was thinking furiously, and he began pacing about. He stopped, folded his hands prayer-like, and brought the fingers to his lips.

By the minute, Philippe's anxiety grew as he prayed for this interminable interview to end and let him go back to finding Leonie.

"Ah, Philippe," said Rufus, "you do not know. There are things. You suspect witchcraft, I can tell, for you fear to tell it to me. But this is not done by Satan's evil, though there are such forces loose in this land. There are also others who are not like us, who come among us from time to time. But folk fear what they do not understand, Philippe, just as you fear what you have seen. Does de Mowbray know of her disappearance?"

"Nay, Sire, she left after de Mowbray returned to Alnwick."

"And tell me, what does he make of the lovely Leonie?"

"He seems fond of her. He offered his protection."

Rufus nodded, his face full of solemnity. "He should. It was he who saved her from her father when she was a babe. De Mowbray is a man of many past evils, but there is a core of honor somewhere in him, as if he hides his honor behind a mask of brutal evil. He himself carried the child to her uncle at Brodin, bringing also her Scottish maid, who had been badly injured. And he vowed to Theobald he would tear him limb from limb if the man ever came within sight of the baby again. My father, too, made a strange vow then, to an old hag. That is why the girl remained in the care of her uncle all these years."

"Theobald did not send her to be fostered, then?"

"Do not give any credit to that man. He had tried to murder both her and her mother, as well as being the most useless of marcher lords."

"Then what happened to Herzeloyde?"

"I suspect de Mowbray knows, but honor or no, he also easily condescends to lying."

"Still, how could the old woman possibly be Herzeloyde, who would not be past middle age?"

Rufus scratched at his golden beard, as if he debated to himself what he would say, and then nodded as if coming to agreement with himself. "Have you heard of the Cailleach?"

"I heard it among the villagers on our wedding night. The village elder, Cyne, tells me it is merely a word for an old woman."

"Not any old woman. *The* old woman. The crone. The hag. The old Celts believed in many things, like the spirits of the trees, of water, and the like, but this old woman is a different sort of being. They say she is a mortal being, though she lives a very long life. But she dies, like any mortal. Then another takes her place."

"But then how could it be Herzeloyde, who was not old?"

"I'm only a king, Philippe. How can I tell? I have asked many questions as discreetly as I could, yet I still know so little. I have thought for some time Herzeloyde was the one chosen, and now I believe it."

"Then you have seen her too."

"She has come to me five times, twice in this year. I have honored my father's promise to her. Information for a favor still to come.

"This time she demanded her payment, a husband for Lady Leonie. She chose you."

"Why me?"

Rufus shrugged. "Who can tell? But her choice was the right one. I knew it in that very moment. But Philippe, the lady must be in grave danger. You must find her."

"But how, Sire, if she can pass through walls? How can anyone do such things, save by magic?"

"I said there are other beings. Do you not imagine a dog must think people strange because they walk on only two legs? These strange folk do things we cannot. 'Tis not magic so much as what comes to them naturally."

Philippe shook his head. "But then how can I find her?"

Rufus's eyes began to gleam. "You must, Philippe. I know you can do it. You have a sense for tracking. If you fail, this kingdom could fall."

Was it so dire? He knew it was dire for Leonie.

But he knew as well that somehow his long-held secret was also a part of this entire mystery. If he told, it would be the end of him. Haps it would take that to save Leonie's life.

Whatever it cost him, he would do.

"Sire," he said, and lowered himself to one knee, "there is something you must be told."

"Tell, then."

"First, I beg you, when I have done, give me leave to find Leonie and bring her back to your safety. After that, I care not what you do to me."

"Do to you, Philippe?" Rufus placed his beefy arms like wings, fists on his hips. "What nonsense is this?"

"A secret, long held, that I know I must confess. I have seen the hag. She has told me the secret stands in the way of Leonie's life, and perhaps your kingdom. So I must say it."

"Up off your knees, then, and tell it like a man."

Reluctantly, Philippe rose to his full height, dwarfing the king. He drew in a deep breath. "It began with Joceline's death. The sorcerer Clodomir had imprisoned her in his tower. I went after him and killed him, but not in time to save Joceline."

"Yes, yes, I know. I also know you believe he is not dead, and that may be so. You have no need to worry over this, Philippe."

"But I do, Sire. I am the only living witness to the truth. Clodomir used Joceline to force me to betray the Conqueror. For that, the sorcerer would trade Joceline's life."

"You didn't!" The color in Rufus's face darkened and matched the fury in his eyes.

"I could not let her die, Sire. My intent was to find a way to overpower him. Still, I did kneel, knowing I would likely fail. But to save me, when he was distracted, Joceline broke free and jumped from the window and died in the flames Clodomir shot to her body."

"You bloody traitor! You set your wife above my father? Your king?" Rufus screamed, his body shaking with rage. "By God's holy face! You would sell his life to a sorcerer! And then come into my court, where I made you my friend!"

"I did. For that I dare not even ask your forgiveness, though I hold you in my highest esteem."

"And of what value is such esteem if it will not even restrain you from treachery? By the Virgin's holy veil, I trusted you! This is how you repay me?"

"Sire, it was my wish to give you my complete loyalty, in penance. Yet I say to you now, before you mete out your punishment, I beg you to give me leave to bring back Leonie and give her over to your care. She must not stay with me, for Clodomir threw his dying curse on me, that any woman I love will die at my own hand. I beg you to take her, and do what you will with me."

"You dare make demands of me? You betrayed my father for the woman you loved. How do I know you won't betray me? Speak!"

"I will not give your life up for Leonie. But I will not give her life up for you."

"And so you would. You love her. Admit it. If you were forced to it, which of us would you save?"

Philippe's jaw locked tightly, unable to say the words. For Leonie's sake, he prayed.

"That is the greatest treason of all, Philippe le Peregrine, that a man should choose his wife, or anyone, over his liege lord. And you stand here unable to say you would not."

"Only allow me one last quest, *Beau Sire*, to find her and bring her to you. Then do with me what you will."

"And you think you can find her?"

"She will go to de Mowbray, for there is no one else she can trust. I will bring her back alive and well. I vow on my life, Sire. "

"It will be, Peregrine. It will be."

He had only that strange sense to direct him, and the thought that she would try to find de Mowbray. Through the night he had followed the whim. In the darkness, the air had grown chilly, a sign of coming winter. He knew she had her cloak, but that would not have kept her very warm. She had her bow, too. That gave him some comfort.

"Close your eyes and open your mind. See what is in your heart."

What had the old woman meant? He had closed off his heart for so many years he hardly knew he had one.

With a heavy sigh, he dismounted at a rapidly rushing river and let his horse drink while he scooped up water for himself. He stood to survey the area, looking for signs. She could not have easily crossed the river, which had narrowed and was mercilessly swift and jagged with boulders. But it flowed east toward the sea, in the direction of Alnwick. He let his mind wander for a while, drifting away from his concentration on the search back to the strange things Rufus had told him.

What was she, then? Did Rufus mean there was a race of men apart from common folk? Or were they not human at all? Could they be demons, and Rufus was wrong about their intent? For a truth, he knew demons existed. And he knew for himself of evil sorcerers.

But he also knew in his heart Leonie was not evil.

Where are you, Leonie? Do not hide from me.

He hungered for her. But he could get no real sense of her. It was as if the sense, or essence, that had been leading him had become blocked. As if she blocked it. He could not blame her. He was the one who had chased her into danger. He barely cared about Rufus's great fear for the kingdom, and even less for his own life, if only he might find her and bring her back safely.

The one thing that was sure was what Rufus would do. Rufus was not a man for torture—most of the time. Likely the ending would be swift.

And so he waited. Waited for the sense. He sat, leaning against the rough bark of a pine, his eyes closed, waiting. His bones ached with weariness, for he had slept very little for weeks.

But no matter how much his body begged for sleep, he could not let it. His mind would not let it.

Leonie, where are you? his heart begged.

"Help! Someone help me!"

Philippe jerked out of his reverie and jumped to his feet, homing in on the sound. Nay—not a sound. It was the sense again, but so strong in his head he thought he'd heard it. With a sharp whistle, he called Tonerre while he tossed aside the last crust of his bread. He launched himself into the saddle and spurred the horse to action.

East. Downstream, into the thick of the forest. But there was no path, and the undergrowth quickly became too dense for the horse. He dismounted and left Tonerre, drawing his sword to slash at the brush in his way. He could hear the sounds of a skirmish now, as he forced himself over shrubs and rough ground, around thick trees, up the steep sides of the river's valley.

At the top of the ravine, trees and undergrowth gave way to broad, undulating ground dotted with scrubby heather and gorse. A shrill scream cut through the air, sending fear slashing into his spine. It was that inhuman sound he'd heard in the forest near Brodin. His heart racing, he sped across the rocky ground toward the clashing and shouting.

Leonie's voice carried over the others, harsh and fierce, and he ran even faster down the far slope. Beyond a stand of alders, he saw thrashing movement. On he ran, his thoughts shouting in his head.

"Hang on, Leonie! I'm coming!"

"Find my bow!"

"Where?"

"The big beech tree. On the hill!"

He spotted the tree ahead of him, to the right. He scrambled over the rocks, jumped a narrow streamlet, and climbed to where the lone beech stood. The ivorywood bow lay on the ground, still strung. The quiver dangled upside down on a low, scrubby bush, the arrows tossed and scattered. He grabbed what he could as he ran, his eyes focused on the brutal sounds coming from beyond the stand of alders.

"*Shoot!*"

"*Shoot where?*"

"*At me.*"

"*Where? I can't see you.*"

"*Shoot!*"

"*I might hit you!*"

"*Do as I say!*"

God and the saints help him. His own words. Philippe gulped down fear for her and let that unknown sense guide him. He aimed the bow upward, aimed at what he did not know beyond the top of the hill, and loosed it to fly to where he could only pray was not her heart.

Was this the way she would die at his hand? He kept running and topped the rise.

Something—it was not human—dropped Leonie from its grasp and toppled to the ground as the arrow struck. For a brief instant, it lay on the ground, then crumbled to dust. Tall, skeleton-like creatures, more bone than flesh, their garments like faded flags tattered in a storm. Were they the creatures de Mowbray had called bone demons? One of the hideous things lunged for her as she bent to grasp the sword of the one that had fallen. She slashed behind her, turning in the action to catch the creature across the bare bones it used for legs.

He caught the flash of her eyes as she spotted him, but she fought like a battle-hardened knight, swinging a huge sword far too heavy for such a slight maiden.

"*Shoot!*"

"*Duck!*"

"*Aim at me! Do as I say!*"

He uttered prayers to every saint he knew as he shot the arrow to the sky, then immediately started running again.

His heart trembled as the arrow flew toward her. Then it veered away and curved back again, then thunked into the bony skull of one of the things just as it snatched her around the chest from behind.

He stopped. Wishing he had taken the time to learn her trick of shooting many arrows quickly, he launched one after another into the air toward the monsters. It seemed not to matter where he aimed, for each one found its enemy in either chest or head. The last arrow gone, he drew his sword and ran again, his battle cry of fury scorching the air.

Leonie broke free of the fiends and ran toward him. He pointed toward the ravine behind him. She sped past him, snatching her bow and thrusting it over her arm onto her shoulder. As she ran, she lifted her open hand in the air, and the arrows and quiver came to her. He raced behind her, keeping an eye on the regathering creatures behind them. He estimated they had killed nearly a dozen of the things, but at least that many followed them now.

She was breathing hard but didn't slow as she followed the trail he had blazed through the underbrush. So did the things coming up behind them.

"That's what attacked me in Brodin wood," she gasped out over her shoulder to him.

"You've remembered?"

"I think—everything. They must be the gholins." She paused at the precipice, searching for the path down.

"Over there," he said, pointing to the way he had come up. "My horse should be down there."

"Not anymore. They have him."

They came to a halt at the edge of a rocky bluff above the raging river. Below and upstream near the narrow bank, the bony creatures surrounded his magnificent steed as it reared and bucked against them. More of the fiends descended the hill behind them. Philippe blew an earsplitting whistle. Tonerre reared, screaming, bucking viciously and trampling any creature unlucky enough to be too close. He broke loose and ran. But in the wrong direction.

"Well, at least they won't get him," Leonie said, still gasping for breath.

"Can you swim?" he asked. The cliff wasn't all that high, and the water looked to be deep and clear of dangerous rocks.

"Admirably. But are you daft? You're wearing mail."

"Trust me. I've done it."

She frowned suspiciously but looked back at the advancing horde. "It can't be done."

"If I say I've done it, then I've done it," he shouted. "Jump!"

With a hearty yell, Leonie flung herself over the cliff. Philippe sheathed his sword and followed.

He hit the icy water immediately after her. The weight of his mail carried him deep into the darkest water, to touch bottom before he could begin to fight toward the surface. The current pulled him down, away, everything but up. He forced all his strength into his arms to pull against the weighty iron as he struggled toward the light above.

Something touched him. A hand. She was pulling on him. She must have dived back under for him. Fiercely he stroked against the raging water. His lungs felt like they were going to burst. The cool blue light appeared above. He fought his way up and broke the surface. The weight of the mail pulled him downward while his arms pushed to keep his head above the rush of water.

She popped up into the air beside him. "I thought you said you could swim with it."

He coughed and sucked in the precious air. "I can. It's going in that's hard."

"Rocks!" she shouted, grabbing his mail at the sleeve and pulling him. "Watch out!"

Too late, he banged against a huge, dark boulder, knocking out his breath. Close by, the water turned milk white, frothing as it raged through a narrow channel, a strid between the boulders, so constricted it forced the water through it faster than an arrow shot. If it dragged him into its power, it would tear him apart.

"Get out of the water, Leonie! Don't let it suck you into that!" He braced himself with his feet and arms against the rock, struggling against the mighty flow.

"Not without you!"

"Do as I say!"

"Some other time!" She climbed upward. Then something pulled on him, a force counter to the powerful current. She could barely hold on to him, but the effort gave him just enough purchase to push himself higher out of the water and drag himself out of the torrent's power onto dry rock. His chest heaved as if he'd been in a battle with death for hours. Every corner of his body felt bruised.

Leonie collapsed on the massive boulder beside him.

"The mail has to go," she said.

"We don't have time. They'll be down on us before we can get it off. Where are they?"

"Across the river. We were carried to the other side, and they don't seem to want to try the water."

"That sounds intelligent of them."

"Trust me, they aren't. There is some sort of creature who commands them, but they aren't all that hard to fight. It's the thing that commands them I'd worry about." She pointed.

Philippe shook his dripping hair out of his eyes and trained them on the far bank.

It looked like a man. It was the right size. But it sat upon its horse, completely clothed in a black cloak with a large, concealing black hood.

"What is it?"

She shook her head. "I only know it has no face."

CHAPTER TWENTY-FOUR

A THICK KNOT FORMED IN LEONIE'S THROAT. THE BLACK cloak swirled around the thing as it dismounted from its restless black horse and strode toward the jumble of rocks on the far side of the strid. It had no eyes, yet she could feel its vile gaze fixed on her.

The entire flow of the river was forced into the very narrow channel. There were rumors about men who dared to jump the strid but missed and were torn apart by the fierce current. But she had no idea what this creature might be able to do.

Instinctively, Philippe jumped to his feet, his hand reaching for his side but finding only empty air. "My sword. It's gone."

"Which makes running a good thought," she replied.

"We need it. I can't defend us without it."

"Too late. You probably lost it when we jumped in the water."

"Nay, I felt it moments ago. It's close by." Urgently, he tried to peer into the frothing water near the strid.

"Come on, run!"

"You run. I have to find it!"

"In the water? You're daft!" But he was also right. Well, there was little sense in pretending she was just a human now. Leonie stretched her arm out over the water and let her senses call the sword, hoping it would respond. She turned her hand palm up. Would it come? She begged for it in her mind.

Out in the deep water, something stirred. With the force of an arrow, the sword shot up, point first, and came to rest on the fast-flowing surface, floating—nay, moving faster than the current!—in their direction with the current.

"God be merciful," he said. "Swords can't float."

She blinked. Her concentration failed her. The sword sank. Leonie slapped her hands against her temples. "Oh, do pardon me, adoring husband," she sneered. "I forgot."

"Leonie, stop that!"

"Make up your mind, brave spouse. This is hard." Turning her palms toward the sky, she tried again, and the sword, still riding with the current, resurfaced. Her fingers beckoned, and it sped toward her.

Philippe stepped into the water and snatched it up, broken belt, scabbard, and all. The fiend in black was starting across the rocks with an assurance that told her it could make the jump over the strid.

"Run, Leonie!" Philippe shouted. "Get up there to that cave."

Frowning, she looked at the cliff behind them, which had probably been the cause of the jumble of rocks that stretched across the river. "What cave?"

"The cave in the cliff. Go!" He had his sword drawn and his feet planted wide, which said he stood for a fight, guarding her while she ran.

He really was daft! "There's no cave! We'd just get trapped in one anyway."

"Up at the top of that rockfall. There's light coming through, so there has to be a way out. Go!"

The thing picked its footing, moving from one rock to another, sidling around larger boulders. Getting closer.

But if she could call Philippe's sword...and the arrows...

"Haps I'll just steal his sword," she suggested. Well, why not try? She held out her hand as she had done before and called to the sheathed sword at the fiend's side.

The black-clad creature stopped. Whatever it was, it focused on her. She wavered, stepping back. It drew the sword and pointed the weapon at her. Blue and red lightning streaks streamed through midair and slammed into her chest. She couldn't move. Couldn't breathe. Not even the muscles of her face could release a scream. Its earthquake-like evil laugh convulsed through her.

"It's a sorcerer! Run, Leonie."

She couldn't even move. Her lungs were burning, fierily demanding breath she couldn't draw.

Philippe leaped in front of her, his huge body like a giant shield, braced and ready for battle.

The power that had imprisoned her broke abruptly. Blocked. Philippe's enormous body stopped it. But it would kill him!

The long streams of blue and red light bounced off him like sunlight reflecting from highly polished steel, back to the creature, knocking it backward. It stumbled, barely saving itself from tumbling into the swift water.

"Run, Leonie!"

She was so glad to move she would have willingly jumped over the cliff into the river again. She scrambled up the scree slope with Philippe at her back, goading her onward. But she still couldn't see a cave. Did he see some shadow and think it was a cave? They were heading into a trap. Every time she slowed down or looked back, he prodded her on.

"Go! Go!" he shouted.

At the top of the scree slope, she put her hands against a solid, nearly vertical rock face. She could climb no farther and the top of the cliff was still beyond their reach.

"What are you waiting for? Get in there!"

"There's nothing here but solid rock!"

With an impatient glower, Philippe stepped past her. Into the rock. She couldn't even gasp before his hand shot out from the rock, grabbed her arm, and pulled her through it. Her Faerie vision began to glow, but there was no space around them. They were inside rock!

Merciful saints, if I am Faerie, what is he?

"Shh." Philippe propped the scabbard against a rock that was there yet was not, its broken belt dangling, drawn sword in his hand, waiting. He seemed to think they were safely hidden against a cave wall. But they weren't.

Haps it might be better if she thought of things his way. Although being one with a rock wasn't that appealing to her, he didn't seem to mind.

But she could see outside the rock, or cave, or whatever, to the creature working its way up the scree of fallen rock. Could it also go through rock?

Philippe reached behind him to touch her, a reassuring touch that also commanded her to stay back against the so-called wall. Best to let him manage things here, since she had no notion what was going on.

With its feet placed broadly on the jagged rock, the creature in the black cloak turned its empty face at them. It knew where they were. Once again drawing its sword, it tested the outer surface, clanging the blade lightly against it, and it rang like a bell.

The beast tipped its hooded head back, showing only black emptiness where a face should be. A roar meant to shake the earth split the air. The beast pounded the hilt's pommel against the rock, up, down, around in circles, but the rock only echoed back its solidity.

With a growl, the creature grasped the sword's hilt and sheathed the weapon, for the first time baring the hilt to view.

A silver snake wound around the black leather, terminating at the pommel in a menacing head with tiny ruby eyes. She'd seen it before.

"Fulk!" she whispered.

The being turned as if it heard. Philippe touched fingers to her lips. She understood she'd made a mistake.

The fiend grasped the sword at the hilt, baring the grip. The silver snake uncoiled from the grip, growing as it moved through the air, toward the rock face. The spoon-shaped head blackened, and eyes like burning embers in a hot fire searched as the head wove back and forth before the rock, seeking its prey. It fixed on Leonie, and its enormous maw gaped, baring sharp fangs as it hissed.

The snake struck faster than lightning. Leonie leaped back. But it hit the stone wall of the cliff. It retreated, shrank, and re-coiled about the hilt.

Enraged, the faceless being pounded its black-gloved fist on the cliff wall. But the rock face held firm. Nothing seemed to be working for the malevolent creature. Fulk—or the fiend that had Fulk's sword—could not reach them.

At last it slammed the sword into its scabbard and climbed down the cliff in the direction of the river.

"Let's go," Philippe whispered when the being disappeared from their sight, and took her hand.

"Go where?"

"Follow the light. It has to lead out."

She considered saying there was no light, but decided just to let him lead the way. After all, going back down to the river didn't seem very appealing.

As long as she continued to follow him, she could see what seemed to be a path through the rock, and it looked very much like a cave, uneven to the point where from time to time they had to climb or descend, sometimes squeezing through narrow slits to broader spaces beyond. But looking around, she saw only the glow she could usually see in the dark. He continued to follow his light in full certainty that it was there.

"What made you call that thing Fulk?" he asked as he walked along his path, taking a moment now and then to run a hand over alabaster spikes of rock that seemed to appear from nowhere when he touched them.

"Have you seen the hilt of Fulk's sword?"

"I don't think so."

"I have. That was Fulk's sword."

"Haps a similar one."

"I would know that snake on the hilt anywhere."

"But that was no man. The thing had no face. And it was commanding those bone demons."

"Aye. You called it a sorcerer, but it seems more like a demon."

"What if it is both? A demon sorcerer?"

"And a man as well? A man who is perhaps not a man at all?"

"I'll wager we'll find out soon enough."

Philippe kept on walking through the cave along a path she could not see. But she followed in silence, not knowing what else to do. Or what had become of the simple, orderly world she had wanted to escape only weeks ago.

"How do you do that thing with the arrows?" Philippe asked as he turned to help her climb over jumbled rock that had appeared from nowhere, but that he obviously saw as clearly as if the cave were really a cave. Something that puzzled her even more, since she knew for a certainty that caves were black as midnight.

She shrugged. "I don't know. I never did it before. I just wanted a weapon, and they came."

"How did you guide the arrows I shot?"

"I've always been able to guide them, when I chose. I sing to them in my mind and they heed me."

"And how do you speak to me without sound?"

"You do the same to me. How do you do it?"

"It is something you do, not me. How do you do it? What are you?"

Leonie glowered. He followed a path through stone and he thought she was strange? Yet he did not even believe that she could not see what he saw. What was the point in answering him?

"And how do you pass through walls?"

"I cannot."

"I saw you."

"You think you saw that. You saw my appearance change so that you could not tell the difference between me and the wall. It's called fading."

"By whom, Leonie? Who calls it fading?"

She clamped her mouth closed to make sure she said no more. He would not believe her anyway. For what seemed like hours they roamed through the rock, and she patiently tolerated his decisions to go this way or that when there clearly was no way at all, for in spite of firm logic, he did keep moving forward.

He stopped and pointed at something somewhat above their heads. "There," he announced.

"Where?"

"I thought you had such excellent sight. Why can't you see anything? Up there. That's the source of the light. We'll have to climb, but it doesn't look hard."

She thought about suggesting that light from that location could not possibly have been bending around all the curves and ups and downs they had taken. On the other hand, he could invade her dreams, read her thoughts, hear things no one else could. And somehow he had stopped the beam of colored lightning from the sorcerer that had immobilized and nearly suffocated her. Why not a little thing like bending light?

Releasing a sigh that sounded more impatient than she had meant, she followed him, climbing up a dark slope, jagged rock pressing into her hands and knees. To her, it was like climbing through muddy water. Above her, he stopped and held out a hand to help her up to his level. With a wan smile, she allowed the assist.

She stood beside him, looking again at sunlight and earth.

Before them stretched a broad, green valley, enclosed by high hills. A gentle beck wandered pleasantly down its length and disappeared into the distance. Masses of trees bloomed in soft pink and white, and sometimes yellow. Fields of wild poppies sprinkled red blotches through summer green grass, spiked with tall plumes of purple lupine, as if it were spring and summer at the same time.

"I don't think we're in England anymore," he said, his voice sounding as dry as her throat felt.

Leonie took a deep breath. "I don't think we're even in September anymore."

CHAPTER TWENTY-FIVE

"WAIT THERE. I WANT TO LOOK AROUND," PHILIPPE SAID AS he stepped into the bright day.

Leonie smirked and followed him anyway, not being thrilled by the possibility of being trapped inside solid rock if he left her behind. She watched the hint of a sneer develop on his lips and decided to ignore that too. But she thought she ought to check to see if the cave was still there.

She glanced back and saw exactly what she expected: no sign of the opening they had just passed through. She tugged on Philippe's arm and pointed. He looked back too.

"Am I right?" she asked. "No cave?"

He frowned. "It has to be there."

"But it's not."

His scowl deepened, then he shrugged. "We have to find our way back to Bosewood. Rufus has come. There could be trouble with Fulk and Durham, and he needs our information."

"Where are we?"

Philippe studied the distant hills and scanned over the beautiful valley. He squinted as he looked into the bright sky. Leonie did the same, and she could not pick out the sun's location. The sky was not blue, but simply pale, and light seemed to ooze from everywhere. She glanced at their feet and saw no shadows. For a moment she wondered if they were no longer alive but did not know it.

Or if they'd found the Summer Land.

If so, she'd best not mention it. He still thought her a witch. She could only guess what he thought about this place. But he was the one who had led them to it, not her—even though he'd probably blame her anyway.

"We'll find out soon enough," he replied. "We were north and a bit east of Bosewood when I found you, but I don't know what river we saw. We don't know what direction we traveled underground, but we entered the cave before noon. It must be midafternoon now. The valley looks too flat to be in the mountains or foothills, so we must be east or south of them, but we could be either east or west of Bosewood. We know Alnwick is east, near the sea, so we'll go in that direction."

But without the sun for reference, he had no way to tell which direction was east. He seemed remarkably reluctant to admit he didn't know. Leonie thought she'd let things go on in whatever way they went on. They had worse problems right now.

She just hoped they weren't within Durham's boundaries, and she suspected he worried about it too.

Philippe picked his way down the slope until they reached a little rivulet that flowed from the high hills to join the beck below. Although the valley had seemed broad and shallow, as they went farther into it, it deepened and became more rounded like a bowl, and the hills surrounding it became more like steep-sided mountains with bare, dark, rocky slopes jutting toward the sky. The grass was fresh, as on a recently rainy early summer day. Lush meadows scattered along the beck, which had joined another and widened. Leonie spotted cattle in one direction, and in another, odd, toylike ponies, unlike any she had seen in the northern country, with gracefully curved and arched backs and necks, their manes and tails either black or a deeper, richer gold than their coats. Black-faced sheep thickly dotted one slope. She saw a shimmering trout leap in the wider brook, which bounced over mossy rocks and was shaded by trees with convoluted branches ending in balls of leaves, not like any she had seen at Bosewood or Brodin or anywhere else.

But no people. The only sign of people, in fact, were the herd animals, which surely must have owners.

As the valley leveled out, Philippe knelt beside the brook and scooped water into his hand. He smelled it. Then he tasted it. "Fresh, I think," he said. "The animals haven't died, and we have nothing else to drink. I think we're safe here."

"I suppose we can't be sure of that, either," she replied, and knelt beside him to taste the water, which was cool and sweet.

"Why are those things after you, Leonie?"

She shook her head, frowning. "I don't know. But the sword in that fiend's hand was Fulk's. When he came courting at Brodin Castle, I saw the hilt. It had a silver snake that coiled about the grip. The snake's head formed the pommel and had ruby eyes. Like the snake in the solar that had gleaming red eyes."

"The snake again."

Leonie pulled her lips into a pout as she studied the grass at her feet. Her tangled hair fell in front of her eyes. How unappealing she must look to him. She had run for miles until her braid had fallen, then fought a gruesome battle, only to run more and jump over a cliff into a raging river. Her hair had dried now and was matted and tangled like the roots of a witch hazel.

She jutted her chin. "I care not if you don't believe me."

"Yesterday, I would have believed nothing you have told me. Today I think there is nothing past believing."

"Is there?" She stood and shook out her rumpled, torn kirtle, realizing she could not even remember what had happened to her cloak. With a disgusted snort, she strode off, headed downstream.

He caught up quickly. She thought it was wise of him that he said nothing more.

Beyond the beck, on the far side, Leonie spotted straight, level lines that contrasted with the hillside behind them. Straight lines meant people. As they progressed, the lines brightened and formed squared shapes, low and long, lighter in color than the hillside beyond it. "That looks like a house."

"What?" He frowned in the direction she pointed.

Leonie leaped over the beck and hiked across the meadow. The house took shape, with sleek round stone columns supporting a reddish roof she thought might be some kind of slate, though slate would be too heavy for such a shallow slope. Brilliant garden colors decorated the surrounding terrain, and she began to see the outlines of a terrace.

Now Philippe could see it too, for his pace quickened. "I'll go ahead. You don't know who the people might be."

Not like any she had known, she suspected. He was more likely than she to be astounded at what they would find. But she ignored his order and strode along beside him, mostly because even with her long legs, she could not outpace him.

The closer they drew to the building, the odder it became. It ceased being white or pale. Bright colors of crimson and gold with touches of blue, green, and darker colors formed angular designs on the walls. The terrace in front of the house was topped by an arbor, with vines growing over it thick enough to produce shade, and heavy bunches of grapes hung all about. At least she thought they were grapes, since she had never actually seen any growing. Around the terrace grew small trees with shiny, bright green leaves, with fruits in shades of gold, red, yellow, and green weighing down the branches.

Beyond the round columns, a table covered in a white cloth stood in the shade of the vines. The heady aroma of freshly cooked pork hit her nostrils, and sharp pangs of hunger struck her belly, reminding her she had not eaten since the night before.

"I wonder who lives here?" she said. Never had she seen such a house, nor such a bountiful display of foods she did not recognize.

"You might ask him," Philippe replied.

Leonie startled as she turned, catching sight of a solemn, bald-pated, dark-haired man, wearing a long, belted tunic of white. She was certain he had not been standing there before.

And he was almost not there now. She could see the outline of the laden table through him. It was almost as if the very aroma from the still sizzling meats wafted through him.

The man bowed and swept his hand before him to show them welcome. Then Leonie saw others like him, many men, but one face repeated, identical in every detail, including the simple swirling embroidery around the necks of their tunics.

"Is this your home?" she asked the man.

Instead of answering, he again bowed and repeated the gesture of welcome, showing them to a long, wide, low couch that reclined before the table.

Two women as ethereal as the men appeared, and they took her bow and empty quiver, which they set aside in an alcove in a frescoed wall. They took her hands and raised them over her head, then pulled her ragged, stained garments up and off. Their deft hands unwound her bound hose and removed them and her tattered shoes.

She glanced at Philippe and saw that two men had also stripped him bare. His sword and mail were set in an alcove of their own. She winced at the sight of so many angry red imprints from his mail on his chest and back. He turned his back to her.

"I wonder if my husband is shy?" she asked. "He seems afraid of showing his body to his wife."

Philippe pivoted at his waist and let his eyes scan her nude body from hair to toe. His eyes brightened to match the beginning of a smile turning up the corners of his mouth. "Haps you would not want to see it just now."

"I know what you have, Philippe le Peregrine. I suspect it is right now at its best."

"I'm suspect my body thinks yours is at its best."

Her heart took a leap. She ought to know better, yet she couldn't help reveling in his words.

Other ghostly figures appeared, bearing folded white garments in their hands, and these were silently slipped over the heads of their amazed guests. Golden cords fastened these soft white tunics, which were exactly like those of the servants, save for the richer embroidery of intertwined gold horses galloping in line against a purple background, bordered in gold along the neck openings and sleeves.

"It's exquisite," she said, fingering the needlework. "I never thought of using the horse motif in my embroidery." She ran her hands over the fabric, wondering how any cloth could ever be made so soft, and for that matter, how people who were as transparent as water might carry it. The smoothness caressed her skin—so much better than her rough, torn kirtle that had survived a dunking and swim in icy water, then grown stiff and chafing as it dried. Her delight bubbled out in laughter, and looking back at Philippe, she saw a wide smile, something that was as rare as dragon's eggs. Her anger melted away as if it had never existed.

"Haps they are not real," Philippe said.

"They could be ghosts."

"But they mean to serve us."

She nodded. "Haps we are dreaming."

Philippe chuckled. "We are getting very good with our dreaming, wife."

A pleasant flush came over her as she remembered.

She followed the translucent servant's motions to recline on the odd couch, which had its head at the food-laden table. She snickered softly. "Whatever might not be real about this place, the food looks tasty enough."

Philippe took a bite of a rich white meat while Leonie savored sweet yellow-red-colored fruit that came apart in sections and squirted juice as she bit into it. Out of curiosity, she squeezed a section over a slab of the tender cooked meat, and as she bit into it, she laughed delightedly at the marvelous combination. She held out a bite to Philippe, and he took it from her fingers with his mouth, letting his tongue graze her fingertips. He grinned, his honey-brown eyes sparkling.

Leonie let her gaze wander around the open terrace, noting a light breeze stirring the grape leaves, and watched as the ghostly servants walked about, filling gold goblets with red wine that had no bitterness, only a rich, sweet warmth. Platter after platter appeared before them. Philippe pulled a grape from a dark purple bunch and popped it into his mouth. His eyes widened, accompanying the hint of a smile. He plucked another and brought it to her lips.

Leonie sank her teeth into the delicate flesh of the grape, and her mouth filled with the most heavenly taste, rich and sweet. She giggled.

"What is different about it?" he asked.

"It's good?"

"No seeds."

"Oh. I have never eaten a grape before."

"Then try this." He picked up a dark red fruit with a skin that looked like old leather, and peeled it. "Eat the seeds."

How peculiar. The seed glistened like a dark ruby. The delicate taste swarmed through her mouth. She hummed in ecstasy.

"A pomegranate," he told her.

"I have heard of them. But they do not grow here, do they?"

"I am not sure where we are," he replied.

"I have never seen a house like this."

"I have, somewhat. In Tuscany and Rome. In Sicily."

"And pomegranates? Grapevines?"

"In Catalonia too."

"You have been many places."

She watched his eyes lose their spark of mischief and become sadly regretful. "Aye."

"It's why they call you the Peregrine."

He looked down at the silver plate and said nothing.

"Sometimes I think there is much you do not tell me about yourself."

"Aye." He let out a sigh. Then once again he cocked his head to eye her from an odd angle, and he laughed. "Another time, haps," he said. "Let us have this dream together. It is too good to waste." He leaned to her and turned her face to meet his kiss, and his fingertips skimmed her cheek. Leonie lost herself in the ripple of sexual delight that ran through her body.

He leaned back again. "Aye, let's enjoy this dream while we have it."

They were behaving like giddy, silly lovers. He didn't love her, she knew. But that was not his fault. Whatever might come, what was wrong with simply enjoying this experience together?

"Do you really think we are in a dream, Philippe? Haps it is your dream, since I have no memories like these."

"If it's a dream, where do you suppose we really are while we're dreaming?"

"I don't remember falling asleep. Usually I have a sense that I'm having a dream."

"Then where did the dream begin?" he asked. "Where did we leave the real world?"

"But what if it's not a dream?"

"How can spring and summer exist at the same time? Where can fruit ripen, yet new blossoms bloom on the vines and trees at the same time?"

He fell silent, she noted, having successfully evaded her probing. With a napkin, he wiped his mouth and set aside the plate.

She, too, was marvelously sated, and sat up on the couch. This place made no sense to her. It was not simply the alien trees or the strange ponies with golden manes, not even this house, which with its transparent servants and pools of water inside the house was the strangest thing of all. It was the way it made them act and feel. All the anger she should have, she couldn't find. And oddly, his seemed gone too. Instead, they seemed to want to frolic like young colts. And make love like wild hares. But she needed her anger. She needed its shield. She would rather lose all her Faerie powers than fall so dangerously in love with him.

She snickered at her own ridiculous ways. Now she was angry because she couldn't stay angry?

The ethereal servants reappeared, and with properly downcast eyes removed the plates and remaining feast. They filed through a door, and Leonie watched, fascinated, as the ghostly figures merged into one man who still was no more substantial than any one of them had been.

As they stood on the smooth flagstone terrace, the man bowed again and waited in the manner of a servant who expected them to pass by him into the chamber beyond. Philippe spoke to the figure, which silently bowed once more, making all the previous motions so exactly that Leonie began to think those were somehow the only movements he could make when someone spoke to him.

She shrugged. She'd had worse dreams in her life.

Beyond the door, many candles burned around a room with a large, rectangular pool of clear water. A series of wide steps descended into the water, and tendrils of steamy vapor rose from the surface. If it was meant to be a heated bath, it was the largest one she could imagine. The closest she had ever seen before was a big wooden tub that might hold two people only if they were avid lovers.

An intriguing idea.

In an adjoining chamber she could see a bed with carved legs and a thick, plump mattress with brightly colored bedding. Through a different door, she thought she saw another pool, and wondered why anyone might need two bathing places. But as she watched, the room changed into a garden terrace with stone benches. She saw flowers form. And bushes in bloom in many colors. Beyond the garden, a small lake transformed, with several low cascades of a small river flowing into it. Such a place of beauty surely could not be found in the wilderness.

Inside, near the steaming pool, more of the strange servants stood by with folded cloths draped over their arms.

Leonie removed her sandals and stuck her toe in the water. "Hot," she said. "I suppose we are expected to bathe."

He knelt beside her and dangled his fingers in the steamy pool. "Aye." He glanced back at her. "Leonie, I want to know. What are you?"

"But you won't tell me what you are," she countered.

"I asked first."

Leonie sucked on her lower lip. She had been waiting for this conversation to come back. Haps the lost anger would return too. "You called me witch. Are you suddenly unsure?"

"I was wrong. But you are not like any woman I have ever known."

"Didn't you say to everyone in Castle Bosewood I was a witch?"

"I said it to no one. I told them you had gone missing. They assumed you must be hiding somewhere inside the castle walls."

"You said it to the king."

"I did not. He guessed you had escaped again, as you did at Brodin. He also guessed my suspicion and told me it was not so, but that you came by your talents naturally through your mother."

Leonie blinked suddenly, staring at him. "What does Rufus know of my mother?"

"It's what he guesses, not knows, but he is far better at gathering hidden information than most people credit him. And he is very good at fitting pieces together to reach the truth. What are you, Leonie?"

"What are you?"

"You're evading me. You know I'm no more than a man. You are something else. No ordinary person can do what you can do."

"Did I not see you walk through solid rock?"

"Why do you insist there was no cave?"

"It's all very well for you to say I saw no cave, but how can you explain why that demon sorcerer creature couldn't see it, or see us in it? Yet we could see him outside. Didn't you hear the ringing of his steel sword and the pommel against the stone?"

"How do you explain being inside a cave if there is no cave?"

"I can't. And tell me what you did to block that lightning power from the thing's sword. It left me paralyzed, yet you bounced it back on him like a mirror."

"It must have been my mail. I am but an ordinary man. But answer me. What are you?"

"You won't believe me. You don't believe anything I say unless someone else confirms it."

"Tell me anyway."

She let out a harsh huff and folded her arms across her chest as if she might shield herself from the onslaught of his questions. But she supposed there was no greater danger in telling him than there was in not doing it. She huffed again. "My father was Theobald of Bosewood, a Norman."

In that infuriating superior way he had, he nodded and smiled. "And?"

"My mother was Herzeloyde of the Summer Land."

"Somerset. I know all that. Tell me the missing pieces."

"If you so desire, sir knight, but you must be patient enough to hear them. Not Somerset. People assume that because Somerset means 'summer land.' She is from the Summer Land, a place humans cannot find unless they are led to it. She is Faerie. Since my father was a mere Norman, I am but a halfling. Beyond that, I know almost nothing."

His eyebrows could not seem to make up their minds which way to go—one arched high while the other furrowed into half of a frown. A smirk formed on his lips, and amusement widened his dark honey eyes. "Aren't the Faerie folk wee creatures who play wicked jokes and mend people's shoes in the night when everyone sleeps?"

Nostrils flaring like an offended horse, Leonie jerked to her feet and turned her back to him. She jerked off the soft wool tunic, tossed it aside and stalked nude to the edge of the pool.

"Leonie, come back here. I am talking to you."

Sneering as she tossed her head, she glared back at him. "Talk to yourself. You may answer yourself too."

She crouched, sprang, dived into the pool, and cruised through the silky water until she reached the center. She turned over and floated on her back, the long tendrils of her hair fanning out all around her head as she absorbed the luxury of the enormous heated bath as if she lay on the softest of beds. Tiring of that, she arched and thrust herself backward, head first and down, deep into the water, and spun beneath the surface like a wheel, rotating back to the surface to float and breathe in the fragrant, steamy air. She dived backward again and swam underwater toward the deeper, far end of the pool.

Still beneath the surface, she felt, rather than heard, a powerful splash and whoosh into the pool. Like a sleek river otter, he caught up to her. His powerful arms snared her in his embrace, and lips found lips in a forceful kiss. They popped up to the air, floating, still in the embrace as his tongue invaded her mouth. Her mind fought her lustful body, wanting to be angry, wanting to shut him out, then just as strongly wanting, needing him, every part of him.

"Damn you," she said when she forced herself free. She grabbed a deep breath and shouted, "Damn you!"

"Aye damn me, lady," he said in raspy tones, kissing her again. He brushed her dripping hair away from her eyes. "Why, because I teased you?"

She felt her anger rising, hotter than passion, hotter than the water. "You think it is funny? You ask me to tell you the truth, but when I do, you ridicule me."

Following an odd impulse, she flung her hands high and twirled them in the air. A stream of arrows flew at his head from all directions. She gasped and rapidly splayed out open hands, spread fingers. The arrows halted in midair. A finger's breadth away, circling his head.

Leonie gulped, heart racing. How did that happen? She could have killed him.

"Haps I was wrong?" he said, his eyes shifting warily around at the halo of arrows.

"A-ah!" she huffed. Leonie splashed her hands against the water. The arrows fell and floated. She scooped them up and sloshed through the water toward the stone steps on the opposite end of the pool. She could hear him shoving through the water behind her, but she disregarded him and pushed herself on through the shallow water to the steps.

"Leonie," he called. From behind her, his arm caught her at the waist. "Put the arrows away. Stay with me here a little longer."

She huffed back at him. "I can think of no reason to."

"Because the water is so warm." He pressed her back to his lean and utterly naked body. "Because it feels as silken as your skin. Because you are so beautiful and I want to be with you."

She stiffened as his hands slid gently up her arms and brushed her massive hair away from her shoulders. But she couldn't resist him. She wanted to but couldn't.

"You lie," she said. Yet she could not stop herself from leaning back in his arms and closing her eyes. She laid the handful of arrows down on the paving of tiny colored ceramic fragments that surrounded the pool. In this odd place that seemed to change as things did in dreams, she couldn't seem to stay mad at him. Somehow the place seemed so real, like some deeply buried memory that had come back to her. But was it?

He must be right. It was only a dream. Then if it was, why should she not enjoy with him what she could not in their real world?

She followed the urging of his hands as he gently tugged her back into the sumptuously warm scented water, and they floated, his arms still around her as he propelled them with leg kicks back into deeper water. He released her and they floated side by side on their backs. Leonie's hair spread out in waves through the water.

"I've decided I like sharing dreams with you," Philippe said in a languid voice.

Leonie just hummed, curiously happy. "At least it's better than running from evil, faceless demons."

At the far end of the pool, a stone carving of a blowsy-cheeked man with a stone mane of wavy hair radiating from his face poured water from his fat-lipped mouth into an alcove of the pool. Stone seats were built into the side of the alcove, and they moved through the water to sit beneath it, letting the warm water cascade over them at their shoulders.

As equals in the water where such things as height did not matter, they locked in an embrace. Leonie's hungry hands stroked his body, roaming over hard muscles, letting the healing touch of her fingers find the dark bruises on his chest where the metal of his mail shirt had cut into him. Aye, she could close wounds again, but now she could even heal bruises. She wondered what else she could do that she never could before. Was this like the arrows that suddenly came when called, or the sword in the water? Or was it part of the magic of this place?

"What are you doing?" he whispered hoarsely, nuzzling into her neck as if he didn't care what she answered.

"Doesn't matter."

"You're making the bruises heal. How do you do that?"

"I don't know. I just do it."

"Is that one of your Faerie skills?"

"I suppose. I've always done it. Ealga would never let me tell anyone. She thought I would be accused of witchcraft."

"She's right. Nobody trusts a witch. Are you sure you're not one?"

"Why would I be a witch? Do you care?"

"Nay. Your touch is like heaven."

"Then hush. Let it be."

He pulled her into his arms, tight against his chest, their limbs entwining in the sleek water, and pulled them to stand beneath the cascade of warm water flowing out of the fountain.

"I love you," he whispered hoarsely. "I love you so much."

Her heart burst into a wild rhythm, echoing like drums inside her head. He loved her? Did he forget and think he was back in time with his Joceline? Perhaps this dreamy place had affected him more than her.

But just for now, she could let even that go. She closed her eyes as his lips found hers once again, slowly, with passion, his tongue exploring yet caressing. She had never thought kissing could be this wonderful. She would give up everything to be kissed like this the rest of her life.

Abruptly he halted. His face looked as if he had been slapped. Then as he pushed away, his face became a mask of purest torment.

"What now?" she asked, and knew she sounded more than a little impatient.

His eyes searched hers, a hungry passion mixing with some terror that made her heart pound in fear. His hands glided slowly from her cheeks over her shoulders, down her arms.

"No. This can't be. Somehow, you must go away," he said. "You must get as far away from me as you can."

"What?" Leonie pushed him back, her passion suddenly turning cold. "Philippe, you are the most confusing man I've ever met. You love me, but you want to get rid of me?"

"It's the only way, Leonie. The only way to keep you safe."

She folded her arms when he tried to pull her back to an embrace. "Oh, do pardon my ignorance, my learned and worldly husband. I am only a lowly woman with no knowledge of the world, yet somehow I think it's not the usual thing for a man who loves his wife to cast her off."

Philippe chewed on his lip while he slowly shook his head. "I have to or you will die. He bowed his head. "Those creatures, the bone demons, whatever they are. They are not your greatest danger."

"Aye, it's Fulk."

"Not even him."

"Then who?"

"I am."

CHAPTER TWENTY-SIX

"OFT HAVE I THOUGHT THAT," SHE REPLIED WITH ROLLED eyes and thinly drawn lips. But his anguished face told her this time he was not joking. Her heart began to melt again.

"Nay, hear me out, Leonie. I would rather die than tell you this, but I must say it. If it angers you, I understand. You should have been told sooner, but I thought I could save you another way."

"Save me? I don't understand."

His hands slid up and down her arms, taking the warm water over her skin. "I know I have seemed angry with you, but I was really angry at myself. I have failed you in the worst possible way. There is a curse on me. It affects you."

"I don't believe you." If anyone would have a problem with curses, it would be her, not him.

"It's true. I can find no way to break it. I've looked for years and can find nothing, but it dooms you."

"But why? Why you? Why me?"

Philippe turned away from her and leaned into the fountain, letting its cascade wash over his face. With a toss of his head, he turned and shook away the water, but the intense pain that clung to his eyes could not be washed away. "You know how Joceline died."

"She was killed by a sorcerer."

"She tried to save me from him, and she did. Clodomir meant to hold her hostage to force me to his will. But she broke free and leaped from the window to prevent me from giving in."

"But you killed him. Everyone says you did."

"I did. But he is not dead."

"Philippe! You are making no sense."

"I cut off his head. But the head rolled across the room and then it began to talk again. Dead though he must be, he laid a curse on me, that I will slay by my own hand any woman I love. Nothing in this world could be more horrible to me than to destroy the woman I love."

Her jaw dropped open, and her heart began to race again, a new terror flooding her. "The dream. I saw it in your dream. You stabbed me but you could not stop the sword."

As she slowly forced her gaping mouth to close, she finally grasped the torment that had driven his strangely volatile nature. "So you thought you could avoid the curse by avoiding a wife."

He nodded and guiltily looked down at the water. "I meant never to marry, nor let any woman close to my heart."

"But how could you love me? You have never even liked me. You have never wanted to be near me."

"You do not know, sweet love. Fear for you drove me from you, whenever I could get away. And soon I realized I could not make myself stay away from you, no matter how desperate I was. I did not mean to ever care for you." He sighed. "I was so angry with your accusation that I was sure I would never even come to like you again. I tried to hold on to the anger, but you kept chasing it away. When Rufus made his demand, I thought I could just send you away to one of your estates. You'd be safe and I would never see you again. But it was not to be. We were forced to be together.

"The hag told me what I must do, but I didn't understand at the time," he said, once again turning his anguished face away from her. "I sought a way to break the curse. She asked instead if there were something I had not told someone. I knew what she meant. I had not told Rufus the truth about Joceline's death because then he would know I had betrayed his father. But I knew when he reached Bosewood I had to tell him. He was furious. So I will return with you and give you over to safety, and then Rufus will do with me whatever he has decided."

"You betrayed him? I don't see how."

"I chose to submit to the sorcerer to save Joceline's life. And I knew I would be used to destroy William. A king has no friends, Leonie. Rufus has told me that many times. A king has courtiers, vassals, allies, all as changeable as the wind. But Rufus broke his own rule and trusted me, a man who is too dangerous to keep at his back."

"But you have served him faithfully. He forgave even Robert de Mowbray and gave him all of Northumbria as well."

He shook his head. "Rufus has never trusted de Mowbray. Rufus needs him in Northumbria because no man can do what he can do. But I betrayed the Conqueror to save Joceline. And I fear I would betray Rufus to save you. I refused to say I would not."

Taking a shaky breath, she reached through the water to him, but he backed away, his face still contorted with his anguish. She hoped he didn't see the trembling in her hand, but knew her hope was in vain.

The one thing she had always wanted was his love. And it would cost either her life or his.

There must be another way. There must be.

"You are not a traitor," she said. "You are a man caught in the jaws of Hell. Rufus will see that."

"I don't think so."

Though he pulled away from her, though her hands were shaking, revealing the cowardice in her heart, Leonie forced herself to move in front of him, cutting off his retreat through the water. She had run from danger before, too many times, driven by the fears that had haunted her all her life. She begged God to give her strength. "I am frightened, aye, for you and for me. But there must be another way, and we will find it."

"Leonie—"

She laid her hands on his chest, then slipped them round him to hold him close as she rested her head on his warm, bare skin. "I will run no more," she said. "I am here, and alive, only because you have saved me so many times. And I have saved you as well. Alone, against powers we can't understand, we are nothing. But together we can fight them. We have already won more than once, and for now, we are safe. This is the Summer Land."

CHAPTER TWENTY-SEVEN

HER GREEN EYES WERE SO ACHINGLY BEAUTIFUL, FILLED WITH anguish so like what he felt for her. She knew what a threat he was to her life, yet all her pain was for him. How could anyone be so forgiving? Never had he wanted a woman so much.

"We can't fight together, my love. It will only make things worse," he said. "I would have you safe."

She leaned her head on his chest. "What do you want, really? Do you mean to punish yourself for loving me? Will it make a difference, Philippe? If you loved me less, would it undo the curse?"

He shook his head. "I don't know."

"If you love me more, will it be more likely to come true? If you hate me tomorrow, will the curse then be undone? For as long as I have known you, I have desired your love, so perhaps it is I who have made this terrible curse, not you."

"It is not your doing."

"Aye. For the same reason it is not yours. Always you have been honorable, but an evil being has taken your very honor and turned it against you. We'll fight him together, for we have never been able to fight him alone. But for now, I beg you, give me what I have so long desired. There is no greater gift than love. We all must die, but I want only to live first. If it is to be, then we cannot stop it, so let us not let our hearts die before it is our time to go."

Slowly his heart and mind settled on the truth he had so long denied. Now he understood the hag was right: his deception was the very root of all their pain. He would never have encountered Leonie without it, nor been a risk to her, for the Conqueror would have beheaded him on the spot. And deservedly so. But now—

"Give me your love, Philippe. It is the one thing my life must have."

Her words were as clear as if he had heard them spoken, just as she could know his words if he meant to send them to her. Yet she must not know his other thoughts, for if she did, one way or another she would stop him from what he knew he must do. So tonight he would, instead, share all his love with her, and take hers for himself. He had nothing else of value to give her.

Tomorrow they must find their way back. And a new deception must begin. She didn't need to know what Rufus would be planning for him this very moment.

"Aye, love, share with me. Give me all your heart."

As he pulled her into an embrace, the wish for a bed, the perfect bed to make love, flashed into his mind. They were in the water, and then they were not. They had not moved, yet everything around them was changing. The steamy water swirled and lifted around them like walls, and then became walls of mellow golden stone glowing in the soft light of candles. The bed he longed for stretched out, low to the floor, deep with pillows, smooth sheets and warm, russet colored blankets. Too much light, fewer candles, he thought, and then the candles winked out and vanished. Together they fell onto the bed, onto inviting, soft sheets that felt like the finest silk, and all thoughts beyond themselves vanished as their minds and bodies moved with one purpose.

He gasped as her hand slid to encompass his rampantly engorged shaft. She would be his love in truth, if only for one final night.

His beloved's face was a mask of passion, eyes closed, lips open for a kiss. Here, in this strange Summer Land, he could deny her nothing of himself, no matter what waited for him in that other world that suddenly seemed to be the one that was unreal. There he was her unwilling enemy, but here, her husband and lover, as they had been in truth only once before.

He would offer her all, share this one moment of need. Mayhap it would make all the rest worthwhile. He gave in to his lust and closed off his thoughts, letting the power of his love conquer him.

Her hand slid over his shaft once again, stroking the flared head in such a way as to bring forth a drop of his seed. He groaned without meaning to, bringing an answering response from her lips. Sensuality twanged between them like a bowstring, passing arrows of lust back and forth.

Her rosy mouth parted in desire and he imagined her taking his shaft between those lips. Sucking him, coating him with her hot warmth. Imagination became reality once again as she bent over him, her curly lion's mane drifting over his nude legs. His flesh trembled as her soft hair danced over it, then as her lips closed around his erection, his blood boiled.

He felt her tongue flick against his heated, turgid flesh and nearly died a little death right then.

"Leonie," he whispered. He shoved his hands through her hair, finding her scalp and massaging it in time with her licks.

She took him farther down now, swallowing him deep into her heat. He meant to give her the best of him, but she clearly wanted to return the favor.

"Leonie," he said again. "Let me give you this pleasure, beloved wife."

She lifted her face. Her skin glowed with exertion. "This is my pleasure, my husband. How I love to feel your hips move, your lusty moans."

"I can deny you nothing." He leaned back and watched her delight in the surrender of his body to her Fae-born prowess.

No woman had ever pleased him so much as this slim, wayward goddess.

She seemed to anticipate his every desire. When he wanted her to touch him more, she stroked his flanks with those long, wonderful fingers. When he wanted speed, her mouth moved up and down on his shaft, guided and enhanced by her slick fingers. When he wanted to watch her work upon his manly parts, she let him pull her hair back so he could see the way he moved in and out of her soft lips.

"My Leonie," he said, his words coming out like strung-out moans. "You are all mine. You are everything to me, for eternity." His shaft tingled, engorged even further, as he spoke the blessed truth. If only eternity would soon come for him, to save her from the curse's power.

He felt her lips curve into a smile, then her fingers slipped between his legs to grasp his sac.

"Saints in Heaven," he gasped.

She rotated his tender balls in her palm. All reason fled before heat and lust. He bent his head back and began to thrust his hips in earnest.

His shaft dipped into her mouth. He felt her suck up and down. One hand joined her mouth. Her hot tongue massaged him.

"Harder," he begged.

She complied, offering him such presumptuous ecstasy that he wondered how he could be outside Heaven at the moment. All his focus tightened into one shiny coin at the base of his cock.

His vision exploded into gold. His senses gone, he mindlessly pumped his cock between her eager lips. His seed flowed into his wife's willing mouth.

Her greedy swallows brought him back to himself, and he knew he'd never heard a sweeter sound than her taking his seed with such alacrity.

"Sweet bride, we've only just begun." Gently, he pulled her away. "You are the most beautiful woman who ever lived," he whispered, reaching for her small, perfect breasts. "We are built so perfectly for one another."

Her eyes widened when she felt his fingers plucking at her nipples. "I feel that in my womb, sir knight."

"And lower?"

She smiled naughtily. "I am wet below. Is that to your pleasure?"

Her lusty nature drew him like a bee to a spring flower. "Greatly," he said. "Do you think I can put a child in you today?"

"Anything is possible, my beloved."

He grinned at her sexy wink. "Would you want that?"

She let her head fall back. Her hair curled and danced down her slender spine. "Pleasure me, husband. Let the rest come as it may. I can think of nothing but tupping and tupping and tupping again." She laughed aloud.

He let his fingers drift down, between her breasts, past her navel, down her belly, into her wiry golden curls. "Shall I take you fast, then? I thought to sup from you first."

When she said nothing to differ, he tugged her forward, pulling her legs until they rested on his shoulders, the nub of her pleasure at his mouth. "Ah, yes, you are a feast."

She cried out, wriggled away, then her soft flesh was full against him. "Again," she begged.

This time, just as he suckled her, he found her opening with his finger and pressed in.

"Sweet Lord!"

His wife convulsed around him, sending a thrill of joy through him. He had made her work much harder for his pleasure. But this only meant she was ready for his shaft all the sooner.

She laughed hoarsely, her body still quivering. "You are a beautiful man," she whispered.

When she had stopped shuddering, he set her gently on the bed, then moved over her.

"Now?" he asked, feeling cool linen underneath his knees.

Her eyes were unfocused. "Now," she agreed. "Give me all of you."

He found her channel, then pushed in gently. His lips found hers and then he entered her mouth with his tongue. He meant to thrust it in time with his shaft, but her tongue swirled around his, joining them intimately. She stroked his back with her fingers and her slim legs wrapped around his buttocks, then slid higher until he felt enveloped in warm, scented femininity.

She liked speed, showing him by the undulations of her hips, so he gave it to her. In and out, slick heat surrounding his hard shaft, his buttocks working under her hands, her fingernails digging into his flesh, her little cries of delight urging him on. Indeed, she was a gloriously wanton creature. His previous ejaculation meant he could last longer this time, so after a while he flipped onto his back, just in time to prevent her from a second climax.

"Oh, Philippe," she protested. "Don't stop!"

"Ride me, beloved wife," he said, "as if I were your warhorse."

"With pleasure, sir," she said as her hips moved on his broad body with all the grace of a dancer.

Only moments passed before he grasped her hips with his fingers, holding her tightly. "I cannot keep this pace in your tight sleeve without losing myself to you."

"We are in the Summer Land. Anything can happen here." She clenched him in her velvet mail, grinning with naughty purpose, and squeezed rhythmically until he lost himself inside her.

He felt her shudders and knew he'd taken her with him. The juices of her pleasure mingled with his seed on his loins. How perfect they were together, and how he wished he could live and have every night be like this.

He slept only as long as it took her to find the will to circle his shaft with her mouth again. If he could break a curse with the power of lovemaking, he was certain they could overcome any obstacle. But it would not come to pass. Aye, Rufus was right—he would give anything to save his dearly beloved. And that would brand him a traitor to any king.

"I have always loved you," Leonie said, drowsing so close to dreaming she was nearly gone.

"I cannot remember not loving you now," he replied. "It was a different world, a different time. I will keep you safe. I swear with my life."

"I know." Her lazy fingers gave one last attempt to run through the crinkly hair on his chest, then stilled.

He tugged his lady wife close, silently sending up a prayer to God that he hoped she did not hear. *Please let me get a child on her in this strange place. Give her hope for a future, since I have none. Make it a good birth, to show another, better man that she can bear strong sons, and help her find a place in this troubled world.*

It had been a day of horrors, of salvation, of revelation. He knew now what she had struggled so long to keep secret, and in some strange way it made sense. It was what she was that the demon sorcerer wanted from her, and he wanted her alive, else he would already have killed her. She was right, that demon and Fulk had to be the same. But she was strong, and she was smart, and she would have Rufus and Robert de Mowbray on her side.

So now he knew her secret, that she was Faerie. But one dread puzzle remained:

How had he done the things he had done?

What was he?

CHAPTER TWENTY-EIGHT

PATIENCE HAD NEVER BEEN RUFUS'S BEST VIRTUE. HE DID NOT, in fact, have any virtues that he could recall, unless it might be that he always did what he believed was best for his realm, regardless of what any others thought. Nor, he mused, did he care what anyone else thought about anything. He was, after all, the king.

But back to the patience, of which he had none. He stood on the ramparts of the unfinished stone curtain wall at Bosewood and frowned out at the horizon, back to the village below the castle, and once again the forests beyond, waiting. He was losing patience even with losing patience.

Something had to be done. But what? The Peregrine had been gone seven days, and no word from him. Rufus had sent out searchers, but no word came back. He had even called on de Mowbray, his most reluctant ally, for the man had a stake in Lady Leonie's life, and in this he knew this most selfish Black Earl would die to save her if he must. A queer situation, but there it was, and Rufus was not one to fail to use such an opportunity.

But God preserve the saints, a full week! He could not hold Durham and his treasured knight, that bedamned Warrior of God, at bay any longer. He had run out of excuses. And if he let them into Bosewood, they would all too quickly discover Leonie had fled her husband, and the husband had followed her into the wilderness. Rufus had a sense for danger, and that sense told him Durham was not to be trusted, even if the evidence had not confirmed his suspicions.

Seven days! If Fulk had captured Leonie, he would have the weapon he needed. And Philippe would be slaughtered for it. But who knew whether Philippe had not simply turned his horse toward Scotland, abandoning them all? If only he knew more.

Yet he could not make himself believe Philippe would betray him. A man should never hold his family more dear than his king, aye. But how many reasons had his own father had to tell him a king must never have friends?

If he, Rufus, had been merely a knight and not a king, if a lady such as the enticing Lady Leonie had ever loved Rufus, would he not have sacrificed anything, even his fealty to his liege for her?

He laughed cruelly. He knew the answer. He knew no such lady would ever love him, but if she did...aye, he understood Philippe le Peregrine all too well.

If only he knew *something*.

In the castle bailey he spotted that little blacksmith's son dashing around like a scurrying little rat. Rufus admired energetic people. Too bad about the boy's great ambition. His grandfather's taint had been too great, too awful. The boy was fortunate his father had been allowed to live and become a blacksmith.

But, Rufus thought, as he rubbed his newly bristling chin, the boy was a bit like the crone. He knew things. Rufus had allowed the boy to come with his brother to Bosewood just for that purpose. He was a born snoop.

He nodded, as if somehow he must confirm his own thought. "Boy!" he shouted down to the bailey.

The boy skidded to a halt and turned to stare up at the rampart, then remembered to bow. "Aye, Sire?"

Rufus beckoned with a hand that circled in the air. The boy ran to the steps and climbed to the rampart, then stopped short and fell to his knees. Ah, his manners had improved.

"Up," Rufus said, knowing the growl of impatience would probably be mistaken for royal displeasure. He motioned for the boy to join him in his quest for the invisible out there somewhere.

"You know something," Rufus said, now breaking eye contact.

"Nay, *Beau Sire*," the boy replied. "I'm just the blacksmith's brother."

"Brother to one, son to another. I know your story, boy. And I know the Lady Leonie has a special interest in you. If anyone knows what happened to her, you would."

He watched the boy's gaze shift to either side so quickly a less astute observer would have missed it. "Aye, I see I am right. Well, then, let me tell you what I know. Do you even know who the lady's mother was? Not her name, but what she was?"

The boy's expression changed to an odd frown with one eyebrow rising rather high.

"I see you don't," Rufus said. "Tell me then, does the lady have a strange way of disappearing, haps as if she has walked through a wall?"

This time the eyes widened. Fear was what Rufus saw now. But fear for what?

"She vanished, lad. Beneath our very noses. I see you will pretend you know nothing, and I value your loyalty for your lady. So I will continue to tell you, and you will listen. She does indeed have that ability, and I believe she came by it through her mother's unusual heritage. It is of no mind to me or to you, but we must not share that knowledge with anyone."

Rufus started down the steps, the boy tagging along as if the two of them were tied together. "But we must find them. Each hour they remain in the wilderness alone they are in more danger. Yet I cannot tell what we must do about it. There is one other who might help us, but I do not know how to find her. Have you seen a very old woman about? Very tall and unusually thin and haggard, hair like old straw? Wears a green mantle?"

"Aye, Sire, I saw her once, the night of the wedding. But not since."

"The wedding, you say." Aye, of course Herzeloyde would attend the wedding she had demanded of Rufus.

"Aye, Sire. She spoke to the Peregrine. Called him Norman lord, said something about his winding path. She's a strange one, *Beau Sire*, strange."

"Aye, so she is, lad," Rufus replied. "I want you to help me find her."

"But I don't know where to look, Sire."

"If you had to find her, where would you begin looking?"

"The village, I guess."

"Then let's go." At the last step, Rufus landed on the hard-packed bailey, already breaking into a fast pace, headed for the gate.

"But, Sire, they will not tell. I mean, I think they don't know. I heard the Peregrine—I mean, my lord of Bosewood—ask the Earl of Northumbria, who told him no one knows where she lives."

"But the Peregrine found her. He told me so. This is important, boy. She's the only hope we have. They've been gone too long, and I fear if we don't go to their aid they won't come back. It may already be too late. So I ask you bluntly, and expect a truthful answer. Will you protect your lady? You've done it before, so I ask now: Will you do anything to save her?"

Sigge's bright blue eyes widened and he swallowed what looked to be a very large lump. "Aye," he said. "You mean Leonie."

"She's in great danger. She was my ward, and the Peregrine is very important to England."

"He's your friend, right?"

"I have been doing some thinking on that. Kings must not have real friends, I'm afraid. A king cannot know if one day he might have to sacrifice someone he loves for the sake of his kingdom. And who can tell when a friend might use the friendship for treachery? But I do not want anything bad to befall either of them. Worse than that, though, it could be the entire kingdom that is at stake. She must not fall into enemy hands, nor must the Peregrine."

The boy's eyes shifted around again. And Rufus saw that the only way to manipulate the boy into giving up what he knew was to play the trustworthy, caring, fatherly sort, as he had at Brodin.

"I see you understand. And nay, I do not expect you to trust me not to send her into harm. You will not say what happened in the forest at Brodin. You did not argue that the lady's accusation was false. Yet you did not help her escape, nor did you do anything to prevent the marriage. You did nothing. Yet I believe quite firmly if you thought the Peregrine were a threat to her, you would have done all you could to keep him from her. You know better, don't you?"

This time, the boy's face became all but contorted with inner pain. Rufus thought it more than interesting that even at this young age, the boy thought, like all men, that he did not reveal his thoughts when they were all but written on his face.

"You know better. You know why she fears him, but you also know he will not harm her. But your loyalty to her tells me I must trust your judgment. So I ask you again, are you with me? Nay, I rescind that. Sigge, son of Harald, I command you. Help me find the old woman."

Rufus strode as if demon-driven to the gate, and with impatient gestures shoved away any who would follow him. Sigge hesitated. Rufus harrumphed—but nay, the boy was unused to royal command and didn't know what was expected of him.

"Come on, boy! Now!" He did not wait, knowing the lad was at least smart enough to comprehend that.

Rufus's army was encamped all over the lower bailey, and as they traipsed down the winding path to the village, Rufus became ever more impatient with those who sought to accompany them. They ought to know when the king didn't want an escort, but it was only with great reluctance he acknowledged to himself a king without escort was a frightening thing. That was their misfortune. He could swing his sword as well as any man who rode with him.

In the village, all the peasants fell to their knees. "Up! Up!" he demanded. "Go on about your business!" But he knew they would only pretend to comply. There were things about being king that were annoying, and this was one of them.

"All right, boy, where shall we start?"

"Don't ask them, Sire. Let me."

Rufus nodded grimly. In no time at all, Sigge had singled out an elderly man standing close enough to an elderly woman to demonstrate she was his wife.

Sigge spoke in the English tongue, as if he were interpreter for a king who knew none of it. The truth was, though, that Rufus knew it well but spoke it only rarely, out of deference to his own position as Norman overlord of all England. He waited through the introduction, which was about as correct as he could expect from a young boy, and waited through the man's very proper fawning. God help him, but how he hated all these little delays.

"Ask him," Rufus said, prodding at the boy's back.

Sigge phrased the request in careful English. Rufus watched as the fellow shook his head.

"No one knows, Sire," old Cyne replied. "She comes, she goes. We never know when or where. 'Tis by her will, not ours."

"Do you know if she does the same in other places?" He shook his head with a frown. That wasn't what he wanted to know, so he might as well get to it. "Is she the Cailleach?"

The entire village seemed suddenly frozen by a gale of silence. Rufus looked around. Jaws dropped open, faces pale as ashes from yesterday's fire. Amazing how well these people understood while all the time pretending they didn't know the Norman tongue.

"It will be our secret," the king said. "I must talk to her. Only she can help Lady Leonie and her husband."

And there she was. Aye, the Cailleach, who figured so completely in the folklore of the North. This time he looked past her aged skin and thinning, brittle hair, and saw the long, slender bones so much like the Lady Leonie's. The likeness was in her very character, even the shape of her ears. How such a young, beautiful woman had aged so far beyond her years, he could not fathom. She would have been little more than a score of years when she had first appeared to his father, yet even then she had been a hag, looking as old and weathered as God's earth.

"You seek me, Red King?"

"I do, and desperately so, old woman." With a fiercely waved hand, he shooed away all watchers but grabbed the boy by the neckline of his tunic when he tried to exit too.

Looking around, Rufus made sure they were alone. "Now, old woman, I tell you with God and this boy as my witness, I know your secret. And as you set up this mess, you must now help us resolve it."

"You have lost them already, Red King?"

"No more of your taunting jokes, old woman. Tell me how to save them."

"I have told you before, I do not know the future. I only know what must be, will be."

"And you have ordered me about before. Why not now?"

"It is not for you to do. You are merely a king. You are not the Almighty God."

Rufus stepped back a pace, as if a blow had stung him. How dare—

"So you really are the Cailleach, then."

"'Tis naught to you, Norman king. Go back to your petty wars. They will live or die. Neither you nor I can change it."

"Your own child—"

"I am Cailleach now. I am mother to all my people, but can touch none. I am who I am, and you are who and what you are. But I am in debt to you and your father forever, as you are in debt to me. Do not meddle in this unless you are called to it, or you could cause irreparable harm."

As Rufus opened his mouth to stammer out some rebuff, knowing he had none that was logical, he heard a howling of air as if they were suddenly in the midst of a great storm. In truth, aye, the wind had gone from naught but a pleasant breeze to a tree-bending violence. He turned in a full circle and realized it whirled about them, all the way around, picking up limbs and dust and swirling so fiercely it became like a dense, dark cloud.

"Run, boy!" he shouted, and the boy began to run, but the wind had become like a wall. Rufus dragged the boy back by his tunic.

"Don't worry, Sire," shouted Sigge against the roar. "I'll save you!"

The last thing Rufus needed, a reckless lad laying down his life in foolishness. He dragged the boy closer, clutching his arms tightly enough to bruise, as the cloud spun about them, tightening its circle around them.

"'Tis magic," he muttered, and drew his sword.

The old woman's shape twisted, undulated, the dun-green color of her mantle brightening and mixing with unexpected colors, and she re-formed. But now—she was young again. Her pale hair hung in dense, tightly waving hanks over her shoulders. Instead of her crooked staff, she held a sword, poised for battle—against the wind.

'Twas the legendary Herzeloyde.

Tighter and tighter spun the whirling cloud of dust, whipping their garments and their hair like wild, flapping pennants. So close! It tugged on the boy. Rufus pulled him close. "Hold on to me!"

"I'll save you, Sire!"

"Sheath the damned knife, boy, before you cut me! Hold tight!"

The twisting demon wind clutched at the boy, pulling him in one direction and Rufus in another. It whisked Herzeloyde into its motion. His great weight surely could hold them to the ground.

Then it picked up speed and caught them up, ripping at their garments. His sword was yanked from his hand and his sword belt broke and spun away. The boy clung tightly. Herzeloyde spun separately, too far from his grasp.

"Save the boy!" she shouted.

That was what he was trying to do.

But how did even a king fight a demon wind?

"Don't let go, boy! Don't let go."

From somewhere in the distance the sound of a baying hound shocked the morning air, penetrating Philippe's lazy dream. He blinked as he stirred, moving his arm from Leonie's waist where she lay beside him. She stirred and sat up, as did he. The sound of the baying hound grew louder.

"Ilse," he said, smiling at a memory of the shaggy hound's huge tongue lapping across his face, and wondered if he would be treated to the tongue swipe again if he lay there any longer.

"Where are we?" Leonie asked, looking around them with a puzzled frown.

Gone. The entire villa, from pillar to bath. The cushioned bed, its sheets as soft as baby's skin, the brightly painted walls, even the mosaic floors, were gone, vanished as if they had never been. A broad, rocky valley spread out into the distance, cupped on three sides by forlorn, tall, barren hills, instead of the verdant meadow and deep-green tree-laden slopes.

Leonie got to her feet and shook out the wrinkles of her kirtle. She bent over to look down at her toes. "My boots are new. The same, but like they were when they were first made. They don't look like they've been through a river and a rocky cave. And the tear in my kirtle is gone."

"You lost your cloak, but you have it now."

"And it looks as bright as it did the day I dyed the wool. That was two years ago."

Philippe examined his sword and sword belt and the buckle that had broken when they jumped into the river. The steel and silver chasing on the blade gleamed and the leather scabbard looked freshly tooled and oiled—surely it had never been dunked.

"There she is!" Leonie shouted. "Ilse!"

The dog loped toward them, her long ears flying.

In the distance, the silhouette of a rider appeared on a horse. It would be de Mowbray, and far behind him like small moving dots near the horizon, his knights. Few horses could run as swiftly as de Mowbray's giant, wild-tempered black.

Philippe broke into a run, Leonie keeping pace. They met the shaggy hound, which jumped first at Leonie then at Philippe, licking first one then the other in the face, then back again as if she couldn't decide who needed it more. Philippe laughed at

Ilse's dancing and prancing, and at Leonie's excited greeting as she futilely dodged the slurping tongue. From the beginning the dog had preferred Leonie, and he laughed, seeing Leonie receiving about three times as many swipes with the wet tongue as he did. He didn't really mind.

De Mowbray's black warhorse raced like the devil drove it, its flying mane flailing the air in rhythm with its rider's thick black curls as they rode up. De Mowbray reined in to an abrupt halt and threw himself out of the saddle.

"By God and the saints!" The man strode up, sweeping a quick bow to Leonie. Almost at the same time he clapped Philippe on the shoulder hard, then grabbed him by both arms. "Where have you been?"

"We were hoping you'd tell us," Philippe replied, grinning, and slapping de Mowbray's back in kind, "since we have no idea." Mild surprise struck him as he realized he had never thought the day would come that he would be so delighted to see this man.

"You're but a few miles north of Bamburgh Castle, lad. I would never have looked for you here, but Ilse would hear of naught else this morning."

"How would she know?" Philippe asked, still chuckling at the bouncing dog with her happily lolling tongue. "If her nose is that good, I'll be begging a pup out of her."

"She's tasked to look after Lady Leonie, I think. She is Herzeloyde's gift."

Philippe exchanged wary glances with Leonie.

"When?" Leonie folded her arms and glared at the earl.

"Now, lass, let's not go into that again. I've told you what I can." De Mowbray turned his horse loose to drink at the brook, watching it with one eye lest it overdrink, or haps, Philippe suspected, to avoid Leonie's intense gaze. "I found your horses north of Bosewood," he said, "and I found signs of a skirmish. But 'twas strange after that. The dog can follow any trail, but it was as if you disappeared from the earth, and she would go no farther, until today. I went back to Bamburgh, and it's there I left the horses. We'd all but given you up for dead."

"So soon?" Leonie frowned back at the man.

De Mowbray's bushy black brow furrowed in the middle. "You've been missing eight days. Rufus is beside himself. His ruddy face has turned as pale as his father's ghost."

Philippe shook his head, sidling a glance at Leonie. "It's not possible. It was only two days ago I left."

De Mowbray eyed them both as if they had lost their minds. "And where have you been that the sun does not set?"

Philippe frowned, puzzled. "Well, in a cave," he said.

"And in the Summer Land," Leonie added.

"Summer Land? You cannot go there. 'Tis forbidden to humans."

"And I'm Faerie, and you know it."

De Mowbray shifted his startled gaze back and forth between them, not once, but several times. "He knows, then?"

"He knows. Stop avoiding me, Lord Northumbria. I want the truth."

"Lass—" The black eyes that were so fierce in battle, so wicked in scheming, were soft and pleading in the face of Leonie's determination. Philippe felt like laughing, but that would not help her cause.

"Tell her." Philippe folded his arms in unity with Leonie. "It's long past time for secrets. She deserves to know."

Ilse sat at the earl's side, panting happily, watching her master's every move. De Mowbray bent and fondled the dog's ears, then turned, pacing, and patted his black steed's mane. He ran his hand over the dark red leather saddle and played with the bridle and reins as if he contemplated jumping into the saddle and fleeing. He ran his hand through his bushy black hair. "'Tis not—"

He huffed, turned away, turned back, then started again. "'Tis not because you're not wanted, lass. But a human can't go there. Things happen, and they're not good things."

"But we've been there."

"You don't understand. You can't go there. It's closed to you." The great bristle of eyebrows that slashed across his forehead folded into such deep furrows that they met in the center. "You couldn't. Unless something's wrong."

"Then haps," Philippe said, lifting an eyebrow as he pushed himself into the middle of the battle, "there's something wrong. Unless there's another place where spring, summer, and autumn happen all at once, where houses from Tuscany sit in England and have hot baths big enough for swimming."

The earl paled.

"And where things that are worn or torn or shattered are made new again," Leonie added. "Tell me, Lord Northumbria, since you know so much, that we were not there."

"Haps you'd best tell me more."

At that, de Mowbray's knights began to ride up, their horses blowing and exhausted, for they were not the quality of the great black stallion. De Mowbray commanded his knights to dismount by the beck and rest their horses.

Philippe told him of finding Leonie and their escape into the river. Leonie told him of the faceless creature and of the unreal bolt of lightning, of the cave that she insisted was not there, yet Philippe knew he had not only seen it but taken her with him inside it. And the astonishing valley at the other end. With each tale they told, the Black Earl's bulging black eyes grew ever wider, and he glanced back and forth to Leonie, then to Philippe.

Philippe pondered. Was Leonie right about him? Was there something different? It seemed impossible, yet those things had happened. How had he stopped that powerful bolt? He'd known it had nearly killed her, yet it had done little more than poke him.

The cave had seemed so real to him that he'd thought Leonie mad for believing it was not. Yet if was not, how had it led to that incredible valley? And it was beyond belief how the mere thought of something would make it appear.

But the most puzzling of all was how he had found her so quickly, not once but at least twice. He'd followed an eerie sense that had led him, first in Brodin Forest, and again this time, directly to her.

How did they share their dreams?

Philippe slid his lowered gaze toward the knights who remained near the beck and realized he could hear their words. He'd always been able to hear what other men could not.

With a quick shake of his head, he brought himself back to the argument.

Black Robert de Mowbray, the great and powerful Earl of Northumbria, was staring at him with his mouth agape.

"Christ and His saints! You're an Annwyn King!"

Something inside him sank to the bottom of his gut. For a moment, even swallowing was beyond him. "A what?"

"That has to be it." De Mowbray rubbed at the thick brush of beard. "Aye, it has to be. I should've known—nay, how could I? You showed nothing of this when you were a babe."

Whatever that thing was in his gut, Philippe thought it had just twisted into a knot.

"What's an Annwyn King?" he asked. "And what do you know of me as a babe?"

With his beefy hands at his temples, de Mowbray shook his head, then paced some more. "Saints!" he growled. "I knew it. I knew it. I knew if I answered even one question, you'd be asking more, and then more. And it will never end."

"What's an Annwyn King?" Philippe said again. "Why should you know about me when I was a babe?"

"Where's my mother?" Leonie demanded.

"More to it," added Philippe, "who is her mother? Is she the Cailleach?"

Leonie turned her shock on Philippe instead of de Mowbray. "The old woman? My mother can't be that old."

De Mowbray sighed. "Aye, lass, she can. She is, but she isn't." With a circling wave of his hand, he summoned his knights. "We'd best be getting on to Bamburgh and send word to Rufus you've been found. I'll tell you as we ride."

De Mowbray gave his orders to his knights more with grunts and pointing than words, something Philippe thought strange for such a windy-worded man. But even as Philippe mounted the horse given up by one of the knights with Leonie boosted up behind him, he made up his mind he wouldn't wait long for answers. Of all things, he knew he was not a king of anything.

Leonie wrapped her marvelous long arms around Philippe's waist, making him wish to be out of his mail and back in the elegant, soft bed in the house in the valley. He thought once more of the curse and swore to himself. Leonie was right. They would live before they died. But she would not die because of him. He would find a way.

They would find a way.

He fully expected De Mowbray would again evade their questions once they were on the move and he was prepared. But the man seemed resigned. He had sighed six times since mounting his great black steed.

Once more he huffed, so loudly this time one of the knights turned to look back with a puzzled frown. But the earl's glower quickly returned the man's attention to the road ahead.

"Might as well," the earl said aloud. "Well, lass, you want the truth. 'Tis not all that pretty a beast, the truth."

"Just tell me." Her jaw jutted.

De Mowbray shook his head slowly, then began. "The old Scots tell many a story about the Cailleach, some true, most mere fancy. It's a word for an old woman, a hag. But she's more than that. She's a meddler of sorts, you might say. Likes to interfere in the affairs of men, but she's not of the world of men. She lives a very long life, far beyond that of any mortal man. But she's mortal, so eventually she dies and a new Cailleach is made. No one knows how. It just happens. The Cailleach is always Faerie, never human. And she does not choose—she is chosen.

"Herzeloyde was living among men as the wife of Theobald when she began her change and she had no choice but to go, but she feared to leave her daughter with her violent husband when she went to the Summer Land. But she couldn't take her, knowing the child was human."

"But I'm only half human."

"There's no such thing, lass. You showed no sign of the Fae blood in you, so you had to be left in this world. You see, when a halfling is born, 'tis known right away what he is, either human or Faerie, never both. The Faerie accept their own kind, but they cannot take a human into their realm."

"But I am both. I have the sight, and I can command weapons. And I have been closing wounds since I was a baby."

"Aye."

"Well, doesn't that make me Faerie then?"

"But there's the rub, you see. When you were born—well, there's never been another like you, to be both human and Faerie, and we didn't know what to do with you. The healing touch is not known among the Faerie. Nor is it human. You're both, and... something more. What that is, none can decipher."

"But I—"

"Wait, I'll get to that. Herzeloyde sent for my help, for Theobald suspected something and beat her so badly her maid thought she would die. Though she was desperately injured, she escaped. I took the child and her nurse and rode to Brodin Castle. 'Twas your uncle, with mine, the Bishop of Coutances, who secretly persuaded William to put his protection on you, and Theobald never dared go near you again. All these years Theobald sulked, looking for a way to avenge himself while his castle rotted about him. And I fear he found his vengeance by allying with the Scottish king and Durham against William's son. But he died before their coup could take place.

"So you see, though I have no love for Rufus, I owe him a debt of gratitude for keeping his father's promise. Though I admit for a while I was afraid he'd sold you out." De Mowbray managed as much of a smile as anyone had ever seen of him.

Philippe could hear the disappointment in her sigh, and he squeezed her hand that wrapped around his waist. "And the Annwyn King?" he asked.

The way de Mowbray shook his head seemed more intended to dislodge a sudden infestation of gnats than to clear the nonsense from his mind. "'Tis another race, like the Faerie, or Sidhe, as they ought to be called. They are more like the people of this world than the one they left behind, yet they are different. Any Faerie can find the portals and enter them, but only an Annwyn King can build a portal. That's what you've done."

"I only took Leonie into the cave. She must have made it happen."

Leonie touched his arm. "Nay, Philippe. I could not see the portal. How could I build it?"

"But you are the Faerie, not I."

"No Faerie can build a portal, Peregrine," said de Mowbray. "That is why Herzeloyde stays close to a portal unless she is called by duty or need. Nay, you must be an Annwyn King, else you are something the likes of which has ne'er been seen. So that is what Herzeloyde sought to protect. But there is something else that escapes us. Tell me more about this sorcerer."

Philippe told him more of the story, though little had gone unsaid before.

De Mowbray's face became grimmer by the minute. "Gholins," he said. "It must take very strong powers to call them up from their graves."

"Fulk," Leonie said.

Stiffening in his saddle as if he'd been stabbed, de Mowbray turned wide eyes on her. "That pious fool? Couldn't be. Nay, wait, tell me more."

"I think the leader is a sorcerer. Leonie thinks he is a demon," Philippe said. "She saw the hilt of his sword. It's Fulk's."

"And he's a man?"

Leonie shook her head and shuddered. "Not a man. Shaped like one, but clothed entirely in black, with a hood that hides the fact that there's only blackness beneath it."

"No face." De Mowbray chewed his lower lip.

"Aye."

The Black Earl raised his hand high to summon the knights behind him and spurred his great warhorse. "Then it's true," he said. "Come, we must return to Bamburgh quickly. There is danger, more danger than I knew."

The warhorses raced across the plain toward the morning sun in the east, and Philippe began finally to see familiar land. The sea came into view and they turned south. In a short time the castle, golden sandstone glowing in the morning sun atop a craggy rock jutting into the sea, came into view as they topped a low hill.

With renewed energy, they spurred on, so close to the castle that even the knights' weary horses could make the last leg of the journey.

At the gate, de Mowbray dismounted and slapped the reins of his horse into a squire's hands. He ran up the steep slope within the bailey, shouting orders, while Leonie and Philippe ran after him.

"What news from Rufus?" he demanded of a knight running along beside him.

"Naught since yesterday, lord," the knight replied. "We sent your word to him, but he has not replied. He must still be at Bosewood."

"And Durham? Scotland?"

"No movement so far, lord."

"Then go find out for yourselves, damn you. Prepare fresh mounts. Summon the knights. And a quick repast—very quick. We ride out within the hour."

With only a bare pause to relieve themselves, de Mowbray and his guests rushed into the hall, where the Black Earl shooed away the servants.

Philippe watched the servants scurry out, having nearly dropped their trays of food on the trestle table. "You don't trust your people?"

"They know my secrets, but they don't need to know yours. Nor what I must tell you next." He grabbed up a chicken leg and took a huge bite, all but crunching through the bone.

"What's your concern?"

"A sorcerer who is a demon, and in addition, a shade. Commanding the gholins. And now you tell me 'tis Fulk, the Warrior of God, Durham's favorite, who's at the bottom of this. If Fulk's a sorcerer, or a demon, or both, then he has the bishop in his thrall. That explains a lot of things."

"The bishop's unexplainable behavior, for one," Philippe agreed. "We thought him insane." Suddenly, the delicious smell of freshly cooked meat lost its appeal. "If Fulk sides with Scotland, then he needs to seize Bosewood to gain control of the pass it guards. So he beguiled the bishop and used him to help his plot."

De Mowbray nodded and bit into a slab of boar meat, talking as he chewed and only pausing to swallow. "Durham also has a powerful army. United with Scotland, they might defeat Rufus."

Leonie set down her plate, too. "I imagined it earlier. If they have Bosewood and can come down through that pass, while Durham and Fulk come from the east, they will trap the king between them."

"Aye. That would be the way."

"Haps you'd explain what a shade is? Some sort of ghost?" Philippe asked, echoing de Mowbray's grim smile, but with narrowed eyes.

"But it's not dead," said the Black Earl. "It's a bodiless spirit that steals the bodies of other creatures for a home, you might say."

Philippe ran a finger over his chin, absently noting its smoothness despite several days in the wild, one more reminder that things were afoot that he couldn't explain or comprehend. "That makes sense, but one other thing doesn't."

One of de Mowbray's black brows lifted, his only response to Philippe.

"Why you?"

De Mowbray's eyes shifted beneath his thick lashes in a way that made the hair on Philippe's neck bristle. But he gave no answer.

Philippe probed further. "Out with it, de Mowbray. Why you? I knew of Black Robert when I was a boy in Normandy. You were known to be wild and cruel, with a mood and heart even darker than your black beard."

De Mowbray released a noisy breath and shifted in his chair. "'Twas true enough," he said.

"Why would Herzeloyde trust such a man with her infant daughter?"

The loud breathing turned to rough grunts and clearing of his throat as the Black Earl shifted in his chair. Abruptly, he jumped up and strode to the narrow lancet window. Philippe watched every move the man made, his shoulders hunching ever so slowly and the great bear of a man ebbing into a slouch as he leaned against the sill. He chewed his lips.

At last he turned to face them, but his eyes looked more to the chamber's vaulted ceiling than to his guests. He sighed once more.

"Robert de Mowbray is dead," he said. "I inhabit his body."

CHAPTER TWENTY-NINE

Leonie's mouth dropped open. "Then you're a shade?"

The frown on Philippe's face increased. "'Twas not what I expected to hear."

"You thought I'd confess to Faerie blood? Wouldn't I make a delightful sprite?"

"It would make more sense to me. You say there is evil in being a shade. Why would Herzeloyde trust you? And how is it you know her?"

"Don't you be impugning Herzeloyde's honor. Make no mistake, there is naught between us that should not be."

The man's voice had taken on an entirely different sound that did not fit the huge, gruff bear of a man. One that was quiet, almost gentle and sad, echoing the lyrical sound of the French language.

"Four lifetimes ago, I was born Valenze of the house of Savoie, on the Piedmont at the foot of the Pyrenees Mountains. There was a Faerie lass I followed into the Summer Land, and like many a man before me, I tarried too long. I returned to the outer world, the world humans know, only to discover I was but a pale wisp of myself, and I could not survive without the body of another. Since then I have been many things. A blacksmith, a soothsayer, even a midwife.

"Black Robert was indeed the vile man you remember. He and his wild friends took it into their bored heads to raid a convent and rape its nuns when I was there. It was at the end of my sojourn in the midwife's body, a very old, sick woman in the care of the nuns, and I was desperate to find a new home for my soul before the old one expired. That's the evil, you see. A shade steals the bodies of others to survive, and he finds a sort of immortality in it. He has only to find a new body when he has the need, and if he chooses wisely, each time he can live a new life again. All men fear death, but to a shade, giving up his soul to death is terrifying. He'll do anything to find that new body."

"Meaning he will kill to take over a man's body?"

"I did not—would not—until then. I had always managed to slip into a body just as life expired, without then expiring with it. 'Tis a tricky thing, you see. Sometimes the body itself dies and can't be revived, and if the shade doesn't escape in time, he dies too."

"How much time?"

"Very little, but it depends on how disintegrated the shade is. I thought I knew exactly how to do it, but that time I had become desperate, for I had failed twice and feared to fail again."

"So you killed de Mowbray."

"'Twas easy enough. An iron candlestand to his head while he was busy raping Sister Isa. His friends fled with only a few dents and broken bones. I could have done as I had done before and merely suppressed that villain or forced him out of his body. But then he might have done the same, haps to one of the nuns, or some other hapless man who would then die. So aye, I killed him. And I took over his life. But I did not know how truly evil the man was until I inhabited his body, for there is much more than just the body that remains, you see, and Black Robert de Mowbray had, it seems, many terrible secrets. I live with them now."

"If you were a knight in battle, you would not hesitate to kill a man," Philippe said.

"And he deserved to die," Leonie added. "If you had not done what you did, other innocent people would have suffered and died."

"Aye. But I thought only of my own life, and only later did I justify what I did. Now I am Robert. The more I live within his body, the more evil I take on. I'm no different from another shade. I am imprisoned by my own fear of death."

"Yet Herzeloyde trusted you with her daughter."

Robert's dark, flashing eyes turned a bitter, barely hidden rage on Philippe. "Do you think I would not do the same to you as I did him, if need be?"

"Haps you would not, when the time came."

"A man is what he does, my friend. I am not just what I have done, but what all those others have done as well. I know my own evil." He chuckled crudely. "But don't you worry, man. I've no designs on your body. And you may be sure, Herzeloyde would rip out my throat if I let harm come to her lovely daughter."

Leonie lowered her head, not quite sure if she ought to laugh along with him or not. For a joke, it seemed very ugly. "But then you do know where to find her," she said.

"'Tis not so much going to where she is—that I can't do. 'Tis more a thing of her coming when she is needed."

"When she appears out of nowhere," Philippe added. "When I went to find her, she appeared inside Cyne's house so suddenly I thought she must have been there all along. But when she left, she passed right through the wall."

"I told you how it was done," Leonie said.

"Aye, now I know."

"So then Herzeloyde came to me and warned me of a great evil that has descended on the land. Those bone demons have been gone for many years. We did not know what they were about again. Now, with this faceless thing commanding them— he is a sorcerer, to be sure. Yet I agree, he is also something else."

"Then a demon as well as a shade?"

"I don't know. I don't know. Haps we should ask instead, what is it they want?"

"They want Leonie," Philippe said. "And Bosewood."

"But I think 'tis something bigger. If 'tis Fulk, as you say, then of course Durham is involved. A year ago, Fulk returned from a pilgrimage to the Holy Land, changed, I thought. The bishop is not the man he once was, but Fulk even more, for he was once a good, if arrogant, man."

"So Rufus has said. And now the three powers come together to battle for the border of England and Scotland. Or is there even more at stake?"

"What if it's not just the border, but England in its entirety?" said Philippe.

"Why not Scotland, too?" Leonie asked. "We do not know what influence he might have on Malcolm Caenmore."

"Haps 'tis so. Haps even more. A shade, as far as I know, must have once gone to the Summer Land or he would not fade. Fading for the Faeriekind is a different sort of thing, for they have the power to control it. But for one of mankind, there is no control. Even though returning to the Summer Land would mark the man's death, there is a yearning to return that is almost unsurpassable. Could be Fulk means to destroy the Summer Land, or perhaps conquer it. That was what happened to the land of Annwyn. A vengeful sorcerer found a way to destroy it, and only those Annwyn who were in the world of man survived. Yet, nay, that would not work with Fulk. Surely he would have enough good sense never to enter there again."

"If he knows Leonie's secret, then haps that's what he really wants from her."

The Black Earl of Northumbria frowned in a pensive way and tugged at his dense black beard.

Leonie frowned and shook her head. "Nay, wait, there is something we're missing."

"What, lass?"

Her brow warped as she pressed a fist to her lips. "Something doesn't make sense." She held up two fingers on her right hand, and mirrored the gesture with her left. "Two sorcerers. Two wives. Each sorcerer wanted the same thing from each of Philippe's wives. Is that not odd? And each used the same method to try to get it."

"You mean to say the two sorcerers are the same?" Philippe asked. "I have never been convinced Clodomir was dead, for his body vanished after I killed him. Is this possible, de Mowbray?"

"A demon might resurrect. And a shade can live many generations, gathering new knowledge from others. A man is not a sorcerer born, but one who sells his soul to the devil for his powers." De Mowbray rose and paced the room.

But Leonie frowned and shook her head. "I can see that they might attack Bosewood to capture it, but why attack us on the road and demand I be given over if it was Philippe they really wanted? Why not take him, especially since they would have had to kill both him and you to do it?"

"Is Fulk such a man who would tell the truth about what he really wants?" But then de Mowbray frowned back. "Still, you are right. Haps you have thwarted them several times, forcing them to change tactics."

"Nay," she countered. "It does not make sense. They did not kill me at Brodin when they could easily do it, nor did they attempt to keep me. Instead, they used me to set a trap for Philippe. Do you think Fulk could have known what decision Rufus would make, or did he expect Rufus to do something else, haps to kill him?"

"Hm, aye. Rufus is a hard one to guess. Haps something else. Haps he thought Rufus would defend his knight, and then

Geoffrey would rise up in rebellion. But how would that help Fulk's cause?"

"And we have already asked ourselves how Fulk could possibly have known of the events at Brodin in time to ride to the crossroads," Philippe added. "A man would have to ride straight through the night to make it to Durham and return to the crossroads in time to catch us there."

"But the gholin the lady saw took on your shape, Peregrine. He could also have taken the shape of someone in the castle. Or haps he was not a gholin, but a shade and a shifter. And that would make him Fulk, the sorcerer, for shades do not keep each other's company. Who knows what ways a sorcerer might have to pass quickly from one place to another?"

The Black Earl sat in his chair, scratched his head, then rose again and paced. He put hands to his lips, paced some more, and pounded one fist into the other hand. Then he shook his head. "I am missing something. Something long ago."

Again he shook his head and huffed.

"Another question, then," Philippe said. "The one you've been avoiding. "What is an Annwyn King and how could I possibly be one? I am French and Norman for many generations and there is no royalty in my ancestry."

"Well, 'tis not that I meant to ignore you, but we have too many questions at once. We have known since your birth of your Annwyn heritage. Such things are watched. But no Annwyn traits have surfaced in any descendant for many generations. A king is so called for his skills, and he would have no kingdom, nor subjects."

Philippe's eyebrows rose. "Long ago?"

"Aye." De Mowbray narrowed his eyes. "Long. Hundreds of years, in man's reckoning. There was something. Before that, even." Then his bulbous black eyes widened as his jaw dropped. "The myths. Something in the myths of Annwyn. Lady Leonie, your Faerie skills have grown greatly in the last few weeks, is it not so? And you had few before? And you, Philippe, none of these traits came upon you before now?"

Leonie nodded.

"Not that I ever noticed," Philippe said. "I've always had very sharp hearing, but naught else."

"And all of these changes occurred after Rufus sent you to Brodin, where you met Lady Leonie for the first time as a grown woman."

Leonie sidled a glance at Philippe, as he did to her.

De Mowbray sat again in his chair, his head shaking so hard both his thick curls and heavy beard bobbed with the movement. "It was only a myth from the distant past told around the fireside at night. The Alchemy of Spirits. I never thought it could be true." And he sat, silent for once, his thick fist drawn up thoughtfully before his mouth.

"But perhaps you might take a moment to share it with us?" Philippe asked.

"Well, 'tis clear you are among those who need to know. The story was that in the old days, matings sometimes occurred that brought about a meshing of the souls, so that both grew in strength and skills beyond what any others have been. Neither one, alone, would have such talent, but together they had the power to rule kingdoms, to create and destroy as none other had done. Eventually the folk of the Faerie realm and the Annwyn planned such unions so that their rulers could protect their folk from the outside world."

"And you think this is what happened for us?"

"'Tis said it could only be one of the Faeriekind and one of the Annwyn, and the Annwyn no longer exist. Yet here you are."

"Clodomir must have known something about it when he took Joceline, then."

"Haps I'm wrong. But a sorcerer, especially one who is also a shade, could be so ancient as to know those things. If he knew the truth, that your ancient blood had surfaced, he would want your talents, even those not yet seen.

"Another thing: a shade's ordinary victim might be trapped at the moment of death. An Annwyn King might be too powerful for a shade, even though he be a sorcerer, to subdue. The victim would have to submit willingly. Your greatest strength is also your greatest weakness. And only to save your beloved could you be forced to submit. But this went untested when Joceline broke free and you caught the sorcerer unguarded. The body, you killed. But not the shade. And now he seeks to become an Annwyn King."

Leonie shivered at the thought. "He might have known about me all along, too. Haps he meant to kill Philippe and take his body, then in that masquerade persuade me to marry him."

"God protect us," de Mowbray said. "God save us and save the people of this earth."

"More than that." Instinctively, Philippe touched the hilt of his sword. "You say a sorcerer destroyed Annwyn and scattered its people."

"You are the last Annwyn King. And you have no idea of your powers. If the sorcerer had taken on your power, how many nations—how many worlds—could such a being destroy?" The Black Earl shoved himself away from the wall where he had been leaning. "Well, you wanted to find out how to break the curse. We need Herzeloyde.

"Come," he said, and took off at a lope across the hall.

As if his retainers read his mind, they appeared quickly to arm him for battle. "Lady Leonie will need a sword," he said to one of them. "The small Breton one will be right for her."

"I have no training in sword fighting, Lord Northumbria. I would not know how."

"You'll know, lass. 'Tis in your blood."

Returning to his long-legged lope, de Mowbray headed out of the hall and across the bailey to the stable where they found both Tonerre and the brown palfrey, as well as the great black stallion de Mowbray rode. Quickly, they mounted.

"I thought you said you didn't know where to find her."

"I don't. But Ilse does." De Mowbray looked down at the grey hound that danced and whined at his feet. "What is't, Ilse? Aye, girl, let's go. On chase, my pretty hound!"

As de Mowbray climbed into his saddle, the hound leaped into the air, her big paws clawing. She rose as if running on the ground, yet there was naught beneath her but air. De Mowbray's huge black stallion followed, and behind came Philippe on Tonerre. Leonie clung with tight fists to her palfrey's mane, not daring to look down. The silent hooves pounded the air as they soared, rising above the oaks, which in the few days they had been gone in the wilderness had turned to rusty red.

CHAPTER THIRTY

I⸀t took Philippe the mere blink of an eye to decide flying should be left to birds, bats, and dragons. Beside him, Leonie's green eyes were round and huge as her lips moved silently in the rhythm of a chant. *"Don't look down. Don't look down."*

"Aye. Don't look down," his thoughts answered. It was not enough to hold the reins, and like Leonie on the palfrey, he wove his fingers through Tonerre's long mane for fear of toppling sideways and to the ground far below. He didn't want to know what trees, hills, and becks looked like from above. But he caught a glimpse of grey-blue expanse in the distance and recognized the sea where it spread out from the brown edge of the cliffs and pale sand beaches. The jutting rocks of Lindesfarne dared poke through the waves far off to his left.

He chuckled and pointed the sea out to Leonie, who just shook her head and fixed her gaze on the palfrey's mane and ears.

He smiled to himself, for he was quickly becoming at ease with the flight and began to look around, absorbing the wind blowing through his hair and whipping his clothes. The lines of grey clouds looked different, reflecting brilliant, sun-like pale mirrors and forming rolling curls far out to sea. The far distant land off his right side rose higher and higher, its color shifting from the aging green and brown of autumn to the stark black and grey of the mountains beyond. He recognized them by their shapes, yet he had never thought what they might look like from above. Haps he might like this riding through the clouds after all.

Ahead of him, de Mowbray sat high and forward in his deep Norman saddle, his bushy black curls blowing like the mane of his great black stallion. He spurred the black onward, though it was clear the stallion loved the flight as much as a lark climbing high into the sky on a summer morn.

"I don't suppose you could explain this," he said to de Mowbray.

The earl laughed, a wild, dark laugh that sent both chill and exhilaration through Philippe. "Ah, there's nothing finer than to soar through the sky after my little hound, is there? 'Tis Ilse's magic, not mine. I have none. But she was born to the Faerie and is built to chase the clouds."

"But we seem to be doing the same."

"We couldn't, not even you, Annwyn King, were it not for Ilse. 'Tis much like the way you could take Leonie into a portal she couldn't see. But Ilse has a dire task, or she wouldn't take us with her. 'Tis to bring us to Herzeloyde, I'll wager."

Beside him, Leonie squeaked. If she had words to tell her thoughts, she neither said nor thought them. Philippe reached out across the air between them and squeezed her hand.

"You will not fall, my love. Ilse would not allow it."

Leonie did not seem persuaded. Still, she raised her head high, and the magnificent curls of her golden hair flayed the wind. Courage, he knew, was facing the world with her kind of boldness. For her sake—no, now he realized the need went far beyond her and him—he had to find a way to block the curse, and more, he must destroy the sorcerer. Fulk was Clodomir, he knew now. And far more dangerous than he had ever imagined before.

He could not let the fiend take Leonie too. He would not let him take the world.

He felt the air growing warmer, and the wind stronger, as they dived through long, flat blankets of clouds. It seemed as if they flew through rain, or water, that hung in the midst of the thick, white substance. Then once again they emerged, now beneath the clouds that partially blocked the sun. Ahead of him, he saw Ilse still descending toward earth, and he began to wonder if they would collide, for they were falling now—in a way. Yet like birds they swooped low and slowed, and came to touch the ground on a rocky, gorse-covered slope.

He patted Tonerre's neck, and the horse shook out his mane, now at a full gallop behind the giant black stallion. Had they been running over ground all this time, they would have been blown. Yet he felt no sweat on Tonerre, barely heard the horse's steady whuffing.

The shaggy hound followed a path into a dark wood, her nose high in the air as if she had caught a scent, and she began to bay. She slowed in a wide glade, and for an instant wandered, the way a dog does when the scent is scattered. Her snuffling sound mixed with a faint whimper, then grew louder and more frantic as she whirled in a wide circle. The dog dashed about, turning to de Mowbray and barking, then went back to her odd, wild dashing about in a wide circle. She leaped into the air, barking, then ran in her wide circuit, as if chasing the air or enclosed in some invisible pen.

Philippe reined in his horse, and apiece with de Mowbray and Leonie, leaped down from the saddle.

One minute the forest beyond the glade had been cleanly sharp, black trunks and dark green branches of pines, with the gold and crimson limes and ash trees standing sharp against the thicket beyond. The next the edges of the glen hazed with a dirty fog, muting the trees as if in a heavy storm. Then, as if they all stood in a quiet, clear glen amid a deep, thick cloud, the world appeared to vanish. Philippe had the dread feeling that the cloud was circling them, yet he could see nothing that even looked like movement, it was so dense. All was silence, save that he could hear their putrid breath and smell the stench of their death-grey rotting flesh and decaying bones.

"Gholins," he whispered.

"Aye." Leonie's fingers played impatiently at the grip on her bow.

"Prepare yourself, magnificent wife. We are going to need your skills."

A *thunk* behind him. He spun around. A sword still quivered where it had struck into the soil, its gold- and garnet-inlaid scabbard flopped beside it.

"Rufus's sword!" Philippe shouted as he yanked it out of the earth. Rufus would have never given it up without a fight.

Another thud, then another. Fallen from the sky, a crude wooden walking stick and a dark green peasant's cloak. A bishop's crosier, its golden crook gleaming in the bright sun flooding into the circle of the open glen. *Clunk* again, and a small dagger.

Leonie dashed up and bent to the dagger, not a man-sized blade, and roughly sheathed. "I gave it to Sigge," she said, pulling it from the sheath.

And the walking stick was the one the old crone had carried. The bishop's crook was obvious.

De Mowbray looked upward, then around, his nostrils flaring. The horses shied and whinnied with the fear of the unknown, as only horses could truly understand. But Philippe felt the same deep chill slide down his spine as he watched the earth-colored fog condense and tighten around them.

Philippe surveyed the ground around them for clues, his gaze expanding farther out toward the trees. Ilse whimpered as she sniffed the tufts of dry grass and lumps of hardened dirt.

"Somehow they've captured all of them. How could they snatch Rufus from inside Bosewood?"

"The bishop was easy, I'll vow," said de Mowbray. "He was already taken in. But Herzeloyde? How could they capture her?"

"Haps the same way he almost caught me," Leonie replied. "I thought he was turning me to stone."

Thunks, screams, yelps, as more objects hit the earth, this time farther away.

The fog thinned. Greyed, faint shadows of human forms splattered before them, then began to rise to their knees. One by one, they took more shape and color.

"Sigge!" shouted Leonie.

Aye, 'twas the little boy, struggling to his knees.

"Leonie!" he shouted back. But with bound hands and feet, he could not stand.

Leonie stepped toward the boy, but pure gut instinct forced Philippe to take her arm and hold her back.

Next appeared Rufus, without his battle gear, similarly bound, fighting against his own rotund shape to right himself onto his knees despite his bonds. And the Bishop of Durham, who cried out, holding up his tied hands in supplication when he saw the group before him. Some unseen force shoved him back to his knees.

"Peregrine!" shouted the king. "By God, now we'll slay these bloodless bastards!"

A club came out of the mist behind the king and struck him upside the jaw. Rufus wavered but stayed on his knees, stocky legs widespread, rage seething in his red-as-beef.

And there, bound like the others, not the crone, but a pale, beautiful woman, utterly the slenderest woman he'd ever seen, her thick, tightly curled hair almost white.

"Herzeloyde." De Mowbray breathed the name, almost as silent as a gasp.

"Mother!"

It could be no other. Now Philippe understood what it was about the woman that held de Mowbray and the villagers in such thrall. But no time for that now.

"Don't move," he said beneath his breath. "The gholins are there, guarding them, so attacking could get them killed."

"Where?" She drew four arrows to place in the hand that gripped her ivorywood bow.

"They're there. I can hear them. A complete circle of them."

CHAPTER THIRTY-ONE

"So CLEVER OF YOU, PEREGRINE."

The voice reverberated through the glen, deep and ominous. The thick, dirty cloud turned to misty fog and began to swirl in bands first grey and white, then deepening into red, violet, and hazy blue, before the swirling bands slowed and became a mist. In a whoosh, the remains of the grimy mist swirled upward and vanished in the air, revealing an army of the gholins, with choking ropes on their captive's necks.

Philippe pressed Leonie behind him, but she moved back to his side. Nay, she was right. It would take all of them at their best to win this fight.

"Four heads," he said.

"Four arrows," she replied. "Now."

Faster than he could determine her movements, she nocked and shot each arrow, and sang them on their way, each striking the bare neck bones of the gholin guards. The severed heads plopped to the ground and the gruesome skeletons crumpled to the grass.

Behind him, Ilse growled and lunged at a gholin that had appeared from nowhere. As de Mowbray whirled around, the gholin swung its club, catching the Black Earl in the head. He groaned and fell forward, face into the grass, blood streaming from the back of his head. Philippe whirled. Others of the ghoulish creatures advanced from all around.

"Defend me!" Leonie shouted as she threw herself to her knees beside de Mowbray, her left hand spreading over the wound to the back of his head. Her right arm extended outward and her hand whirled in the air, fingers splayed out to call her arrows back and sending them flying to their prey around the circle. The gholin backed away from Philippe's swinging sword, but Leonie called back her arrows and struck again while rising from beside de Mowbray's sprawled body. God help them, he hoped she succeeded. They could not afford to lose the man now.

All around them the gholins held back, some again falling to Leonie's arrows.

"You have no chance, Peregrine," said the disembodied deep voice again, echoing as if it bounced off walls.

Philippe swung his gaze around but saw naught. But a smudge appeared, stretched long and tall, darkened. Human features. A Norman helm. Legs and body in mail, covered by a dark tabard, long black cloak tossing as if in a storm, yet there was no wind. From the dark hood, he could at first see no face. But he needed no face to know who this fiend was.

"*Fulk. Clodomir.*" It was Leonie's thought. She stood again beside him, and he could hear de Mowbray groaning and shuffling as if he might be able to rise.

"*Aye.*" Odd, he thought, that the gholins attacked only de Mowbray. They wanted the earl dead, but not him or Leonie. Nor the four prisoners by the trees.

As Leonie drew the sword de Mowbray had given her, Philippe sent up another prayer to the Almighty that her Faerie skills would extend to the cutting edge as well.

"You have no chance," Clodomir growled out like a wolf. "Submit to me or your king will die. And the witch as well."

"I think you will kill them anyway."

The sorcerer's laugh roared like an ominous wave sweeping over a ship's bow. "You need not worry. I have uses for them. But I will dispose of them if I find it necessary."

Philippe glimpsed Rufus's narrowing eyes that said this was a fight that went far beyond kings and kingdoms. Rufus would never forgive him for giving in, no matter the stakes. But the king was helpless in his bonds, and although Philippe was under a death sentence, he was still sworn to protect Rufus.

The boy, Leonie's favorite child, and the woman who was her mother, who she now saw for the first time in her own memory. Lumps constricted in his throat. He had to save them all. But how?

Beside the king a shimmering light, wobbling in layers, enveloped the woman with the long, pale hair. Her body shifted its shape, shrank and re-formed into the tall, gaunt, wizened Cailleach. Her gnarled hands grew smaller and smaller until the binding ropes loosened and slipped from her wrists. Once free, the crone shimmered again and returned to the shape of the proud warrior woman of unearthly beauty.

"Black Earl!" she shouted. "Awake!"

De Mowbray's struggling body shifted. He groaned; his body glowed and twisted, darkened and reshaped. Writhed like trapped eels in an eel net. A tumultuous growl and he rose up, now a huge black dog as big as a warhorse, enormous eyes round and glowing, black as Satan's kiss.

"Leonie!" shouted Herzeloyde as she raised her hand high in the air.

Leonie sent the small sword to fly to Herzeloyde's hand just as the black moor hound, joined by shaggy Ilse, ripped through rotten-fleshed gholins with their mighty teeth. Philippe swung both his sword and the king's as Leonie called back her arrows and pitched them yet again, then snatched up a dropped club to slam it against the gholins that grabbed at her. Her dagger in one hand and the club in the other, she slashed and pounded against the demons like a war maiden.

Herzeloyde sliced through bodies of the gholins, which fell all about her and were strewn like harvest straw from the raging bite of the black moor hound. Rufus shouted to be set free to join the fray, but none had time for him as they pushed their way closer to the prisoners. Frantically, the bishop worked at Rufus's ropes while Rufus's hands attempted to free the bishop. Philippe had seen both of them fight. He would welcome either as an ally.

Leonie glanced at the king and directed the dagger to him, an easy catch. All of one motion, he grasped it between his bound hands and spun around to cut loose the bishop, who then freed him. Philippe threw Rufus his sword. The bishop grabbed a fallen cudgel.

The little dagger hit the ground in favor of better weapons. Sigge, forgotten by the real warriors, spotted the dagger and worked it between his hands to cut them free. A gholin came up behind the king with his cudgel.

"I'll save you, Sire!" he shouted, and the boy, still hobbled at the ankles, sprang forward between the king's short legs and stabbed the creature's foot. Rufus stumbled, but the gholin fell into a tangled pile of bones.

Rufus was not one to be slowed down for more than a nod to the boy, and he yanked the blade from the ground and tossed it back to Sigge.

The gholins kept coming. But only a few could fight at once, for there was no room. Philippe desperately wanted to send Leonie away from the fray, but he could not even put her behind him, for his back was as endangered as his front. But they moved, inch by putrid inch, amid the din of clanging blades and shouts of agony, closer to their allies, until they could form an outward-facing ring to defend themselves in all directions. Slaying the slow-moving gholins that moved the circle closer, ever closer, to the black-cloaked sorcerer.

Philippe turned, the sorcerer in his sight as he bore down on the evil creature.

From the emptiness beneath the black hood, two crimson eyes began to glow, and the shape of a face traced itself in the darkness. The sorcerer raised his sword and pointed it, as if welcoming battle. The hood fell back, revealing the blackened face of the man called the Warrior of God, but the red eyes glowed with the light of Hell. Fulk.

Fury filled Philippe from bones to brawn and rushed through his veins as he raised his sword and swung.

The streak of blue light swept from Fulk's sword tip and seized Leonie from her fight, tossing her through the air into Philippe's advancing blade.

Philippe pulled back, but too late. Her shriek was little more than a startled gasp as the sword point pierced her at the waist. She crumpled to the ground. Philippe dropped his sword and fell to his knees beside her.

Around them, the tableau of warriors came to a sudden halt, frozen as they were.

"Leonie!" He grabbed her, trying to lift her, trying to turn time back, trying to undo what he knew deep in his heart had been destined. Nothing mattered now, save her.

Her green eyes glazed, then she closed them, her head drooping. *"Do not speak. Hear me. Place my hands on the wound. Hurry, while I still have strength."*

Involuntarily, he nearly spoke. But he grasped her thought and laid her on the ground, taking her hands and laying them, interlaced, over the wound.

"My love—forgive me."

"Nay—listen. Don't let him know you hear me. Don't let him know what I can do."

"Oh, my love." Silence rang loudly around him as if his ears still echoed from the chaos and clamor of battle hours after it

was done. He glanced around and saw all those embattled were frozen in their positions as if time itself had stopped.

"You cannot save her," roared Fulk's dark voice. "None of your petty human tricks can save her. Only I can. She will die, Peregrine, unless you kneel to me in submission. Quickly now, decide. She can live. It is in your hands if you act before she is gone."

Leonie lay as limp as if dead, eyes closed. *"'Tis a lie. The curse is a lie. This is by his hand, not yours. But my hand will undo it."*

Her bright blood seeped and spread, covering her garments, covering him. Doubt hung heavy in his heart. *"Can you?"*

"Trust me. But do not let him know. You are the key to all. If he steals your body, he will have the power to enter and destroy the Summer Land, and England and Scotland as well. Kill him for me, my Peregrine."

"He cannot be killed."

"He can. Only you can do it. You have the powers he does not. He knows you can open the portals. Use it against him. Make him think you give him what he wants."

"You waste valuable time, Peregrine. She will soon be dead, and then you can do nothing for her. Will you lose her by your own hand, Peregrine? As you did Joceline? You should know by now you cannot stop me. I will always win."

Philippe touched Leonie's cheek, smearing her blood as he did so. *"My love. I will win. I will kill him. For you."*

"You are my only love, Peregrine. Forever. I will live for you."

He had no choice but to believe. Any other was beyond bearing. He rose from his knees, a man empty of all save his immense hunger for vengeance. But he wiped it from his face and bade God and whatever powers had bestowed the Annwyn skills upon him to guide him. What he would do, he knew not. He dropped his sword to the grass and walked toward the sorcerer.

Nearby Rufus stood, his sword still in midswing, his pale eyes stricken with horror. Herzeloyde was caught in midgasp as she beheaded a gholin, but she could see the daughter she had been forced to abandon soaked with blood on the ground. And de Mowbray, no longer the black dog, had stopped in his stride toward the bleeding Leonie.

I am the Peregrine. The Annwyn King. The lover of the beautiful Faerie Leonie of Bosewood. For her, I will win.

"Kneel to me, Annwyn King."

"I am naught but a man."

"Hah. Even I know you know the truth by now. Kneel to me and submit to my will."

If he did, the sorcerer-demon-shade would enter his body and mind. Philippe drew from Leonie's mind the image of her fighting the demon that had possessed her. She had won then. He could too. He would let this demon in and then fight it to the death.

He knelt. He felt the sorcerer drawing near and begged God for the strength he needed. As the long, craggy fingers reached out, coming closer, he steeled himself.

Nay, wait! That wouldn't work! If the fiend took his body, he could enter the Summer Land without dying. If Philippe let him in, the sorcerer would become the Annwyn King as well as have a body that could survive inside the portal—which he couldn't do now.

Philippe called up a fierce stroke of will and slammed shut his mind like a massive iron portcullis crashing down. The sorcerer hit it like a ballista into a stone wall. In an instant mind flash, Philippe built the portal. He lunged, grappling the sorcerer, and flung both of them through the portal into the Summer Land.

Still gripping the creature, he forced the portal shut. The shade screamed, a high, agonizing sound. He went limp and collapsed.

The blackness of the demon shade faded from the body. It was nothing. A body of a man. A shell. No spirit, no soul. No demon, shade, or sorcerer left.

Aye. His Annwyn heart told him. The evil was gone. The body was only that of Fulk, the true man, who had been rightly known for his piety.

Philippe grabbed the body by one arm, and as he reopened the portal, he dragged it out into the green glade. The mist and sun sparkled on an earth that had the scent of a new spring day.

Like frozen branches released in a thaw, the arrested tableau came to life again. Bodies of gholins dropped to the earth among those already slain.

Leonie still lay in a wide pool of her blood. Still and quiet.

His heart in his throat, Philippe dropped Fulk's body and raced toward her, all else forgotten, shouting as he ran, but not even an eyelash moved. He knelt and gently scooped her into his embrace, and her hand dropped limply away.

"Leonie! You promised me!" he cried, and nestled his tear-soaked cheek next to hers.

"I'm here."

"Leonie!" Sigge screamed. "You can't die, Leonie! Wake up!" The little boy hopped, ankles still tied, until Rufus grabbed him by the waist and ran with him to Leonie's side.

"Tell them."

He kissed her cheek and smoothed her wildly rumpled hair, loving the very touch. "She's still with us, just exhausted."

"A wound like that," Herzeloyde, no longer the ethereally beautiful Faerie warrior, said in a scratchy voice. "The healing itself might have killed her."

"'Tis the Alchemy of Spirits," said the Black Earl to her. "Whatever she was before, now she is far greater."

"Aye, I see that now. Tell her for me, Annwyn King, that I have loved her always, and have regretted every moment that I have been forced to leave her."

"Tell her for me, my love, I know. I understand. Always will she be my beloved mother."

Philippe looked up at the crone. "She gives you her love. She cannot yet talk."

Giant tears flooded down the old hag's face. "I long so desperately to touch my child, but it is my *geas* that I am forbidden to touch those I love. I did not ask to be taken from her, but it cannot be otherwise. I only beg forgiveness, and give my great gratitude for all those who have loved and protected where I could not."

"She knows," he said. "There is no forgiveness, for none is needed."

Beside the crone stood de Mowbray, his face heavy with sweat. But Ilse sneaked between the warriors, whimpering, and suddenly swiped her tongue over Leonie's face. Leonie grimaced and jerked back. Her eyes popped open.

The odd company of warriors laughed. Philippe tightened his embrace and laughed with them.

"Aye," de Mowbray added, "'Tis a miracle she's survived. And she had already used some of her energy on me."

Rufus knelt down too. "Lady, I thought you were gone. How could you have survived? I don't understand. What is all of this about? The old woman here, I deduced. And I know of your connections to her. But the rest?"

The Black Earl shifted his jaw about and frowned. He huffed a sigh. "She has a talent for closing wounds," de Mowbray said. "But 'tis a chancy thing. She's failed before. 'Twould have been a dire thing if she'd saved me, then lost herself."

"Her Faerie blood, then? But Philippe? What was that?"

"He's of the old race of Annwyn, long gone and scattered. No one has ever seen the powers pass on beyond the second generation. But these last few weeks it's come out, not just as one with the blood, but an Annwyn King. 'Tis how he can build the Summer Land portals."

Rufus stepped back, and his eyes turned bright and rounded like two pale moons. "The Peregrine, a king? I cannot believe it. Just who are his subjects?"

"I have none, Sire," Philippe said, feeling his face heat like a young girl's.

"'Tis a matter of skills and talent, not of subjects, Red King," said the Cailleach. "Annwyn is no more."

"So this is why you chose him?"

The old woman chuckled, her voice as rough as sandstone. "I told you I cannot foretell. But if you were a mother seeking a husband for your daughter, and looking out over that silk-skirted group you call your household knights, which one would you choose?"

A cynical frown furrowed the king's face. "I'll never believe you do not lie when it suits you, old woman." Then, with narrowed eyes, Rufus faced Philippe. "Well, Peregrine, have you made your choice?"

Philippe startled. He'd never thought he had anything to say in that matter between him and the king. "I have, Sire."

"And to whom do you owe your allegiance?"

"I am bound by law, loyalty, honor, and friendship to my king. I am bound by law, loyalty, honor, and love to my wife. Never will I give over either to the enemy, with or without a fight."

"And if you should have to choose?"

"I will not choose. That is something I have learned from my Leonie. There is always another way."

Philippe waited for the characteristic purple rising in the king's face that meant his rage was about to boil over. But this time, Rufus merely stared, then raised a hand to stroke his copper-colored beard.

"Well. One must protect one's family," he said. The king's face turned to a dark frown as he turned to de Mowbray. "And you," he said, raising a finger to point, then shook his head. "Nay, don't even try to explain. That I do not want to know."

The Bishop of Durham had said little. But now he knelt beside the body of Fulk. "I loved this man," he said. "He was like a son to me. How did he deceive me so? He led those bone beings against me—against us."

It was de Mowbray who joined the bishop on his knees beside the body. "That was not Fulk. That sorcerer killed Fulk and stole his body when he was on pilgrimage, then planted demons in your mind so you thought his own thoughts. That evil is destroyed. But now here is Fulk's body back, free of evil. Take him home and bury him with Christian dignity, for Fulk was a good man, worthy of what he was called, worthy of our tears."

The bishop's head bowed and nodded slowly as a tear trailed down his cheek.

Rufus let something rumble in his throat, and then he cleared it. "Come, all of us together. Lady Leonie, can you rise?"

"Soon," she said, though Philippe could see she was still weak.

"Well, then, we shall all kneel to where you are. You, too, boy. You are old enough and brave enough to save your king's life, so you must join this pledge."

The boy worked his face into a solemn frown and got down on his knees.

"What we have seen here today must not be told, for the sake of all those we protect. We shall come up with a suitable lie. A battle with an incursion across the border, in which Fulk was killed. That would do it. The Scots won't like it, but how can they tell one border raid from another? We shall claim a whirlwind caught us up, which it most certainly did, and it was by God's grace we survived, which is most certainly true. But we were lost and wandered until we all chanced to meet in time to do battle."

The hands joined, one atop another, in the center of the circle. Philippe sighed his relief, anxious to get Leonie back to safety where she could rest.

"And now you, you rapscallion," Rufus said to Sigge. "What do you have to say for yourself?"

Sigge's face fell. "I'm sorry, Sire. Whatever it was I did."

"You are sorry for saving your king's life? Then you are not the boy I thought you were. Where is that audacious lad? It cannot be this one. How could such a lad become a knight?"

"I—"

"A blacksmith's son? It is not done."

"But my grandfather—"

"A traitor. You, however, are not that man. Nor was your father, whose honor and integrity are beyond question. But you are half Saxon. And still a blacksmith's son. They will not accept you. They will harass you and brutalize you. You will have no friends."

"I don't care, *Beau Sire*. I'll be the best knight there ever was, and I'll never, ever let you down."

"But you must first be a page."

"I'll take him." The Bishop of Durham and the Earl of Northumbria spoke at once.

"He's mine," Philippe said. "My lady has already spoken for him, and I must honor that."

For the first time that day, the Bishop of Durham smiled. "Fulk has no heirs, nor wife. It would please him to have such a brave, loyal lad as his heir."

"Hm. Well, I shall think on that. You would have to take the land in tenancy. And he needs a Norman name. Ah, I have it. His father's Norman name, which he gave up so many years ago. Emilien. One who seeks the highest cause. You'd best live up to it, boy."

Sigge-Emilien screamed his joy. But Philippe caught him around the mouth with his hand. "Decorum, Emilien. On your knees quickly and kiss the hand of your monarch."

Philippe left the king and his vassals and at last turned back to his beloved. She sat on the grass where only minutes before a battle had raged and she had fought for her own life. Alive and smiling, though fatigue still held its grip on her, she held up her hand to him. He lifted her to standing and into his embrace. There were no words, no way to say his deep emotions, how desperately he wanted her, forever.

"*It's over.*" Her golden hair, her scalp wet with perspiration, rested against his chest.

"*I love you, for all that you are, forever. It's good that we still have company so you can rest...for now. Already I hunger for you so desperately that I would take you now if they were not here.*" He could not stop caressing her, her face, her hair, her back, nor quit the kisses wherever he could find a place for them.

"*I am well now. I love you, my Philippe. Forever.*" Her caresses were as urgent as his.

"Don't they talk to each other?" Rufus said.

"Methinks they are talking," said de Mowbray. "Haps, not with words."

Rufus harrumphed. "Those two need a bed."

De Mowbray burst into a raucous laugh. "I know just the place. Ilse, my lass, fly them off to Bamburgh, where there's a chamber fit enough for an Annwyn King and his Faerie bride."

Ilse's wild, switch-like tail swung so hard her hips went with it. She whined and bounced with eagerness for the flight.

Philippe laughed. "Sorry, girl. I know how you love to fly. But I have another idea. Sire, if you'll see the boy back to Bosewood, I think you can all manage without us for a few days."

"Aye," said Rufus. "Likely Malcolm's been set back a bit without Fulk. But where are you going?"

Philippe grinned back at his king. "I know a beautiful valley where it's always summer."

"Not again," de Mowbray said with a groan. "I suppose you'll be wanting me to meet you."

"Send Ilse for us."

Philippe could have done it with a mere thought, but he waved his hand in a wide circle to build a portal. Now that he knew how it was done, they would not have to bother with long walks through caves. Taking Leonie's hand, they stepped inside.

And out to a green meadow, sheltered by tall mountains and blossoming with checkered lilies and red poppies. Hand in hand, they approached the villa with its red-tiled roof and brightly colored walls, stretched out atop the low hill, surrounded by its orchard of ever blooming and ripening fruits.

At the terrace decorated with festoons of purple grapes, Philippe stopped and moved his arm to her waist. Her lithe body leaned into his as her arm embraced him. Hungry desire was already consuming him.

"Ah, glorious husband, it is such a beautiful place you've made."

He laughed. "Glorious, am I?"

"Oh, most glorious," she replied.

Behind the villa, the cascades he had barely noticed the last time tumbled with a soothing murmur into the lake. His thoughts had been of the steaming bath inside and how many ways they could make love in it, but he suspected the newly decorated terrace with its stone benches draped in heavy tapestries and topped with thick, tasseled pillows must have come from her thoughts.

Or did it need both of them together to make this place?

"Then, precious bride—for you are most precious to me—what else would you like?"

She smiled up at him. "It needs music, I think. From a bard's harp."

From inside the villa, tones rising then falling like the cascades of water, echoing off the marble walls, came the warm, mellow music of a harp.

THE END

ACKNOWLEDGMENTS

THE DAYS HAVE PASSED WHEN AN AUTHOR PENNED HIS STORY alone, unguided by any but his muse. Now writers share with others—critique partners, focus groups, editors, friends who do what we call cold reads, and—now that there are e-books—fans and reviewers who interact with writers in ways they never could before. I'm so grateful to all those who helped me get this book the way I wanted it.

To Heather Hiestand for great plot-storming, Sophia Johnson for her vivid feel for the medieval paranormal romance, Barbara Rae Robinson for her nitpickiness, and Vonnie Alto and SamMarie Ashe for unfailing support. To Rowena Williamson for sharing her Scottish Deerhounds with me. To the Wet Noodle Posse for their thorough and ceaseless flogging. And most of all, to Eleni Caminis and the author team at Montlake who do such a marvelous job of making a book blossom.

Many, many thanks.

ABOUT THE AUTHOR

A NATIVE OF ILLINOIS, DELLE Jacobs has been crafting stories since the tender age of four. She earned a degree in geography from the University of Oklahoma and worked as a cartographer until eventually becoming a social worker specializing in troubled teens and families. Everything changed, however, once she began writing books in 1993, and by 2004, literary success convinced her to quit her day job and focus full time on writing. She is a seven-time finalist for the Romance Writers of America's Golden Heart Award, which she won an unprecedented three times, in addition to numerous other writing awards for her novels, including *His Majesty, the Prince of Toads*, *Lady Wicked*, *Sins of the Heart*, and *Aphrodite's Brew*. Along the way she discovered a knack for designing e-book covers, which is a great way to get her creative juices flowing when her book characters are being particularly uncooperative. She lives today in southwest Washington State with her family.

Made in the USA
Charleston, SC
12 November 2012